ALEXANDER: CHILD OF A DREAM

DR VALERIO MASSIMO MANFREDI is an Italian historian, journalist and archaeologist. He is the Professor of Classical Archaeology at the University of Milan, and a familiar face on European television. He has published seven novels, including the bestselling Alexander trilogy, for which the American Biographical Institute voted him Man of the Year in 1999. He is married with two children and lives in a small town near Bologna. He is currently at work on a screenplay for a major Hollywood studio.

IAIN HALLIDAY was born in Scotland in 1960. He studied American Studies at the University of Manchester and worked in Italy and London before moving to Sicily, where he now lives. As well as working as a translator, he currently teaches English at the University of Catania.

Also by Valerio Massimo Manfredi

ALEXANDER: THE SANDS OF AMMON

VALERIO MASSIMO MANFREDI

ALEXANDER

CHILD OF A DREAM

Translated from the Italian by Iain Halliday

PAN BOOKS

First published 2001 by Macmillan

This edition published 2001 by Pan Books
an imprint of Pan Macmillan Ltd
Pan Macmillan, 20 New Wharf Road, London N1 9RR
Basingstoke and Oxford
Associated companies throughout the world
www.panmacmillan.com

Associated companies throughout the world

ISBN 978 0 330 51858 1

1 3 5 7 9 8 6 4 2

A CIP catalogue record for this book is available from
the British Library.

Typeset by Set Systems Ltd, Saffron Walden, Essex
Printed and bound in the UK by
CPI Mackays, Chatham ME5 8TD

Visit **www.panmacmillan.com** to read more about all our books and to buy
them. You will also find features, author interviews and news of any author
events, and you can sign up for e-newsletters so that you're always first to hear
about our new releases.

To Christine

ALEXANDER

CHILD OF A DREAM

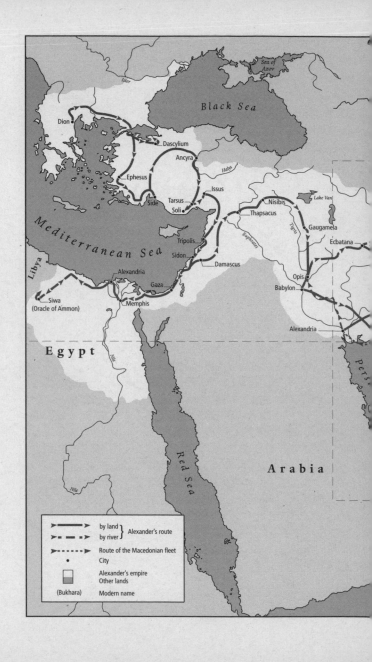

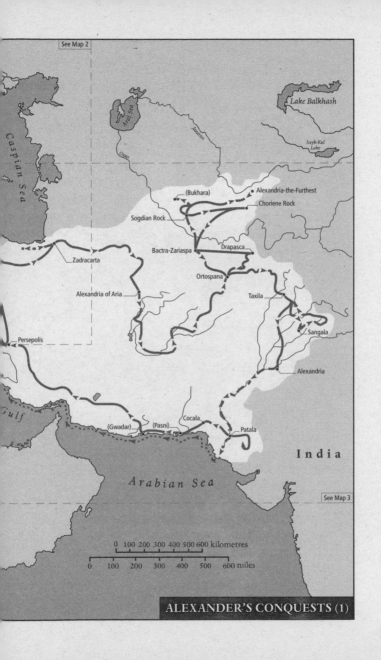

See Map 2

Lake Balkhash

Aral Sea

Caspian Sea

Issyk-Kul Lake

Jaxartes

Oxus

(Bukhara)

Alexandria-the-Furthest

Choriene Rock

Sogdian Rock

Bactra-Zariaspa

Drapasca

Zadracarta

Ortospana

Alexandria of Aria

Taxila

Persepolis

Sangala

Alexandria

Gulf

(Gwadar)

(Pasni)

Cocala

Patala

India

Arabian Sea

See Map 3

0 100 200 300 400 500 600 kilometres

0   100   200   300   400   500   600 miles

ALEXANDER'S CONQUESTS (1)

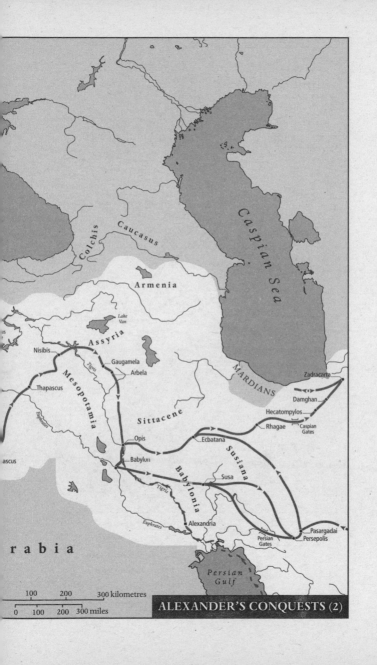

ALEXANDER'S CONQUESTS (2)

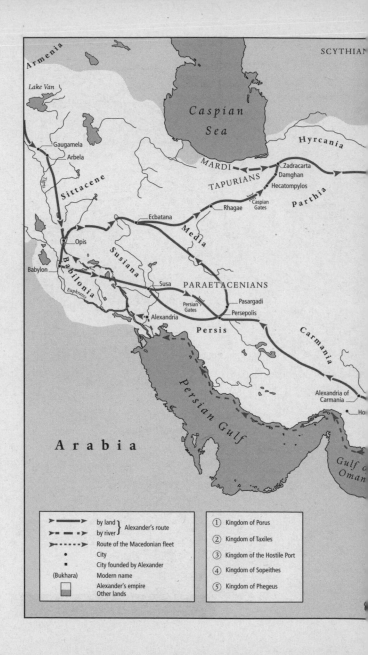

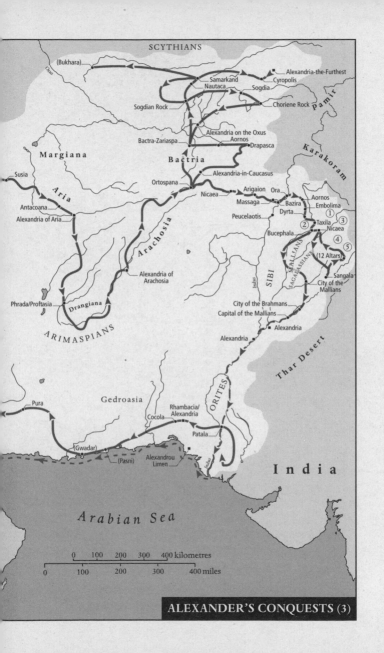

SCYTHIANS

(Bukhara)
Oxus
Samarkand
Nautaca
Sogdian Rock
Bactra-Zariaspa
Margiana
Alexandria on the Oxus
Aornos
Drapasca
Bactria
Ortospana
Alexandria-in-Caucasus
Susia
Aria
Antacoana
Alexandria of Aria
Arachosia
Nicaea
Arigaion Ora
Massaga
Peuceolaotis
Bazira
Dyrta
Aornos
Embolima
①
Taxila ③
② Nicaea
Cyropolis
Alexandria-the-Furthest
Sogdia
Choriene Rock
Pamir
Karakoram

Alexandria of Arachosia
④ ⑤
(12 Altars)

Phrada/Proftasia
Drangiana
Sangala
City of the Mallians

ARIMASPIANS

City of the Brahmans
Capital of the Mallians
Alexandria

Alexandria

Pura
Gedrosia
Rhambacia/Alexandria
Cocola
ORITES
Patala

(Gwadar)
(Pasni)
Alexandrou Limen

Indus
SIBI
MALLIANS
SAGALASSIANS

Thar Desert

India

Arabian Sea

0   100   200   300   400 kilometres
0   100   200   300   400 miles

ALEXANDER'S CONQUESTS (3)

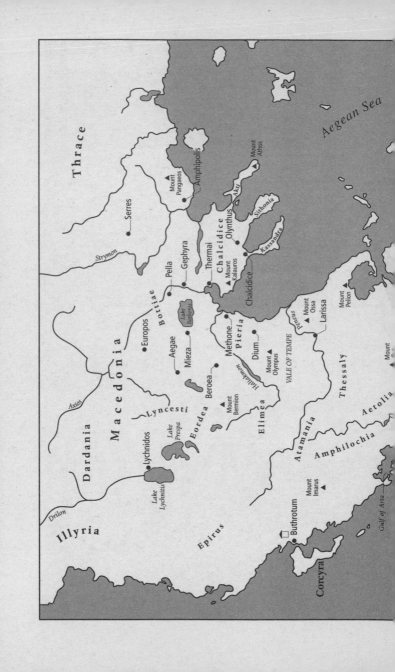

ANCIENT GREECE

PROLOGUE

THE FOUR MAGI slowly climbed the paths that led to the summit of the Mountain of Light. They came from the four corners of the horizon, each carrying a satchel containing fragrant wood for the rite of fire.

The Wise Man of Sunrise wore a cloak of pink silk that shaded into blue and his feet were clad with deerskin sandals. The Wise Man of Sunset wore a crimson gown streaked with gold and from his shoulders hung a long stole made of byssus and embroidered in the same colours.

The Wise Man of Midday had a purple tunic decorated with golden ears of wheat and wore snakeskin slippers. The last of them, the Wise Man of the Night, was dressed in black wool woven from the fleece of unborn lambs and dotted with silver stars.

They moved as though the rhythm of their walk were marked by a music that only they could hear and they approached the temple at the same pace, covering equal distances even though the first was climbing a rocky slope, the next was walking along a level path and the last two progressed along the sandy beds of dried-up rivers.

They reached the four entrances of the stone tower at the same instant, just as dawn draped the immense deserted landscape of the plateau in pearly light.

They bowed and looked into one another's faces

through the four entrance arches, and then they moved towards the altar. The Wise Man of Sunrise began the rite, arranging sandalwood branches in a square; next came the Wise Man of Midday who added, diagonally, bundles of acacia twigs. Onto this base the Wise Man of Sunset heaped cedar wood, gathered in the forest of Mount Lebanon and stripped of its bark. Last of all the Wise Man of the Night laid branches of seasoned Caucasian oak, lightning-struck wood dried in the highland sun. Then all four drew their sacred flints from their satchels and together they struck blue sparks at the base of the small pyramid until the fire began to burn – weak at first, faltering, then ever stronger and more vigorous: the vermilion tongues becoming blue and then almost white, just like the Celestial Fire, like the supernal breath of Ahura Mazda, God of Truth and Glory, Lord of Time and Life.

Only the pure voice of the fire murmured its arcane poetry within the great stone tower. Not even the breathing of the four men standing motionless at the very centre of their vast homeland could be heard.

They watched on enrapt as the sacred flame took shape from the simple architecture of the branches arranged on the stone altar. They stared into that most pure light, into that wonderful dance of fire, lifting their prayer for the people and for the King: the Great King, the King of Kings who sat far away in the splendid hall in his palace, the timeless Persepolis, in the midst of a forest of columns painted purple and gold, guarded by winged bulls and lions rampant.

The air, at that hour of the morning, in that magic and solitary place, was completely still, just as it had to be for the Celestial Fire to assume the forms and the motions of its divine nature. It was this nature which drove the flames ever higher towards the Empyrean, their original source.

But suddenly a powerful force breathed over the flames and quenched them; as the Magi watched on in astonishment, even the red embers were suddenly transformed into black charcoal.

There was no other sign, not a sound except the screech of a falcon rising up into the empty sky; neither were there any words. The four men stood dumbstruck at the altar, stricken by this most sad omen, tears welling in silence.

*

At that same moment, far away in a remote western land, a young woman trembled as she approached the oaks of an ancient sanctuary. She had come to request a blessing for the child she now felt move for the first time in her womb. The woman's name was Olympias. The name of her child came on the wind that blew impatiently through the age-old branches, stirring the dead leaves round the bases of the giant trunks. The name was:

ALÉXANDROS

1

OLYMPIAS HAD DECIDED to visit the Sanctuary of Dodona because of a strange premonition that had come to her as she slept alongside her husband – Philip II, King of the Macedonians, who lay that night in a wine- and food-sated slumber.

She had dreamed of a snake slithering slowly along the corridor outside and then entering their bed chamber silently. She could see it, but she could not move, and neither could she shout for help. The coils of the great reptile slid over the stone floor and in the moonlight that penetrated the room through the window, its scales glinted with copper and bronze reflections.

For a moment she wanted Philip to wake up and take her in his arms, to hold her against his strong, muscular chest, to caress her with his big warrior's hands, but immediately she turned to look again on the *drakon*, on the huge animal that moved like a ghost, like a magic creature, like the creatures the gods summon from the bowels of the earth whenever the need arises.

Now, strangely, she was no longer afraid of it. She felt no disgust for it, indeed she felt ever more attracted and almost charmed by the sinuous movement, by the graceful and silent force.

The snake worked its way under the blankets, it slipped

between her legs and between her breasts and she felt it take her, light and cold, without hurting her at all, without violence.

She dreamed that its seed mingled with the seed her husband had already thrust into her with the strength of a bull, with all the vigour of a wild boar, before he had collapsed under the weight of exhaustion and of wine.

The next day the King had put on his armour, dined with his generals on wild hog's meat and sheep's milk cheese, and had left to go to war. This was a war against a people more barbarous than his Macedonians: the Triballians, who dressed in bearskins, who wore hats of fox fur and lived along the banks of the Ister, the biggest river in Europe.

All he had said to Olympias was, 'Remember to offer sacrifices to the gods while I am away and bear me a man child, an heir who looks like me.'

Then he had mounted his bay horse and set off at a gallop with his generals, the courtyard resounding with the noise of their steeds' hooves, echoing with the clanging of their arms.

Olympias took a warm bath following her husband's departure and while her maidservants massaged her back with sponges steeped in essence of jasmine and Pierian roses, she sent for Artemisia, the woman who had been her wet-nurse. Artemisia was aged now, but her bosom was still ample, her hips still shapely and she came from a good family; Olympias had brought her here from Epirus when she had come to marry Philip.

She recounted the dream and asked, 'Good Artemisia, what does it mean?'

Artemisia had her mistress come out of the warm bath and began to dry her with towels of Egyptian linen.

'My child, dreams are always messages from the gods, but few people know how to interpret them. I think you should go to the most ancient of the sanctuaries in Epirus, our homeland, to consult the Oracle of Dodona. Since time immemorial the priests there have handed down the art of reading the voice of the great Zeus, father of the gods and of men. The voice speaks when the wind passes through the branches of the age-old oaks of the sanctuary, when it makes their leaves whisper in spring or summer, or when it stirs the dead leaves into movement around the trunks during autumn and winter.'

And so it was that a few days later Olympias set off towards the sanctuary that had been built in a most impressive place, in a green valley nestling among wooded mountains.

Tradition had it that this was among the oldest temples on earth – two doves were said to have flown from Zeus's hand immediately after he chased Cronus, his father, from the skies. One dove had lighted on an oak at Dodona, the other on a palm tree at the Oasis of Siwa, in the midst of the burning sands of Libya. And since then, in those two places, the voice of the father of the gods had made itself heard.

'What is the meaning of my dream?' Olympias asked the priests of the sanctuary.

They sat in a circle on stone seats, in the middle of a green meadow dotted with daisies and buttercups, and they listened to the wind through the leaves of the oaks. They seemed rapt in thought.

Then one of them said, 'It means that the child you will bear will be the offspring of Zeus and a mortal man. It means that in your womb the blood of a god has mixed with the blood of a man.

'The child you will bear will shine with a wondrous energy, but just as the flame that burns most brightly consumes the walls of the lamp and uses up more quickly the oil that feeds it, his soul may burn up the heart that houses it.

'Remember, my Queen, the story of Achilles, ancestor of your great family: he was given the choice of a brief but glorious life or a long and dull one. He chose the former, he sacrificed his life for a moment of blinding light.'

'Is this an inevitable fate?' Olympias asked, apprehensively.

'It is but one possibility,' replied another priest. 'A man may take many roads, but some men are born with a strength that comes to them as a gift from the gods and which seeks always to return to the gods. Keep this secret in your heart until the moment comes when your child's nature will be fully manifest. Be ready then for everything and anything, even to lose him, because no matter what you do you will never manage to stop him fulfilling his destiny, to stop his fame spreading to the ends of the earth.'

He was still talking when the breeze that had been blowing through the leaves of the oaks changed, almost suddenly, into a strong, warm wind from the south. In no time at all it was strong enough to bend the tops of the trees and to make the priests cover their heads with their cloaks.

The wind brought with it a thick reddish mist that darkened the entire valley, and Olympias too wrapped her cloak around her body and her head and sat motionless in the midst of the vortex, like the statue of a faceless god.

The wind subsided just as it had begun, and when the mist cleared, the statues, the pillars and the altars that embellished the sacred place were all covered in a thin layer of red dust.

The priest who had spoken last touched it with his fingertip and brought it to his lips: 'This dust has been brought here on the Libyan wind, the breath of Zeus Ammon whose oracle sits among the palms of Siwa. This is an extraordinary happening, a remarkable portent, because the two most ancient oracles on earth, separated by enormous distances, have spoken at the same moment. Your son has heard voices that come from far away and perhaps he has understood the message. One day he will hear them again within the walls of a great sanctuary surrounded by the desert sands.'

After listening to these words, the Queen returned to the capital, to Pella, the city whose roads were dusty in summer and muddy in winter, and there she waited in fear and trembling for the day on which her child would be born.

*

The labour pains came one spring evening, after sunset. The women lit the lamps and Artemisia sent word for the midwife and for the physician, Nicomachus, who had been doctor to the old King, Amyntas, and who had supervised the birth of many a royal scion, both legitimate and otherwise.

Nicomachus was ready, knowing that the time was near. He put on an apron, had water heated and more lamps brought so that there would be sufficient light.

But he let the midwife approach the Queen first, because a woman prefers to be touched by another woman at the moment when she brings her child into the world: only a woman truly knows of the pain and the solitude in which a new life is made.

King Philip, at that very moment, was laying siege to the city of Potidaea and would not have left the front line for anything in the world.

It was a long and difficult birth because Olympias had narrow hips and was of delicate constitution.

Artemisia wiped her mistress's brow. 'Courage, my child, push! When you see your baby you will be consoled for all the pain you must suffer now.' She moistened Olympias' lips with spring water from a silver bowl, which the maids refreshed continuously.

But when the pain grew to the point where Olympias almost fainted, Nicomachus intervened, guiding the midwife's hands and ordering Artemisia to push on the Queen's belly because she had no strength left and the baby was in distress.

He put his ear to Olympias' lower belly and could hear that the baby's heart was slowing down.

'Push as hard as you can,' he ordered Artemisia. 'The baby must be born now.'

Artemisia leaned with all her weight on the Queen who let out one frightfully loud cry and gave birth.

Nicomachus tied the umbilical cord with linen thread, then he cut it immediately with a pair of bronze scissors and cleaned the wound with wine.

The baby began to cry and Nicomachus handed him to the women so that they could wash and dress him.

It was Artemisia who first saw his face, and she was delighted: 'Isn't he wonderful?' she asked as she wiped his eyelids and nose with some wool dipped in oil.

The midwife washed his head and as she dried it she found herself exclaiming, 'He has the hair of a child of six months and fine blond streaks. He looks like a little Eros!'

Artemisia meanwhile was dressing him in a tiny linen tunic because Nicomachus did not agree with the practice followed in most families by which newborn babies were tightly swaddled.

'What colour do you think his eyes are?' she asked the midwife.

The woman brought a lamp nearer and the baby's eyes shone as they reflected the light. 'I don't know, it's difficult to say. They seem to be blue, then dark, almost black. Perhaps it's because his parents are so different from each other . . .'

Nicomachus was taking care of the Queen who, as often happens with first-time mothers, was bleeding. This eventuality having been a worry to him beforehand, he had had snow gathered from the slopes of Mount Bermion.

He made compresses of the snow and applied them to Olympias' belly. The Queen shivered, tired and exhausted as she was, but the physician could not afford to let himself feel sorry for her and he continued to apply the ice-cold compresses until the bleeding stopped completely.

Then, as he took off his apron and washed his hands, he left her to the care of the women. He let them change her sheets, wash her with soft sponges steeped in rose-water, change her gown with a clean one taken from her clothes chest, and give her something to drink.

It was Nicomachus who presented the baby to Olympias: 'Here is Philip's son, my Queen. You have given birth to a beautiful boy.'

Then he went out into the corridor where a horseman of the royal guard was waiting, dressed for a journey: 'Go, fly to the King and tell him his child is born. Tell him it's a boy, that he is beautiful, healthy and strong.'

The horseman threw his cloak over his shoulders, put the strap of his satchel over his head and ran off. Before he disappeared at the end of the corridor, Nicomachus shouted after him, 'Tell him too that the Queen is well.'

The cavalryman did not even stop and an instant later there came the noise of a horse neighing in the courtyard below and then the clatter of galloping which soon faded to silence along the roads of the sleeping city.

2

ARTEMISIA TOOK THE BABY and put him on the bed alongside the Queen. Olympias lifted herself up on her elbows, her back resting on the pillows, and she looked upon her child.

He was beautiful. His lips were full, his features delicate, his complexion rosy. His hair, a light brown colour, shone with golden reflections and at the very centre of his forehead was what the midwife described as a cowlick – a small tuft of hair that stood up above the rest.

His eyes appeared blue, but deep in the left one was a sort of black shadow that made it seem darker as the light changed.

Olympias lifted him up, held him to her and rocked him until he stopped crying. Then she bared her breast to feed him, but Artemisia moved closer and said, 'My child, the wet-nurse will take care of that. Don't ruin your breasts. The king will soon be back home from the war and you will have to be more beautiful and desirable than ever.'

Artemisia held out her arms to take the baby, but instead of giving him to her, Olympias moved him towards her breast and fed him with her milk until he fell asleep peacefully.

In the meantime the messenger continued his gallop to

13

reach the King as quickly as possible. He came to the river Axios in the middle of the night and spurred the horse on across the bridge of boats that united the two banks. It was still dark when he changed his mount at Thermai and he continued on towards the interior of the Chalcidice peninsula.

Dawn found him on the coast where the vast gulf blazed with the rising sun like a mirror set before a fire. He wove his way up the mountainous mass of the Kalauros, through an increasingly harsh and bitter landscape, among impervious rocks which here and there formed sheer cliffs above the sea, fringed below by the white boiling spume of the sea.

*

The King was besieging the ancient city of Potidaea, which for almost half a century had been under Athenian control. He was doing this not because he wanted conflict with Athens, but because he considered the city to be in Macedonian territory and it was his intention to affirm his domination throughout the region that extended between the Gulf of Thermai and the Bosphorus. At that moment, cramped in an assault tower together with his warriors, Philip – armed, covered in dust, sweat and blood – was about to launch the decisive attack.

'Men!' he shouted. 'If you are truly worthy soldiers, now is the time to prove it! I will give the finest horse in my stables to the first who has the guts to attack the enemy walls together with me, but, by Zeus, if I see even just one of you turn weak-kneed when the time comes, I swear I will flay him skinless. And I will do it personally. Do you hear me?'

'We hear you, King!'

'Now then, let us begin!' ordered Philip as he nodded to his men to take the brakes off the winches. The bridge came down on the walls that had already been breached and half demolished by the battering rams and the King rushed forward – shouting and striking out with his sword, so quickly that it was difficult to keep up with him. But his soldiers knew well that their King always kept his promises and all as one they pushed forward too, barging one against another with their shields and sending the enemy reeling down from the sides and the battlements. This was an enemy already weakened by the hardships of the siege, by the sleepless nights and the fatigue of months and months of continuous fighting. Behind Philip and his guard the rest of the army came flowing, engaging in brutal hand-to-hand combat with the last defenders who were barricading the roads and house entrances.

At sunset Potidaea, brought to its knees, asked for truce.

*

It was almost night when the messenger arrived, having exhausted another two horses. When he looked down from the hills surrounding Potidaea he saw a circle of fires around the walls and he could hear the shouts of the Macedonian soldiers celebrating their victory.

He dug his heel into the horse's ribs and in no time at all he reached the encampment. He asked to be taken to the King's tent.

'What's it about?' asked the officer on guard, from the north judging by his accent. 'The King is busy. The city has fallen and its government has sent a delegation to negotiate.'

'The Prince is born,' replied the messenger.

The news brought the officer instantly to attention. 'Follow me,' he said.

The King was still in his battle armour and was sitting in his tent surrounded by his generals. Just behind him was his deputy, Antipater. All around them were the representatives of Potidaea who rather than negotiating were in fact listening to Philip dictate his conditions.

The officer, realizing that his intrusion would not be tolerated, but that any delay in announcing such an important event would have been tolerated even less, said immediately: 'Sire, news from the palace – your son is born!'

The delegates from Potidaea, pale and drawn, looked at one another, stood up from the stools they had been told to sit on and moved aside. Antipater took up position with his arms crossed over his chest, the posture of one who awaits orders or a word from the King.

Philip had been interrupted in mid-sentence, 'Your city will be required to provide a . . .' and he had continued, with quite a different voice, 'a . . . son.'

The delegates, who failed to understand what was happening, looked at one another dumbstruck, but Philip was already on his feet, his chair crashing to the floor; he pushed the officer aside and grabbed the messenger by the shoulders.

The flames from the lamps sculpted his face into the

sharpest light and shadow, igniting his gaze. 'Tell me what he looks like,' he ordered with the same tone he had used in ordering his warriors to their death for the glory of Macedonia.

The messenger felt hopelessly at a loss, realizing that he had only three words to give his King. He cleared his throat and announced in a stentorian voice: 'Sire, your son is beautiful, healthy and strong!'

'And how do you know? Have you seen him?'

'I would never have presumed, Sire. I was in the corridor, as ordered – my cloak, my satchel and my weapons ready. Nicomachus came out and said . . . these were his very words, "Go, fly to the King and tell him his son is born. Tell him he is beautiful, healthy and strong." '

'Did he say the boy looks like me?'

The messenger hesitated, then replied, 'No, he did not say so, but I am sure he looks like you.'

Philip turned towards Antipater who came forward to embrace his King, and just then the messenger remembered he had heard something else as he was running down the stairs in the palace.

'The physician also said that . . .'

Philip turned suddenly. 'What?'

'That the Queen is well,' concluded the messenger in a single breath.

'When did it happen?'

'The night before last, just after sunset. I flew here without stopping – I haven't eaten, I only drank from my flask and only ever dismounted to change horses . . . I could not wait to bring you this news.'

Philip came back and clapped him on the shoulder.

'Get something to eat and drink for our friend – whatever he wants. And make sure he has a good night's sleep because he has brought me the best of news.'

The emissaries congratulated the King and sought to take advantage of the auspicious moment to conclude their negotiations to some extra advantage, given that Philip's mood had improved so much, but the King said firmly, 'Not now,' and out he went, followed by his field adjutant.

He immediately summoned the commanders of his army's forces; he had wine brought and asked them all to drink with him. Then he issued orders: 'Sound the trumpets for fall in. Have my army lined up in perfect order – infantry and cavalry. I want them all assembled here.'

The noise of the trumpets resounded throughout the camp and the men, many of them already drunk or half naked in the tents with prostitutes, scrambled to their feet, put on their armour, took up their spears and hurried to fall in because the noise of the trumpets was as urgent as the voice of the King himself shouting into the night.

Philip was already standing on a podium, surrounded by his officers, and when the ranks were formed the eldest soldier, as custom dictated, shouted, 'Why have you summoned us, Sire? What do you require of your soldiers?'

Philip stepped forward. He had put on his iron and gold parade armour with a long white cloak; his legs were sheathed in greaves of embossed silver.

The silence was broken only by the snorting of the horses and by the calls of nocturnal animals attracted by the camp fires. The generals standing alongside the King could see that his face was red, as if he had been sitting by the camp fire, and his eyes were moist.

'Men of Macedon!' he roared. 'In my house, in Pella, the Queen has borne me a son. I declare here before you now that he is my legitimate heir and I entrust him to you. His name is

ALÉXANDROS!'

The officers gave the order to present arms: the infantry raised their *sarissae*, enormous battle pikes, twelve feet in length, and the cavalry lifted up to the sky a forest of javelins, while the horses stamped their hooves and neighed as their teeth ground into the bit.

Then, in rhythmic unison, they all began to shout the Prince's name:

Aléxandre! Aléxandre! Aléxandre!

and they beat the handles of their spears against their shields, sending the clamour up to the stars.

They believed that in this way the glory of Philip's son would rise, with their voices, like the tumult made by their weapons, up to the home of the gods, among the constellations of the firmament.

When the assembly was dismissed, the King returned together with Antipater and his adjutants to the tent where the delegates from Potidaea were still waiting for him, patient and resigned. Philip confessed, 'My only sadness is that Parmenion is not here to rejoice with us now.'

Indeed, at that moment General Parmenion was encamped with his army in the mountains of Illyria, not far from Lake Lychnidos, their mission being to secure the Macedonian border in that area. Later some would say that on the very day Philip received news of the birth of his son, he had conquered the city of Potidaea and had received news of another two victories: Parmenion's against the Illyrians and that of his four-horsed chariot in the races at Olympia. For this reason the fortune tellers said that the child born on the day of three victories would surely be invincible.

In truth Parmenion defeated the Illyrians at the beginning of the summer and soon after came the Olympic games and the chariot races, nevertheless Alexander was born into a wonderfully auspicious year and the omens pointed towards a future more akin to a god's than a man's.

The Potidaean delegates tried to resume their negotiations where they had left off, but Philip gestured to indicate his deputy: 'General Antipater knows my feelings on the matter, speak with him.'

'But, Sire,' Antipater intervened, 'it is absolutely imperative that the King should . . .'

Before he had even finished the sentence Philip had put his cloak on his shoulders and whistled for his horse. Antipater followed him, 'Sire, this campaign has involved months of siege and fierce battle to reach this point and you cannot . . .'

'Of course I can!' exclaimed the King, leaping onto his horse and spurring it on. Antipater shook his head and was turning to go back into the royal tent when Philip called out, 'Here! Take this,' and he slipped the seal ring from his finger and threw it to his second in command. 'You'll need it. Make sure it's a good treaty, Antipater, this has been a most costly war!'

He caught the ring with the royal seal and stood for an

instant watching his King gallop through the camp and exit by the northern gate. He shouted to the guardsmen: 'Follow him, you idiots! How can you let him leave alone? Move, damn you!'

As the guards set off at full tilt, Antipater could still see Philip's cloak gleaming in the moonlight on the mountainside and then he was gone. He returned to the tent, had the increasingly bewildered delegates from Potidaea sit themselves down, and said, as he himself took a stool, 'Well, where were we?'

*

Philip rode all through the night and all through the next day, stopping only to change mount and to drink, with his horse, from streams or springs. He came within sight of Pella after sunset, just as the last rays gave a purple hue to the far off snow-coloured peaks of Mount Bermion. Down on the plain herds of galloping horses flowed like a sea swell and thousands of birds descended to sleep on the quiet waters of Lake Borboros.

The evening star shone so brightly as to compete in splendour with the moon which was rising slowly from the liquid surface of the sea. This was the star of the Argeads, the dynasty that since Hercules' time had reigned over these lands, an immortal star, more beautiful than any other in the sky.

Philip drew rein, pulling up his horse to contemplate and invoke the star. 'Watch over my son,' he said from his heart, 'let him reign after me and let his children reign after him and his children's children after that.'

Then he went up to the palace, unannounced,

exhausted and soaked in sweat. A buzz of activity greeted him: a rustling of women's clothes as they fussed along the corridors, a clanking of arms among the guards.

When he looked in through the door of the bed chamber, the Queen was sitting on a grand, high-backed armchair, her naked body only just covered by an Ionian undergown gathered into the finest pleats; the room was perfumed with Pierian roses and Artemisia was holding the boy in her arms.

Two attendants undid the shoulder plates of the King's armour and unhooked the sword from his side so that he might feel the child's skin on his. He took Alexander in his arms and held him tenderly, the baby's head nestled between his father's neck and shoulder. He felt his son's lips on the hardened scar tissue there, he breathed the scent of his lily-soft skin.

Philip closed his eyes and stood upright and immobile in the middle of the silent room. In that moment the roar of battle, the creaking wood of the siege engines, the furious galloping of the horses all faded away; he simply stood stock still and listened to his son's breathing.

3

THE FOLLOWING YEAR Queen Olympias bore Philip a baby girl who was given the name Cleopatra. The child looked like her mother and really was most beautiful, so lovely that the maids played with her as if she were a doll, dressing and undressing her continuously.

Alexander, who had started walking three months previously, was only allowed into his sister's room several days after the birth, and he bore with him a small gift the nurse had prepared. He approached the crib carefully and stood there looking at Cleopatra, his eyes wide open with curiosity, his head leaning to one side. A maid came closer, worried that the boy might be jealous of the new arrival and might harm her, but Alexander took his sister's hand and squeezed it as though he actually realized that this little baby was united to him by a deep and special bond and that for some time she would be his only companion.

Cleopatra gurgled and Artemisia said, 'See? She's very pleased to meet you. Why don't you give her your present?'

Alexander unhooked a metal ring with small silver bells from his belt and started to shake it in front of the baby who seemed to stretch out her hands to grab it. Olympias was very much moved as she watched them: 'Wouldn't it be wonderful if we could stop time right now?' she said, thinking out loud.

For a long time after the birth of his children Philip was involved continuously in bloody wars. He had secured the borders to the north where Parmenion had defeated the Illyrians; to the west was the friendly realm of Epirus, ruled over by Aribbas, Queen Olympias' uncle; to the east a series of campaigns had ensured that the warlike Thracian tribes had been quashed, extending Macedonian control as far as the banks of the Ister. Then he had taken possession of almost all the cities the Greeks had founded on his coasts: Amphipolis, Methone, and Potidaea, participating in the internecine struggles that tormented the Hellenic peninsula.

Parmenion had tried to warn Philip of the danger of this policy and one day, during a council of war the King had called in the palace armoury, he decided to speak up:

'You have built a powerful, united realm, Sire, and you have given the Macedonians pride in their nation; why do you seek now to become involved in the Greeks' internal struggles?'

'Parmenion is right,' said Antipater. 'Their conflicts make no sense. They're all fighting against one another. Yesterday's allies fight each other tooth and nail today and whoever loses forms an alliance with his worst enemy simply to spite the victor.'

'What you say is true,' admitted Philip, 'but the Greeks have everything we lack: art, philosophy, poetry, drama, medicine, music, architecture, and above all else – political science, the art of government.'

'You are a king,' objected Parmenion, 'you have no

need of science. It is enough for you to give orders, and you are obeyed.'

'For as long as I have the strength,' said Philip. 'For as long as no one slips a knife between my ribs.'

Parmenion did not reply. He well knew that no Macedonian king had ever died of natural causes. It was Antipater who broke the silence that had become as heavy as lead.

'If you are determined to put your hand into the lion's mouth then there's nothing I can say to change your mind, but I would advise you to act in the only way that has any chance of success.'

'And that would be?'

'There is only one force in Greece stronger than all others, only one voice that can impose silence . . .'

'The sanctuary of Apollo at Delphi,' said the King.

'Or rather, its priests and the council that governs them.'

'I know,' said Philip in agreement. 'Whoever controls the sanctuary controls much of Greek politics. These are difficult times, however, for the council: they have declared a sacred war against the Phocaeans, accusing them of having farmed lands that belong to Apollo, but the Phocaeans have taken them by surprise and appropriated the temple treasure, using the money to pay for thousands and thousands of mercenaries. Macedonia is the only power that can change the outcome of this conflict.'

'And you have decided to go to war,' concluded Parmenion.

'With one proviso: if I win I want the Phocaeans' seat and vote together with the presidency of the council of the sanctuary.'

Antipater and Parmenion understood that not only had the King already thought out his plan, but he would implement it whatever the cost and they made no attempt to dissuade him.

*

It was a long, bitter conflict with advances and reverses on both sides. Alexander was three years old when Philip was badly defeated for the first time ever and was forced to pull back his troops. His enemies accused him of fleeing, but Philip retorted: 'I did not retreat, I only stepped back to take a better run up, lower my head and butt my opponent – like an angry ram.'

This was Philip. A man of incredible strength of spirit and determination, of indomitable vitality, with a sharp and restless mind. But men of this stamp grow to be ever more alone because they find themselves increasingly incapable of giving anything to those around them.

When Alexander began to be aware of what was happening around him, and when he realized who his father and mother were, he was about six years old. He already spoke with conviction and understood complex and difficult reasoning.

Whenever word reached him that his father was in the palace, he would slip out of the Queen's rooms and walk to the chamber where Philip sat in council with his generals. They all seemed old to the boy, scarred as they were by the infinite number of battles they had survived, and yet they were little more than thirty years old, apart from Parmenion who was almost fifty and whose hair was almost completely white. Whenever Alexander saw the white-haired general he started chanting a rhyme he'd learned from Artemisia:

> The silly old soldier's off to the war
> And falls to the floor, falls to the floor!

And then Alexander himself would tumble to the floor amidst the laughter and to the delight of onlookers.

But it was his own father Alexander observed most carefully, studying his bearing, the way he moved his hands and his eyes, the tone and timbre of his voice, the way in which he dominated the strongest and most powerful men of the realm with the power of his gaze alone.

Alexander would move closer while his father led a council – step by step, little by little – and when Philip reached the high point of his speech or his debate, Alexander would try to climb up onto his knees, as though he hoped that no one would notice at that critical moment.

Only then did Philip seem to be aware of his son and he would hold him close to his chest, without a pause, without losing the thread of his speech, but he saw that his generals changed their posture, he saw their eyes turn to the child and their expressions melt into a light smile, whatever the gravity of the topic he had been dealing with. And Parmenion would smile too, thinking of the rhyme and Alexander's antics.

Then, just as he had arrived, the child would leave quietly. Sometimes he went to his room hoping that his father would come to him there. On other occasions, after waiting for a long time, he would go and sit on one of the palace balconies, staring at the horizon. He would remain there, speechless and motionless, under the spell of the immensity of sky and earth.

And when in those moments his mother approached quietly, she would see the shadow that darkened his left eye deepen slowly, almost as if a mysterious night were falling in the young Prince's soul.

He was fascinated by weaponry, and more than once the maids found him in the armoury attempting to unsheathe one of the King's heavy swords from its scabbard.

One day, while he was staring at a giant set of bronze armour that had belonged to his grandfather Amyntas III, Alexander sensed someone behind him. He turned and found himself in front of a tall, wiry man with a goatee beard and two deep, haunted eyes. He said his name was Leonidas and that he was to be his tutor.

'Why?' asked Alexander.

And that was only the first in a long series of questions that Leonidas would find himself unable to answer.

From then on Alexander's life changed profoundly. He saw his mother and sister less often and saw more and more of his tutor. Leonidas began by teaching him the alphabet, and the following day he found the child writing his name correctly with the point of a stick in the ashes in the hearth.

He taught him to read and to count, things that Alexander learned quickly and easily, but without any particular interest. But when Leonidas began to tell him stories of gods and men, stories of the birth of the world, of the struggles of giants and titans, he saw Alexander's face light up as he listened enrapt.

The child's spirit inclined towards mystery and religion.

One day Leonidas took Alexander to the temple of Apollo near Thermai and allowed him to offer incense to the statue of the god. Alexander took great handfuls and threw it on the brazier, but his teacher shouted at him: 'Incense costs a fortune! You will be entitled to waste as much as you wish when you have conquered the countries that produce it.'

'And where are these countries?' asked the child to whom it seemed strange that one might have to be miserly where the gods were concerned. Then he asked, 'Isn't it true that my father is a great friend of the god Apollo?'

'Your father has won the sacred war and has been nominated head of the council of the sanctuary of Delphi, seat of the oracle of Apollo.'

'Is it true that the oracle tells everyone what they must do?'

'Not quite,' replied Leonidas, taking Alexander by the hand and leading him into the open air. 'You see, when people are about to do something important, they ask a god for advice: "Should I do it or not? And if I do it, what will happen?" for example. Then there is a priestess called the Pythia and the god replies through her, as if he were using her voice. Do you understand? But the words are always obscure, difficult to interpret, and that is why priests exist – to explain the words to the people.'

Alexander turned back to look at the god Apollo standing erect on his pedestal, rigid and immobile, his lips pulled into that strange smile, and he understood why the gods need men in order to be able to speak.

On another occasion, when the royal family had travelled to Aegae, the old capital, in order to offer sacrifices at the tombs of previous kings, Leonidas took Alexander to a tower of the palace from which they had a view of the summit of Mount Olympus covered with storm clouds, being struck by bolts of lightning.

'You see,' he tried to explain, 'the gods are not the statues you admire in the temples: they live up there in an invisible house. They are immortal up there, they sit and dine on nectar and ambrosia. And those lightning bolts are thrown by Zeus himself. He can hit anyone and anything in any part of the world.'

Alexander, his mouth gaping, looked long and hard at the awesome mountain top.

The following day an officer of the palace guard found him outside the city, walking briskly along a path that led towards the mountain.

'Where are you going, Prince Alexander?' the officer asked as he dismounted.

'There,' replied the child, pointing to Mount Olympus.

The officer picked him up and took him back to Leonidas, who was sick with fright and fretting about the terrible punishment the Queen would inflict on him if anything ever happened to her son, his pupil.

Throughout that year Philip had to contend with serious illness – a result of the hardships he had endured during his military campaigns and the unsettled life he led when he was not in battle.

Alexander was pleased because it meant he saw more of his father and was able to spend more time with him. Nicomachus was responsible for overseeing the King's treatment and from his clinic in Stagira he had two assistants sent who would help gather the herbs and roots for his medicines from the surrounding woods and mountains.

The King was put on a strict diet, almost completely without wine, to the point where he became unapproachable and indeed when he was in a bad mood only Nicomachus dared come near him.

One of the two assistants was a fifteen-year-old boy and his name too was Philip.

'Get him out of here,' the King ordered. 'Another Philip here gives me no pleasure whatsoever. I know what we'll do! I'll appoint him as my son's physician, under your supervision, of course.'

Nicomachus agreed, being well used by now to the whims of his King.

'What is your son Aristotle doing?' Philip asked Nicomachus one day as he was drinking a decoction of dandelion, grimacing as it slithered down his throat.

'He's living in Athens and studying with Plato,' replied the physician. 'In fact, I am told he is the best of Plato's students.'

'Interesting. And what is the topic of his research?'

'My son is like me. He is attracted by the observation of natural phenomena rather than by the world of pure speculation.'

'And is he interested in politics?'

'Yes, of course, but here too he demonstrates a particular inclination towards the various manifestations of political organization rather than political science true and proper. He collects constitutions and makes comparative studies of them.'

'And what does he think of monarchial rule?'

'I don't think he has any opinion on the matter. For him the monarchy is simply a form of government typical of certain communities rather than others. You see, Sire, I think that my son is interested in knowing the world for what it is rather than establishing a series of principles that the world should conform to.'

Philip forced down the last sip of the decoction under the vigilant gaze of his physician, which seemed to command, 'Every last drop.' Then he wiped his mouth with the edge of his royal cloak and said, 'Keep me informed about that boy, Nicomachus, because I'm interested in him.'

'I will. I'm interested in him too – he's my son.'

During this period Alexander spent as much time as possible with Nicomachus because he was an affable man and full of surprises, while Leonidas was somewhat cantankerous and terribly strict.

One day he entered the physician's surgery and saw Nicomachus examining his father's back and measuring his pulse at his neck.

'What are you doing?' he asked.

'I am checking the speed of your father's heartbeat.'

'And what is it that moves the heart?'

'Vital energy.'

'And where is this vital energy?'

Nicomachus looked in the boy's eyes and read there an insatiable hunger for knowledge, a wonderful intensity of feeling. He brushed the boy's cheek with his finger while Philip – intent and fascinated by the scene – watched on.

'Ah! No one knows the answer to that one,' said Nicomachus.

4

PHILIP WAS SOON back on his feet and engaged in the business of government with his energies fully restored, disappointing those who had even gone so far as to suggest that he had died.

Alexander was not pleased because this meant he no longer saw his father so often, but it meant he became interested in getting to know other youngsters – some his age, others a little older – the children of Macedonian nobles who frequented the court and lived in the palace in accordance with the King's specific wishes. For Philip this was a way of keeping the kingdom united, of binding together the most powerful families, with all the tribal and factional chiefs under one roof – the King's.

Some of these youngsters also attended Leonidas' lessons – Perdiccas, Lysimachus, Seleucus, Leonnatus and Philotas, General Parmenion's son. Others, who were older, such as Ptolemy and Craterus, already bore the title 'Page' and were directly dependent on the King for their education and their training.

Seleucus at this stage in his life was quite small and thin, but Leonidas liked him because he was good at his schoolwork. He was particularly well versed in history and mathematics and for his age was surprisingly wise and well balanced. He could do complicated sums in increasingly shorter times and he enjoyed competing with his companions, often besting them.

His dark, deep eyes lent him a penetrating look and his unkempt hair was a sign of a strong and independent, though never rebellious character. During lessons he was often keen to get himself noticed for his remarks, but he never tried to ingratiate himself with his teacher and neither did he do anything to charm or flatter his superiors.

Lysimachus and Leonnatus were the most undisciplined because they came from the interior and had grown up free out in the woods and the prairies, taking the horses out to graze and spending much of their time outdoors. Living cooped up within four walls was like life in prison for them.

Lysimachus, who was a little older, was quicker in adapting to this new life while Leonnatus, who was only seven, looked like a little wolf because of his rough appearance, his red hair and the freckles over his nose and around his eyes. When punished he reacted by kicking and biting, and Leonidas tried taming him by making him go hungry and locking him up while the others were playing; he even made ample use of his willow cane. But Leonnatus had his own form of revenge in that every time he saw the teacher appear at the end of a corridor he would shout out a rhyme at the top of his voice:

Ek korì korì koróne!
Ek korì korì koróne!

'Here he is, here's the old crow!' and all the others would join in, including Alexander, until poor Leonidas went red with rage and lost his temper, chasing them and brandishing his cane above his head.

When he fought with his companions, Leonnatus simply had no concept of the idea of losing and he even came to blows with those bigger than him, the result being that he was always covered in bruises and scratches, almost always unpresentable on official occasions or at court ceremonies. This was quite the opposite of Perdiccas, who of the group was the most conscientious, always present both in class and on the games and training fields. He was only a year older than Alexander and, together with Philotas, they often played the same games.

'When I grow up I'm going to be a general like your father,' Perdiccas used to say to Philotas, who of all his friends was the one who was most like him.

Ptolemy, almost fourteen, was quite stocky and well developed for his age. The first spots were appearing on his face together with a few wiry hairs, and he had funny features dominated by a large nose and hair that was always ruffled. His companions poked fun at him, saying that he'd started growing nose-first, and this upset him no end. He would lift up his tunic to show off other protuberances that were growing no less rapidly than his nose.

Apart from these moments of excess in his high spirits, Ptolemy was a good boy, very fond of reading and writing. One day he let Alexander come to his room and showed him his books. He had at least twenty of them.

'So many!' exclaimed the Prince as he went to touch them.

'Stop right there!' said Ptolemy as he blocked him.

'They're delicate objects: papyrus is fragile and it disintegrates easily; one has to know the right way to unroll and roll them. They have to be kept in a well-ventilated and dry place with a mousetrap nearby because mice love papyrus and if they get hold of the scrolls – that's the end of that. They can polish off two books of the *Iliad* or a tragedy by Sophocles in one night. Wait just a moment and I'll get one for you.' He took out a scroll marked with a small red card.

'There. You see? This is a comedy by Aristophanes. It's called *Lisistrata* and it's my favourite. It tells of an occasion when the women of Athens and Sparta were truly fed up with all the wars that kept their menfolk away from home and they were all desperate for . . .' he stopped when he saw Alexander's face, his mouth gaping. 'Well, let's skip that, you're too young for these things. I'll tell you all about it some other time, all right?'

'What's a comedy?' asked Alexander.

'Haven't you ever been to the theatre?' asked Ptolemy, shocked.

'Children aren't allowed. But I know that it's like listening to a story, only there are real men with masks on their faces and they pretend to be Hercules or Theseus. Some of them even pretend to be women.'

'More or less,' replied Ptolemy. 'Tell me, what are your teacher's lessons about?'

'I can add and subtract, I know the geometrical figures and I can distinguish the Great Bear from the Little Bear in the heavens as well as more than twenty other constellations. And then I can read and write and I've read Aesop's fables.'

'Mmmm . . .' observed Ptolemy, carefully putting the scroll back in its place. 'Kids' stuff.'

'And then I know the entire list of my ancestors, both on my father's and on my mother's side. I am a descendant of Hercules and of Achilles; did you know that?'

'And who were Hercules and Achilles?'

'Hercules was the strongest hero in the world and he carried out twelve labours. Shall I tell you about them? The Nemean lion, the Hind of Cery . . . Ceryne . . .' The boy couldn't quite get his tongue round it.

'I see, I see. You're very good. But if you like I can read you some of the beautiful things I have here in my study . . . what do you think? And now, why don't you run along and play? Did you know there's a boy who's just arrived here in Pella and who's just your age?'

Alexander's face lit up. 'Where is he?'

'I saw him in the courtyard kicking a ball around. He's a strong-looking specimen.'

Alexander ran down as fast as he could and sat under the portico to watch the new guest without daring to speak to him.

All of a sudden the boy kicked a little harder and sent the ball rolling to Alexander's feet. The newcomer ran after it and the two youngsters found themselves face to face.

'Do you want to play with me? It's better when two play. I'll kick it and you catch it.'

'What's your name?' asked Alexander.

'Hephaestion, and yours?'

'Alexander.'

'Right. Come on then, up against that wall. I kick first

and if you catch the ball you get a point, then it's your turn to kick. If you don't catch it I get a point and I get to kick again. Understand?'

Alexander nodded in agreement and they started playing; soon the courtyard was filled with their shouting. They only stopped when they were dead tired and dripping with sweat.

'Do you live here?' Hephaestion asked as he sat on the ground.

Alexander sat down beside him. 'Of course. This is my palace.'

'Don't tell tales. You're too little to have a palace this big.'

'The palace is mine because it belongs to my father – King Philip.'

'By Zeus!' exclaimed Hephaestion, waving his right hand in a gesture of amazement.

'Do you want to be friends?'

'Of course, but to become friends we have to exchange some token of friendship.'

'What's a token of friendship?'

'I give you something and you give me another thing in exchange.'

Hephaestion rooted in his pocket and pulled out a small white object.

'Gosh! A tooth!'

'Yes,' whistled Hephaestion through the gap where one of his front teeth had been. 'It fell out a few nights ago and I almost swallowed it. Here – it's yours.'

Alexander took it and immediately felt at a loss because he had nothing to give in exchange. He fumbled in his pockets while Hephaestion stood there in front of him holding his hand out in expectation.

Alexander, finding himself completely lacking in a gift of equal significance, gave a deep sigh, gulped, and then put his fingers into his mouth and took hold of a tooth that had been wobbling for some days but which was still quite solid.

He began to rock it backwards and forwards, pushing and pulling hard and holding back tears of pain until it finally came out. He spat out a gob of blood, washed the tooth in the drinking-water fountain and handed it to Hephaestion.

'There you are,' he mumbled. 'Now we're friends.'

'Until death?' asked Hephaestion, pocketing his token.

'Until death,' replied Alexander.

*

Summer was already coming to an end when Olympias told her son that there was to be a visit from his uncle, Alexander of Epirus.

He knew he had an uncle – his mother's younger brother – and he knew that they shared the same name. But even though Alexander had seen his uncle on previous occasions, he had no real recollection of him because he had been so young.

Prince Alexander saw his namesake arrive on horseback one evening, accompanied by his escort and his tutors.

He was a handsome boy of twelve with dark hair and deep blue eyes; he carried all the trappings of his dignified rank: a ribbon of gold around his hair, a purple cloak and in his right hand an ivory sceptre, because he too was a king, albeit a young one and of a country that was all mountains.

'Look!' exclaimed Alexander, turning to Hephaestion who was sitting next to him with his legs dangling over the balcony. 'That's my uncle, Alexander. He has the same name as me and he's a king too, did you know that?'

'King of what?' asked his friend, swinging his legs.

'King of the Molossians.'

He was still speaking when Artemisia grabbed him from behind. 'Come here! You have to get ready now to meet your uncle.'

Alexander kicked his legs because he didn't want to leave Hephaestion, but Artemisia carried him bodily to his mother's bath chamber where she undressed him, washed his face, made him put on a tunic and a Macedonian cloak trimmed in gold, put a ribbon of silver around his head and then stood him up on a chair to admire him. 'Come on, little King. Your mother's waiting for you.'

She led him to the royal antechamber where Queen Olympias was waiting, already dressed and perfumed and with her hair arranged. She was stunning: her black eyes contrasted with her flame-coloured hair and the long blue stole embroidered with golden palmettes along the edges covered a *chiton* tunic in the Athenian style, slightly low-cut and held up on her shoulders with a thin cord, the same colour as the stole.

Her cleavage, which the *chiton* left partly visible, was beautifully embellished with a large drop of amber, as big as a pigeon's egg, set in a capsule of gold in the shape of an acorn – a wedding present from Philip.

She took Alexander by the hand and went to sit on the

throne alongside her husband who was ready to receive his young brother-in-law.

The boy entered at the bottom of the hall and bowed first to the King, as protocol required, and then to the Queen, his sister.

Philip was full of pride as a result of his military successes, and rich because of the gold mines he had occupied on Mount Pangaeos. Indeed, he was fully aware of being the most powerful lord of all the Hellenic peninsula or perhaps even the most powerful in the world after the Persian emperor. For these reasons he increasingly behaved in such a way as to inspire awe in his visitors, both in the finery of his clothes and the splendour of the ornaments he wore.

Following the ritual greetings, the young King of Epirus was led to his apartments so that he could make himself ready for the banquet.

Alexander, too, would have liked to take part, but his mother told him he was still too young and that he and Hephaestion could play with the ceramic soldiers that she had had made for him by a potter in Aloros.

That evening, after the banquet, Philip invited his brother-in-law to a private room to talk about politics and Olympias was doubly offended – firstly because she was the Queen of Macedon and secondly because the King of Epirus was her brother.

In truth, Alexander was only King in name, not in fact. Epirus was actually in the hands of his uncle, Aribbas, who had no intention of stepping down, and only Philip, with his strength, his army and his gold, would ever have the power to install Alexander firmly on the throne.

To do so was certainly in Philip's interests because he would thus keep the young King tied to him and at the same time dampen Olympias' ambitions. She often felt that her husband neglected her and in the exercise of power she had found some satisfaction in a life that was otherwise colourless and monotonous.

'You must be patient for a few more years,' explained Philip to the young King. 'Just for the time it will take me to drum some sense into all the cities on the coast that are still independent and to make sure the Athenians understand who is strongest in this area. I have nothing against them as such, it's just that I do not want them in the way here in Macedon. And I want control of the straits between Thrace and Asia.'

'Whatever you say, my dear brother-in-law,' replied Alexander, who felt flattered at being treated, at his age, like a real man and a real king. 'I realize that there are more important things for you than the mountains of Epirus, but if one day you are able to help me, I will be grateful to you for the rest of my life.'

Although only just adolescent, the youngster had a fine head on his shoulders and Philip was most favourably impressed.

'Why not stay here with us?' he asked. 'The situation in Epirus will be increasingly dangerous for you and I would rather be sure that you are safe. Your sister, the Queen, is here, and she has your best interests at heart. You will have your apartments, your royal income and all the prestige befitting your rank. When the time comes I will personally accompany you to take possession of your father's throne.'

The young King accepted willingly and so he remained in the palace at Pella until Philip completed the political and military programme through which Macedon was to become the richest, the strongest and the most feared state in Europe.

In her resentment Queen Olympias had gone to her rooms where she waited for her brother to come and say goodnight and pay his respects before retiring. From a room nearby came the voices of Hephaestion and Alexander playing with their toy soldiers and shouting:

'You're dead!'

'No I'm not! *You're* dead!'

Then their voices subsided into silence. The energies of the little warriors soon dwindled into sleep as the moon made its appearance in the sky.

5

ALEXANDER WAS SEVEN and his uncle, the King of Epirus, was twelve when Philip attacked the city of Olynthus and the Chalcidicean League, the association which controlled the large trident-shaped Chalcidice Peninsula. The Athenians, allies of Olynthus, sought to negotiate, but Philip proved to be quite intractable.

'Either you leave here or you will have to chase me out of Macedon,' was his answer, which on the face of it did not leave much room for manoeuvre.

General Antipater tried to make Philip consider other aspects of the problem and as soon as the Athenian envoys, all of them furious, left the council room, he said, 'This attitude, Sire, will only help your enemies in Athens, especially Demosthenes.'

'I am not afraid of him,' said the King, shrugging his shoulders.

'Yes, but he is an excellent orator as well as a skilful politician. He is the only one to have understood your strategy. He has noticed that you no longer use mercenary troops, that you have created a national army which is united and motivated, and you have made this the key feature of your reign. He is convinced that this makes you Athens' most dangerous enemy. An intelligent opponent always merits consideration, Sire.'

Right there and then Philip was lost for words. All he said was, 'Keep an eye on Demosthenes through some of our men in Athens. I want to know everything he says about me.'

'It shall be done, Sire,' replied Antipater, and he immediately alerted their informers in Athens, telling them to make sure they sent news of Demosthenes' activities rapidly and effectively. Every time a text of the great orator's speeches arrived in Pella, however, there was trouble. The King always asked for the title first.

'*Against Philip*,' came the inevitable reply.

'Again?' he would shout, his temper boiling. These readings would upset him so much that if the bad news arrived just after a meal, it meant instant indigestion. He would stride up and down the room like a caged lion while his secretary read the speech out loud, and every now and then he would interrupt, shouting, 'What was that? Damnation! Repeat it . . . read that bit again!' His reaction was so fierce that the secretary came to feel that the words he was reading were actually his own.

The thing that drove the King to distraction more than anything else was Demosthenes' insistence on calling Macedon 'a barbaric or second-class state'.

'Barbaric?' he shouted, sweeping everything off the table onto the floor. 'Second-class? I'll show him second-class!'

'You must bear in mind, Sire,' the secretary pointed out, trying to calm him, 'that, as far as we know, the people's reaction to these diatribes of Demosthenes is rather luke-warm. The people of Athens are more interested in knowing how problems in land ownership and the distribution of lands to the peasants of Attica will be resolved.

They could not care less about Demosthenes' political ambitions.'

The passionate speeches against Philip were followed by others in favour of Olynthus, an attempt to convince the people to vote for military aid for the besieged city, but even this approach brought negligible results.

The city fell the following year and Philip razed it to the ground to provide a clear, unequivocal message for whoever dared challenge him.

'This really will give Demosthenes good reason to call me a barbarian!' he shouted, when Antipater invited him to reflect on the consequences, in Athens and in Greece, of such radical action.

Indeed, this drastic decision made the conflicts in the Hellenic peninsula even more acute: throughout Greece there was no city or village that did not have both a pro-Macedonian and an anti-Macedonian faction.

Philip, for his part, felt ever closer to Zeus, father of all the gods, in terms of glory and of power. He felt this way even though the continuous conflicts into which he threw himself 'like an angry ram', to use his own words, were beginning to take their toll. He drank heavily during the intervals between one campaign and the next and he let himself go in excesses of all kinds during binges that lasted from dusk to dawn.

Queen Olympias, however, was becoming increasingly withdrawn, dedicating herself to caring for her children and to religious worship. Philip came to her bed rarely now and when he did there was no satisfaction for either of them. She was cold and distant and he would leave humiliated by the meetings, realizing that his desperate and hurried passion left the Queen unmoved and numbed.

Olympias was a woman whose character was no weaker than her husband's, and she guarded her own dignity jealously. In her brother, and in her son especially, she saw the young men who one day would be the true custodians of that dignity, restoring to her the prestige and the power that were hers by right and which Philip's arrogance stripped from her, day by day throughout his reign.

Official religious functions constituted an obligation for the Queen, but they were clearly lacking in any real meaning for her. She was sure that the gods of Olympus, if they had ever existed, had no interest in human affairs at all. She was more intrigued by other cults, especially that of Dionysus, a mysterious god capable of taking hold of the human mind and transforming it, dragging it into a vortex of violent emotion and atavistic feeling.

Word was that she had been secretly initiated and that by night she took part in the god's orgies which involved drinking wine mixed with potent drugs and dancing to the point of exhaustion and hallucination, all this to the rhythm of primitive musical instruments. In this state she felt as though she were running through the woods at night, her fine royal vestments left torn to rags on the branches as she chased wild beasts, caught them and ate their still-throbbing flesh. Then she would fall exhausted, succumbing to a leaden sleepiness, on what seemed to be a blanket of fragrant moss.

And in this state of semi-consciousness she saw the divinities and the creatures of the woods come timidly out of their dens: the nymphs with their skin as green as the leaves of the trees, the satyrs with their bristly coats, half-men and half-goats, approaching a simulacrum of the god's gigantic phallus, crowning it with ivy and vine-leaves, soaking it with wine. And then the orgy exploded, all of them drinking undiluted wine and throwing themselves into feral couplings that would lead them into direct contact, in that frenetic ecstasy, with Dionysus himself, possessed by his spirit.

Others came closer furtively, their phalluses enormously erect, avidly ogling Olympias' nudity, eager to satisfy their animalistic lust . . .

And so the Queen, in secluded places known only to the initiates, abandoned herself to the depths of her wildest and most barbaric nature, to the rites that liberated the most aggressive and violent elements in her soul and body. Apart from these more extreme manifestations her life in truth consisted of all the usual things expected of any woman and spouse, and she was able to return to that life as though closing a solid interior door that cut out all memory and all feeling.

In the quiet of her rooms she taught Alexander all that a young boy could possibly learn of those cults; she told him of the adventures and journeys of the god Dionysus who had travelled – together with his cortege of satyrs and sileni wearing crowns of vine-leaves – as far as the land of tigers and panthers, as far as India.

But if his mother's influence was important in moulding Alexander's spirit, even more so was the daunting education administered according to his father's will and wishes.

Philip had ordered Leonidas, official director of the boy's schooling, to organize his son's learning without neglecting anything and so, as Alexander progressed, other teachers, trainers and instructors were summoned to court.

As soon as Alexander was able to appreciate poetry, Leonidas began to read him the works of Homer, particularly the *Iliad*, because it presented the codes of honour and bearing that were appropriate to a royal prince of the house of the Argeads. In this way the old teacher began to win not only the minds of Alexander and his young companions, but their hearts too. However, the rhyme that announced Leonidas' arrival in class was still to be heard echoing through the corridors of the palace:

Ek korì korì koróne!
Ek korì korì koróne!

'Here he is, here's the old crow!'

Together with Alexander, Hephaestion listened to the poetry of Homer, and the two boys, enrapt, pictured in their minds' eye all those extraordinary adventures – the story of the titanic struggle in which the strongest men and the most beautiful women in the world had taken part, joined even by the gods themselves, all of them with parts to play and sides to take.

By now Alexander was perfectly aware of who he was, of the universe that rotated around him and the destiny for which he was being prepared.

The models presented to him were those of heroism, of resistance to pain, of honour and respect for one's word, of sacrifice to the point of offering one's life. And he followed these models day after day, not out of the diligence of the disciple, but out of his own natural inclination.

Gradually his nature revealed itself for what it was: at one and the same time it displayed the brutal aggressiveness of his father – the royal temper that could flash like lightning – together with the mysterious charm of his mother, her curiosity for the unknown, her hunger for mystery.

He cherished his mother deeply. It was an almost morbid bond, while he held his father in limitless esteem. Over time, however, this admiration gradually evolved into a desire for competition, an ever stronger will to emulate him. Indeed, there came a day when the frequent news of Philip's successes seemed to sadden rather than please Alexander. He began to think that if his father conquered everything, then there would be no space left for him to demonstrate his own worth and valour.

He was still too young to be able to understand just how big the world is.

Occasionally, on entering Leonidas' classroom along with his companions for their lessons, he would bump into a sad-looking youngster, perhaps thirteen or fourteen years of age, who always rushed off without stopping to speak.

'Who is that boy?' he asked his teacher one day.

'That's no concern of yours,' replied Leonidas, briskly changing the subject.

6

EVER SINCE BECOMING KING, Philip's greatest ambition had been to bring Macedon into the Greek world, but he well knew that to achieve this goal would inevitably require the use of brute force. For this reason he had dedicated all his resources to making his country a modern power, pulling it up out of its condition as a tribal land of herdsmen and livestock farmers.

He had developed agriculture on the plains, bringing skilled experts from the Greek islands and cities of Asia Minor, and he had intensified mining activity on Mount Pangaeos, extracting up to a thousand talents per annum of gold and silver.

He had imposed his authority on the tribal leaders and made them dependent on him either through force or through matrimonial alliances. He had also created an army the likes of which had never been seen before, consisting of enormously powerful heavy infantry, extremely mobile light infantry and squadrons of cavalry that had no reason whatsoever to fear any force in the Aegean area.

But all this had not been enough for him to be accepted as Greek. And not only Demosthenes, but also many other orators and men of politics in Athens, Corinth, Megara and Sicyon continued to call him Philip the Barbarian.

For the Greeks the Macedonian accent, which was influenced by the speech of the uncivilized peoples pressing on Macedon's northern borders, was something laughable. Macedonian excesses in drinking, eating and lovemaking during their feasts, which regularly deteriorated into orgies, were similarly scorned. A state still based on blood ties rather than rights of citizenship, ruled over by a king who governed absolutely and was above all laws, was considered barbaric.

Philip attained his objective when he finally defeated the Phocaeans in the sacred war and had them expelled from the council of the sanctuary, the noblest and most prestigious assembly of all Greece. The two votes held by their representatives were assigned to the King of Macedon, who was also granted the great honour of being appointed president of the Pythian Games, the most important after the Olympics.

This was the crowning glory of ten years of concerted effort and it coincided with the tenth birthday of his son, Alexander.

In that same period a great Athenian orator by the name of Isocrates delivered a speech in which he praised Philip as protector of the Greeks and as the only man who could ever hope to quash the barbarians of the Orient, the Persians who for over a century had threatened Hellenic civilization and freedom.

Alexander was kept fully informed of these events by his teachers and the news worried him greatly. He felt grown up enough now to take on his role in the country's history, but he well knew that he was still too young to be able to act.

As the Prince grew, his father dedicated more and more time to him, almost as though he considered him a man, while still keeping him out of his most daring projects. Philip's objective was not in fact domination of peninsular Greece: that was only a means. His ambitions lay much further, beyond the sea, towards the limitless territories of all Asia.

Sometimes, during his periods of rest in the palace at Pella, he would take Alexander up to the highest tower after dinner and would point towards the eastern horizon, where the moon was rising over the wave-furrowed sea.

'Do you know what's over there, Alexander?'

'Asia, Father,' came the reply. 'The land where the sun rises.'

'And do you know how big Asia is?'

'My geography teacher, Cratippus, says it's bigger than ten thousand stadia.'

'He's wrong, my son. Asia is a hundred times bigger than that. When I was fighting on the River Ister, I met a Scythian warrior who spoke Macedonian. He told me that beyond the river there extends a plain, vast as a sea, and then mountains so big they pierce the sky with their peaks. He explained that there are deserts so wide it takes months to cross them and that on the other side there are mountains rich in precious gemstones – lapis lazuli, rubies, cornelian.

'He told me that on those plains run herds of thousands of fiery-tempered horses, indefatigable, capable of running for days over the infinite expanses. "There are regions," he said, "gripped in the ice, locked in the dark bitterness of night for half the year, and then others burned up by the blazing sun throughout the seasons, places where not even a blade of grass grows, where the snakes are poisonous and the sting of a scorpion kills in an instant." That is Asia, my son.'

Alexander looked at his father, saw his eyes smouldering with dreams and understood what was burning in his soul.

More than a year had passed since that night in the tower when one morning Philip suddenly entered Alexander's room: 'Put on your Thracian trousers and get yourself a rough woollen cloak. No insignias and no ornament. We leave immediately.'

'Where are we going?'

'I have already had them prepare the horses and the food; we'll be away for some days. I want to show you something.'

Alexander asked no more questions. He dressed as he had been told to, looked in for a moment at the door of his mother's apartments to say goodbye, and quickly went down into the courtyard where a small escort from the royal cavalry and two steeds were waiting.

Philip was already on his mount. Alexander jumped onto his own horse and they all galloped out of the palace through the open gate.

They rode for several days towards the east, first along the coast, then through the interior, then again on the coast. They passed Thermai, Apollonia and Amphipolis, stopping at night in small country inns and eating traditional Macedonian food – roast goat's meat, game, mature sheep's milk cheese and bread baked in the embers of the fire.

After leaving Amphipolis they started weaving their way up a steep path until, quite suddenly, they saw a desolate landscape there before them. The mountain had been stripped of its wooded cover, and everywhere there were mutilated trunks and carbonized tree stumps. The land, laid bare by the destruction of its greenery, was pitted with excavations in several places and at the entrance to each cave-like hole there stood enormous piles of rubble, like giant anthills.

A relentless drizzle began to fall and the cavalry escort pulled their hoods over their heads as they urged the horses forward. The main bridleway soon forked into a labyrinth of pathways on which a multitude of ragged and emaciated men were walking, their skin darkened and wrinkly, all carrying heavy baskets full of rocks.

A little way beyond, a column of dense black smoke rose into the sky in lazy coils, spreading a thick soot over the entire area which made breathing difficult.

'Cover your mouth with your cloak,' Philip abruptly ordered his son.

A strange silence lay everywhere and there was not even any sound from the movement of all those feet, muffled as they were by the thick mud the rain had made of the dust.

Alexander looked around in amazement: this was how he had imagined Hades, the kingdom of the dead, and the sight brought some lines from Homer to mind:

There lie the realm and region of the Men of Winter hidden in mist and cloud. Never the flaming eye of Helios lights on those men at morning, when he climbs the sky of stars, nor in descending earthward out of heaven, ruinous night being rove over those wretches.*

Then, suddenly, the silence was broken by a dark, rhythmic noise, almost like the fist of a giant Cyclops beating monstrously on the tormented slopes of the mountain. Alexander spurred his horse on by digging in his heels; he wanted to see what was making the tremendous noise which now seemed so strong as to make the ground shake.

They came over a rocky crest, and Alexander saw ahead of him the point where all the pathways came to an end. There was a gigantic machine, a sort of tower of large wooden beams and uprights, and it supported a pulley at its highest point. A hemp rope held a colossal drop hammer, made of iron, while at the other end the rope was wrapped around a winch operated by hundreds of poor souls. They pushed the winch to make the rope turn around the drum, thus raising the hammer inside the wooden tower.

When the hammer reached the top, one of the overseers unhooked the brake, freeing the drum of the winch which then spun in the opposite direction because of the weight of the hammer. The hammer fell freely to earth, smashing the rocks that were tipped inside continuously from the baskets carried bodily across the mountain.

The men gathered the smashed mineral material, filled other baskets with it and then took it away along other paths to an open area. Here it was crushed more finely in

* *The Odyssey*, Book XI (translated by Robert Fitzgerald).

mortars and then washed in the waters of a torrent, channelled through a series of weirs and ramps, separating the gold granules and dust from the smashed rock.

'These are the mines of Mount Pangaeos,' Philip explained. 'With this gold I have armed and equipped our army, I have built our palaces, I have developed Macedon's strength.'

'Why have you brought me here?' asked Alexander, his profound distress apparent in his voice. While he was asking the question one of the labourers collapsed to the ground and almost ended up beneath his horse's hooves. An overseer made sure the man was dead, then nodded to another two poor wretches who put their baskets to one side, took the body by the feet and dragged it away.

'Why have you brought me here?' Alexander asked again. And Philip saw the leaden sky reflected in the dark expression on his son's face.

'You have not yet seen the worst of it,' he replied. 'Do you feel up to going underground?'

'I am not afraid of anything,' stated the boy.

'Follow me then.'

The King dismounted and moved towards the entrance of one of the caves. The overseer who challenged him, holding up his whip, suddenly stopped in shock, recognizing the golden star of the Argeads on Philip's chest.

Philip simply nodded and the overseer stood back, lit a lantern and prepared to guide them underground.

Alexander followed his father, but as soon as he entered the cave he felt himself suffocating in the unbearable stench of human urine, sweat and excrement. They had to crouch, sometimes with their backs almost bent double, in a narrow passageway full of the din of continuous hammering, of a general breathlessness, of coughing, of the guttural rattles of death.

The overseer stopped occasionally where a group of men were working with their picks to extract the mineral-bearing rock. Here and there they stopped at the edge of a pit and down at the bottom the feeble glow of a lantern illuminated a bony back, joined to skeletal arms.

Once or twice the miners, down in these pits, on hearing the approach of footsteps or voices, lifted their heads and so Alexander witnessed the masks of men disfigured by fatigue, by illness and by the horror of living such a life.

Further on, at the bottom of one pit, they saw a corpse.

'Many of them commit suicide,' the overseer explained. 'They throw themselves on their picks or stab themselves with their chisels.'

Philip turned to look at Alexander. The Prince was silent and apparently numbed by this experience, and the darkness of death had fallen over his eyes.

They exited on the other side of the mountain through a narrow passage, and there were the horses and their escort waiting for them.

Alexander stared at his father. 'What have these people done to deserve this?' he asked, his face waxen pale.

'Nothing,' replied the King. 'Apart from being born.'

7

THEY REMOUNTED THEIR HORSES and went down to the pass through the rain which had started falling once more. Alexander rode in silence alongside his father.

'I wanted you to know that there is a price to be paid for everything. And I wanted you to know exactly what type of price as well. Our grandeur, our conquests, our palaces and our finery . . . all this must be paid for.'

'But why them?'

'There is no why or wherefore. The world is governed by fate. When they were born it was written that they would die in that way, just as our own destinies were established at our births, and the outcome will be kept hidden from us until the final moment.

'Only man, among all living things, is capable both of rising up to touch the dwelling of the gods, and of sinking lower than a beast. You have already seen the home of the gods, you have lived in the home of a king, but I felt it was right that you should see what fate may have in store for a human being. Among those wretches there are men who perhaps one day were chiefs or nobles, and who have suddenly been plunged into this misery by fate.'

'But if this is the destiny that may await all men, why not be merciful for as long as fortune smiles upon us?'

'That is what I wanted to hear you say. You must be

merciful whenever you can, but remember that nothing can be done to change the nature of things.'

At that moment Alexander saw a girl just slightly younger than himself coming up the path; she was carrying two heavy baskets full of broad beans and chickpeas, probably for the overseers' meal.

The Prince dismounted and stood in front of her: she was thin, barefoot, her hair dirty, her big dark eyes full of sadness.

'What is your name?' he asked her.

The girl did not reply.

'She probably cannot speak,' observed Philip.

Alexander turned to his father. 'I can change her fate. I want to change it.'

Philip nodded. 'You can, if you wish, but remember that your actions will not change the world.'

Alexander had the girl climb onto the horse, behind him, and he covered her with his cloak.

The sun was setting when they reached Amphipolis once more, and they spent the night in the house of a friend of the King. Alexander ordered that the girl should be washed and dressed and then he sat and watched her as she ate.

He tried to speak to her, but she replied in monosyllables and nothing of what she said was comprehensible.

'It must be some barbarian tongue,' Philip explained. 'If you want to communicate with her, you'll have to wait until she learns Macedonian.'

'I will wait,' replied Alexander.

The following day the weather improved and they

continued on their return journey, once again crossing the bridge of boats over the Strymon, but on reaching Bromiskos, they turned to the south along the peninsula of Mount Athos. They rode throughout the day and at sunset reached a point where they could see before them an enormous trench which had been carved through the peninsula from one side to the other. Alexander pulled in the reins of his charger and sat immobile, speechless, looking at the gigantean work.

'Do you see this canal?' his father asked. 'It was excavated almost one hundred and fifty years ago by Xerxes, the emperor of the Persians, to allow the passage of his fleet and to avoid the risk of its being shipwrecked on the cliffs of Mount Athos. Ten thousand men laboured on it, working shifts through day and night. And before this the emperor had had a bridge of boats built across the Bosphorus, uniting Asia with Europe.

'In a few days' time we will receive a delegation from the Great King of the Persians. I wanted you to have some inkling of the power of the empire with which we are negotiating.'

Alexander nodded and stared at the colossal feat for a long time without speaking; then, seeing his father set off once more, he dug his heels into the flanks of his horse and followed on behind.

'There's something I'd like to ask you,' said Alexander as he rode alongside Philip.

'I am listening.'

'There is a boy in Pella who comes to Leonidas' lessons, but he does not sit with us. On the few occasions I have met him he has avoided speaking to me and he is usually so very sad, melancholic even. Leonidas won't explain who he is, but I am sure you must know.'

'He is your cousin, Amyntas,' replied Philip without turning. 'Son of my brother who died in battle fighting an Illyrian tribe. Before you were born he was heir to the throne and I governed in his place as regent.'

'You mean *he* should be king?'

'The throne belongs to whoever is able to defend it,' replied Philip. 'Remember that. And in our country whoever has come to power has always eliminated all pretenders to the throne.'

'But you let Amyntas live.'

'He is my brother's son, and he poses no threat to me.'

'You have been . . . merciful.'

'If you like.'

'Sire?'

Philip turned; Alexander only called him 'Sire' when he was angry with him or when he wanted to ask a very serious question.

'If you were to die in battle, who would be the heir to the throne – Amyntas or myself?'

'The worthier of the two.'

The boy asked nothing else, but the reply made a deep impression on him and marked his soul for ever.

They reached Pella three days later and Alexander gave Artemisia the job of looking after the girl he had saved from the horrors of Mount Pangaeos.

'From now onwards,' he affirmed, with a certain childish haughtiness, 'she will be in my service. And you will teach her everything she needs to know.'

'But does she at least have a name?' asked Artemisia.

'I know not. I, however, will call her Leptine.'

'That's nice . . . suits a little girl.'

That day news came of the death of old Nicomachus. The King was most sorry because he had been an excellent physician and had brought his son into the world.

In any case Nicomachus's surgery was not closed, even though his son, Aristotle, had taken quite a different direction in life and was then in Asia, in the city of Atarneus, where he had founded a new school of philosophy on the death of his teacher, Plato.

It was Nicomachus's young assistant, Philip, who continued to work in the surgery and he practised the profession with great skill and ability.

The youngsters who lived at court with Alexander had grown by now in both body and spirit and the inclinations they had displayed as infants were now for the most part consolidated. Those companions who were close to Alexander's age, such as Hephaestion, who was by now his inseparable friend, Perdiccas and Seleucus, had become close to him and they formed a compact group, both in play and in study. Lysimachus and Leonnatus, with the passing of time, had adapted to communal life and they found outlets for their energies in games of physical effort and skill.

Leonnatus, especially, was keen on wrestling and for this reason he was always untidily dressed and covered in scratches and bruises. Older companions such as Ptolemy and Craterus were young men by now and had already for some time been receiving tough military training in the cavalry.

In this period a Greek by the name of Eumenes came to join the group. He worked as an assistant in the King's chancellery and was much appreciated by virtue of his intelligence and wisdom. Philip wanted him to have the same schooling as the other youngsters and so Leonidas found a place for him in the dormitory. Leonnatus, however, immediately challenged the newcomer to a wrestling match.

'If you want to earn your place here, you have to fight for it,' he said, taking off his *chiton* and strutting around bare-chested.

Eumenes did not even look at him. 'Are you crazy? I wouldn't even dream of it.' And he set about sorting out his clothes in the chest at the foot of his bed.

Lysimachus started making fun of him. 'I told you. This Greek is just a little fart.' Even Alexander started laughing.

Leonnatus gave the new lad a push and sent him rolling across the floor. 'Come on then, are you ready to fight or what?'

Eumenes got up angrily, straightened his clothes and said, 'Just a moment, I'll be right back.' He walked to the door, leaving them all speechless. As soon as he was outside he approached a soldier on guard duty on the upper balcony of the palace, a Thracian built like a bear. Eumenes pulled out some coins and put them in the soldier's hand. 'Come with me, I have a job for you.' He entered the dormitory and pointed to Leonnatus: 'See that one there with the freckles and the red hair?' The giant nodded. 'Good. Pick him up and give him a good hiding.'

Leonnatus realized immediately that the odds were stacked against him and he shot through the Thracian's legs much as Ulysses must have done in giving the Cyclops Polyphemus the slip before taking off down the stairs.

'Does anyone else have anything to say?' asked Eumenes, starting to sort out his personal effects once again.

'Yes. I do,' said Alexander.

Eumenes stopped and turned towards him: 'I'll listen to you,' he said, with evident respect in his voice, 'because you're the master here, but none of these birdheads has any right to call me "little fart".'

Alexander burst out laughing. 'Welcome to the gang, Mister Secretary General.'

From that moment onwards Eumenes was truly part of the group and he became ring leader in all sorts of jokes and pranks carried out at the expense of people throughout the palace, but more often than not it was their teacher, old Leonidas, who took the brunt of it all: lizards in his bed and live frogs in his lentil soup for example. Such activities constituted revenge for the tutor's liberal use of the cane when his pupils failed to apply themselves sufficiently to their studies.

One evening Leonidas, who still directed their schooling, announced proudly that the following day their King would receive the Persian envoys and that he, too, would take part in the diplomatic proceedings because of his knowledge of Asia and the customs of the peoples there. He told them that the oldest among them would serve in the King's guard of honour, wearing dress armour, while the youngest would carry out similar duties alongside Prince Alexander.

The news created much excitement among Leonidas'

pupils: none of them had ever seen a Persian before and what they knew of Asia came from their readings of Herodotus or Ctesias or the famous diary of Xenophon the Athenian – the *Anabasis*, also known as the 'march of the ten thousand'. They all set to polishing their weapons and preparing their ceremonial clothes.

'My father once spoke to a man who was on the expedition of the ten thousand,' Hephaestion recounted, 'a man who saw the Persian armies line up against him at the battle of Kunaxa.'

'Can you imagine, lads?' Seleucus joined in. 'A million men!' and he put his hands in front of his face, opening them out like fans as though representing the huge advance of the warriors.

'And the scythed chariots?' Lysimachus exclaimed. 'They fly like the wind across the plains, with scythes sticking out from underneath the carriage and from the hubs of the axles, and they mow down men like wheat. I wouldn't like to find myself up against them on the battlefield.'

'Tricks that create more fuss and panic than they cause real damage,' Alexander said. Up until that moment he had been quiet, listening to his friends' comments. 'Xenophon says so in his diary. Anyway, we'll all have a chance to see how the Persians really handle their weapons because my father the King has organized a lion hunt in Eordaea, in honour of our guests.'

'Oh! And are the little ones to be allowed along as well?' Ptolemy giggled.

Alexander took up position in front of his elder class-mate: 'I am thirteen years of age and I am afraid of nothing and of no one. Try saying that once more and I'll send your teeth down your throat.'

Ptolemy bit his lip and the others stopped laughing. They had all learned not to provoke Alexander, even though he was not particularly well developed from a physical point of view. More than once he had demonstrated surprising energy and a lightning speed in his movements.

Eumenes piped up and suggested they should have a game of dice for their weekly allowance and that was the end of the argument. Much of the money ended up in Eumenes' pockets because he was truly fond both of gambling and of gold.

Having cooled off a little, Alexander left his companions to their games and went to visit his mother before retiring. Although she still held considerable power at court as mother of the heir to the throne, Olympias now lived a very secluded life. Her meetings with Philip were limited almost exclusively to those occasions required by protocol.

In the meantime the King had married other women for political reasons, but he still respected Olympias and, had she been less cantankerous and difficult, he would perhaps have shown that the passion he once held for her had not withered completely.

The Queen was sitting on a high-backed chair with armrests near a lamp with five flames, a papyrus scroll open on her knees. Her room, outside this circle of light, was completely dark.

Alexander entered briskly and quietly: 'What are you reading, Mother?'

Olympias lifted her head: 'Sappho,' she replied. 'Her

poetry is wonderful and her feelings of solitude are so close to my own . . .'

She stood and walked to the window to look out at the starry sky and recited the lines she had just read, her voice vibrant and melancholic:

> 'Night is midway through its course,
> The moon and the Pleiades have set
> And I lie in my bed . . . alone.'*

Alexander moved towards his mother, and in the hesitant light of the moon he saw a tear tremble for a moment on her eyelash before descending slowly, leaving a track down her pale cheek.

* Sappho, fragment 168.

8

THE MASTER OF CEREMONIES ordered the fanfare to be
sounded and the Persian dignitaries made their impressive
entrance into the throne room. The head of the delegation was the Satrap of Phrygia, Arsames, accompanied by
the province's military governor and other notables who
followed some steps behind.

They were flanked by an escort of twelve Immortals,
the soldiers of the imperial guard, all chosen for their
daunting stature, their majestic bearing and the dignity of
their lineage.

The Satrap wore a soft tiara, the most prestigious
headdress after the rigid tiara, which only the Emperor
himself was allowed to wear. His gown was of green
byssus embroidered with silver dragons and he wore it
over a pair of elaborate trousers and on his feet were
antelope-skin slippers. The other dignitaries were also
dressed in incredibly rich and refined vestments.

But what most attracted the attention of the onlookers
were the Great King's Immortals. Almost six feet tall and
olive-skinned, they sported frizzy black beards and their
hair had been sumptuously dressed and curled with a
calamistrum. They wore ankle-length gowns of golden
samite over tunics of blue byssus and trousers of the same
colour embroidered with golden bees. Over their shoulders

they carried their deadly double-curved bows and their quivers of cedar wood, inlaid with ivory and silver.

They moved forward in a slow rhythmic march, touching the floor with the shafts of their spears which terminated in golden pommels in the shape of pomegranates. Hanging at his hip each Immortal wore the most beautiful weapon that any armourer in the known world had ever made – the dazzling *akinake*, a solid gold dagger sheathed in a scabbard which carried embossed patterns of rampant griffins with eyes of rubies. The scabbard was also made of the purest gold and hung from a swivel joint hooked onto the Immortals' belts. This meant that the weapon swayed freely with each step they took and the glinting light of the precious metal lent yet more rhythm to the majesty of the warriors' movement.

Philip, who had been expecting a display of grandeur of this type, had prepared an appropriate welcome – each side of the room was lined with two rows of thirty-six *pezhetairoi*, the well-built soldiers of his heavy front-line infantry. Encased in their bronze armour, they presented their shields, emblazoned with the silver star of the Argeads, and they gripped their *sarissae*, pikes twelve feet in length with shafts of cornel-wood. Their bronze heads were polished like mirrors and almost touched the ceiling.

Alexander, dressed in his first suit of armour – a suit which he himself had designed for the craftsman who made it – was surrounded by his personal guard and stood on a stool at his father's feet. On the other side, at Queen Olympias' feet, sat his sister, Cleopatra, only just adolescent and already stunningly beautiful. She wore an Attic *peplum* gown that left her arms and shoulders bare as it fell into elegant folds around her young breasts, and her feet were clad in sandals made of ribbons of silver.

On reaching the throne, Arsames bowed to the royal couple before moving aside to allow the dignitaries to come forward with the gifts they bore: a belt of knitted gold with aquamarines and tiger-eyes for the Queen, and an inlaid Indian breastplate made out of a turtle shell for the King.

Philip had the master of ceremonies move forward with his gifts for the Emperor and the Empress: a Scythian helmet in gold and a Cypriot necklace of coral set in silver.

On completion of the formalities the guests were invited into the adjacent chamber where they sat on comfortable divans for discussion of the agreement that was on the day's agenda. Alexander was allowed in as well, because Philip wanted him to begin to have an idea of the responsibilities of a man of government and how a relationship with a foreign power should be managed.

The negotiation regarded a quasi-protectorate Philip wanted to exercise over the Greek cities of Asia, with continued formal recognition of Persian sovereignty over the region. The Persians, on their part, were worried about Philip's advance towards the Straits, pivotal point between two continents and confluence of three great territories: Asia Minor, Asia true and proper, and Europe.

Philip tried to present his case without creating too much alarm among the delegation: 'I have no interest in disturbing the peace of the area around the Straits. My only objective is to consolidate Macedonian hegemony between the Adriatic Gulf and the western coast of the Black Sea, something which will certainly bring stability to the Bosphorus, a throughway for traffic and trade that is clearly vital for all of us.'

He gave the interpreter time to translate and watched the expressions on his guests' faces as one by one his words passed from Greek to Persian.

Arsames displayed no emotive reaction. He turned to Philip and looked him in the eye as though they both spoke the same language and said: 'The problem that the Great King would like to solve regards your relationship with the Greeks of Asia and with certain Greek dynasties on the eastern shores of the Aegean. We have always favoured the independence of these peoples and we have always wanted the Greek cities to be governed by the Greeks . . . they are our friends, you understand. It is our opinion that such independence is a wise solution – on the one hand it respects their traditions and their dignity, while on the other it protects both their interests and ours. Unfortunately,' he began again after having waited for the interpreter to finish, 'we are dealing with a border area that has always been a source of friction and bitter conflict or even full-blown war.'

The discussions were beginning to touch on more difficult points and Philip, in order to lighten the atmosphere somewhat, nodded to the master of ceremonies. Some extremely good-looking young people were brought in – male and female, all of them scantily clad. They proceeded to serve sweets and spiced wine cut with snow from Mount Bermion, snow which had been kept in jars in the royal cellar. The silver cups were covered with a light frosting which gave the metal a sort of opaque patina and transmitted to the eye, before the hand, a pleasant

sense of coolness. The King let the foreigners help themselves before picking up where they had left off.

'I know exactly what you mean, my Illustrious Guest. I
realize that in the past there have been many bloody wars
between the Greeks and the Persians without there ever
having been any definitive solution. But I would like to
remind you that my country and my ancestors, our kings,
have always worked as mediators, and I therefore beg you
to tell the Great King that our friendship with the Greek
states of Asia is simply the result of an awareness of our
common origins, of our mutual religion and the ancient
bonds of hospitality and family relations . . .'

Arsames listened with the same sphinx-like expression,
the make-up around his eyes lending him a strange statuesque immobility, and Alexander, from his vantage point,
watched the guest and his father trying to understand what
it was exactly that the other was hiding behind the screen
of perfunctory words.

'I do not deny,' Philip began again after a short while,
'that we are very much interested in trade with those
cities, and we have even more interest in their considerable
experience in all fields of knowledge. We want to learn
how to build, to navigate, to control the flows of the
waters of our land . . .'

The Persian, strangely, spoke before the interpreter had
finished, 'And what can you offer in exchange?'

Philip hid his surprise ably, waited for the translation of
the question and, still imperturbable, replied: 'Friendship,
gifts, and products that Macedon alone can provide – the
wood of our forests, magnificent horses and strong slaves
from the plains along the River Ister. I simply want all the

Greeks who live around our sea to look up to the King of Macedon as their natural friend. No more than this.'

The Persians seemed to be happy with what Philip was telling them and in any case they realized that even if he was lying, the simple truth was that right now he could not afford to start any aggressive projects and that fact was enough, for the moment.

As they left the chamber to go into the banqueting hall, Alexander moved closer to his father and whispered: 'How much truth is there in what you told them?'

'Almost none,' replied Philip, coming out into the corridor.

'Which means that they too . . .'

'They have not told me anything of any real substance.'

'Of what use are these meetings then?'

'For sniffing each other out.'

'For sniffing each other out?' asked Alexander.

'Exactly. A real politician has no need of words, he places more trust in his nose. For example, do you think he prefers girls or boys?'

'Who?'

'Our guest, obviously.'

'Well . . . I really wouldn't know.'

'He likes boys. He gave the impression he was watching the girls, but out of the corner of his eye he was watching that blond boy serving the iced wine. I'll tell the master of ceremonies to make sure the Satrap finds him in his bed. The boy comes from Bythnia and speaks Persian. Perhaps in this way we'll find out more about our guest's true thoughts. After the banquet you can act as guide and show them the palace and the grounds.'

Alexander nodded and when the time came he willingly carried out his task. He had read a lot about the Persian empire, he knew the *Education of Cyrus* by the Athenian Xenophon almost by heart. He had also read Ctesias' *Persikà*, a historical work which was full of imaginative exaggeration, but nevertheless interesting because of its notes on customs and landscape. This, however, was the first ever occasion on which Alexander had had the opportunity to talk to real flesh-and-blood Persians.

He was accompanied by an interpreter and showed the guests the palace and the apartments of the young nobles, where he made a mental note to make sure he tore a strip off Lysimachus because his bed had not been made properly. He explained that the offspring of the Macedonian aristocracy were educated at court together with himself.

Arsames commented that the same practice existed in their capital, Susa. In this way the King not only ensured the loyalty of the tribal chiefs, but he simultaneously reared an entire generation of noblemen who were closely bonded with the throne.

Alexander showed them the stables of the chargers of the *Hetairoi*, the aristocrats who served in the cavalry and who indeed bore the title, 'Companions of the King'. Together they watched the training of some superb Thessalian horses.

'Magnificent animals,' commented one of the dignitaries.

'Do you have such beautiful horses?' asked Alexander, somewhat ingenuously.

The dignitary smiled. 'Have you never heard, Prince, of the Nysaean steeds?'

Alexander, embarrassed, shook his head.

'They are animals of incredible beauty and power which are allowed to graze only on the highlands of Media; the grass that grows there is extremely rich in nutritional properties and is called *medica*. The flowers, purple in colour, are the richest part of the plant and the Emperor's horse is fed exclusively on medica flowers, gathered one by one by his stable lads, served fresh in spring and summer and dried during autumn and winter.'

Alexander, charmed by this story, tried to imagine what a horse fed on flowers alone must be like.

They then went to visit the gardens where Queen Olympias had planted all the known varieties of Pierian rose, which at that time of year gave off a most delicate and intense perfume.

'Our gardeners make infusions and essences for the ladies of the court with them,' said Alexander. 'But I have read of your gardens, which we Greeks call "paradises". Are they really so beautiful?'

'Our people's origins lie in the steppes and the arid highlands of the north and so gardens have always been dreams for us. In our language we call them *pairidaeza*; they are enclosed within huge walls and are criss-crossed by complex systems of irrigation channels which keep the grassy swards green throughout the year. Our noble families grow all types of local and exotic plants and they stock them with ornamental animals from all parts of the empire: pheasants, peacocks, parrots, but even tigers, white leopards, black panthers. We strive to recreate the perfection of the world as it was when it came fresh from the hands of our god, Ahura Mazda, may his name be praised eternally.'

Alexander then took them in a closed carriage to see the capital and its monuments, the temples, the porticoes, the squares.

'But we also have another capital,' he explained. 'Aegae, near the foothills of Mount Bermion; that is where our family comes from and our Kings rest there. Is it true that you have more than one capital as well?'

'Oh yes, young Prince,' replied Arsames. 'We have four capitals. Pasargadae is the equivalent of your Aegae, seat of the first Kings. There, on the windblown plateau, stands the tomb of Cyrus the Great, founder of the dynasty. Then there is the summer capital, Ecbatana, in Elam, on the Zagros mountains, white with snow for most of the year. The walls of the fortress there are covered in tiles made of enamelled sheets of gold and when the sun sets the whole building shines like a jewel against the background of pure snow. It is truly a most moving spectacle, Prince Alexander. The third capital is Susa, where the Great King resides during winter, and the fourth, capital of the year's end, is the sublime Persepolis, built on high and perfumed with cedar and incense, resting on a forest of purple- and gold-coloured columns. The royal treasure is kept there, and there are no words to describe its wonder. I hope you will visit it one day.'

Alexander listened enrapt; in his imagination he could almost see those fabled cities, those gardens of dreams, the treasure of centuries, those limitless landscapes. When they returned to the palace, he had the guests sit on stone benches and called for cups of hydromel to be served. As they drank he asked, 'Tell me, how big is the Great King's empire?'

The Satrap's eyes lit up and his voice resounded with feeling, like that of a poet who sings the beauty of the land of his birth: 'The Great King's empire extends to the north to the point where man cannot live because of the cold and to the south to where man cannot live because of the heat. He reigns over one hundred nations – from the frizzy-haired blacks who dress in leopard skins, to the straight-haired blacks who wear tiger skins.

'Within the limits of the empire there are deserts that no one has dared cross, there are mountains that no human foot has ever dared to climb, so high their summits reach almost to the moon. Earth's four largest rivers, sacred to the gods and to men, run through the empire: the Nile, the Tigris, the Euphrates and the Indus, and a thousand others like the majestic Choaspes or the wild Araxes, which rushes into the Caspian Sea, a mysterious sea whose limits remain unknown, so big that it reflects one fifth of the sky . . . And there is a road that from the city of Sardis crosses half of the empire's provinces as far as the capital Susa: a road all paved in stone, with gates of gold.'

Suddenly Arsames went quiet and looked straight into Alexander's eyes. In the Prince's gaze he saw a powerful longing for adventure and the light of an invincible vital force. He understood that in this young man there burned a soul more powerful than any he had ever come across in his life. And then he remembered the tale of an event that had taken place many years previously, an occurrence that had been much talked of in Persia: one day, inside the Temple of Fire on the Mountain of Light, a sudden breath had come from nowhere and had quenched the sacred flame.

And he was afraid.

9

THE HUNT BEGAN at first light and, in accordance with the King's wishes, even the younger members of court were there to take part: Alexander with his friends Philotas, Seleucus, Hephaestion, Perdiccas, Lysimachus and Leonnatus, as well as Ptolemy, Craterus and others.

Eumenes had also been invited, but he asked to be excused on account of a stomach upset and he showed a note from Philip the physician, prescribing absolute rest for a few days together with an astringent cure based on hard-boiled eggs.

King Alexander of Epirus had sent for a pack of hounds from his kennels. These were special hunting dogs with an excellent sense of smell which were set loose now by the beaters who had taken up position the night before on the edge of a wood up on the mountain. The ancestors of these hounds had been brought from the East more than a hundred years before and had settled extremely well in Epirus. The best kennels were in the land of the Molossian people, and so the hounds, too, became known as Molossians. Their strength, their large build and their ability to withstand pain made them the best possible breed of dog for hunting big animals.

The herdsmen had reported the presence of a lion in the area, a male which had already carried out several massacres among the sheep and the cattle. Philip had waited deliberately for this special occasion to give chase to the beast – to initiate his boy into the only pastime befitting an aristocrat and to offer his Persian guests a diversion worthy of their rank.

They had set out from Pella three hours before dawn and as the sun rose they found themselves at the foot of the mountains separating the valley of the Axios from the valley of the Ludias. The beast was hiding somewhere in the midst of the oak and beech woods that covered the massif.

The King nodded and the chief huntsmen blew their horns. The sound, intensified by its echo, travelled high to the wooded peaks and the beaters heard it. They egged the dogs on, following on foot, and then they too set about making noise, beating the metal rings on their javelins against their shields.

The valley resounded with the howling of the pack of Molossians and the hunters readied themselves, forming a semi-circle over an arc of perhaps fifteen stadia.

At the centre was Philip with his generals: Parmenion, Antipater and Cleitus the Black. The Persians were all arranged on the right flank and everyone was amazed at the transformation in their appearance. No more embroidered tunics and showy gowns, now the Satrap and his Immortals were dressed and equipped like their nomadic ancestors of the steppes: leather breeches, jerkin, hard cap, two javelins in a holster, a double-curved bow complete with quiver and arrows. To the left of Philip stood King Alexander of Epirus, lined up together with Ptolemy and Craterus, and after them came the youngest hunters – Alexander, Hephaestion, Seleucus and the others.

Wisps of fog floated down along the river, spreading like a gossamer veil over the green, flower-filled plain, which for the most part was still in the shadow of the mountain. Suddenly a great roar ripped through the peaceful dawn, drowning out the far-off barking of the dogs – the horses neighed excitedly, stamping and snorting, so that it was difficult to keep them still.

Somehow no one moved; they all managed to wait for the lion to come out into the open. But first there came another roar, louder this time, and immediately another one echoed from farther away, from the river – the lioness was with her mate!

Finally the big male came out of the wood and, finding himself surrounded, he gave forth an even more powerful roar that seemed to shake the very mountain and this time scared the horses. The female soon appeared as well: the two beasts were reluctant to move forward because of the hunters facing them, but neither could they turn back because of the approach of the beaters. They made a dash in the direction of the river.

Philip gave the signal for the start of the chase and everyone rushed onto the plain just at the moment when the sun came over the crest of the mountain and flooded the valley with light.

Because of their position, Alexander and his companions were closest to the riverbank, and, anxious to demonstrate their courage, they spurred their chargers on to intercept the lions.

The King in the meantime was worried that the youngsters were heading towards serious danger and he set off, his javelin poised in his hand, while the Persians widened the semi-circle, pushing their mounts ever more quickly to prevent the lions from turning back into the wood and facing the dogs.

Alexander, excited by the chase, was now very close and was just about to let fly at the exposed flank of the male with his javelin when the hounds burst out of the wood. The lioness, frightened, turned suddenly in the other direction and leaped at the hindquarters of his mount, bringing it heavily to the ground.

The lioness was immediately surrounded by the dogs and was forced to relax its grip, so that the horse was on its feet in a flash and fled, kicking and neighing and spilling blood over the grass as it galloped away.

Alexander stood and confronted the lion. The Prince was unarmed now, having lost his javelin in the fall, but just then Hephaestion arrived, brandishing his weapon and managing to wound the beast superficially, making it roar in pain.

The lioness ripped open the throats of several hounds and then turned towards her mate, who by then was furiously attacking Hephaestion. The boy defended himself valiantly with his javelin, but the lion was striking out wildly, roaring and lashing its own flanks with its tail.

Philip and Parmenion were closer now, but everything was happening so very quickly. Alexander managed to pick up his javelin and take aim, without realizing, however, that the female was ready to pounce once more.

At that moment one of the Persian warriors, the one furthest away, lifted his bow without even stopping his horse, pulled back the string and let fly: the lioness leaped just as the arrow whistled through the air – it thudded into her side and she fell to the ground, mortally wounded.

Philip and Parmenion had reached the male now and coaxed him away from the boys. The King struck first, but Alexander and Hephaestion immediately came back to attack once more, wounding the lion this time, so that all Parmenion had to do was administer the final blow.

All around the dogs howled and wailed as though possessed, and the beaters let them lick the blood of the two beasts so that they would remember the scent for the next hunt.

Philip dismounted and embraced his son: 'You gave me a fright, my boy, but you also made me tremble with pride. One day you certainly shall be King – a great King.' And he also embraced Hephaestion, who had risked his life to save Alexander's.

When the excitement had died down a little and the chief huntsmen had started skinning the two beasts, everyone remembered the crucial moment, the moment when the lioness had pounced.

They turned and saw the foreigner, one of the Immortals, immobile on his horse, his big double-curved bow still in his hand, the weapon that had struck down the lioness at a distance of over one hundred feet. He was smiling, showing off a double row of the whitest teeth in the midst of his thick black beard.

Only then did Alexander realize he was covered in bruises and grazes and he saw that Hephaestion was bleeding from a superficial but painful wound, inflicted by the lion's claws. He held his friend tightly and had him taken immediately to the surgeons so that they could treat his injuries. Then he turned to the Persian warrior who was watching him from far off, from astride his Nysaean steed.

Alexander walked towards the man who had saved his life and when just a few paces away he looked into his eyes and said, 'Thank you, O Foreign Guest. I shall never forget this.'

The Immortal did not understand Alexander's words because he had no Greek, but he understood the meaning perfectly. He smiled again and bowed his head, then he dug his heels into the flanks of his horse and sped off to join his companions.

The hunt resumed shortly after and it carried on until sunset, when the final signal was given. The bearers piled up all the prey that had fallen to the prowess of the hunters – a stag, three boars and a pair of roe bucks.

As evening fell all the hunters met under a great canopy which had been set up by the servants in the middle of the plain. As they laughed and shouted, reliving the exciting moments of the day, the cooks slipped the game off the spits and the carvers cut it into slices and served the diners – first the King, then the guests, then the Prince and then the others.

The wine soon began to flow copiously and even Alexander and his friends were given some. Their deeds that day were ample proof of the fact that they were men now.

At a certain point the women arrived too: flute players,

dancers, all very expert in animating the banquet with their dancing, their lewd jokes and their youthful energy in making love.

Philip was particularly merry and he decided that all of his guests should join in a game of *kottabos*, asking the interpreter to translate for the Persians:

'You see that girl there?' pointing to a dancer who was stripping off just at that moment. 'You have to hit her right between the legs with the last drops of wine left at the bottom of your cup. Whoever hits the bullseye will have her as his prize. Here, like this, watch!' He slipped his index and middle finger through one of the handles and threw the wine towards the girl. The drops hit one of the cooks in the face and everyone burst out laughing: 'You have to fuck the cook now, Sire! The cook! The cook!'

Philip shrugged his shoulders and tried again, but even though the girl had moved closer and was a sitting target by now, the King's aim seemed a trifle skewed.

The Persians were not used to drinking undiluted wine and the majority of them were already rolling on the floor under the tables. As for Arsames, the guest of honour, he couldn't stop fondling the young blond boy who had kept him company the night before.

Other attempts were made, but the *kottabos* was not much of a success because the guests were simply too drunk for such a game of skill and they all grabbed the first girl who happened their way, while the King, as host, grabbed the one he'd promised as a prize. The feast degenerated, as usually happened, into an orgy – a tangle of semi-naked, sweating bodies.

Alexander stood up and, donning his cloak, moved away from the canopy and walked down to the river. There was the noise of the water gurgling among the stones, and the moon just then was rising over the crest of Mount Bermion, giving a silver tint to the water and spreading a slight opaline brightness across the plain.

The bellowing and the groaning from the canopy had subsided slightly now, while the voice of the forest was becoming stronger – rustlings, beatings of wings, whispers and then, suddenly, a song. A whistling as though from a secret source, a ringing that at first was muffled and then increasingly brighter and acute, like the playing of a mysterious harpist in the fragrant depths of the wood. The song of the nightingale.

Alexander stood there in rapture as he listened to the melody of the little songster, oblivious to the passage of time. Suddenly, however, he realized there was someone next to him and he turned. It was Leptine. The women had brought her with them to help prepare the tables.

She was watching him, her hands crossed in her lap, her gaze clear and serene, just like the sky above them. Alexander brushed her face with a caress, then he had her sit down near him and held her tightly in his arms, in silence.

*

At first light they started back to Pella with the Persian guests who had been invited to stay for the formal banquet that was to be served on the following day.

Queen Olympias immediately summoned her son on

his return, and when she saw him with bruises and scratches all over his arms and legs, she hugged him fitfully. But he pulled away, embarrassed.

'They told me what you did. You could have died.'

'I am not afraid of death, Mother. The power and the glory of a king can only be justified if he is ready to give his life, whenever the moment comes.'

'I know. But what has happened still makes me tremble with fear. I beg you to keep your daring under control, please take no more pointless risks. You are still a boy, you have more growing to do, you must put more strength in your limbs.'

Alexander stared at her steadfastly, 'I must go onward to meet my destiny and my journey has already begun. I know this for certain. What I do not know, Mother, is where that journey will take me and when it will come to an end.'

'No one knows this, my son,' said the Queen, her voice quavering. 'Destiny is a god whose face is obscured by a dark veil.'

10

THE DAY AFTER the Persians' departure, Alexander of Epirus entered his nephew's room carrying a small bundle in his arms.

'What is it?' Alexander asked.

'It's a poor little orphan. His mother was killed by the lioness the other day. Do you want him? He has a fine Molossian pedigree and if you're good to him he will repay the kindness a thousand times.'

He opened the bundle and there was a fine tawny-coloured puppy with a lighter coloured patch on his forehead. 'His name is Peritas.'

Alexander picked the dog up, sat it down on his knees and began to stroke it. 'It's a fine name. And he's a lovely puppy. Can I really keep him?'

'He's all yours,' his uncle replied. 'But you'll have to look after him. He hadn't even been weaned.'

'Leptine will take care of all that. He'll grow quickly and will be my hunting dog and my companion. Thank you very much.'

Leptine was enthusiastic about the task she was given and she set to it with a great sense of responsibility. The signs of her nightmarish infancy were slowly fading and she seemed to bloom more and more with every day that passed. Her complexion was lighter and brighter, her eyes clearer and more expressive, her brown hair, flashing with copper-coloured streaks, ever shinier.

'Will you take her to bed when she's ready?' asked Hephaestion, giggling.

'Perhaps,' replied Alexander. 'But that is not the reason why I lifted her from the dirt in which I found her.'

'No? Why did you do it then?'

Alexander did not reply.

*

The following winter was particularly harsh and more than once the King suffered from bouts of sharp pain in his left leg – an old wound which continued to make itself felt despite the passing of the years.

Philip the physician applied stones heated on the fire and wrapped in woollen cloths to absorb excess humidity and he rubbed the area with oil of turpentine, from the terebinth tree. Sometimes he physically forced the King to bend his knee until his heel touched his buttock and this was the exercise the King hated more than any other because it was the most painful. But the danger was that the leg, already a little shorter than the other one, might continue to shrink.

There was no mistaking when the King was in pain and was reaching the end of his tether because he would start roaring like a lion and then came the noise of plates and cups being smashed – unequivocal proof of his having thrown all the ointments, tisanes and medicines prescribed by his namesake physician against the wall.

Occasionally Alexander would leave the palace at Pella

to shut himself away at Aegae, the ancient capital up in the mountains. He would have a big fire lit in his room and would sit for hours contemplating the snow that fell in blankets over the peaks, the woods of blue fir and the valleys.

He liked to watch the smoke rising from the shepherds' cabins on the slopes and from the houses in the villages, savouring the profound silence that in certain moments of the evening or the morning reigned over that magical world suspended between heaven and earth. When he went to bed he would lie awake for a long time, his eyes open in the darkness, listening to the howling of the wolves, echoing like a lament through far-off hidden valleys.

On clear days at sunset he would admire the summit of Mount Olympus as it turned red, and the clouds driven by the north wind sailing lightly towards far-off worlds. He watched flocks of birds migrating and wished he could fly with them over the ocean waves or up to the bright globe of the moon on the wings of the falcon or the eagle.

And yet at those very moments he knew that none of this was possible and that he too, one day, would sleep under a great tumulus in the Valley of Aegae, just like the Kings who had come before him.

He knew that his childhood was coming to an end and he would soon be a man, and this thought brought with it both melancholy and feverish excitement. These moods came according to whether he was contemplating the dying light of the winter sunset with its last purple flash across the mountain of the gods, or whether he was watching the vortex of ardent flames in the bonfires that the peasants lit on the mountains to transmit energy to the sun as it disappeared below the horizon for another night.

Peritas curled up at his master's feet near the fire and watched, whining as though he actually understood everything that was going through Alexander's mind.

Leptine, meanwhile, was away in some other part of the palace and she only appeared when called for – to prepare his dinner or for a game of battlefield, a board game played with small ceramic soldiers. She had become quite good at it, to the point where she sometimes succeeded in beating her royal opponent. When that happened her face would light up, her eyes smiling: 'I'm better than you!' she would say, laughing. 'You should make me a general!'

One evening when he saw that she was particularly happy, Alexander took her hand and asked, 'Leptine, can you remember nothing of your infancy? What was your name? Where did you come from? Who were your parents?'

The girl's face suddenly darkened, she bowed her head in confusion and started shaking as though a sudden chill had gripped her limbs. That night Alexander heard her shouting in her sleep, more than once, in an unknown tongue.

*

Many things changed with the return of spring. It was in this season that King Philip began to concern himself with spreading his son's fame both within and beyond Macedon. He therefore presented Alexander to the assembled army more than once and even took him along on several brief military campaigns.

On these occasions Philip allowed Alexander to have the most beautiful and expensive weapons made by his own armourer. He ordered Parmenion to make sure that Alexander was always protected by the most valiant soldiers, but to let him onto the front line so that he could sniff, as he put it, the smell of blood.

The soldiers jokingly referred to Alexander as 'King' and Philip as 'General', as though the father were subaltern to the son, and this pleased the Sovereign enormously. Philip also asked many artists to create portraits of Alexander, making medals, busts and tableaux of them to be given as gifts to friends and especially to the foreign delegations or those of the Greek cities of the peninsula. In these images Alexander was always represented according to the accepted canons of Greek art as an *ephebe*, a young military recruit, with the finest features, his golden locks ruffled by the wind.

The young Prince was becoming more handsome by the day. His natural body temperature was higher than normal, which meant that his face was never marked with the sorts of skin problems typical of adolescence. His complexion was smooth, full and free of imperfections with a rosy tint on his cheeks and on his chest. His hair was thick, soft and wavy, his eyes large and expressive and he had a curious way of tilting his head slightly towards his right shoulder which lent a peculiar intensity to his gaze, as though he were scrutinizing others into the depths of their souls.

One day Philip called him to his study, an austere room

the walls of which were covered in shelves, some carrying chancellery documents, others carrying the literary works the King enjoyed reading.

Alexander appeared immediately, leaving Peritas outside; the puppy followed him everywhere and even slept in his room.

'This is a most important year, my son. This is the year in which you will become a man.' Philip ran his finger across Alexander's upper lip: 'Yes ... there's some fluff appearing here and I have a present for you.'

He picked up a small boxwood case, inlaid with the Argeads' sixteen-point star, and handed it to Alexander. The Prince opened it and there was a bronze razor, sharpened to perfection, together with a hone for keeping it so.

'Thank you. But I don't think you called me here just for this.'

'No. Indeed,' replied Philip.

'Why then?'

'You will soon be leaving Pella.'

'Are you sending me away?'

'In a certain sense.'

'Where am I to go?'

'To Mieza.'

'That's nearby. Little more than a day's journey. Why?'

'You will spend the next three years there to complete your education. There are too many distractions here at Pella: court life, the women, the banquets. At Mieza, instead, I have prepared a beautiful place – a garden through which runs a stream of the clearest water, a wood of cypresses and bay trees, rose bushes ...'

'Father,' Alexander interrupted, 'what's wrong with you?'

Philip was startled. 'Me? Nothing. Why?'

'You're talking of roses, of woods . . . it's like listening to a bear recite the poetry of Alcaeus.'

'My son, what I am trying to tell you is that I have prepared the most beautiful and welcoming place I possibly can for you. There you will continue with your schooling and your formation as a man.'

'You have seen me ride, fight, hunt lions. I know how to draw, I know my geometry, I speak Macedonian and Greek . . .'

'These things are not enough, my boy. Do you know what the Greeks call me, after my having won their accursed sacred war, after my having secured their peace and prosperity? They call me Philip the Barbarian. And do you know what this means? It means that they will never accept me as their guide and leader because they feel only contempt for me, even though they are afraid of me.

'Behind us we have limitless plains peopled by barbarous and fierce nomadic tribes. In front of us are the cities of the Greeks – shining and reflected in the sea, where man has reached the highest levels of excellence in the arts, in science, in poetry, in engineering, in politics. We are like someone who sits at the campfire on a winter's night – our face is lit up and our chest is warmed by the fire, but our back is exposed to the dark and the cold.

'For this reason I have fought to keep Macedon safe within firmly defined borders, and I will do all that is in my power to make sure my son appears to the Greeks as a Greek – in his thinking, in his habits, even in his physical image. You will have the most refined and complete education that any man alive today could possibly have. You will be able to consult the greatest living mind in the eastern and western Greek world.'

'And just who is this extraordinary personage?'

Philip smiled. 'He is the son of Nicomachus, the physician who brought you into this world. Your new tutor is the most famous and the most brilliant of Plato's disciples. His name is Aristotle.'

11

'MAY I TAKE ANYONE WITH ME?' Alexander asked after listening to his father's plans.

'Any of the servants.'

'I want Leptine. And my friends?'

'Hephaestion, Perdiccas, Seleucus and the others?'

'I'd like them to come.'

'They will accompany you, but there will be special lessons which only you may attend, lessons that will make you different from the others. Your tutor will decide on the order of teaching, the subjects you'll study with the others and those which are reserved for you alone. The discipline will be strict: no disobedience of any kind will be tolerated, nor distractions or lack of effort. And if you deserve it you will receive your punishment just as your companions will.'

'When am I to leave?'

'Soon.'

'How soon?'

'The day after tomorrow. Prepare your things, get the girl ready, choose which other servants you require and spend some time with your mother.'

Alexander nodded and stood in silence. Philip looked at his son closely and saw that he was biting his lip to hide his tears.

He came closer and placed a hand on Alexander's shoulder: 'It has to be done, my boy, believe me. I want you to become Greek, I want you to be part of the only civilization in the world which creates men rather than servants, a repository of the most advanced learning, a culture which speaks the language of the *Iliad* and the *Odyssey*, which represents the gods as men and the men as gods. This does not mean that you will betray your origins, because you will remain Macedonian to the depths of your soul: the sons of lions will always be lions.'

Alexander still had nothing to say and kept his hands busy with the case containing his new razor.

'We have never been very close, my son,' Philip began again as he ruffled Alexander's hair with his big, calloused hand. 'There has been no time. You see, I am a soldier and I have done what I could for you: I have conquered a realm that is three times as big as the one I inherited from your grandfather Amyntas and I have made the Greeks, the Athenians in particular, realize that here in Macedon there is a great power which they must respect. But I am not able to mould your mind, neither are the teachers you have had so far here in the palace. They have nothing more to teach you.'

'I will do as you wish,' Alexander said. 'I will go to Mieza.'

'I am not sending you into exile, my son; we will see each other, I will visit you, and your mother and sister will also be able to come sometimes. I simply wanted to make ready a suitable place for your studies. Naturally your weaponry instructors will also go with you, together with your riding instructor and your chief huntsman. I do not want a philosopher, I want a king.'

'As you wish, Father.'

'One more thing. Your uncle Alexander is leaving us.'

'Why?'

'Up till now he has simply been playing the role of King, like an actor in a theatre. He wore the sovereign's cloak and crown while his kingdom remained in the hands of Aribbas. But your uncle is twenty years old now: it's high time he began his life's work. I will get rid of Aribbas and put Alexander on the throne of Epirus.'

'I am glad for him, but I'll be sorry to see him go,' said Alexander, used as he was to listening to his father's plans as though they had already been put into effect. He knew that Aribbas had the support of the Athenians and that there was an Athenian fleet at Corcyra, with a contingent of infantry ready to land.

'Is it true that the Athenians are at Corcyra and are getting ready to invade? You'll end up in direct conflict with them.'

'I have no quarrel with the Athenians, in fact I hold them in great esteem. But they must understand that coming near my borders is like putting their hand straight into the lion's mouth. As for your uncle, I too am sorry that he has to leave. He's a fine young man and an excellent soldier and . . . I get on with him better than I do with your mother.'

'I know.'

'It seems to me there's nothing more for us to discuss. Do not forget to say goodbye to your sister, and your uncle of course. And Leonidas as well. He is not a famous philosopher, but he is a good man who has taught you all he was capable of teaching and he is as proud of you as if you were his own son.'

From the other side of the door came the sound of Peritas scratching, trying to find a way in.

'I will,' replied Alexander. 'May I go now?'

Philip nodded and then went to the desk, as though looking for some document. But the simple truth was that he did not want his son to see his eyes brimming with tears.

12

ALEXANDER WENT TO VISIT his mother the following day at sunset. She had just finished her meal and the maid-servants were clearing up. The Queen gestured for them to stop and had a chair brought.

'Have you eaten?' she asked. 'Can I get you something?'

'I've already had supper – your brother's farewell feast, Mother.'

'I know . . . I know, I'll say goodbye to him in person before retiring. So . . . tomorrow is an important day for you.'

'It looks that way.'

'Are you sad?'

'A bit.'

'You mustn't be. Do you realize how much your father's spending on moving half the Academy to Mieza?'

'Why half the Academy?'

'Because Aristotle isn't alone. Together with him there's his nephew and disciple Callisthenes, together with Theophrastus, the great scientist.'

'How much is he spending?'

'Fifteen talents a year for three years. Zeus knows he can afford it – the Pangaeos mines bring in a thousand a year in gold. Between helping friends, corrupting enemies and financing his projects, he's put such quantities of gold into circulation that over the last five years prices through-out Greece have increased fivefold! Even the price of philosophers.'

'I see you're in a bad mood, Mother.'

'And why shouldn't I be? You're going, my brother's going. I'll be left here alone.'

'But Cleopatra will still be here. She loves you, and indeed I really think she's like you. She's so young yet she already has a strong, determined character.'

'Yes,' Olympias nodded. 'Of course.'

Then there was a long silence. From the courtyard came the sound of the rhythmic marching of the guards who were starting the night watch.

'Don't you agree, Mother?'

Olympias shook her head. 'No, that's not the problem. The truth is that of all Philip's decisions this is certainly the wisest. It's just that my life is so difficult, Alexander, and it gets worse every day. Here at Pella I've always been looked upon as "the foreigner"; they've never accepted me and for as long as your father loved me everything was bearable . . . enjoyable even. But now . . .'

'I think my father . . .'

'Your father is a king, my son, and kings are not like other men: they have to marry when the interests of their kingdoms require it – once, twice, three times even – or they have to reject their wives for the same reason. They are required to fight interminable wars, they have to plot, to make and unmake alliances, to betray friends and brothers if necessary. Do you really believe there is a place for a woman like me in the heart of a man like that? But do not feel sorry for me. After all, I am still a queen, and the mother of Alexander.'

'I will think of you every day, Mother. I will write and I will come to visit you whenever possible. But remember that my father is better than many other men – better than most of those I know.'

Olympias stood up. 'I know,' she said, and she moved closer to him. 'May I embrace you?'

Alexander held her to himself and felt the warmth of her tears on his cheeks, then he turned towards the door and left. The Queen returned to her chair once more and sat there motionless for a long time, staring into space.

*

As soon as Cleopatra saw her brother she burst into tears and put her arms around his neck.

'Hey!' exclaimed Alexander. 'I'm not going into exile, I'm only off to Mieza. It's just a few hours' march away and you'll be able to come and visit sometime – Father has said so.'

Cleopatra dried her tears and blew her nose. 'You're just saying that to keep my spirits up,' she sobbed.

'Not in the slightest. And then there are the boys here at court. I've heard that one or two have started showing an interest in you.'

Cleopatra shrugged her shoulders.

'You mean you don't like any of them?'

She made no comment.

'Do you know what I've heard?' asked her big brother.

'What?' she asked, suddenly full of curiosity.

'That you like Perdiccas. Others are saying that you like Eumenes. I find myself wondering whether you don't perhaps like both of them.'

'You're the only one I love!' and she threw her arms around his neck once more.

'That's a fine lie,' said Alexander, 'but because I like the idea so much I'll pretend it's the truth. Anyway, even if there is someone you like there's no harm in it. You mustn't get any strange ideas of course – it'll be Father who decides on your marriage and your husband, when the right time comes, and if you happened to be in love with someone else you would suffer terribly.'

'I know.'

'If it were up to me I'd let you marry whoever you wished, but if I know our father he won't let any political advantage to be drawn from your marriage slip past him. And there is no man alive who would not do everything possible to marry you. You really are so beautiful! So, will you promise to come and visit me?'

'I promise.'

'And you won't start crying as soon as I walk through that door over there?'

Cleopatra nodded while the tears streamed silently down her cheeks. Alexander gave her one last kiss and left.

He spent the rest of the evening with his friends who had prepared a farewell celebration and he got drunk for the first time in his life. All the others followed suit, but, not being used to drinking, they all felt ill and vomited. Peritas, so as not to be left out of the debauchery, cocked his leg and peed on the floor.

When Alexander tried to make his way to his bed

chamber, he realized that walking was no easy venture. But at some stage someone appeared in the dark with a lamp, gave him a shoulder to lean on and helped him into bed. This person wiped his face with a damp cloth, and moistened his lips with pomegranate juice before leaving. She reappeared shortly afterwards, this time bearing a steaming cup, and made him drink a camomile infusion before tucking the blankets around him.

And in a glimmer of awareness Alexander recognized her – it was Leptine.

*

Mieza in itself was an enchanting place, nestling in the foothills of Mount Bermion in the greenest of hollows, crossed by a stream and surrounded by woods of oak. The residence that Philip had prepared was so beautiful that Alexander wondered if the gardener hadn't learned some secrets from their Persian guests, so as to create here in Macedon a 'paradise' like their Elam or Susiana.

An old hunting lodge had been completely restored and altered so as to create within it living quarters for guests, together with study rooms communicating with the libraries, an odeon for music and even a small theatre for dramatic performances. Everyone knew how highly Aristotle thought of the dramatic arts – tragedy in particular and comedy too.

There was a study room for the classification of plants and a pharmaceutics laboratory, but what amazed Alexander more than anything else was the drawing and painting studio and the foundry communicating with it. It was equipped with all the latest tools and materials arranged in an orderly way on its shelves: clay, wax, lead, copper, silver, all with the Argead sixteen-point star hall-mark guaranteeing weight and provenance.

Alexander knew he was quite good at drawing and he had been expecting a small, bright studio with a few white-lead slates and some charcoal sticks. But these impressive facilities seemed to him to be somewhat excessive.

'The guest we've been expecting has arrived,' explained the custodian, 'but your father has given me strict orders to tell you nothing. It's to be a surprise.'

'Where is he?' asked Alexander.

'Come.' The custodian led him to a ground-floor window that looked out into the building's internal courtyard. 'There he is,' said the custodian, pointing to the eldest of a group of three people walking under the eastern wing of the portico.

He was a man of about forty – slim, erect in his gait and measured and contained, almost studied, in his bearing. His eyes were small and lively and followed every gesture of his companions and it seemed even the movements of their lips, but at the same time he missed nothing of all that existed and happened around him.

Alexander was immediately aware that this man was observing him without having looked at him directly even for an instant. He went outside and stood in front of the door waiting for the guest to finish a half-circuit of the portico before reaching that spot.

Soon Alexander found himself facing Aristotle: his eyes were grey, nestling under a high and broad forehead, marked by two deep frown lines. His cheekbones were prominent and were further accentuated by his lean face.

His mouth was regular and shaded by a thick moustache and a very neat beard which functioned as a sort of frame, granting his expression an aura of thoughtful intensity.

Alexander could not help but notice that the philosopher combed his hair up from the back of his neck to cover the considerable baldness afflicting the top of his head. Aristotle realized what Alexander was looking at and for an instant his gaze turned icy cold. The Prince immediately lowered his eyes.

The philosopher offered his hand and said, 'I'm pleased to meet you. I would like you to meet my assistants: my nephew Callisthenes who studies literature and cultivates history, and Theophrastus,' he added, indicating the companion who stood to his left. 'You will perhaps already have heard of his ability in zoology and botany. The first time we met your father at Assus, in the Troad, Theophrastus was immediately taken with the fine shafts of the *sarissae*. And when the King had finished speaking, Theophrastus whispered in my ear, "Cut from a strong cornel tree in August by the light of the new moon – seasoned, polished with pumice and beeswax. What harder and more flexible material can there be in the plant world?" Isn't that extraordinary?'

'Indeed it is,' confirmed Alexander as he let go of Aristotle's hand and then shook hands with the assistants, first Callisthenes, then Theophrastus, respecting the order in which his tutor had named them.

'Welcome to Mieza,' Alexander continued. 'I would be honoured if you were to have lunch with me.'

Aristotle had not stopped studying the Prince from the first moment he had seen him and he was deeply impressed. 'Philip's boy', as he was known in Athens, had an intense depth to his gaze, a wonderful harmony in his features, and a vibrant, sonorous timbre to his voice. Everything in the young Prince declared a burning desire to live and to learn, a great capacity for commitment and application.

At that moment Peritas' celebratory barking erupted into the courtyard and the dog began biting at the strings of Alexander's sandals, interrupting the wordless communication between tutor and pupil.

'He's a beautiful puppy,' Theophrastus remarked.

'His name is Peritas,' said Alexander, bending over to pick him up. 'My uncle gave him to me as a present. A lioness killed his mother in the last hunt we took part in.'

'He is very fond of you,' Aristotle noted.

Alexander made no reply and led them to the dining room. He had them all take their places comfortably and then he too stretched out gracefully. Aristotle was opposite him.

A servant brought the jug and basin for washing and passed them a towel as well. Another began serving the meal: hard-boiled quails' eggs, broth and boiled hen, bread, roast pigeon meat and wine from Thasos. A third servant placed a bowl containing Peritas' food on the floor near Alexander.

'Do you really think Peritas is fond of me?' asked Alexander, watching his puppy happily wagging his tail as he ate eagerly from the bowl.

'Most certainly,' replied Aristotle.

'But wouldn't that mean then that a dog has feelings and therefore has a soul?'

'That question is bigger than you,' remarked Aristotle, peeling an egg. 'It's bigger than me too. A question which has no certain answer. Remember one thing, Alexander, a good teacher is one who gives honest answers.

'I will teach you to recognize the characteristic features of animals and plants, to subdivide them all into their species, to use your eyes, your ears, your hands to recognize the depths of the nature that surrounds you. This means that you must also recognize, as far as is possible, the laws that govern nature.

'Look at this egg. Your cook has boiled it and thus has put an end to its future, but within this shell there was a potential bird – able to fly, nourish itself, reproduce, migrate distances of tens of thousands of stadia. As an egg it is none of all this, yet it carries within itself all the features of its species, its form we might say.

'Form works in matter with various results, or consequences. Peritas is one of those consequences, just as you are, just as I am.'

He bit into the egg. 'Just as this egg would have been had it been allowed to become a bird.'

Alexander looked at Aristotle. The lesson had already begun.

13

'I'VE BROUGHT YOU A PRESENT,' announced Aristotle as he entered the library. In his hands he held a wooden box which appeared to be very old.

'Thank you,' said Alexander. 'What is it?'

'Open it,' the philosopher suggested as he handed it to him.

Alexander took the box, placed it on a table and opened it: inside were two large scrolls of papyrus, each one complete with a small white card tied to the scroll batons and bearing lettering in red ink.

'The *Iliad* and the *Odyssey*,' exclaimed Alexander enthusiastically. 'It's a wonderful present. Thank you so much. It's just what I've wanted for so long now.'

'Rather old editions, among the first copies of the Athenian version by Pisistratus,' explained Aristotle, showing him the headings of the scrolls. 'When I was at the Academy I had three copies transcribed at my own expense. I am glad to make you a present of one of them.'

The custodian, who was well within earshot, found himself thinking that indeed Aristotle could well afford it with all the money Philip was giving him, but he kept his thoughts to himself as he went on preparing the materials the philosopher had requested for the day's lessons.

'To read of the heroes of days gone by and their deeds

is an essential part of a young man's education, and so too are the tragedies,' Aristotle continued. 'The reader, or the spectator, cannot help but admire the great and noble deeds as they bear witness to the generous behaviour of those who suffer and even give their lives for their communities and for their ideals, or pay high prices for their own mistakes, or those of their ancestors. Don't you agree?'

'Yes, of course,' Alexander concurred, carefully closing the box. 'There is one thing, however, which I would like to know from you: why do I have to be educated in the Greek manner? Why can't I simply be a Macedonian?'

Aristotle sat down. 'That's an interesting question, but in order to answer it I have to explain to you what it means to be Greek. Only in this way will you be able to decide whether you really want to apply yourself and to learn from my teaching. To be Greek, Alexander, is the only truly worthy way of life for a human being. Do you know the myth of Prometheus?'

'Yes . . . he was the Titan who stole fire from the gods to give it to men and free them from their misery.'

'That's it, that's the myth. Now, when mankind freed itself from the darkness, attempts were made to organize life in communities and in essence three ways of doing this developed: with one person only in command, a system which goes under the name of monarchy; with more than one but only a few people in command, known as oligarchy; and then the system by which all citizens exercise power, known as democracy. And this is the greatest manifestation of what it means to be Greek.

'Here, in Macedon, your father's word is law; those

who govern in Athens, however, have been elected by the majority of the citizens, so that in this way a cobbler or a stevedore can stand up in the assembly and ask that measures already approved by the government of the city be withdrawn, if they find enough people to support their motion.

'In Egypt, in Persia, and in Macedon too, there is only one free man – the King. All the others are slaves.'

'But the nobility . . .' Alexander made an attempt to get a word in.

'The nobility too. Certainly, they have more privileges, they have more pleasant lives, but they too must obey.' Aristotle fell silent then because he saw that his words had struck their mark and he wanted to make sure there was sufficient time for them to work their way into the boy's soul.

'You have given me the works of Homer as a present,' Alexander replied eventually, 'but I already know them in part. And I well remember that Ulysses made a speech in the assembly of the warriors just before Thersites took the floor and offended the gods and earned himself a hiding from Homer's hero. Ulysses had this to say:

> Shall we all wield the power of kings? We can not,
> and many masters are no good at all.
> Let there be one commander, one authority,
> holding his royal staff and precedence
> from Zeus, the son of crooked-minded Cronos:
> one to command the rest.

These are Homer's words.'

'Yes . . . you are right. But Homer recounts tales of

ancient times, when kings were indispensable and they were so because things were different back then. In those times there were continuous attacks from the barbarians, wild beasts and monsters in a natural world that was still wild and primitive. I made you a present of Homer's poetry so that you might grow by reading and developing your noblest feelings – friendship, value, respect for your word once given. But today's man, Alexander, is a political animal. There is no doubt of that. The only context in which man can grow is in the *polis*, in the city as conceived of by the Greeks.

'It is freedom that allows each and every soul to express itself, to create, to generate greatness. You see, the ideal state would be one in which everyone knows how to lead as they grow old, after having obeyed diligently as young men.'

'That is what I am doing now and what I will do in the future.'

'You are just one person,' replied Aristotle. 'I am speaking of the many thousands of citizens who live as equals under the protection of law and justice, that protection which grants honour to whoever deserves it, which regulates trade and commerce, which punishes and reforms those who have committed errors. A community like this is held together not by blood ties, but by laws under which all citizens are equal. The law corrects the flaws and the imperfections of individuals, limits conflict and competition, rewards the will to do and to achieve, encourages the strong, supports the weak. In a society like this the shame lies not in being humble and poor, but rather in doing nothing to improve one's condition.'

Alexander sat in silence, meditating.

'Now I will give you tangible proof of the things I have told you,' Aristotle began again. 'Come with me.'

He went outside through a side door on the external side of the building and walked to a small window that looked into the foundry workshop.

'Look,' he said, pointing inside, 'can you see that man?'

Alexander nodded. In the workshop he saw a man of about forty, wearing a short work tunic and a leather apron; nearby were a couple of assistants, one about twenty, the other about sixteen years of age. All three were busy arranging tools, preparing the large chain that was to hold the crucible, stoking the forge.

'Do you know who that is?' asked Aristotle.

'I have never seen him before.'

'He is the world's greatest living artist. He is Lysippus of Sicyon.'

'The great Lysippus . . . I saw one of his sculptures once in the sanctuary of Hera.'

'And do you know what he used to be before he became what he is today? A labourer. He worked as a labourer for fifteen years in a foundry, for two obols per day. And can you guess how he became the great Lysippus? Thanks to his city's system of government. It is the city which makes space for talent, which allows each and every man to grow like a healthy plant.'

Alexander studied the new guest who all told looked quite powerful: wide shoulders, muscled arms and the wide, knobbled hands of a man who has worked hard for a long time.

'Why is he here?'

'Come. Let's meet him and he himself will explain.'

They entered by the main door and Alexander greeted the sculptor.

'I am Alexander, son of Philip, King of Macedon. Welcome to Mieza, Lysippus. I am honoured to meet you. This is my tutor, Aristotle, son of Nichomachus, from Stagira. In a certain sense he too is Macedonian.'

Lysippus introduced his assistants, Archelaus and Chares, but as he spoke Alexander felt the sculptor's eyes on his face. Lysippus' gaze explored the Prince's features, drawing and redrawing them in his mind.

'Your father has commissioned me to make a portrait sculpture of you in bronze. I would like to know when you will be able to pose for me.'

Alexander looked towards Aristotle, who smiled and said, 'Whenever you want, Lysippus. I can easily teach while you create his likeness . . . that is if I am not a distraction to you.'

'Not at all,' replied Lysippus, 'it will be a privilege for me to listen to you.'

'What do you think of the lad?' the philosopher asked after Alexander had left the foundry to show the rest of the building to Archelaus and Chares.

'He has the countenance and the features of a god.'

14

LIFE IN MIEZA was marked by extremely regular rhythms. Alexander and his companions were woken every morning before sunrise. Breakfast consisted of raw eggs, honey, grated cheese, wine and flour, a mixture they called 'Nestor's cup' which came from an ancient recipe described in the *Iliad*. Then they went out with their riding instructor for an hour or two.

After the riding lesson the young men worked with their weapons instructor who trained them in wrestling, running, fencing, archery, spear-work and javelin throwing. The rest of their time was then spent with Aristotle and his assistants.

Sometimes the arms master, rather than instructing them in the usual things, took them hunting together with the house guests. The surrounding woods were rich in wild boar, stags, roe-deer, wolves, bears, lynxes and even lions.

One day, on their return from a hunt, Aristotle met them at the entrance dressed in a strange way – he was wearing high leather boots that came halfway up his legs and an apron with a bib. He inspected the animals they had killed and chose a female boar that was obviously pregnant.

'Please have that brought to my laboratory,' he said to

the chief huntsman and nodded to Alexander to follow him. This meant that the lesson about to take place was for the Prince alone.

The tutor's orders were immediately carried out and the boar was placed on a table alongside which Theophrastus had arranged a series of surgical instruments, all perfectly sharpened and polished.

Aristotle asked for a scalpel and turned to the young Prince, 'If you're not too tired I'd like you to help with this operation. You'll learn many important things. Over there are the materials necessary for writing,' he added, pointing to pen, ink and some sheets of papyrus on a lectern, 'that way you'll be able to take notes and remember everything you see during the dissection.'

Alexander put his bow and quiver down in a corner, took up the pen and the papyrus and moved towards the table.

The philosopher made an incision along the sow's belly and, inside the animal's uterus, there appeared six small boars. He measured them one by one.

'Two weeks from being born,' he observed. 'Here, this is the uterus, or the matrix where the fetuses take form. This internal sack here is the placenta.'

Alexander managed to control his initial repugnance for the smell and the sight of the bloody innards and began to take notes and even to draw.

'You see? The organs of a pig or a boar, which is the same thing, are very similar to those of a human being. Look: these are the lungs, the bellows that allow us to breathe, and this membrane which separates the upper part of the innards, the nobler part, from the lower part is the *phren* and the ancients believed that this housed the soul. In our language all the words that indicate the activity of thought or of reasoning or even madness, which is the degeneration of thought, derive from the term *phren*. A membrane.'

Alexander would have liked to ask what moved the *phren*, what regulated its rhythmic rising and falling, but he already knew the answer – 'There are no simple answers to complex problems.' And he chose to say nothing.

'Now this is the heart: a pump like the one used to empty the bilges on ships, but infinitely more complicated and efficient. This is the home of feeling and intellect because its movement accelerates if a man is under the influence of anger or love, or simple lust. In truth, my heart's movement accelerates even if I simply walk up the stairs, and this demonstrates that it is the centre of all functions in the life of man.'

'Indeed,' Alexander agreed, staring in bewilderment at his tutor's bloody hands as they rooted through the innards of the boar.

'A plausible hypothesis might be that when life's intensity increases it is necessary for the blood to circulate more quickly. And there are two systems of circulation – the one that comes from the heart and the one that goes back to the heart, completely separate, as you can see. In this respect,' he added, placing the scalpel on the tray, 'we are very much like animals. But there is one thing in which we are clearly different,' he added.

'Hammer and chisel,' he then said to Theophrastus who immediately handed over the instruments, and with a few sharp, expert blows Aristotle opened the animal's skull. 'The brain. Our brain is much larger. I have always thought that all those twists and turns were to help disperse body heat, but man does not seem to produce any more heat than any of the animals. It is a problem I will have to give some thought to . . .'

Aristotle had finished and he passed the instruments to Theophrastus to clean. He then washed his hands and asked Alexander for his notes and sketches.

'Excellent!' he said. 'I couldn't have done better myself. Now you may consign this beast to the butcher. I am very partial to sausage and offal, but unfortunately for some time now I haven't been able to digest them very well. Have them grill me some chops for supper, if you don't mind.'

On another occasion Alexander found Aristotle intent on the same operation, but this time with a much smaller subject – a ten-day-old hen's egg.

'My sight isn't what it used to be and so I have to ask Theophrastus for help. Pay attention because one day you'll have to help me.'

Theophrastus held the incredibly sharp and slender blade between thumb and index finger and was using it with remarkable precision. He had removed the albumen and had isolated the fetus within the yolk.

'At ten days it is already possible to make out the chick's heart and lungs. Can you see them? You've still got good eyes, can you see them?'

Theophrastus indicated the small clots of blood his tutor was talking about.

'I can see them,' said Alexander.

'There you are, the same process accounts for the development of a plant from its seed.'

Alexander stared into Aristotle's small, darting grey eyes. 'Have you ever done this with a human being?' he asked.

'More than once. I have dissected weeks-old fetuses. I used to pay a midwife who carried out abortions for the prostitutes in a brothel in the Kerameikos quarter of Athens.'

The young man went pale.

'It's important not to be afraid of nature,' said Aristotle. 'Did you know that the closer all living beings are to the moment in which they were conceived then the more alike they are?'

'Does that mean that all life forms share the same origin?'

'Perhaps, but not necessarily. The facts are, my boy, that there is an abundance of matter, while life is brief and our means of enquiry are limited. Do you see why it is difficult to give answers? Humility is what's required. One must study, describe, catalogue, take one step after another, reach ever greater levels of knowledge. Just as when one climbs up a stair – one step at a time.'

'Certainly,' confirmed Alexander, but in his expression there was an anxiety that belied his words, as if his desire to know the world could in no way be reconciled with the patient discipline propounded by his tutor.

*

For a long time Lysippus did no more than attend some lessons. And while Aristotle was speaking, or while he was busy with one of his experiments, the sculptor drew sketches of Alexander's face, both on sheets of papyrus and on wooden boards whitewashed with plaster or with white lead. Then, one day, he approached Alexander and said, 'I'm ready.'

From then onwards Alexander had to spend at least an hour every day in Lysippus' studio for the definitive sittings. The artist had arranged a block of clay on a support and modelled a portrait in it. His hands ran fretfully over the damp clay, searching, chasing forms that glimmered in his mind, forms recognized for an instant in the face of his model or evoked in the sudden light of his gaze.

Then the hands suddenly destroyed the thing they had modelled, taking the matter back to its formless state to begin again immediately, vigorously, determinedly in reconstructing an expression, an emotion, the flash of an intuition.

Aristotle looked on fascinated, following the dance of the sculptor's hands over the clay, the mysterious sensitivity of those enormous blacksmith's hands as they created, moment by moment, an almost perfect imitation of life.

It's not him, the philosopher thought in those moments. It's not Alexander . . . Lysippus is modelling the young god he imagines to be there in front of him, a god with the eyes, lips, nose, the hair of Alexander, yet he is something else, he is more and is less at the same time.

The scientist observed the artist, studied his intent, feverish gaze, the magic mirror that absorbed the real and reflected it transformed, recreated first in his mind and then through his hands.

The clay model was ready after only three sittings during which Lysippus had reworked the boy's likeness a thousand times. Then he began the model in wax which would confer its ephemeral form to the eternal bronze.

As the sun's light began to descend towards the crest of Mount Bermion, it spread a golden luminosity through the room just as the artist turned the mobile base of the support, showing Alexander his portrait.

The young man was astounded at the sight of his own effigy, finely reproduced in the light tones of the wax, and he felt a wave of emotion rush to his heart. Aristotle also moved towards the work.

There was much more than a portrait in those proud and yet at the same time graceful forms, in the trembling chaos of the hair that framed, almost besieged the face of superhuman beauty, the majestic, serene forehead, the long eyes, suffused with a mysterious melancholy, the sensual and imperious mouth, the sinuous and neat contours of the lips.

There was a deep silence at that moment, a great peace in the room pervaded by the gentle liquid light of the evening, and in Alexander's mind there resounded the words of his tutor telling of how form models matter, of the intellect that regulates chaos, of the soul that makes its own mark on the flesh, perishable and ephemeral.

The Prince turned towards Aristotle who was contemplating with his small, grey sparrow-hawk eyes a miracle that failed to fit any of the categories known to his genius and he asked, 'What do you think?'

The philosopher started and turned to look at the artist who had slumped down on a stool, as though the energy spent in such a wildly prodigious manner over the past few days had completely run out all of a sudden.

'If God exists,' said Aristotle, 'he has Lysippus' hands.'

15

LYSIPPUS REMAINED AT MIEZA through spring of that year and Alexander became friends with his assistants, who told him wonderful stories about the art and character of their master.

The young man posed for the sculptor again, this time for a full-figure work, and even on horseback, but one day on entering the studio at a moment when Lysippus happened to be out, he noticed among the drawings heaped untidily on the table an extraordinary portrait of Aristotle.

'Do you like it?' came the voice of the sculptor who suddenly appeared at his shoulder just then.

'I'm sorry,' said Alexander, slightly startled. 'I didn't want to nose through your things, but this drawing is magnificent. Did he sit for you?'

'No, I sketch him a little now and then while watching him speak or walk. Would you like to have it?'

'No. You keep it. Perhaps one day you will be asked to create a statue of him as well. Don't you think a wise man merits that more than a king or a prince?'

'I think they both deserve it, if the king or the prince are wise men too,' replied Lysippus with a smile.

Every now and then Alexander received visits, and for some months he was able to spend more time with his friends because their physical and military activities were increased, especially during those periods when Aristotle was absent due to his research or special missions on Philip's orders. On other occasions Alexander himself would go to Pella to see his parents and Cleopatra, who became more beautiful by the day.

Back at Mieza he would fall back into his routine studies and exercises which kept him increasingly busy, absorbing all his physical and mental energies. Aristotle's methodical approach to his own research was also the inspiration behind his way of organizing his pupil's studies.

He had had a solar clock set up in the courtyard and a hydraulic clock in the library, both of which were constructed to his own design, and with them he measured the duration of the lessons or laboratory sessions so that all the disciplines received the correct amount of time.

In one wing of the building he was nurturing a fine collection of medicinal plants, stuffed animals, insects, butterflies and minerals. There was even some bitumen which some friends from Atarneus had sent from the Orient, and Alexander was amazed when his tutor ignited it and it burned with an extremely hot but smelly flame.

'I think olive oil is much better,' he commented. And Aristotle agreed with him.

His tutor collected all sorts of things in his obsession with cataloguing everything that was knowable in nature and he had even traced out a map of the thermal water sources spread throughout the various parts of the country, studying their healing properties. Philip himself had found some relief for his leg in the warm mud baths of a spring in Lyncestis.

In the school at Mieza an entire wall of shelving was dedicated to a collection of animals found preserved in stone, fish for the most part, but also plants, leaves, insects and even a bird.

'It seems to me that this is proof that there really was a flood, given that these fish have been found up on the mountains around us here,' said Alexander, an observation that was anything but stupid.

Aristotle would have liked to provide another explanation, but he had to admit that, for the moment at least, the myth of the flood was the only story that might explain the phenomenon. In any case, this point seemed to be of secondary importance: in his opinion it was necessary to collect those objects, measure them, describe them and draw them so that someone, in years to come, might find a scientific explanation based on incontrovertible data.

His relationship with Alexander was a source of great satisfaction to Aristotle: Philip's boy was always asking questions and this is precisely what every teacher hopes for from his pupils.

In the political field Aristotle had begun collecting – and continued now with the help of his assistants and of Alexander himself – the constitutions of various states and cities both eastern and western, both Greek and barbarian.

'Is your aim to collect all the constitutions that exist in the world?' Alexander asked him.

'If only that were possible,' sighed Aristotle, 'but I fear it is an unrealizable feat.'

'What is the aim of your research? To discover the best constitution of them all?'

'Impossible,' replied the philosopher. 'Firstly because there are no points of reference to help establish which is the perfect constitution, despite the things my tutor Plato had to say on this subject. My aim is not so much to reach an ideal constitution as to observe how each community is organized according to its own requirements, the environment in which it has developed, the resources it has at its disposal, the friends and enemies it has to deal with.

'This obviously implies that there cannot be an ideal constitution, but the fact is that the democratic codes of Greek cities are the only ones that can possibly govern the lives of free men.'

Just at that moment Leptine crossed through the court-yard holding an amphora full of water to her hip and for an instant Alexander had a vision of the hell that was Mount Pangaeos.

'And the slaves?' he asked. 'Can there be a world without slaves?'

'No,' replied Aristotle. 'Just as there will never be a loom that weaves cloth on its own. When this is possible, then a world without slaves will be possible, but I don't believe that will ever happen.'

Then one day the young Prince asked his tutor the question he hadn't dared ask up to that moment: 'If the democratic code of the Greek cities is the only one worthy of free men, then why have you accepted the job of educating the son of a king and why are you Philip's friend?'

'No human institution is perfect, and the Greek city system has one huge problem – war. Many cities, even though supported by democratic codes, seek to prevail over the others, to win new markets for themselves – more fertile lands, more advantageous alliances. This leads to continuous wars that wear down their best energies and privilege the age-old enemy of the Greeks: the Persian empire.

'A king like your father has it in him to become the mediator of all this discord and these internecine struggles. He can make sure a sense of unity prevails over the seed of division and can be a superior arbiter and guide who, if necessary, knows how to impose peace, even through the use of force. Far better a Greek king who saves Greek civilization from destruction, than continuous war with everyone against everyone else and, ultimately, domination and slavery under the barbarians.

'These are my thoughts. For this reason I have accepted the job of educating a king. Otherwise there would be no sum of money sufficient to buy Aristotle.'

Alexander was satisfied with this answer which he felt to be just and honest. With the passing of time, however, he realized that there was an unresolvable contradiction growing within himself: on the one hand the education he was receiving, and which he supported fully, pushed him towards moderation in his behaviour, in his thinking and his desires, in his attitude towards art and knowledge; on the other hand his nature, in itself bold, pushed him to follow the archaic ideals of the warrior's values, something akin to the prowess that he found in the Homeric poems and in the words of the tragic dramatists.

Alexander's ancestry, on his mother's side, was from Achilles, the hero of the *Iliad*, the irrepressible enemy of Troy, and this was for him a natural fact. Reading the *Iliad*, which he even kept under his pillow and to which he always dedicated the last moments of the day, stimulated his spirit and his imagination and roused in him an uncontainable excitement. At that time his intense friendship with Hephaestion found expression in a physical intimacy that had been developing gradually ever since their youth. It had started as a form of curiosity for their own bodies, but grew as they reacted to their harsh upbringing and the severity of the punishments inflicted upon them so that they then sought a more gratifying, more personal relationship.

Only Leptine was able to calm him on these occasions. For some time now he had allowed her to become very close to him and at times he sought and obtained even greater intimacy. It was perhaps being deprived of the affection of his mother and his sister, but it was also the need for contact with hands that knew how to caress, how to dispense light, subtle pleasure that grew sweetly to the point where it put fire in his eyes and in his limbs. Every evening Leptine would prepare a warm bath and let the water flow over his shoulders and his torso, she would stroke his hair and his back until he let himself go altogether.

These moments of abandon were ever more often accompanied by an unsettling desire to act, to leave the peace of the retreat and to follow in the footsteps of the great men of history. This primitive rage, this yearning for physical conflict sometimes began to find expression even in his day-to-day actions. On one occasion he went out hunting with his companions and ended up in a fight with Philotas over a roe-buck they both claimed to have struck first; Alexander got his friend in a stranglehold and would have killed him if the others hadn't stopped him.

On another occasion he almost slapped Callisthenes because he had cast some doubt on the veracity of Homer's works.

Aristotle observed him attentively and with some

concern; there were two natures in Alexander – the young man of refined culture and insatiable curiosity who asked thousands of questions, who knew how to sing, draw and recite the tragedies of Euripides, and then there was the wild and barbaric warrior, the implacable exterminator who was increasingly coming to the fore during the hunts, the races, the war exercises and the training sessions in which his ardour got the upper hand to the point of bringing the tip of his sword to the throat of the man standing there before him.

At those moments the philosopher believed he understood the mystery of the gaze that would suddenly darken, of the disturbing shadow that thickened deep down in his left eye, like the dark night of the chaos of creation. But the moment was still not right to let the young Argead lion loose.

Aristotle felt that he still had much to teach him, that he had to channel his extraordinary energies, to provide him with a purpose and an aim. He had to equip that body, born for the wild violence of battle, with a political mind capable of conceiving a plan and seeing it through to conclusion. Only in this way would he ever complete his masterpiece, just as Lysippus had.

*

Autumn passed and winter arrived and the messengers brought the news to Mieza that Philip would not be returning to Pella. The Kings of Thrace had found a second wind and were waiting to be taught a lesson.

So the army had to face the terrible rigours of winter in those remote lands scourged by the freezing winds that blow across the limitless snow-covered plains of Scythia and the ice-covered peaks of the Haemon.

It was a frighteningly demanding campaign in which the soldiers had to deal with a difficult enemy fighting on home territory and used to surviving in even the most arduous conditions. But when spring returned the immense territory extending from the shores of the Aegean to the great Ister river was completely at peace and incorporated into the Macedonian empire.

The King founded a city at the centre of those wild lands and gave it his name, Philippopolis, thus giving free range to Demosthenes' irony; from Athens he dubbed it 'city of thieves' or 'city of delinquents'.

Spring saw the return of the green pastures of Mieza together with the shepherds and cowherds who moved up from the plain towards the mountain meadows.

One day, after sunset, the peace of Mieza was broken by horses approaching at full gallop, and then by brisk orders given in agitated voices. A horseman of the royal guard knocked at the door of Aristotle's study.

'King Philip is here. He wants to see his son and to speak to you.'

Aristotle got to his feet quickly and went to greet the illustrious guest. He almost ran along the corridor, giving rushed orders to all those he met, telling them to prepare a bath and supper for the King and his companions.

When the philosopher arrived in the courtyard, Alexander had already beaten him in the rush to meet Philip.

'Father!' he cried as he ran towards the King.

'My son!' exclaimed Philip, holding Alexander long and hard in his arms.

16

ALEXANDER PULLED AWAY from his father's embrace to take a good look at him. The Thracian campaign had certainly left its mark: his skin had been burned by the frost, there was a large scar over his right eyebrow, the eye itself was half closed, and his hair had turned white.

'Father, what has happened to you?'

'It was the hardest campaign of my life, my boy, and indeed the winter was an enemy more vicious and ruthless than the Thracian soldier's, but now our empire extends from the Adriatic to the Black Sea, from the River Ister to the Thermopylae Pass. The Greeks will have to recognize me as their leader.'

Alexander would have liked to ask a thousand other questions there and then, but he saw the servants and the maids rushing to take care of Philip and he said, 'You need a bath, Father. We will continue our conversation over supper. Is there anything special you would like the cook to prepare?'

'Is there any roe-buck?'

'As much as you can eat, and wine from Attica.'

'So we can drink to Demosthenes' health then.'

'To Demosthenes, Father!' exclaimed Alexander and he ran to the kitchen to make sure that everything was made ready to perfection.

Aristotle joined the King in the bath chamber and sat and listened to what he had to say while the handmaids massaged his shoulders and scrubbed his back.

'It is a tonic bath with sage. You'll feel much better for it. How are you, Sire?'

'Exhausted, Aristotle, and there's still so much to do.'

'If only you could stay here for one or two weeks – I can't say that I'd be able to restore your youth, but I could certainly get you in good shape: a diet to clean out your system, massages, thermal baths, exercises for your leg. And that eye . . . the wound has not been treated correctly. I must examine you, as soon as you have a moment to spare.'

'Ah! But I cannot allow myself any of these luxuries, and the military surgeons do what they can. I do want to thank you for the winter battle diet you researched for our soldiers; it worked out very well and the results were excellent. I believe it saved many lives.'

The philosopher bowed his head slightly.

'I am in trouble, Aristotle,' the King began again. 'I need your help.'

'Speak.'

'I know that you do not agree, but I am preparing to occupy all the cities near the Straits that are still tied to Athens. Perinthus and Byzantium will be tested: I must know whose side they are on.'

'If you force them into a choice, they will choose Athens and you will have to use force against them.'

'I have engaged the services of the best military engineer available today, and he is designing huge machines, some ninety feet high. They are costing me a fortune, but it will be worth it.'

'Anyway, my opinion would do nothing to dissuade you.'

'No, indeed.'

'So why do you ask for my advice?'

'Because of the situation in Athens. My informers tell me that Demosthenes is setting up a pan-Hellenic League against me.'

'That's understandable. In his eyes you are the most dangerous of Athens' enemies and a threat to the independence and democracy of the Greek cities.'

'If I had wanted to take Athens, I would have done so already. Instead I limited myself to establishing my authority in the area that comes under direct Macedonian influence.'

'You razed Olynthus to the ground and . . .'

'But the people of Olynthus had made me angry!'

Aristotle raised his eyebrows and sighed, 'I understand.'

'So . . . what can be done about this League? If Demosthenes succeeds, I will be forced to confront them with my army in open battle.'

'For the moment I do not believe there is any danger of that. The discord, the rivalry and the envy among the Greeks are all so strong that nothing will come of it, I think. But if you persist with your aggressive policy, you will only succeed in uniting them. Just as happened at the time of the Persian invasion.'

'But I am not a Persian!' the King thundered. And he beat his fist on the edge of the bath, causing a little storm to break out in there.

As soon as the waters calmed down, Aristotle spoke again: 'That makes no difference. Since time immemorial whenever a power has achieved hegemony all other powers have become allies against it. The Greeks are extremely fond of their total independence and they are ready to do anything to preserve it. You understand, don't you, that Demosthenes is even capable of making a deal with the Persians? For them there is more value in preserving their independence than in preserving ties of blood and culture.'

'Certainly. I should really just wait quietly and see what happens.'

'No. You must realize that every time you take some military initiative against Athenian lands or allies then you create difficulties for the friends you have in the city because they are immediately marked as traitors or are suspected of having been corrupted.'

'As indeed some of them have been,' said Philip impassively. 'In any case I know I am right and therefore I will continue along this road. I have to ask you a favour, however. Your father-in-law is Lord of Assus; should Demosthenes start negotiating with the Persians then he may come to hear of it.'

'I will write to him,' Aristotle promised. 'But remember, if you are determined to continue this way then sooner or later you will find yourself having to face Demosthenes' coalition. Or something very similar.'

The King was very quiet. He stood up and the philosopher could not help noticing the fresh scars on his body while the women dried him with towels and dressed him in clean clothes.

'How is my boy doing?' asked Philip suddenly.

'He is truly one of the most extraordinary people I have ever met in my life. But with the passing of each day it becomes more and more difficult to keep him under control. He keeps track of your endeavours and is champing at the bit. He wants some glory to bask in now, to show his worth. He is afraid that when his turn comes there will be nothing left to conquer.'

Philip shook his head and smiled. 'As if these were real problems . . . I'll speak to him. But for the moment I want him to remain here. He must complete his education.'

'Have you seen Lysippus' portrait of your son?'

'Not yet, but I've heard it's wonderful.'

'It is. Alexander has decided that in the future only Lysippus will be allowed to make his likeness. It really has had a remarkable effect on him.'

'I have already ordered that copies should be made for all the cities allied with us, for public display. I want the Greeks to see that my son has grown up in the foothills of the mountain of the gods.'

Aristotle accompanied him into the dining chamber, but it would perhaps be better to call it a refectory. Indeed, the philosopher had abolished the dining beds and the low tables and had had tables and chairs introduced, just as in poor people's homes or under military tents. This arrangement seemed to him to be more appropriate for the atmosphere of study and containment that he strove to maintain at Mieza.

'Have you noticed whether he has any relations with girls? It's about time he started,' observed the King as he walked along a corridor.

'His is a very reserved temperament, almost shy. But there is that girl, I think her name is Leptine.'

A frown spread over Philip's forehead. 'Continue.'

'There's not much to tell. She is devoted to him, as if he were a god. And she is certainly the only female to have complete access to him at any hour of the day and night. I know nothing more.'

Philip scratched his chin through his bristly beard. 'I wouldn't like him to produce a bastard with that servant. Perhaps it's best if I send him a "companion" who knows the trade. That way there won't be any complications and she'll be able to teach him a few interesting things.'

By now they had reached the entrance to the dining room and Aristotle stopped walking. 'I wouldn't, if I were you.'

'But she wouldn't bother your work at all. I'm talking about a person with a first-rate education and excellent experience.'

'That's not the point,' said the philosopher. 'Alexander has already let you choose his tutor and his portraitist because he loves you and because he is very mature, for his age. But I don't believe he would allow you to go beyond this, to violate his private life.'

Philip mumbled something incomprehensible and then said, 'I'm hungry. Is there nothing to eat in this place?'

*

They all ate together happily and Peritas sat under the table gnawing at the roe-buck bones they threw to the floor for him.

Alexander wanted to hear all the details of the Thracian campaign. What were the enemy's weapons like and how did they fight? How were their villages and cities fortified? And he wanted to know how the two enemy kings – Cersobleptes and Theres – had fought.

Then, while the servants were clearing up, Philip addressed all those present: 'Now, allow me to give you permission to take your leave and to wish you all good-night. I would like to spend some time alone with my son.'

Everyone stood up, said goodnight in turn and retired. Philip and Alexander were left alone in the lamplight, in the large empty hall, sitting opposite each other. All that could be heard, from under the table, was the sound of bones being chewed and broken. Peritas was fully grown now and had teeth as strong as a lion.

'Is it true that you are leaving immediately?' asked Alexander. 'Tomorrow?'

'Yes.'

'I had hoped you would stay for a few days.'

'I hoped so too, my son.'

There then followed a long silence. Philip never justified his decisions.

'What are you going to do?'

'I am going to occupy the Athenian settlements on the Chersonese Peninsula. I am building the biggest assault machines ever. I want our fleet in the Straits.'

'Athens' grain passes through the Straits.'

'Exactly.'

'That will mean war.'

'Not necessarily. I want them to respect me. If there is to be a pan-Hellenic League it must be understood that I and I alone can be its chief.'

'Take me with you, Father.'

Philip stared into his son's eyes. 'The time is not right, my son. You have to complete your studies, your education, your training.'

'But I . . .'

'Listen. You have had some limited experience of a military campaign, you have displayed courage and ability in hunting and I know that you are extremely skilful with your weapons, but believe me when I say that the things you will have to face one day will be a thousand times more demanding. I have seen my men dying of cold and exhaustion, I have seen them suffer atrocious ordeals, with their bodies torn apart. I have seen others plummet from great heights while climbing city walls and then I listened to them cry out in unbearable pain . . . I listened until silence came.

'And look at me, look at my arms: they look like the branches of a tree that a bear has sharpened his claws on. I have been wounded eleven times – crippled and half-blinded. Alexander, Alexander, you see the glory, but war is above all else horror. It is blood, sweat, excrement; it is dust and mud; it is thirst and hunger, unbearable frost and unbearable heat. Let me face all this for you, for as long as I am able. Stay here at Mieza, Alexander. For one more year.'

The young man said nothing. He knew that those words admitted of no reply. But his father's wounded, drawn gaze pleaded with him to understand and not to hate him for this decision.

Outside, from far away, there came the rumble of thunder and yellow flashes of lightning suddenly lit up the edges of the great storm clouds gathering over the dark peaks of Mount Bermion.

'How is Mother?' asked Alexander all of a sudden.

Philip lowered his eyes.

'I hear you have taken a new wife. The daughter of a barbarian king.'

'A Scythian chief. I had to do it. And you will do the same when it is your turn.'

'I know. But how is Mother?'

'Well. Under the circumstances.'

'I'll be off then. Goodnight, Father.' He stood up and walked towards the exit, followed by his dog. And Philip envied the animal that would keep his son company, that would hear the rise and fall of his breathing all through the night.

It began to rain – a few large, heavy drops that grew quickly in number. The King, alone now in the empty room, got to his feet. He went out under the portico just as a blinding flash of lightning illuminated the wide court-yard and was immediately followed by a deafening thunderclap. He leaned against a column and stood there motionless watching the rain fall in sheets.

17

THINGS WORKED OUT exactly as Aristotle had predicted: driven into a corner, Perinthus and Byzantium declared their support for Athens and Philip replied by besieging Perinthus, a city on the northern coast of the Hellespont, built on a rocky promontory and linked to the mainland by an isthmus.

He had made his camp on a plain from which he was able to dominate the entire situation and every evening he called his generals to a meeting: Antipater, Parmenion and Cleitus, known as 'the Black' because of his black hair, black eyes and dark complexion. He was also almost always in a black mood, but he was an excellent officer.

'Have they decided to negotiate a surrender – yes or no?' asked the King as he entered, even before sitting down.

'No,' said Parmenion, 'and in my opinion they are not even entertaining the possibility. The city is cut off by land thanks to our trenches, but they continue to receive supplies by sea from the Byzantine fleet.'

'And there's nothing we can do about it,' added the Black. 'We do not have control of the sea.'

Philip beat his fist on the table. 'I couldn't care less about control of the sea!' he shouted. 'In a few days' time my assault towers will be ready and I will destroy their walls. I want to see just how courageous they'll be then!'

The Black shook his head.

'What's the problem with that?'

'Nothing. It's simply that I do not believe it will be so easy.'

'So you don't, eh? Well just listen to this: I want those damned machines ready to move within two days at the most, otherwise I'll be kicking backsides from the chief engineer all the way down to the lowliest joiner. Have you all understood?'

'We understand perfectly, Sire,' replied Antipater with his usual patience.

Philip's anger managed to work miracles in certain situations. In three days the machines began their march towards the walls, groaning and creaking: they were self-standing towers higher than the fortifications of Perinthus, functioning by means of a system of counterweights, and each one could carry hundreds of soldiers with their catapults and battering rams.

The besieged citizens understood what was coming, and the memory of what had happened at Olynthus, the city reduced to ashes by the King of Macedon's fury, intensified their energies. They dug pits and burned the machines with night raids. Philip had them rebuilt and dug counter-pits to weaken the foundations of the walls while the battering rams were at work non-stop, day and night, with the entire city resounding to the deafening blows.

Finally the walls gave way, but the Macedonian generals were greeted by a bitter surprise. Antipater, the eldest and most respected of them all, was given the job of breaking the bad news to the King.

'Sire, the walls have collapsed, but I advise you not to send the foot soldiers in.'

'No? And why ever not?'

'Come with me and see for yourself.'

They went to one of the towers, climbed up to the very top, and Philip was left speechless by the sight beyond the walls. The citizens of Perinthus had joined together all the buildings in the row of houses on the first terrace of the city, effectively creating a second wall. And because Perinthus was completely terraced, it was obvious that this technique would be repeated to infinity.

'Damnation,' growled the King as he came down the tower, back to earth.

He went off to his tent and stayed there for days, sulking and racking his brains as he tried to think up a way out of the blind alley he'd ended up in. But there was more bad news to come and all his chiefs of staff came together to communicate it.

'Sire,' announced Parmenion, 'the Athenians have signed up ten thousand mercenaries using money provided by the Persian governors of Asia Minor and they have already been brought ashore at Perinthus.'

Philip lowered his head. Unfortunately the eventuality so feared by Aristotle had come to pass – Persia was now aligned directly against Macedon.

'This really is trouble,' commented the Black, as if the atmosphere weren't already gloomy enough.

'But that's not all,' added Antipater.

'What else is there?' shouted Philip. 'Am I expected to pull the words out of your mouths with pincers?'

'It's quite simple,' continued Parmenion. 'Our fleet is blocked in the Black Sea.'

'What?' shouted the King even more loudly. 'And what exactly was our navy doing in the Black Sea?'

'They were trying to cut off a convoy of grain for Perinthus, but the Athenians realized what was happening and in a surprise move, under cover of night, they blocked the Bosphorus with their fleet.'

Philip collapsed onto a chair and held his head in his hands. 'One hundred and thirty ships and three thousand men,' he murmured. 'I cannot possibly do without them!' he shouted as he suddenly stood up and started pacing the tent with his long strides.

Meanwhile, on board their ships in the Bosphorus, the Athenian crews were singing victory songs and every evening, as darkness fell, they would light fires in braziers and reflect the glow off their polished shields so that the Macedonian ships could not attempt to make use of the darkness in trying to run the blockade. But they did not know that when Philip was trapped and unable to make use of brute strength, he turned to his cunning, which made him doubly dangerous.

One night the captain of an Athenian trireme which was patrolling the western coast of the Straits saw a small Macedonian boat coming downstream, trying to keep as close as possible to the shore in order to remain unseen.

The skipper ordered the light from the brazier to be directed towards the shore and the sloop was immediately visible, fully illuminated by the bright rays reflected off the shield.

'Stop where you are,' ordered the officer, 'or I'll have you sunk!' And he asked the helmsman to turn to starboard and to aim the big bronze ram of the trireme against the side of the small vessel.

The men in the boat were frightened and stopped rowing and when the Athenian captain told them to come closer they did so and climbed on board.

There was something strange about the way they behaved, and in their appearance, but when they opened their mouths to speak the Athenian officer had no doubts – they were certainly Macedonian and not Thracian fishermen, as they had claimed to be.

He had them searched and hanging round the neck of one he found a leather cylinder with a message inside. This was definitely his lucky night! He asked one of his men to bring a lamp while he read:

Philip, King of the Macedonians, to Antipater.

Hail, my General Lieutenant!

We find ourselves now with an opportunity to inflict a crushing defeat on the Athenian fleet in the Bosphorus. Send one hundred ships on ahead from Thasos and block the southern exit from the Hellespont. I will send my fleet down from the south and we will have them in a pincer move. There will be no escape for them. You must be at the mouth of the Straits on the first night of the new moon.

Take good care.

'Gods above!' exclaimed the captain as soon as he had finished reading. 'There's no time to lose.'

He immediately ordered the helmsman and the oarsmen to turn back and row at full strength towards the middle of the Straits where the flagship was floating at anchor. He went aboard and asked to speak to the Navarch, the admiral, an elderly officer of great experience by the name of Phokion, and he gave him the message that had been intercepted. The officer read it quickly and then passed it to his scribe, a competent man who had worked for years as secretary to the Athenian assembly.

'I have seen other letters from Philip in our archive and this is certainly from his hand. And the seal is his too,' he added after having examined the document carefully.

Shortly afterwards, from the prow of the flagship, the Navarch had a shield flash the signal for all the ships of the fleet to withdraw.

They arrived off Thasos some three days later only to discover that there was no sign of Antipater's fleet, which was not really so surprising because Antipater had never actually had a fleet. But in the meantime the Macedonian royal ships had been able to travel down the Bosphorus and the Hellespont peacefully and find shelter in a safe port.

In one of his speeches against Philip, Demosthenes had named him 'the Fox'; when he heard what had happened he realized that never had such a name been more deserved.

The Macedonian King abandoned the siege of Perinthus as autumn began and marched north to punish the Scythian tribes who had refused to send him reinforcements. He defeated and killed their king, Atas, a man who went into battle in person even though he was more than ninety years old.

On the return journey, however, in the midst of winter now, Philip's army was attacked by the fiercest of the Thracian tribes, the Triballians. The Macedonians suffered terrible losses and had to abandon all their loot. The King himself was wounded and was barely able to lead his soldiers back to the homeland, fighting to open up the road all the way.

He returned to the palace at Pella sorely tested by his labours and by the stabbing pains from his wounded leg – exhausted and almost unrecognizable. But that very same day he called a session of the council and asked to be informed about events in Greece and in Macedon during his absence.

There was no good news, and had he been able to find the slightest reserve of energy he would have been a raging bull.

Instead he resolved that all he could do was sleep on it and the following morning he called Philip the physician and said to him, 'Take a good look at me. What do you think?'

The doctor studied him up and down, took note of his dull complexion and his lifeless gaze, the dry, cracked lips, the quavering voice: 'You're in terrible shape, Sire.'

'You don't mince your words,' observed the King.

'What you need is a good doctor. When you need people to worship and flatter you, you well know where to look for them.'

'You're right. Now, listen to me. I am prepared to drink

any concoction you wish, to have my back broken and my neck twisted by your masseurs, to have your enemas up my rear end, to eat stinking fish instead of red meat for as long as you want, to drink pure spring water until there's a colony of frogs in my belly, but for the sake of the gods, get me back on my feet because at the beginning of summer I want my roar to be heard as far as Athens and beyond.'

'Will you follow my instructions faithfully?' asked the physician diffidently.

'I will obey.'

'And you won't throw my medicines and my infusions at the wall?'

'I will not.'

'Come to the surgery then. I have to examine you.'

*

Some time had passed when one quiet spring evening, Philip appeared in the Queen's apartments unannounced. Olympias, warned by her maids, took a quick look at herself in the mirror before going to meet him on the threshold. 'I am pleased to see you have recovered, Sire. Come in, sit down; it is an honour for me to receive the King of Macedon here in these rooms.'

Philip sat and for a while was silent with his eyes lowered. 'Is all this formality necessary? Can we not converse like husband and wife who have been together for many years?'

' "Together" is no longer such an appropriate word,' replied Olympias.

'Your tongue is more cutting than a sword.'

'That's because I have no sword.'

'I have come to speak to you.'

'I will listen.'

'I have to ask you a favour. My recent campaigns have not been successful. I have lost many men and have wasted precious resources. In Athens they think I am finished and they listen to Demosthenes as though he were some kind of oracle.'

'So I hear.'

'Olympias, I do not want a direct conflict now and I don't want to do anything that might lead to one either. For the moment good will must prevail. The desire to somehow undo the rift, the damage . . .'

'How can I help you?'

'I cannot send a mission to Athens at this juncture, but I thought that if you were to do it – the Queen – then that might change many things. You have never undertaken any initiative against them. Some Athenians even maintain that you are a victim of Philip.'

Olympias made no comment.

'To cut things short, it would be like an embassy from a neutral power, don't you think? Olympias, I need time, please help me! And if you don't want to help me, think of your son. It is his kingdom I am building, his hegemony over the entire Greek world – that is what I am preparing.'

He fell silent and composed himself after his emotional plea. Olympias turned towards the window as if seeking to avoid his gaze and she too was silent for a moment. Then she said, 'I will do it. I will send Oreos, my secretary. He is a wise and prudent man.'

'An excellent choice,' Philip said approvingly. He simply had not expected such accommodation.

'What else can I do for you?' the Queen asked again, but the tone was one of cold dismissal.

'I wanted to tell you that in a few days' time I will go to Mieza.' At this news Olympias suddenly changed expression and her pale cheeks flushed pink. 'I am going there to bring Alexander home,' he added.

The Queen hid her face in her stole, but she could not hide the emotions that came over her in that moment.

'You haven't asked whether I've eaten or not,' Philip said to her.

Olympias lifted her moist eyes. 'Have you eaten?' she repeated mechanically.

'No. I . . . I was hoping that you might have asked me to stay here with you this evening.'

The Queen lowered her head. 'I don't feel well today. I am sorry.'

Philip bit his lip and left, slamming the door.

Olympias leaned against the wall as though in a faint and listened to her husband's heavy steps resound along the corridor and fade away to nothing down the stairs.

18

THE MEADOW WAS FLOODED with spring light and dotted with flowers as Alexander ran across it. Half naked and barefoot, he moved quickly against the wind that blew through his hair and brought with it a slight smell of sea spray.

Peritas was running alongside, checking his pace so as not to overtake his master and lose him. Now and again he barked to attract Alexander's attention and the Prince turned towards the dog and smiled, but without stopping.

It was one of those moments in which Alexander gave free rein to his spirit, in which he flew like a bird, galloped like a steed. It was then that his ambiguous and mysterious centaur-like nature – violent and sensitive, dark and sunny at one and the same time – seemed to find expression in harmonious movement, in a sort of initiatory dance under the shining light of the sun or in the sudden shade of a cloud.

With each stride his sculpted body first contracted and then extended in a long movement, his golden hair bounced soft and bright on his back like a mane, and his graceful arms accompanied the rise and fall of his chest in the brisk labour of his running.

Philip watched him in silence, sitting immobile on horseback at the edge of the wood. Then, when he realized they were close now and heard the dog's barking suddenly increase on spotting him, he spurred on his steed and came alongside his son, waving his hand, smiling even, but without stopping him, enchanted as he was by the power of that running and the wonder of those indefatigable limbs.

Alexander stopped on the bank of a small river and dived into the water; Philip dismounted and waited for him. The boy leaped out of the stream together with the dog and they both shook the water from their bodies. Philip embraced his son hard and felt Alexander's equally strong grip – tangible proof that his child had become a man.

'I have come to collect you,' he said. 'We're going home.'

Alexander looked at him in disbelief. 'Is that the King's word?'

'The King's word,' assured Philip. 'But the day will come when you will remember this period of your life with regret for its ever having come to an end. I never had such fortune; I had no songs, nor poetry, nor wise lectures. And this is why I am so tired, son, for this is why my years weigh so heavily on me.'

Alexander said nothing and they walked together through the meadow, towards the house: the young man followed by his dog, the father holding his horse by its bridle.

Suddenly, from behind a hill that hid the view of the Mieza retreat, there came the sound of a horse neighing. It was an acute, penetrating sound, a powerful call like that of a wild beast, or a chimerical creature. And then there came the sound of men shouting, calling, and powerful hooves all shod with bronze that made the earth tremble.

The neighing came again, more acute and angrier this time. Philip turned towards his son and said, 'I have brought you a present.'

They reached the top of the hill and Alexander stopped in amazement: below, there before him, a black stallion reared up onto its hind legs, shining with sweat like a bronze statue under the rain, held by five men with ropes and bridles in their hands, all trying to keep the animal's formidable power under control.

It was blacker than a raven's wing and it had a white star on its forehead in the shape of a bucranium, an ox's skull. With every movement of its neck or its hindquarters it scattered the grooms to the ground and dragged them across the grass like lifeless puppets. Then, head down, it leaped onto its front hooves, kicking out wildly with its hind legs, whipping the air with its tail while the long mane flowed from one side of its neck to the other, shining in the light.

Around the wondrous animal's mouth was a bloody froth and every now and then it stopped struggling, its neck bowed so as to inhale as much as possible, filling its chest with air and then exhaling like a breath of fire, like a dragon blowing. And again it neighed, shook its splendid neck, stretched the tightened muscles that swelled its withers.

Alexander, as though struck by a whip, suddenly came to and shouted, 'Leave it! Let that horse free, by Zeus!'

Philip put a hand on his shoulder. 'Wait a little while more, my boy, wait until we have broken it in. Just a little patience and it will be yours.'

'No!' shouted Alexander. 'No! Only I can tame it. Leave it! I'm telling you to let it go.'

'But it will escape,' said Philip. 'My boy, I paid a fortune for that horse!'

'How much?' Alexander asked. 'How much did it cost, Father?'

'Thirteen talents.'

'I'll bet you the same amount that I can break it in! But tell those fools to let it go! I beg you!'

Philip looked at him and saw that he was very nearly out of his mind with emotion, the veins in his neck were thick and swollen like those of the raging stallion.

He turned to the men and gave the order, 'Let it loose!'

They immediately obeyed. One by one they undid the ropes and the bridles. The animal ran off onto the plain straight away. Alexander ran after it and managed somehow to catch up as the King and his grooms watched on in disbelief.

Philip shook his head and mumbled, 'Oh, by the gods, the boy's heart will burst, his heart will burst.' Peritas, held by one of the men, bared his teeth and growled and barked but the groom quietened him and gestured to the others to listen. They all heard Alexander speaking to the horse in the midst of their breathless running – shouting something, his words snatched away by the wind as was the neighing of the stallion which somehow seemed to be replying.

And suddenly, when it seemed the young man must

collapse because of the effort, the steed slowed down, trotted for a while and then started walking, shaking its head and breathing deeply.

Alexander once again approached it slowly, with the sun behind him. He could see it now, fully illuminated, he could see its wide, black forehead with the white mark in the shape of an ox's skull.

'Bucephalas,' he whispered. 'Bucephalas . . . there, that's your name, that's it. What do you think . . . do you like it? Like this name, do you?' And he came closer and closer, to the point where he could almost touch it. The animal shook its head, but still it did not move and the boy put out his hand and touched its neck, delicately, and then the cheek and its muzzle, as soft as moss.

'Do you want to run with me?' he said. 'Do you want to run?'

The horse neighed and lifted its proud head and Alexander understood that it was saying yes. He stared into its burning eyes for a moment and then leaped swiftly onto its back and shouted, 'Go, Bucephalas!' And he touched its belly with his heels.

The animal sped off at a gallop, stretching its shining back, lengthening its head and its legs and its long tail. He ran as fast as the wind across the plain as far as the wood and the river, and the hammering of his hooves was like thunder.

They stopped in front of Philip, who found himself wondering whether to believe his eyes.

Alexander slipped to the ground. 'It's like riding Pegasus, Father, it's as though he had wings. Achilles' horses, Balius and Xanthus, children of the wind, must have been like this. Thank you for the gift,' and as he said this he stroked the horse on its neck and sweaty chest. Peritas began to bark, jealous of what he felt must be a new friend of his master and Alexander petted him too, to reassure him.

Philip looked on in amazement, struggling to take in all that had happened. Then he kissed Alexander on the head and said, 'My son, you must seek out another kingdom for yourself. Macedon alone is clearly not big enough for you.'

19

'DID YOU REALLY pay thirteen talents for him?' Alexander asked as he rode alongside his father.

Philip nodded. 'I think it's the highest price ever paid for a horse. It's the most handsome animal that Philonikos's stables in Thessaly have produced in many years.'

'He's worth more,' said Alexander, stroking Bucephalas' neck. 'No other charger in the world would be worthy of me.'

They ate with Aristotle and Callisthenes. Theophrastus had returned to Asia to continue with his research, occasionally sending news of his discoveries to his master.

Sitting with them at the table were two ceramic painters Aristotle had called from Corinth, not to paint pots, but to work at another, much more delicate that job which Philip himself had commissioned – a map of the known world.

'May I see it?' asked the King impatiently when they had finished eating.

'Certainly,' replied Aristotle. 'Indeed, it is thanks to your conquests that we have been able to include all these different lands.'

They moved to a spacious, well-lit room dominated by the large map, painted on a tanned ox skin fixed by means of some studs to a wooden board of the same size. The colours used by the artists to represent seas, mountains, rivers and lakes, gulfs and islands were bright and striking.

Philip looked at it spellbound. His gaze ran over its lines from the eastern to the western extremities – from the Pillars of Hercules to the spread of the Scythian Plain, from the Bosphorus to the Caucasus, from Egypt to Syria.

He stroked it gently with his fingers, almost afraid to touch it, searching for countries – friends and enemies alike. His eyes shone as he recognized the city he had recently founded in Thrace and which bore his name – Philippopolis. Thus it was that he finally saw a physical representation of his dominion.

Towards the east and the north the map faded into nothing, just as it did towards the south and the endless sands of the Libyans and the Garamantes.

On a table to one side were many sheets of papyrus which the artists had used for preparatory sketches. Philip looked at some of them, lingering over a drawing that represented the earth.

'Do you think it is round?' he asked Aristotle.

'I don't think so. I know so,' replied the philosopher. 'The shadow projected by the earth onto the moon during eclipses is round. And if you watch a ship sail away from port, first of all you see its hull disappear, then the mast. If you watch a ship approaching port it happens the other way round.'

'And what's down there?' the King asked, pointing to an area marked with the word *antipodes*.

'Nobody knows. But the lands there are probably equal in surface area to our own. It's a question of equilibrium.

The problem is that in truth we still do not know the full extent of the northern regions.'

Alexander turned towards Aristotle and then his gaze fell, enchanted, on the provinces of the vast empire that was said to extend from the Aegaen Sea to India. The passionate words of the Persian guest who three years previously had described his homeland came back to the Prince's mind. He imagined himself on Bucephalas, galloping over those endless highlands, flying over mountains and deserts to the ends of the earth, beyond the waves of the river Ocean which Homer had said encircled the entire world.

The sound of his father's voice and the touch of his hand placed on his shoulder interrupted Alexander's reverie. 'Sort all your things out, my son, tell your servants to prepare your baggage, everything you want to take back home, to Pella. And say goodbye to your tutor. You will not see him again for some time.'

Having said this the King moved off, leaving them to bid each other farewell.

'This period has flown by,' said Aristotle. 'I feel as though I arrived here at Mieza yesterday.'

'Where will you go?' asked Alexander.

'I will stay here for a while. We have collected much material and so many notes and observations which will all need careful arranging. It will take some time. And I am also doing some research on the transmission of illnesses from one body to another.'

'I am glad you are staying, that means I'll be able to come and visit now and then. I have so many questions still to ask you.'

Aristotle looked at him and for a moment he read all those questions in the changing, disquieting light of the Prince's gaze.

'The questions you still have in you, Alexander, are those to which there is no answer . . . or if there are answers you can only hope to find them in your own soul.'

The light of that spring afternoon illuminated all the scattered sheets covered with notes and drawings, the painters' bowls with their paints and brushes, the big map of the known world and the small, grey serene eyes of the philosopher.

'And then, where will you go?' asked Alexander again.

'First to Stagira, to my home.'

'Do you think you've succeeded in making a Greek of me?'

'I think I have helped you become a man, but above all else I have understood one thing: you will never be Greek nor Macedonian. You are Alexander. I have taught you all I can and now you must go your own way and no one can tell you where it will take you. The only sure thing is that whoever chooses to go with you will have to abandon everything – home, love, homeland – for an adventure into the unknown. Farewell, Alexander, may the gods protect you.'

'Farewell, Aristotle. May the gods keep you safe as well, if they want some light to shine through the darkness of this world.'

That was how they took their leave of each other, with a long gaze. They were never to see each other again.

*

Alexander was awake until late that night, prey to a deep perturbation that prevented him falling off to sleep. From his window he looked out at the quiet countryside and the moon which illuminated the still white peaks of Bermion and Olympus, but in his ears he could already hear the metallic clangour of weapons, the neighing of horses as they thundered along at full gallop.

He thought of Achilles' glory, so great it had warranted Homer's song. His mind was full of the fury of battle and the clash of arms, but he could not understand how all this could inhabit his soul together with the teachings of Aristotle, the works of Lysippus, the odes of Alcaeus and Sappho.

Perhaps, he thought, the answer lay in his origins, in the nature of Olympias, his mother – wild and melancholic at one and the same time – and in his father's nature – amiable and ruthless, impulsive and rational. Perhaps it lay in the nature of his people who behind them had the wildest of barbaric tribes and before them the luminous cities of the Greeks with their temples and their libraries.

The next day he would rejoin his mother and his sister. How much had they changed? And how much had he changed? What would his position be now in the palace at Pella?

Seeking to calm the tumult in his soul with music, he picked up his lyre and sat on the windowsill. He played a song that he had heard sung many times by his father's soldiers at night around the watch fire. It was a rough song, just like their mountain dialect, but it was full of passion and nostalgia.

Then he realized that Leptine had come into his room,

called by the melody, and she was now sitting on the edge of the bed, listening.

The moonlight caressed her face, her shoulders and her smooth white arms. Alexander put the lyre down while Leptine, with the most delicate of gestures, bared her chest and held out her arms to him. He lay down beside her and she pulled him to her, holding his head between her breasts as she stroked his hair.

20

ALEXANDER WAS PRESENTED to the assembled army three days after his return to Pella. Alongside his father, dressed in his armour and astride Bucephalas, he inspected the troops. First, from the right, came the heavy cavalry of the *Hetaîroi*, the 'King's Companions', the noble Macedonians of all the mountain tribes, then the infantry of the *pezhetairoi*, the so-called 'Foot Companions', made up of farmers from the lowlands who together formed the formidable phalanx. They were arranged in five lines and the soldiers in each line carried *sarissae* of progressively increasing lengths so that when they were all lowered all the points appeared in the front row.

An officer shouted the order to present arms and a forest of iron-clad spears stood proud to pay homage to the King and his son.

'Remember, my boy, the phalanx is the anvil and the cavalry is the hammer,' said Philip. 'When an enemy's army is driven up against that barrier of spikes there's no escape for him.'

Then, on the left flank, the 'Vanguard', the leading squadron of the royal cavalry, rode by; these were the men and horses that were sent out at the crucial moment in the battle to inflict the hammer blow that would shatter the opponent's lines.

The cavalrymen shouted, 'Hail, Alexander!' and they beat their javelins against their shields – homage reserved exclusively for their leaders.

'You are their commander,' Philip explained. 'From now on you will lead the Vanguard into battle.' Just at that moment a group of cavalrymen dressed in magnificent armour, their heads protected and adorned with shining helmets bearing high plumes, broke ranks. The bits in the mouths of their chargers were made of silver, their caparisons were of purple wool and they stood out from the others by virtue of their size and the nobility of their bearing. They set off immediately at a gallop as though in a furious charge and then, at a given signal, they performed a wide, striking and perfect turn. The rider at the pivot of the turn held his charger still while the others continued riding at ever greater speeds so that the last outrider did not have to slow down at all.

Once the spectacular manoeuvre had been completed, they set their animals off again at a gallop, shoulder to shoulder, head to head, leaving a trail of thick dust behind them, then pulled to a dramatic halt in front of the Prince.

An officer shouted in a stentorian voice, 'Alexander's troop!' And then he called their names one by one: 'Hephaestion! Seleucus! Lysimachus! Ptolemy! Craterus! Perdiccas! Leonnatus! Philotas!'

Alexander's friends!

With the roll call finished they all raised their javelins and shouted, 'Hail, Alexander!' Finally, violating protocol, they surrounded him, almost pulling him down from his horse, and held him in what seemed to be an endless embrace in full view of the King and his soldiers, motion-less in their ranks.

The friends thronged around their Prince, shouting for joy, tossing weapons into the air, jumping and dancing like madmen.

When the parade was dismissed Eumenes also joined the group; because he was Greek he was not actually part of the army, but in the meantime he had become Philip's private secretary and thus played a vital role at court.

That very evening Alexander attended a banquet which his friends had prepared in Ptolemy's house. The room had been prepared spectacularly and painstakingly: the benches and tables were made of inlaid wood decorated with gilded bronze, the lamp holders were beautiful Corinthian sculptures of bronze in the shape of young girls. From the ceiling hung other lamps in the form of vases with lattice-work that projected a curious play of light and shadow onto the walls. The platters were all of solid silver, finely worked around the edges. The food had been prepared by cooks from Smyrna and Samos, Greek in terms of taste, but also refined connoisseurs of Asian cuisine.

The wines came from Cyprus, Rhodes, Corinth and even from far off Sicily, where the colonial farmers were now surpassing their counterparts in the motherland in terms of the quality and excellence of their produce. They were served from a gigantic Attic crater, almost a hundred years old, decorated with a dance of satyrs chasing semi-naked maenads. Each table was equipped with a bowl decorated by the same artist with rather suggestive symposium scenes: nude female flute players in the arms of young men drinking and wearing crowns of ivy, almost a sort of foretaste of what the evening had in store.

On making his entrance Alexander was welcomed with an ovation and the host went towards him bearing a beautiful cup with two handles, brimming with Cypriot wine. 'Well, Alexander! After three years of fresh water at Mieza you must have tadpoles swimming around in your belly. At least we got out of there before you did! Drink some of this and it'll sort you out.'

'So, what exactly did Aristotle teach you in his secret lessons?' Eumenes asked.

'And where did you get that horse?' Hephaestion chipped in. 'I've never seen anything like it.'

'I'll bet you haven't,' commented Eumenes without waiting for Alexander's reply. 'It cost thirteen talents. I signed the payment order.'

'Yes,' confirmed Alexander. 'It was a present from my father. But I won the same amount of money from him betting that I would manage to break it in. You should have seen it,' he continued, his excitement growing, 'there were five of them holding him and the poor animal was terrified, they were pulling him by the bit, hurting him.'

'And what did you do?' asked Perdiccas.

'Me? Nothing. I ordered the idiots to let him go and then I ran after him . . .'

'That's enough talk of horses!' shouted Ptolemy in an attempt to bring some order to the commotion the friends were creating as they all crowded round Alexander. 'Let's talk about women! And take your places because supper's ready.'

'Women?' Seleucus shouted even more loudly. 'Did you know that Perdiccas has fallen in love with your sister?'

Perdiccas blushed and gave Seleucus a push that sent him rolling across the floor.

'Really!' Seleucus insisted without getting up. 'I've seen him making eyes at her during an official ceremony. A bodyguard with the look of love in his eyes! Ha!' and this time he rolled around with laughter.

'And you haven't heard this,' Ptolemy added. 'Tomorrow he has to lead the escort that will take the Princess to offer the initiatory sacrifice to the goddess Artemis. I wouldn't trust him at all if I were you.'

Alexander saw that Perdiccas had turned scarlet and sought to save his embarrassment by changing the subject: 'Well, lads! Just one thing . . . I want you all to know that I'm pleased to see you again and I am proud that you, my friends and companions, are all part of Alexander's troop!' He lifted up the cup and drank its contents in one gulp.

'Wine!' ordered Ptolemy. 'Pour wine for everyone,' and then he clapped his hands and while the guests took up reclining positions on their dining beds, servants poured the wine from the crater and others began serving the food: partridge on skewers, thrush, mountain hens, duck and then a fine rarity – pheasant.

At his right hand Alexander asked for his dearest friend, Hephaestion, to his left, Ptolemy, his host.

After the game came a quarter of veal – roasted and cut into pieces and served individually by the carver while the servants brought in baskets of fragrant, freshly baked bread together with shelled walnuts and boiled ducks' eggs.

The flautists entered with their instruments and began

to play. They were all beautiful and exotic women – Mysian, Carian, Thracian, Bythnian – and they all wore their hair tied up with coloured ribbons or bonnets fringed with silver and gold. They were dressed in imitation of the Amazons, with short tunics and bows and quivers over their shoulders, props used in the theatre.

After the first song some of them put down their bows and then, after the second song, their quivers and then took off their leggings and their tunics so that they were completely naked, their young bodies shining with perfumed oils under the light of the lamps. They began to dance to the sound of the flutes and the drums, floating in front of the tables and among the diners' beds.

The friends had all stopped eating, but they continued drinking and were now in a state of total excitement. Some of them stood up, took off their clothes and joined in the dance with the accelerating rhythm of the drums and the tambourines carrying them inexorably towards a climax.

Suddenly Ptolemy grabbed a girl by the hand, stopping her gyrations and manoeuvring her so that Alexander could get a good look.

'She's the most beautiful of the lot,' he said. 'I've grabbed her for you.'

'And for me?' asked Hephaestion.

'Do you like this one?' Alexander asked as he stopped another striking girl, this one with red hair.

Ptolemy had given orders to the servants to fill the lamps in such a way that some of them would have run out of oil before others, leaving the room in a sort of half shadow.

The youngsters fondled one another as they lay on the dining beds, and on the rugs and the skins that covered part of the paved floor. Meanwhile the music of the flautists continued to ring against the frescoed walls, almost giving rhythm to their excited panting and the surging of their gleaming bodies in the glow of the few lamps that were still burning in the corners of the great room.

Alexander left in the deep of the night, prey to an uncontrollable excitement and headiness. It was as though a long-repressed force had suddenly been let loose and was dominating him completely.

He stopped on a terrace of the palace that was exposed to the northerly wind to clear his mind a little and he stood there gripping the parapet until he saw the moon set behind the mountains of Eordaea.

Down there, lost in the darkness, was the peaceful retreat of Mieza and perhaps Aristotle was burning the midnight oil as he followed the subtle thread of his own thinking. It seemed as though years had passed since he had left his tutor.

*

He was woken up by a guard a little before dawn and he dragged himself up to a sitting position, holding his throbbing head in his hands.

'I hope you have a good reason for having woken me up, because if not . . .'

'The reason is that the King has called you, Prince. He wants you to go to him straight away.'

The young man struggled to stand, somehow managed

to reach the wash basin and dipped his head in it several times. Then he threw a cloak over his naked shoulders, tied his sandals and followed his guide.

Philip met him in a room of the royal armoury and it was immediately clear he was in a foul mood.

'Something very serious has happened,' he said. 'Before your return from Mieza I had asked your mother to help me in a delicate mission: an embassy to Athens, an attempt to stymie a plan of Demosthenes' that might have proved damaging for our policies. I thought that an envoy from the Queen might have had more chance of being heard and of obtaining something. Unfortunately I was wrong. The envoy was accused of being a spy and was tortured to death. Do you realize what this means?'

'That we must declare war on Athens,' replied Alexander, who on seeing his father had to some extent recovered his senses.

'It is not quite so simple. Demosthenes is trying to form a pan-Hellenic League to lead into war against us.'

'We will defeat them.'

'Alexander, it is time you learned that weapons are not the solution to all problems. I have done everything in my power to be recognized as the guiding light of a pan-Hellenic alliance, not to be seen as its enemy. I have an ambitious project: to make war in Asia against the Persians, to defeat and to push back beyond the Aegean coasts the age-old enemy of the Greeks and to acquire control of all the trade routes which reach our shores from the East. In order to achieve these aims I must affirm myself as the undisputed leader of a great coalition that unites all the forces of the Greek states. And I must do so in such a way that in all the important cities the party that supports me comes out on top, not the party that wants me dead. Do you understand?'

Alexander nodded. 'What will you do?'

'I will wait for now. During my last campaign I suffered considerable losses and I must rebuild those parts of our army which were annihilated in the war on the Hellespont and in Thrace. I am not afraid of fighting, but I prefer to do it when the chances of winning are higher.

'I will have all our informers in Athens, Thebes and other cities in Greece alerted so that we have constant news on the development of the political and military situation. Demosthenes needs Thebes if he wants to entertain the slightest hope in any battle against us because Thebes has the strongest land forces after our own. Thus we must decide on the right moment to try to prevent the consolidation of this alliance. It shouldn't be so difficult in that the Athenians and the Thebans have always hated one another. And in any case, should the alliance go ahead then we must strike with all the strength and speed of a lightning bolt.

'Your education is over, Alexander. From now on you will be kept closely informed of everything which affects us. Day or night, fair weather or foul. Now I must ask you to go to your mother and tell her the news of the death of her envoy. She was fond of him, but do not spare her the details, I want her to know everything.

'And you will have to be ready from now on: the next time you lead your troop it won't be on a lion or a bear hunt . . . it will be war.'

Alexander left to go to his mother's apartments and met

Cleopatra in the corridor, dressed in a beautiful Ionian embroidered *peplum*, and accompanied by two maidservants carrying a bulky chest as she went down the stairs.

'So it's true you're off on a journey,' he said.

'Yes, I'm going to the Sanctuary of Artemis to offer all my childhood toys and dolls to the goddess,' replied his sister, indicating the chest.

'Quite, you are a woman now. Time certainly flies. Are you dedicating them all to her?'

Cleopatra smiled, 'Not exactly all of them . . . do you remember that Egyptian doll with the jointed arms and legs and its little case of make-up, the one Father gave me for my birthday?'

'Yes, I think I do,' replied Alexander, forcing his memory somewhat.

'Well, I'm going to keep that one. Do you think the goddess will forgive me?'

'Oh, I have no doubt about that. Have a safe journey, Little Sister.'

Cleopatra kissed him on the cheek and then, followed by her handmaids, went down the stairs quickly to the guard house where a carriage and her escort, led by Perdiccas, were waiting.

'But I don't want to travel in a carriage,' she complained. 'Can't I ride a horse?'

Perdiccas shook his head. 'I have my orders . . . and with you dressed like that, Princess?'

Cleopatra lifted the hem of her *peplum* up to her chin and showed him that underneath the finery she was wearing a short *chiton*. 'See? Don't you think I look like the Queen of the Amazons?'

Perdiccas went crimson. 'I see, Princess,' he admitted, swallowing.

'Well?' Cleopatra let the *peplum* fall back to her ankles.

Perdiccas sighed. 'You well know that I cannot deny you anything. But let's manage it this way. Climb into the carriage for now and then when we've travelled some distance from the palace and no one can see us, we'll make the switch. You can have one of my guards' horses and he can take your place in the carriage – he won't mind travelling with your handmaids.'

'Wonderful!' exclaimed the girl.

They set off just as the sun began to show behind Mount Rhodope and they took the road leading to the north towards Europos. Artemis's temple stood halfway along an isthmus that divided two identical lakes. It was a place of remarkable natural beauty.

As soon as they were out of sight of the palace, Cleopatra shouted for the carriage to stop, took off her *peplum* to the amazement of all members of the escort and mounted one of the guards' horses, having had the guard in question take her place in the carriage. They set off again to the general accompaniment of the handmaids' giggling.

'See?' observed Cleopatra. 'It's much more fun this way for all of us.'

Perdiccas nodded, trying to keep his eyes on the road ahead, but he couldn't help turning to look at the Princess's naked legs and the swaying movement of her hips, all of which made him dizzy.

'I'm sorry to have created all this fuss,' the girl apologized.

'No trouble,' replied Perdiccas. 'Actually . . . I volunteered for this job.'

'Really?' Cleopatra asked, lowering her head as she looked straight at him.

Perdiccas nodded again, feeling ever more embarrassed.

'I am most grateful. I am also especially pleased that you chose to accompany me. I have heard that you are very brave.'

The young man felt his heart leap, but he sought to keep a hold on himself not only out of good breeding, but also because he was aware of his men watching him.

When the sun was high they stopped to eat in the shade of a tree and Perdiccas asked Cleopatra to change her clothes and switch places with the guard again: they weren't far from the sanctuary now.

'You're right,' the girl agreed. She got the guard out of the carriage and put on her ceremonial *peplum* again.

They reached the temple in the afternoon. Cleopatra entered, followed by the handmaids with the chest, and they all walked forward until they were under the statue of Artemis. It was beautiful and very old, made of carved wood and painted. They laid the toys, the dolls and the miniature amphorae and bowls at its feet. Then she invoked the goddess: 'Virgin goddess, here at your feet I leave these tokens of my youth and I beg you to understand if I should ever prove to have neither the strength nor the will to remain a virgin like you. I beg you to be happy for these gifts, and please do not envy me if I choose to enjoy the pleasures of love.' She left a generous offering for the priests of the sanctuary and took her leave.

The place was incredibly beautiful: the small temple,

surrounded by rose bushes, stood in the midst of a green meadow and was mirrored in the twin lakes that opened up to the right and left, as blue as two eyes reflecting the sky.

Perdiccas moved closer. 'I have had rooms made ready for you and your handmaids for tonight here in the guest apartments of the sanctuary.'

'And what about you?'

'I will guard over your sleep, my Lady.'

The girl lowered her head. 'All night?'

'Of course, all night. I am responsible for . . .'

Cleopatra lifted her eyes and smiled. 'I know you are very good, Perdiccas, but I'll be sorry if you have to stay awake all night. I thought you might . . .'

'What are you thinking, my Lady?' asked the young man, his heart thumping.

'That if you get bored, you might come up and talk to me for a while.'

'Oh, that would be a great pleasure and an honour and . . .'

'I'll leave the door open, then.'

She gave him a mischevious smile and ran to join her handmaids who were playing with a ball in the meadow, among the blooming roses.

21

NOT LONG AFTER Alexander's return to Pella, the council of the sanctuary at Delphi asked Philip to intervene for the temple of Apollo against the city of Amphissa, whose inhabitants had started unauthorized farming of lands belonging to the god. Just as the King was about to start considering what might be the real objective behind this new sacred war, he received important news from Asia.

It came directly from one of his spies, a Greek from Cilicia by the name of Eumolpus who had some commercial interests in the city of Soloi and had reached Pella by sea via the port of Thermai. The King received him alone, in his private office.

'I have brought you a present, Sire,' the spy announced as he placed a precious lapis lazuli statuette of the goddess Astarte on Philip's table. 'It is antique and very rare and represents the Aphrodite of the Canaanites. It will protect your virility for a long time to come.'

'Thank you, my virility is indeed very dear to me, but I hope you haven't made such a long journey just for this.'

'Of course not,' replied Eumolpus. 'I bring important news from the Persian capital: the Emperor Artaxerxes III has been poisoned by his doctor on orders, it would seem, from a court eunuch.'

Philip shook his head. 'These castrated specimens are

treacherous. They once wanted to give one to me, but I declined the offer. They're envious of everyone and anyone who still has the possibility, denied them, of fucking. It's perfectly understandable after all. Your news confirms I did the right thing.'

'The eunuch's name is Bagoas. It seems it was a crime of jealousy.'

'Castrated and buggered to boot. It's only natural, I suppose,' said Philip. 'And what's going to happen now?'

'It already has happened, Sire. This Bagoas has convinced the court nobles to offer the crown to Arses, son of the recently departed Artaxerxes, and Atossa, one of his wives. Here he is,' he said as he pulled a coin from his pocket and passed it Philip across the table. 'It's freshly minted.'

The King studied the profile of the new Emperor, marked by an enormous nose shaped like a bird of prey's beak. 'He doesn't look too reassuring. He looks as though he might be even worse than his father, and he was already a tough character. Do you think he'll last?'

'Who knows?' sighed Eumolpus, shrugging his shoulders. 'It's difficult to say. Our observers, however, are all agreed that it is Bagoas who wants to govern through Arses and so the new Emperor will last for as long as Bagoas wants him to.'

'It all makes sense. I will send my greetings to the new King and to the ball-less Bagoas and we'll see what they make of it. Keep me informed of everything that happens at court in Susa and you'll have no cause for complaint. Stop by to see my secretary now and he'll pay you what we agreed on. And then tell him to come and see me.'

Eumolpus took his leave ceremoniously and disappeared, leaving Philip to meditate on what had to be done next. When Eumenes appeared the King had already made up his mind.

'You called, Sire?'

'Sit down and write.'

Eumenes grabbed a stool, a tablet and a stylus, while the King started dictating:

Philip, King of Macedon, to Arses, King of Persia, King of Kings, Light of the Aryans and so on and so on . . . Hail!

King Artaxerxes, third of this name, your father and predecessor, greatly offended us with no provocation on our part. He mustered and paid mercenary troops and put them to work for our enemies while we were busy with the siege of Perinthus and the war against Byzantium.

These actions brought us terrible losses. For this reason we now demand payment of compensation to the value of . . .

Eumenes lifted his head as he waited for the figure.

. . . five hundred talents.

Eumenes couldn't help but whistle.

If you fail to respect our request we will be forced to consider you an enemy, with all that such an eventuality will inevitably involve.

Take good care and so on and so on . . .

'Transcribe it onto papyrus and bring it to me for the seal. It must be sent with a fast messenger.'

'By Zeus, Sire!' exclaimed Eumenes. 'This is the most peremptory letter I have ever read. Arses will have no choice but to reply with the same tone.'

'That's exactly what I want,' affirmed the King. 'Let's say that the message will take a month or two to reach its destination and a month or two to come back; this will give me just enough time to sort things out in Greece. After that I'll take care of the eunuch and his little boy. Make sure Alexander reads this letter and find out what he makes of it.'

*

Alexander read the letter and realized that his father had now truly made his mind up to invade Asia and was simply looking for a pretext to spark off a war.

He returned to Mieza as soon as he was free of the multitude of affairs his return to Pella had involved: participation in governmental meetings, receptions of foreign guests, embassies and delegations, and assemblies of the army, fundamental for relations between the crown and the nobles who supported it.

Aristotle had already left, but his nephew Callisthenes was still there working on the natural history collection and the two studies the philosopher had expressly dedicated to his royal pupil: one on monarchy and another on colonization, in which he theorized on the diffusion throughout the world of the model of the Greek city-state, the only true vehicle of freedom, an experiment in spiritual and material civilization.

Alexander stayed there for a few days anyway, just to rest and meditate. He took his meals together with Callisthenes, a cultured young man who had considerable knowledge of the political situation in the Greek states.

His passion for history had led him to procure not only the great classic works of Hecataeus of Miletus, Herodotus and Thucydides, but also those of the western historians such as Philistus of Syracuse who recounted the history of the Greek cities of Sicily and Italy, a land where new powers were emerging, such as the city of Rome, founded by the Trojan hero Aeneas and visited by Hercules on his return journey from far-off Iberia.

After supper they would sit outside, under the portico, and talk until late. 'While your father was fighting the Scythians, the council of the sanctuary at Delphi declared a new sacred war against the inhabitants of Amphissa.'

'I know,' replied the Prince. 'Neither of the two sides, however, is strong enough to decide the dispute. The Thebans are supporting Amphissa, but they refuse to expose themselves because they are afraid of the council's disapproval. The situation is becoming critical again, especially with regard to what Athens will decide to do. The council has already sent an official request for an intervention and I don't think they'll have to ask my father twice.'

Callisthenes poured some wine for them both. 'The council is led by Thessalians who are your friends . . . if I know your father, I wouldn't be at all surprised if he hadn't arranged this whole manoeuvre.'

Alexander looked straight at him as he nonchalantly

sipped the wine in his cup. 'Does this mean you have been eavesdropping, Callisthenes?'

The young man put his cup down on the table. 'I am a historian, Alexander, and I think I have been a good pupil of my uncle, just as you have been. You must not be surprised if I make use of the means of logic rather than listen to second- or third-hand gossip.

'Now. Let me guess. Your father well knows that public opinion in Athens is not in favour of the Thebans, but he also knows that Demosthenes will try everything possible to make sure the Athenians change their minds and support Thebes in its stand with Amphissa against the council of the sanctuary, which is to say against Philip.

'Demosthenes, for his part, knows that only by uniting the forces of Athens and Thebes is there any hope of avoiding the definitive consolidation of Macedonian hegemony over Greece and therefore he will do anything to make a pact with the Thebans, even if it means challenging the Greeks' highest assembly of worship and the oracle of the god Apollo.'

'And how will the Thebans act, in your opinion?' asked Alexander, curious to know his companion's view in depth.

'It will depend on two factors: the Athenians' manoeuvres and the performance of the Macedonian army in central Greece. Your father will try to apply as much pressure as possible on the Thebans to prevent them from allying with Athens. He knows very well that if they do ally then he will be facing the most powerful land forces combined with the strongest naval power in all Greece, too much even for the King of Macedon.'

Alexander was quiet for a while, as if listening to the noises of the night as they came to them from the nearby forest, and Callisthenes poured him some more wine.

'What will you do when you have finished your work here at Mieza?' Alexander asked after having taken a sip.

'I think I will join my uncle in Stagira, but I would very much like to follow the war from close at hand.'

'You can follow me, if you like; if my father asks me to join him.'

'I would be most happy to,' replied Callisthenes, and it was clear that he had been hoping for such a proposal. It was an arrangement that satisfied both their ambitions.

'Come to Pella then, when you have finished your work here at Mieza.'

Callisthenes accepted enthusiastically. They took leave of each other late in the night after having talked at length about philosophical matters. The next day the young man gave his guest the two works by Aristotle that he had promised, each one with a handwritten letter from the philosopher.

*

Alexander returned to the palace three days later, towards evening, in time to take part in the war council called by his father. The generals Antipater, Parmenion and Cleitus the Black were present, together with the commanders of all the main units in the phalanx and the cavalry. Alexander was there as commander of the Vanguard.

On the rear wall of the council room was a map of Greece that Philip had had made some years before by a geographer from Smyrna and the King explained, with the help of this visual aid, what he planned to do.

'I do not want to attack Amphissa immediately,' he stated. 'Central Greece is dangerous and impervious territory where it is easy to end up imprisoned in narrow valleys, with all possibility of escape suddenly removed, and to find oneself pinned down by the enemy. The first thing we must do therefore is to take hold of the key cities to this region – Kithinion and Elatea. Then we will decide what is to be done.

'Our troops are already under way and are marching through Thessaly. Parmenion and I will join them soon, we set out tomorrow. Antipater will retain command of the troops that will remain here to protect Macedon.'

Alexander waited anxiously for the King to communicate the tasks that had been reserved for him in the war operations, but he was to be disappointed.

'I will leave the Argead seal to my son so that he may represent me in my absence. Each and every act issued by him will have the value of a royal decree.'

The young Prince was about to stand up, but one look from his father kept him seated. At that moment Eumenes entered and handed the seal to Alexander, who slipped it onto his finger and said, without much enthusiasm, 'I am grateful for the honour you have bestowed upon me and I will strive to be worthy of it.'

Philip turned to his secretary. 'Read the commanders the letter I sent to the new King of the Persians. I want them to be aware that some of them might just have to leave soon for Asia to clear the way for us.'

Eumenes read the letter with his clear voice but in a solemn tone and when he had finished the King continued, 'If the reply is as I expect it will be, Parmenion might cross the Straits and take the eastern shore in preparation for our invasion of Asia. In the meantime we will concentrate on teaching the Greeks once and for all that there can be only one pan-Hellenic League – with me as leader. This is all I have to communicate to you. You may now return to your activities.'

Alexander waited for them all to leave at the end of the council so that he could talk face to face with his father.

'Why are you intent upon leaving me in Pella? I have to lead the Vanguard in battle, not in parades. And Antipater is certainly capable of looking after the affairs of state in your absence.'

'I have thought long and hard before taking this decision and I have no intention of changing it now. The government of the country is more difficult and perhaps more important than the war. I have many enemies, Alexander, not only in Athens and Thebes, but in Pella and in Macedon, not to mention Persia, and I need to know that I am leaving behind a stable situation, in good hands, while I am doing battle far away. And I trust you.'

The young man lowered his head, finding it impossible to object in any way to those words. But Philip understood how his son felt and began again: 'The seal you have been given is a sign of one of the highest honours in the whole world and bearing that seal requires much greater abilities than those required in leading a cavalry squadron.

'It is here, in the palace, that you will learn to be a king, not on the battlefield; politics is the king's profession, not the use of the spear and the sword. Nevertheless, should the moment arrive when the final clash cannot be avoided, if I find myself in need of all the force I can muster, I will send for you and *you* will lead the Vanguard into battle, no one else. Come on, don't look like that, I have prepared a surprise for you to keep your spirits up.'

Alexander shook his head. 'What have you been up to, O father of mine?'

'You'll see,' said Philip, with a smile on his face. Then he stood up and left the council room. Shortly afterwards Alexander heard him call his squire in a loud voice, ordering him to bring his horse, bridled, and to alert the guard. The Prince went to look out from the loggia that overlooked the courtyard just in time to see Philip gallop off into the night.

Alexander remained in his study until late that night preparing for the following day's duties. Then, just before midnight, he extinguished the lamp and went towards his apartment. As soon as he entered he called for Leptine, but the girl did not reply.

'Leptine!' he repeated, losing his patience. She must have fallen ill or perhaps she was angry with him for some reason. Then another voice came from the darkness of his bed chamber, 'Leptine has had to go away. She'll be back tomorrow.'

'By Zeus!' exclaimed Alexander on hearing the unknown voice coming from the depths of his own room. He put his hand to his sword and went in.

'It's not that sword you'll be wanting to thrust into me,' said the voice. And there before him, sitting on his bed, was a stunningly beautiful girl he had never seen before.

'Who are you and who gave you permission to enter my room?' he asked.

'I am the surprise that your father, King Philip, has organized for you. My name is Pancaspe.'

'I am sorry, Pancaspe,' replied Alexander, pointing to the door, 'but if I wanted this type of surprise I'd be quite capable of organizing it for myself. Farewell.'

The girl got to her feet, but rather than moving towards the door, with a flick of her wrist she undid the hooks that held her *peplum* and stood there before Alexander, naked except for a pair of leggings made of silver ribbons.

Alexander's arm, which an instant previously had been raised to indicate the door, fell limply to his side and, speechless, he feasted his eyes on her. She was the most beautiful woman he had ever seen in his life, so beautiful she took his breath away and made the blood rush through his veins. Her neck was soft and smooth, her shoulders straight, her breasts firm and erect, her thighs shapely and smooth as though sculpted from Paros marble. He felt his tongue go dry against his palate.

The young woman moved closer, took him by the hand and led him towards the bath chamber. 'May I undress you?' she asked as she began unhooking his *chiton* and his small military cloak, his *chlamys*.

'I'm worried that Leptine will be furious and that . . .' Alexander began to stutter.

'Perhaps, but you will certainly be happy and satisfied. I assure you.' The Prince was now also naked and the girl clung to him with all her strength, but as soon as she felt the extent of his remarkable reaction she pulled away and led him into the bath.

'It will be even better in here. You'll see.'

Alexander acquiesced and she began to stroke him with a skill and dexterity that up until that moment had simply been unimaginable for him. She excited him almost to the point of climax and then retreated delicately to begin her caresses again in more marginal areas of his body.

When she felt that he was truly exploding with excitement she slipped out of the bath and went to lie down on the bed, dripping perfumed water under the golden light of the lamps. She opened her legs and the young man dived on her, but she whispered in his ear, 'That must be how you use the battering ram when you have to bring down the walls of a city. Let me be your guide here and you'll see . . .'

Alexander let her take the lead and he felt himself sinking into pleasure like a stone into water, a pleasure that grew ever stronger and more intense until the explosion came. But Pancaspe still wanted more and she began to stimulate him again with her moist, burning mouth before she mounted him and took the lead once more, slowly this time, in their second dance of love. And that night the young Prince understood that pleasure could take him a thousand times higher than his experience with Leptine's rough and ingenuous lovemaking.

22

From the moment Philip left, Alexander received dispatches every day without fail, keeping him informed of operational progress. This was how he learned that Philip in his very first move had achieved his aim by occupying Kithinion and then Elatea towards the end of summer.

Philip, King of Macedon, hails Alexander.

Today, third day of the month of Metageitnion, I occupied Elatea.

My achievements breed panic in Athens because everyone there felt sure I planned to lead my army against them and that I would force the Thebans to march with me too. But Demosthenes convinced the citizenry that my intention was simply to put pressure on Thebes to prevent them from forging an alliance with Athens. And he persuaded them to send him to Thebes with a delegation to do that very thing, to forge an alliance. I too have decided to send an embassy to the city to persuade them not to do so. I will keep you informed.

Take good care of yourself and your mother the Queen.

Alexander sent for Callisthenes who had joined him in the palace just a few days previously. 'Things are proceeding more or less as I had foreseen,' he said. 'I have just received a despatch from my father on the progress of his expedition. Two embassies – one Athenian, the other Macedonian – will now attempt to persuade the Thebans to make an alliance with one or the other. Who do you think will win?'

Callisthenes arranged his cloak over his left arm with a rather pompous gesture and said, 'Predicting events is always a dangerous exercise, an occupation more befitting a seer than a historian. Who is leading the Athenian embassy?'

'Demosthenes.'

'In that case he will win them over. There is no greater orator in Greece today. Get ready to leave Pella.'

'What do you mean?'

'That the day of the final clash is nigh and your father will want you at his side in the battlefield.'

Alexander looked into his eyes. 'If this happens you will write the history of my deeds, when the moment comes.'

*

The Prince was well aware now of just how right his father was: administering political power was more demanding than fighting in the field. Everyone at court felt it their duty to give him advice, because he was so young, and everyone believed they could influence his decisions, especially his mother.

One evening she invited him to supper in her apartments under the pretext of giving him a cloak she had embroidered for him.

'It's wonderful,' Alexander said as soon as he saw it and then added, even though he had immediately recognized the refined craftwork typical of Ephesus, 'You must have spent months working on it.'

There were only two couches and low tables, arranged alongside each other.

'I thought Cleopatra might have been here with us this evening.'

'She has caught a chill and is running a slight temperature. Please excuse her. But make yourself comfortable, please. Supper is ready.'

Alexander stretched out on his couch and took a few almonds from a platter while a girl began serving a soup of goose meat and a type of bread baked under the embers of the fire. His mother's meals were always rather simple and frugal.

Olympias took a reclining position as well and had the girl serve her a bowl of soup.

'Well: tell me, how do you feel about sitting on your father's throne?' she asked after having taken a few spoonfuls.

'No differently than when I sit on any other chair,' replied her son without attempting to hide his slight irritation.

'Don't talk round the question.' Olympias gave him a reproving stare. 'You know exactly what I mean.'

'I know, Mother. But what can I say? I try to do my best, to avoid making mistakes, to look after the affairs of state diligently.'

'Admirable,' observed the Queen.

A handmaid placed a bowl of legumes and salad on the

table in front of her and proceeded to season it with oil, vinegar and salt.

'Alexander,' Olympias began again, 'have you ever considered that your father might suddenly pass away?'

'My father fights in the front line with his soldiers. It's a possibility.'

'And if it should happen?'

The handmaid poured some wine, took the bowl away and returned with a skewer of cooked crane meat and a cup of pureed peas which the Prince declined with a simple movement of his hand.

'I'm sorry, I'd forgotten that you hate peas. Well . . . have you thought about this eventuality?'

'I would be most sorry. I love my father.'

'But that is not what I meant, Alexander. I am talking about the succession.'

'No one has any right to put my succession to the throne in doubt.'

'For as long as your father is alive and for as long as I am alive . . .'

'Mother, you are thirty-seven years old.'

'That means nothing. Fate can strike anyone. What I mean is that your cousin Amyntas is five years older than you and he was heir to the throne before your birth. Someone might propose him as candidate in your place. And what's more, your father has another son by one of his . . . brides.'

Alexander shrugged his shoulders. 'Arrhidaeaus is a poor halfwit.'

'A halfwit, but he still has royal blood in his veins. He still might cause you problems.'

'So what should I do, in your opinion?'

'Now that your father is far away you hold the power. You have access to the royal treasure, you can do what you want. All you have to do is pay someone.'

Alexander's mood darkened. 'My father let Amyntas live, even after my birth, and I have no intention of doing what you are suggesting. Never.'

Olympias shook her head. 'Aristotle must have filled your head with his notions about democracy, but things are different for kings. A king has to be sure of his succession – don't you understand that?'

'Enough, Mother. My father is alive, you are in good health and that's the end of it. If one day I should find myself in need of help, I will turn to your brother, the King of Epirus. He loves me and will support me.'

'Listen . . .' Olympias insisted.

But Alexander's patience had come to an end; he quickly got to his feet and kissed his mother hurriedly on the cheek. 'Thank you for the meal, Mother. I must go now. Goodnight.'

He went down into the internal courtyard of the palace and inspected the guard before going back up to see Eumenes who was busy in his study arranging the King's incoming correspondence.

'Any news of my father?' he asked.

'Yes, but all's quiet. The Thebans still haven't decided whose side they're on.'

'What is Amyntas up to these days?'

Eumenes looked at him with surprise written all over his face. 'What do you mean?'

'Exactly what I said.'

'Well . . . I don't know. I think he's off hunting in Lyncestis.'

'Fine. When he returns give him a diplomatic mission.'

'Diplomatic? But what type of diplomatic mission?'

'You choose. There must be some type of mission suitable for him, surely? In Asia, in Thrace, in the islands. Wherever you like.'

Eumenes started objecting. 'Really . . . I wouldn't know what to . . .'

But Alexander had already left the room.

Λ

Philip's envoys arrived in Thebes in late autumn and were admitted to speak in front of a full citizens' assembly in the theatre.

The council wanted the citizenry to be able to evaluate the two proposals by comparing them without a long interval between the two presentations, so that same day the Athenian embassy was also admitted to the city, led by Demosthenes himself.

Philip had discussed the proposals to be presented to the Thebans at some length with his chiefs of staff, and he firmly believed them to be so advantageous that they would surely be accepted. He had no plans to ask them to form an alliance with him, fully aware that Thebes was behind Amphissa, the city against which the sacred war had been declared: their neutrality would have been enough for him. In exchange he offered considerable economic and territorial gains. Were they to refuse, he would threaten waste and ruin of their city. Who could possibly be crazy enough to refuse?

The leader of the Macedonian delegation, Eudemus of Oreus, concluded his presentation with sapient doses of flattery, threats and blackmail; and then he left the theatre.

Shortly afterwards he met a Theban friend and informer who led him to a vantage point from which he could see and hear what was happening in the assembly. He realized that Philip would ask him to report on things he had heard himself rather than giving him second-hand news.

The assembly took the briefest of pauses, just long enough to ensure that the Macedonians did not meet the Athenians – thus avoiding any brawling. Demosthenes' delegation then entered the theatre.

The great orator was austere in appearance, philosophical, with a thin, lean body and expressive eyes below a forehead that bore a perpetual frown. It was said that as a youngster he had had problems with elocution and a weak voice and that his ambition to become an orator had led him to practise by declaiming verses from Euripides on the rocky seashore during storms. It was well known that he never spoke without notes because he was not a good improviser, and no one was surprised when he pulled out a bundle of sheets from under his cloak.

He began to read in a studied voice and spoke at length of the various stages in Philip's irresistible advance, of his continual violations of pacts and agreements. At a certain point, however, his passion took over and he came out with an eloquent plea:

'But do you not realize, citizens of Thebes, that the sacred war is simply a pretext, as was the previous one and the one before that? Philip wants your neutrality because he wants to divide the forces of free Greece and to bring down the strongholds of freedom one by one. If you leave the Athenians to stand alone against him, it will be your turn next and then you too will succumb.

'And in just the same way, if you take on Philip alone and you lose, Athens will not be able to defend itself alone. He wants to divide us because he knows full well that only our united forces can stand up to his aggression.

'I know that there have been many causes of conflict and even war between us, but these were all conflicts between free cities. Today we have a tyrant on the one hand and free men on the other. There can be no doubt about your choice, Thebans!

'As a token of our good faith we will cede command of our land troops to you while we retain sole control of the fleet and we undertake to finance two thirds of the total expenses.'

There came a murmuring from the rows of the assembly and the orator realized that his words had hit their mark. He then prepared to deliver the final blow, well aware of the risk he was about to run – possible repudiation by his own government.

'For over half a century,' he began again, 'the cities of Plataea and Thespiae, although part of Boeotia, have been allies of Athens, and Athens has always guaranteed their independence. Now we are willing to bring them under your control, to convince them to accept your authority, if you will accept our proposal and unite with us in the battle against the tyrant.'

Demosthenes' passion, his inspired tone, the timbre of his voice, the force of his arguments, all combined to help him achieve his desired aim. When he fell silent, breathless and with sweat dripping from his forehead, many in the assembly stood up to applaud him and they were joined by others and then more again until the entire theatre was paying tribute to him in a long ovation.

What had convinced them, above and beyond the energy of the Athenian orator, had been the arrogance of Philip's envoy on top of the Macedonian intimidation and blackmail. The President of the assembly ratified the decisions taken and called upon his secretary to inform the embassy of the King of Macedon that the city of Thebes had unanimously rejected both their requests and their offers and called upon them to leave Boeotian territory by sunset the following day, on pain of being arrested and tried as spies.

Philip became a raging bull when he heard the news because he had never imagined that the Thebans were crazy enough to challenge him while he was virtually at the gates of their territory. But he had to accept the results of the debate.

When his rage had quietened he sat down, pulling his cloak up around his knees as he did so, and mumbled a thank you to Eudemus of Oreus who in the end had simply carried out his King's orders. The envoy, who had remained standing until that moment, bearing witness to the King's fury, saw that the worst was over and asked for permission to take his leave before moving towards the door.

'Wait!' Philip called him back. 'What is Demosthenes like?'

Eudemus stopped on the threshold and turned back.

'A bundle of nerves that cries out "Freedom!"' he replied. And he left.

*

Philip barely had time to get over the shock when the new allies were already in action. Theban and Athenian light troops occupied all the mountain passes so as to block any enemy military initiative towards Boeotia and Attica. The King, finding himself in trouble because of the bad weather and the general situation which had become decidedly difficult and risky, resolved to return to Pella leaving a contingent in Thessaly under the command of Parmenion and Cleitus the Black.

Alexander took command of a division of the royal guard and went to meet his father at the border with Thessaly. From there he escorted him home.

'Do you see what I meant now?' Philip said to him after they greeted each other. 'There was no rush. We still haven't gone into action and the game is wide open.'

'But it looks as though everything is going against us. Thebes and Athens are allies now and they have already achieved important successes.'

The King waved his hand as though chasing away some source of minor irritation. 'Ah!' he exclaimed. 'Leave them to dream and enjoy the sweetness of their successes. Their awakening will be much more bitter. I have never sought a direct conflict with the Athenians and I have asked the Thebans to keep out of this matter. But they have dragged us by the hair into this war and now I have to teach them who's the strongest. There will be more deaths, more devastation: all of this is repugnant, but I am left with no choice.'

'What do you think you will do?' Alexander asked.

'I will wait for spring, for now. Making war in warm weather is a bit easier, but above all else I want to have enough time to think about this situation. Remember, my boy, I never fight for the pleasure of wielding weapons. War, for me, is simply politics by other means.'

They continued for a while in silence, the King apparently observing the countryside and the people at work in the fields. Then, out of the blue, he asked, 'By the way, how was that surprise I arranged for you?'

23

'I REALLY DON'T understand my father!' exclaimed Alexander. 'We have a chance to win the day by dint of force of arms and he chooses instead the humiliation of a match with the Athenian orator – only to come out of it the loser. He could have attacked first and negotiated later.'

'I agree,' replied Hephaestion. 'I think it was a big mistake. Strike first, parley later.'

Eumenes and Callisthenes were following behind on their horses at the same pace, and the group was travelling in the direction of Pharsalus to deliver a message from Philip to the allies of the Thessalian League.

'But I understand his reasoning perfectly,' Eumenes joined in, 'and I approve of it. You well know that your father lived in Thebes for over a year as a hostage when he was a youth, in the house of Pelopidas, the greatest Greek strategist of the last hundred years. He was deeply impressed with the political system of the Theban city-state, its formidable military organization and its rich culture. Out of this experience in Thebes during his formative years came the desire to spread Hellenic civilization throughout Macedon and to unite the Greeks in one large confederation.'

'Just as things were at the time of the Trojan War,' observed Callisthenes. 'This is what your father has in mind – first unite the Greek states and then lead them against Asia as Agamemnon did against the empire of King Priam, almost a thousand years ago.'

At these words Alexander piped up, 'A thousand years ago? A thousand years have passed since the Trojan War?'

'Just five years to go before the thousandth anniversary,' Callisthenes replied.

'It must be a sign,' murmured Alexander. 'It's got to be a sign.'

'What do you mean?' Eumenes asked.

'Nothing. But doesn't it seem strange to you that in five years' time I'll be the same age Achilles was when he set out for Troy and this will coincide with the thousandth anniversary of the war sung by Homer?'

'No, it doesn't seem strange,' replied Callisthenes. 'History sometimes reproduces, at a distance of many years, the same combinations of circumstance that generate great achievements. But nothing ever repeats itself in exactly the same way.'

'Is that true?' asked Alexander. And for a moment he frowned as though lost in following fleeting, far-off images in his mind.

Hephaestion put his hand on Alexander's shoulder. 'I know what you are thinking about. And whatever you decide to do, wherever you decide to go, I will follow you. Even to hell. Even to the ends of the earth.'

Alexander turned and looked him in the eye. 'I know,' he said.

*

They reached their destination around sunset and Alexander received the honours befitting the heir to the throne of Macedon. Then, together with his friends, he went to the dinner which the representatives of the Thessalian Confederation had organized for him. At that time Philip also held the title of *Tagos*, President of the Confederation, and indeed he was actually head of two states – of one as King and of the other as President.

The Thessalians, like the Macedonians, were heavy drinkers, but during the dinner Eumenes did not touch a drop and he made the most of this advantage in striking a deal with a rather merry nobleman for the purchase of some horses. The terms and conditions of payment he managed to win were extremely beneficial both for himself and for Macedon.

The next day, his mission accomplished, Alexander left again with his friends, but not far along the road he changed his clothes, dismissed the guard and took the southward road.

'Where are you going?' asked Eumenes, surprised at this change of plan.

'I'm going with him,' said Hephaestion.

'Yes, but where to?'

'To Aulis,' replied Alexander.

'The port from which the Achaeans set sail for the war against Troy,' commented Callisthenes matter of factly.

'Aulis? But you must be mad!' exclaimed Eumenes. 'Aulis is in Boeotia, in the very midst of enemy territory.'

'But I want to see the place and I will see it,' affirmed the Prince. 'No one will notice us.'

'I repeat, you're mad,' continued Eumenes. 'You will most certainly be noticed: as soon as you open your mouths they'll notice your accents, and if you don't open your mouths they'll wonder why. And then your portrait, Alexander, has been distributed in many cities. Do you realize what the consequences will be if you're caught? Your father will be forced to make a deal, to abandon his plans or, if things go well, to pay a ransom that will cost him as much as a defeat in war. No, I won't have anything to do with this madness. Let's pretend I haven't even heard you speak of it. Actually, let's say I haven't even seen you – you left in silence before dawn.'

'That's fine,' nodded Alexander. 'And don't you worry: Aulis is only a few hundred stadia into Boeotian territory. We'll be there and back in two days. And if anyone does stop us, we'll say that we are pilgrims on our way to consult the oracle at Delphi.'

'In Boeotia? But Delphi is in Phocis.'

'We'll tell them we got lost!' shouted Hephaestion as he kicked his horse and set off at a gallop.

Callisthenes looked at his one remaining travelling companion, unsure as to what he should do.

'What are your intentions?' Eumenes asked him.

'Me? Well, if on the one hand my deep fondness for Alexander leads me to want to follow him, on the other hand the natural prudence which is most becoming to a . . .'

'I see,' Eumenes cut him short. 'Stop!' he shouted. 'May Zeus strike the pair of you down with a thunderbolt if you don't stop.' Alexander and Hephaestion did as he asked and Eumenes set off after them saying, 'At least I haven't got a Macedonian accent and, if necessary, I can pass as a Boeotian oaf.'

'Ha! There's no doubt about that!' said Hephaestion.

'Go ahead and laugh,' grumbled Eumenes as he urged his horse into a trot. 'If King Philip were here he'd make you laugh with the help of a few lashes across your back. Come on, let's go, let's get a move on.'

'What about Callisthenes?' asked Alexander.

'He'll come, he'll come,' replied Eumenes. 'Where else can he go on his own?'

They passed the Gates of Thermopylae the following day and Alexander stopped to visit the tombs of the Spartan soldiers who had fallen one hundred and forty years previously during their battle with the Persian invaders. He read the simple inscription in Laconian dialect that commemorated their ultimate sacrifice and he stood in silence listening to the wind blowing in from the sea.

'How ephemeral is the destiny of man!' he exclaimed. 'All that is left of the thunder of a momentous clash which shook the whole world and an act of heroism worthy of Homer's verses are these few lines. All is quiet now.'

They travelled through Locris and Phocis without much trouble in just a couple of days, and entered Boeotia along the sea road. In front of them was the coast of the island of Euboea, its form sculpted by the noonday rays of the sun and the dazzling waters of the Euripus strait. A small fleet of a dozen triremes was cruising offshore and on their sails, full of wind, they could make out the owl symbol of Athens.

'If only that navarch had any idea of who is standing here on this beach watching his ships go by,' murmured Eumenes.

'Let's go,' said Callisthenes. 'Let's get this journey over with as soon as possible. We are close now.' But deep down he was afraid that Alexander might decide to ask them to accompany him on some even more reckless mission.

Just as they reached the top of a hill the small bay of Aulis appeared suddenly before them. Opposite, on the Euboean shore, the city of Chalcis shone white in the distance. The water was intensely blue and the woods of holm-oak and oak that covered the slopes of the hill came down almost as far as the sea, giving way first to the low bushes of myrtle and strawberry-tree and then a slender line of pebbles and red sand.

A lone fishing boat sailed the sea opposite the deserted port from which the thousand Achaean ships had set off.

The four young men dismounted and looked on in silence at that place which was so like a thousand other points along the Hellenic coastline, and yet was so different. At that moment Alexander recalled the words of his father as he held him – he was still a boy – on the gallery of the palace at Pella and told him about far-off, limitless Asia.

'This place could never hold a thousand ships,' observed Hephaestion, breaking the magic of the silence.

'No,' admitted Callisthenes. 'But for the poet they could never have been any fewer. A poet, Hephaestion, sings not to narrate human events as they occur, but to make sure that we have the opportunity of living the emotions and the passions of our heroes even at a distance of centuries.'

Alexander turned towards him, his eyes brimming with feeling. 'Do you think there might exist somewhere in our time a man capable of feats that could inspire a poet as great as Homer?'

'Poets create heroes, Alexander,' said Callisthenes, 'it doesn't work the other way round. And poets are only born when the sea, the sky and the earth are all in harmony.'

On entering Thessaly on their way back, they came across a unit of the royal guard that had been sent out to look for them, and Eumenes had to spin some tale about his having fallen ill and the others having decided not to abandon him: no one believed it. But the trip to Aulis had provided Alexander with proof of the fact that his friends were ready to follow him, even when they were afraid, as Eumenes and Callisthenes had indeed been. Apart from this, however, he had also realized that being away from Pancaspe was a considerable strain and he really was looking forward now to seeing her naked on his bed, in the golden light of the lamps.

But the return to Pella was interrupted by events: the situation had suddenly worsened and the King, having mobilized the army, was marching towards Phocis to take the passes. Time had not made any of the contenders any wiser and once again the cry of war drowned out all other voices.

Alexander was summoned to his father's tent that same evening and Philip asked nothing about his son and heir's late return from the mission in Thessaly; he simply showed him the map he had on his table and said:

'Chares, the Athenian commander, with ten thousand mercenaries on his payroll, has been seen on the road between Kithinion and Amphissa, but he does not know that we are here. I will march all night and tomorrow morning I will personally rouse him from his slumber. You must hold this position and you must not leave it for any reason. As soon as Chares has been taken care of I will come back this way, through the Krissos valley, and I will cut the Athenians and the Thebans off in their mountain passes. They will be forced to abandon their positions and retreat to their first stronghold in Boeotia.' He placed his index finger on the map at the point where he thought his enemies would retreat to. 'And you will meet me there with your cavalry. At Chaeronaea.'

24

CHARES' MERCENARY ARMY, surprised at dawn, was wiped
out by Philip's assault troops and the cavalry dispersed the
few remaining survivors. The King, rather than march on
Amphissa, turned back, as he had said he would, and cut
off the passes held by the Athenians and the Thebans,
leaving them with no option but to retreat.

Alexander was informed three days later that Philip was
taking up position on the Plain of Chaeronaea with command of twenty-five thousand foot soldiers and five thousand cavalrymen; his instructions were to join his father as
soon as possible. He left his servants to strike camp and to
take care of the baggage train and had the departure signal
sounded before dawn. The idea was to march while the
temperature was not yet too high and to maintain a pace
that would not tire the horses too much.

He inspected the Vanguard by torchlight, astride Bucephalas, and his companions – each commanding individual
divisions – all lifted their spears in salute. They were fully
armed and ready for the off, but it was clear that some of
them hadn't slept at all, those who had never before lived
through such a crucial day.

'Remember, men!' he exhorted them. 'The phalanx is
the anvil, the cavalry is the hammer and the Vanguard
is . . . the hammerhead!' Then he spurred Bucephalas over

towards Ptolemy, who was commanding the first division to the right, and told him their battle cry – *Phobos kái Deimos*.

'The horses of the god of war!' Ptolemy repeated. 'No battle cry was ever more appropriate.' And he gave it to the first rider on his right, asking him to pass it on among the ranks.

Alexander nodded to the trumpeter who sounded the departure and the squadron moved in unison. Alexander first, Hephaestion second, and then all the others. Ptolemy's division brought up the rearguard.

They forded the Krissos before dawn and as the sun rose over the plain they saw the tips of the *sarissae* of the Macedonian army glinting in the sun, like shining heads of grain in a ripe field.

When Philip spotted them coming he dug his heels into his charger and sped to join his son. 'Hail, my boy!' as he clapped him on the back. 'It's all working out just as I had imagined. There they are waiting for us. Arrange your men on the left flank and then come to me. I am discussing the battle plan with Parmenion and the Black and we were waiting for you to conclude. You've arrived just in time. How do you feel?'

'Hail, Father. I feel fine and I'll be with you in an instant.'

He went to his squadron and led them round to the left to line up. Hephaestion extended his hand and arm towards the hill and exclaimed, 'Oh, gods above, look! Your father has us facing the Thebans' Sacred Band: can you make them out down there? They're the ones with the blood-red tunics and cloaks. They're tough, Alexander, no one has ever beaten them before.'

'I see them, Hephaestion. We'll beat them. Arrange the men in three lines. We'll attack in waves.'

'Great Zeus!' shouted Seleucus. 'Do you know why they're called the Sacred Band? Because each one of them has made a solemn vow to a companion whereby they will never leave each other until death parts them.'

'That's right,' Perdiccas confirmed. 'And they also say that they're all lovers, which is an even greater bond.'

'But their love for one another won't protect them from our strength,' said Alexander. 'Hold your positions until I come back.'

He spurred his horse on until he reached Philip, Parmenion and the Black who had all pulled back to a small plateau which afforded a fine general view of the battlefield. Opposite them, a little to the right, they could see the acropolis of Chaeronaea with its temples.

At the centre and on the left, up on a range of hills that dominated the plain, the Athenian forces were all lined up, with the Thebans immediately behind them. Their shields glinted as they reflected the light of the rising sun on its way up into the spring sky, partially filled with large white clouds. Out on the Thebans' far right was the crimson splash of the Sacred Band.

To his right Philip had deployed two divisions of 'shieldsmen', the assault troops who three days previously had eliminated Chares' army, directly under the King's command. They took their name from their shields which were adorned with Argead stars in copper and silver.

At the centre, under the command of Parmenion and the Black, the twelve battalions of the phalanx were lined up in five rows forming a barrier of lances, an impenetrable wood of iron spearheads, staggered along an oblique line. On the left flank was the entire force of the Companion cavalry which terminated with the Vanguard, Alexander's squadron.

'I'll attack first,' said Philip, 'and I will engage the Athenians. Then I'll start moving back and if they follow me then you, Parmenion, will bring up a battalion of the phalanx into the breach, splitting the enemy forces into two, and then you'll let the other six battalions loose. The Black will follow you with the rest of the army.

'Then it'll be your moment, Alexander: you will thrust the cavalry into the Theban right flank and your Vanguard will attack the Sacred Band. If you manage to break through, you know what has to be done.'

'I know perfectly, Father: the phalanx is the anvil and the cavalry is the hammer.'

Philip held him to his breast for a moment and suddenly there came a vision of himself standing upright in the half-shadow of the Queen's room in Pella as he held a newborn baby. 'Be careful, my son,' he said. 'In battle the blows come from all directions.'

'I'll be careful, Father,' replied Alexander. Then he jumped up onto Bucephalas and galloped past the massed battalions which were already arranged in battle formation until he reached his division. Philip followed him with his gaze for a while, then he turned to his field adjutant: 'My shield,' he said.

'But, Sire . . .'

'My shield,' he repeated, peremptorily.

The field adjutant helped him slip his arm through the straps of the shield, the only one to carry the Argead star in pure gold.

From the top of the hills there came the sharp sound of trumpets and immediately afterwards the continuous music of the whistles, taking its rhythm from the roll of the drums, and all of this accompanied the soldiers on their march. The movement of the front line as it came down reflected the sun in a thousand flashes of fire and the heavy strides of the infantry clad in their iron armour sent a sinister rumble through the valley.

On the plain the phalanx stood still and silent. The horses out on the extreme left snorted and shook their heads, their bronze bits clattering.

The Vanguard was already lined up in a wedge and Alexander took position as first horseman before all the others, keeping his eyes fixed on the right flank of the enemy lines, the invincible Sacred Band. Bucephalas was unsettled now – raking the ground with his front hooves, snorting loudly through his nostrils, lashing his flanks with his tail.

A cavalryman reached Philip just as he was about to give the signal to attack. 'Sire,' he shouted as he jumped to the ground from his mount, 'Demosthenes has taken up position in the Athenian infantry lines.'

'I don't want him killed,' the King said. 'Pass this order to all my soldiers.'

He turned round to look at his shieldsmen: faces dripping with sweat under the visors of their helmets, eyes staring fixedly at the glinting of the enemy's weapons, limbs tight in the muscle-clenched wait for the attack. This was the moment when they each contemplated death, the moment in which the desire to live was stronger than any other thing. It was the moment in which they had to free themselves from anxiety's grip and throw themselves into the assault.

Philip raised his sword, gave his war cry and his men followed him, shouting like a horde of wild beasts, driving all fears from their chests, anxious only to throw themselves into the turmoil, into the reel of battle, forgetting everything, even themselves.

They advanced at a run while the officers shouted at them to keep in step, to maintain order in the lines so as to meet the clash compact and steadfast.

They were very close now and the Athenians continued to march in time, shoulder to shoulder, shield to shield, their spears extended forwards, pushed on by the continuous, sharp sound of the whistles, by the obsessive roll of the drums, shouting, at each stride:

Alalalài!

The crash of the impact exploded like a bronze thunderclap throughout the valley: it rolled over the hillsides and penetrated the sky itself, pushed up on high by the shouting of twenty thousand soldiers caught up in the fury of battle.

Philip, instantly recognizable by means of his gold star, fought in the front line with indefatigable passion, striking out with his sword and his shield. He was flanked by two giant Thracians armed with double-edged axes, awe-inspiring on account of the bristly red hair on their heads, the hair all over their bodies and the tattoos covering their faces, their arms and their chests.

The Athenian front wavered under the fury of the assault, but a high-pitched, penetrating sound like the cry of a hawk pushed them onward, gave them heart: it was the voice of Demosthenes, inciting them above the music of the whistles and the drums, shouting, 'Athenians! Be brave! Fight, men! For your freedom! For your women and for your children! Send the tyrant back where he belongs!'

The fighting became even more violent and many soldiers in the two sets of lines fell, but Philip had given orders that no one was to stop and loot the bodies until the battle was over. Everywhere the search was on for a breach to thrust and wound, to wield and swing the metal in thinning out the enemy masses.

The front-line infantrymen's shields were covered in blood now, dripping copiously from the edges to the soil which was already slippery and littered with dying bodies – for every man who fell, a soldier from the line behind would simply move forwards to take his place and keep the battle going.

Suddenly, on a signal from Philip, the trumpeter sounded a command and the two battalions of shieldsmen started retreating, leaving their dead and their wounded where they lay in the field. They gave way slowly, keeping their shields high, exchanging blow for blow with their spears and their swords.

On seeing their enemy draw back, the Athenians, at an advantage because of their more favourable position, doubled their efforts and goaded one another on with more shouting; the foot soldiers in the second and third lines pushed their companions ahead with the aid of their shields.

Before attacking, Philip had issued his orders and when the lines of the shieldsmen, moving backwards, reached the level of the rocky outcrop which stood at some one hundred paces towards the left, they turned and started running.

At that point the Athenians, caught up in the fury of combat, drunk on the shouting, the blood and the clangour of arms, excited at the prospect of victory which now seemed to be firmly in their grasp, set off chasing their enemies with every intention of annihilating them. Their commander, Stratocles, rather than trying to have them keep ranks, shouted at the top of his voice telling them to chase their enemies all the way back to Macedon.

More trumpets sounded off to the left and an enormous drum, hung between two carriages, sent out its thunderous voice all across the vast plain. Parmenion gave the signal and the twelve battalions of the phalanx began advancing together in a slow march, staggered along an oblique line.

The Thebans too, at that sight, threw themselves into an attack in tight-knit ranks, bearing before them their heavy ash-wood spears, but soon the leading Macedonian battalion wedged itself between the Athenian front line, disorderly now because of their mad dash to catch the shieldsmen, and the extreme left flank of the Theban lines.

Philip abandoned his shield, dented and dirty with blood, to his attendant before jumping onto his horse and galloping off to Parmenion. The General was staring fixedly and anxiously at the Sacred Band which was still marching in step, apparently indifferent to everything that was going on – inexorable, bristling with iron spearheads.

In the centre the first Macedonian battalion which was advancing uphill was already struggling with the incline and when a division of Theban infantry rushed to close the breach, the *pezhetairoi* lowered their pikes and mowed down their counterparts in the head-on clash, without any physical contact. Then they pushed on even further, their strides following in time to the thunderous rumble of the huge drum that guided them from the plain.

And behind came the others, lined up obliquely, up to the third line bearing their *sarissae* lowered, while the foot soldiers in the rear guard carried them upright, rising and falling in their rhythmic march like ears of grain in the wind. And the threatening clanking of metal weapons that accompanied the heavy marching made its way to the ears of the enemy as they came down on the other side, and to them it sounded like an omen, like the sound of death.

'Now,' the King gave the order to his General, and Parmenion used a polished shield to send a signal to Alexander – three flashes to unleash the cavalry and give free rein to the assault of the Vanguard.

The Prince held his spear firmly and shouted, 'Three waves, men!' And then, even louder, '*Phobos kái Deimos!*' as he dug his heels into Bucephalas' sides. The stallion set off at a gallop across the field which by now was full of shouting and of dead bodies, black as a fury from hell, carrying its rider encased in his shining armour, his high crest blowing in the wind.

The Vanguard, its ranks closed, kept close behind him; the chargers, excited by Bucephalas' haste, galloped on in response to the incitement of their horsemen and the piercing cry of the trumpets.

The Sacred Band closed ranks and its men planted the shafts of their spears in the soil, directing the iron heads at the approaching charge. But as soon as it was within range, Alexander's squadron let fly a swarm of javelins just before performing an about turn; immediately there came the second wave and then the third before the first came once more. Many of the Theban soldiers were forced to abandon their shields which were now full of enemy javelins and to fight without protection. Alexander then had the Vanguard form itself into a wedge shape once more and he took up position at its head before guiding them straight against the enemy lines, spurring Bucephalas on among the ranks of the Sacred Band, striking out left and right with his spear and then, when he had abandoned his shield, with his sword as well.

Hephaestion provided cover on the flank, lifting up his shield to protect Alexander, his own men close behind him.

For every warrior of the Sacred Band who fell, another appeared to take his place, like a body suddenly growing new limbs, closing up the wall of shields and responding, blow by blow, with inexhaustible energy, with dauntless, tenacious courage.

Alexander pulled back and called to Hephaestion: 'Lead your men over to that side, open a breach and then attack the Theban centre from behind. Leave the Sacred Band to me!'

Hephaestion obeyed and advanced with Perdiccas, Seleucus, Philotas, Lysimachus, Craterus and Leonnatus, wedging their cavalry between the Sacred Band and the rest of the Theban troops. Then they performed a wide turn, just as they had done on the parade ground for Alexander, and they caught the enemy from behind, pushing them towards the forest of spikes of the phalanx which was still advancing relentlessly.

Before the sun reached its zenith the battle was won. Alexander came to Parmenion with his sword in hand and his armour still covered in blood. Even Bucephalas' chest and flanks were red.

'The Sacred Band is no more.'

'Victory on all fronts!' exclaimed Parmenion.

'Where is the King?' asked Alexander.

Parmenion turned towards the plain which was still veiled in the thick dust raised by the battle and he pointed to a lone man who despite a limp was dancing like a lunatic through a multitude of corpses.

'There he is,' he said.

25

Two thousand Athenians fell in the battle of Chaeronaea and many others were taken prisoner. Among these was the orator Demades who was brought before the King still wearing his armour and bleeding from a wound to his arm. Demosthenes had managed to flee through the passes that led to the south towards Lebadeia and Plataea.

But the heaviest losses were inflicted on the Thebans and their Achaean allies at the centre of the battlefield. Alexander's cavalry, after wiping out the Sacred Band, caught the central troops from behind and forced them onto the phalanx's barrier of iron spikes, resulting in a massacre.

Philip's rage was directed especially towards those Thebans he felt had betrayed him. He sold the prisoners as slaves and refused to hand over the bodies of their dead for burial. It was Alexander who made him see reason.

'Father, you yourself once told me to show clemency whenever possible,' he pointed out after the frenzy of the victory had subsided. 'Even Achilles returned Hector's body to the old King Priam after his tearful pleas. These men fought like lions and gave their lives for their city. They deserve respect. Tell me what possible advantage there is in treating the dead in this way.'

Philip did not reply, but it was clear that his son's words had had some effect.

'And there's a prisoner, an Athenian officer out there who wants to speak to you.'

'Not now!' roared Philip.

'He says that if you refuse to see him he will let himself bleed to death.'

'Fine! That'll be one less to worry about.'

'As you wish. I'll take care of it then.'

He went out and called for two shieldsmen: 'Take this man to my tent and call for a surgeon.'

The soldiers carried out their orders and the Athenian was laid down on a makeshift bed before being undressed and washed.

One of the shieldsmen soon came back to the tent with bad news: 'Sire, the surgeons are all busy with our soldiers, trying to save the most seriously wounded, but if you issue specific orders they will come.'

'It doesn't matter,' replied the Prince. 'I will take care of it. Bring me a knife, a needle and thread, and heat some water and bring some clean bandages.' The men looked at him in amazement, the patient even more so.

'I'm afraid we'll have to make do,' Alexander said to him. 'I can't let a Macedonian soldier die to save one of the enemy.'

Callisthenes came in just then and saw the heir to the throne of Macedon with an apron tied round his waist, washing his hands.

'But what . . .'

'Let's keep this to ourselves, shall we? But since you also attended Aristotle's anatomy classes, you can help me.

Wash the wound with wine and vinegar and then get the needle and thread ready . . . I can't see for the sweat in my eyes.'

Callisthenes got to work briskly and the Prince began by inspecting the wound: 'Pass me the scissors – it's a ragged cut.'

'Here you are.'

'What's your name?' Alexander asked the prisoner.

'Demades.'

Callisthenes' eyes widened. 'But this is the famous orator,' he whispered into his friend's ear. Alexander, however, did not seem the least bit startled by the revelation.

Demades could not help but grimace as the make-do surgeon cut into his flesh, and then asked for the needle and thread. Alexander held the needle in the flame of the lamp before starting to sew, while Callisthenes held the edges of the wound together.

'Tell me about Demosthenes,' the Prince asked in the meantime.

'He . . . he is a patriot,' replied Demades through clenched teeth, 'but we see things differently.'

'In what sense exactly? Put your finger here,' he added, indicating the point, and Callisthenes, his assistant surgeon, obediently put his finger on the thread that now had to be knotted.

'In the sense . . .' the patient started to explain before holding his breath, '. . . in the sense that I was against going to war alongside the Thebans and I said so publicly.' He let out a deep sigh of relief as Alexander finished tying the knot.

'It's true,' whispered Callisthenes. 'I have copies of his speeches.'

'I've finished,' said the Prince. 'We can bandage it now.' Then, turning to Callisthenes, 'Have a real physician see him tomorrow. If the wound should swell up and become infected it'll have to be drained and it's best if a real surgeon takes care of that.'

'How can I thank you?' asked Demades, lifting himself up on the camp bed.

'You may thank my teacher, Aristotle, for it was he who taught me these things. But as far as I understand you Athenians did not go out of your way to keep him with you.'

'Aristotle left because of an internal problem in the Academy . . . it was nothing to do with the city itself.'

'Listen. Can the assembled army pass a motion here and now granting you a political position?'

'Yes . . . in theory. There are probably more people eligible to vote here than there are in Athens at the moment.'

'Speak with them then and make sure you are the representative charged with negotiating peace terms with the King.'

'Are you serious?' Demades asked in amazement as he got dressed.

'You may take clean clothes from my chest. As far as the rest is concerned, I'll speak with my father. Callisthenes will find you somewhere to sleep.'

'Thank you . . . I . . .' Demades only just had time to stutter these words because Alexander had already left.

He went to his father's tent and found Philip sitting

with Parmenion, Cleitus the Black and some battalion commanders, eating his supper.

'Hungry?' the King asked him. 'There's some partridge.'

'There are thousands of them,' Parmenion explained, 'they take to the air off Lake Kopais in the morning and then spend the day rooting for food along the riverbanks.'

Alexander took a stool and sat down.

The King had calmed down and seemed to be in a good mood.

'Well then, what do you make of my lad, Parmenion?' he said, clapping his hand on his son's shoulder.

'Magnificent, Philip – he led that charge better than any experienced member of the Companions could have handled it.'

'But General, your son, Philotas, also fought with great courage,' said Alexander.

'What have you done with that Athenian prisoner?' asked the King.

'Do you realize who he is? He's Demades.'

Philip jumped to his feet. 'Are you sure?'

'Ask Callisthenes.'

'By the gods! Send a surgeon immediately to take care of him; he has always spoken in favour of our policies.'

'I've already stitched him back up, otherwise he'd already be dead. I've granted him a certain amount of freedom of movement within the camp. I think he'll bring you a proposal for a peace plan tomorrow. As I understand it you'd rather avoid a war with Athens.'

'Yes. To defeat a seafaring city means assuming mastery of the seas and that's something we are certainly not ready for, as was made painfully clear to me at Perinthus and

Byzantium. If you have any suggestions I'll gladly listen to them and I'll explain my own ideas to you. Finish your meat, it's getting cold.'

*

Back in Athens the survivors of Chaeronaea initially spread nothing but despair. When they recounted the defeat and described the dead and the prisoners, the city was full of much wailing and consternation because many people had no idea whether their loved ones were dead or alive.

Later the atmosphere changed when the terrible realization of what might happen next began to take hold; even sixty-year-olds were called to arms and slaves were promised their freedom if they too agreed to fight for Athens.

Demosthenes, still exhausted and wounded, exhorted the Athenians to fight to the last and proposed that the rural population of Attica should be brought within the city walls. But all this proved to be immaterial because an escorted envoy from Philip reached the city a few days later and asked to be allowed to present a proposal for a peace treaty to a plenary assembly. The representatives of the people were amazed to see that the citizens held prisoner at Chaeronaea had already ratified the proposal and indeed it carried the signature of Demades.

The envoy entered the large semi-circle where the Athenians were sitting out in the open under the rays of the springtime sun and, having obtained permission to speak, began: 'Your fellow citizen Demades, who is still a guest of King Philip, has negotiated for you a treaty that contains conditions I think you will find advantageous.

'The King is not your enemy, indeed he admires your

city and its wonders greatly. It was with deep regret that he was forced to go into battle against you. But he was simply complying with the request made by the god of Delphi.'

The assembly did not react as the orator had expected – they all fell silent, anxious to hear the real conditions of the treaty. The envoy continued.

'Philip will now relinquish any idea of exploiting his advantage in this situation, he will recognize your possession of all the islands in the Aegean and he will return Oropus, Thespiae and Plataea, cities which your leaders ceded to the Thebans, thereby betraying an age-old friendship.'

Demosthenes, sitting in one of the front rows, near the government representatives, whispered to his nearest neighbour, 'But don't you see that this way he's keeping hold of all our cities on the Straits? The cities he hasn't named.'

'It could have been much worse,' came the reply. 'Let's hear what else he has to say.'

'The King asks neither for compensation nor for a ransom,' continued the envoy. 'He will return your prisoners and he will return the remains of your dead so that you may bury them decently. His son, Alexander, will personally take charge of this sorrowful mission.'

The emotional reaction of the assembly to this news convinced Demosthenes that he had no hope left. Philip had touched their deepest feelings and he was intent upon sending the Prince himself to carry out this act of clemency. Nothing was more harrowing for a family than to know that the body of their own son lay unburied on a battlefield, prey to the vultures and the dogs and deprived of any funeral rites.

'Now we'll hear what he wants in exchange for all this generosity,' whispered Demosthenes again.

'In exchange Philip asks only that the Athenians should become his friends and allies. He will meet all the representatives of the Greeks in Corinth, in autumn, to put an end to the infighting, to establish a lasting peace and to announce a grand plan that has never been attempted before now, a plan which envisages the participation of all the Greek peoples. This means that Athens will have to dissolve its maritime league and enter into the great pan-Hellenic League – the only true league, which Philip is now building. He will put an end to the centuries-old internecine conflicts of the peninsula and will free the Greek cities of Asia from the Persian yoke.

'I leave you now to decide wisely, Athenians, and when you are ready let me know your answer so that I may refer it to he who has sent me.'

*

The proposal was approved by a large majority, despite Demosthenes' passionate speech in which he called on the city to fight to the very end. The assembly, in any case, sought to reassure him of the high esteem in which it held him by making it his duty to pronounce the funeral oration for those who died in battle. The treaty, which already bore Demades' signature, was countersigned by all the representatives of the government and was sent back to Philip.

As soon as the King heard the news, he sent Alexander to Athens with the convoy of chariots carrying the ashes and the bones of the dead who had already been cremated on the battlefield. The prisoners had identified many of the corpses, and on the basis of their information Eumenes had had the name of the deceased and his family inscribed on each of the small urns.

The unknown soldiers were all grouped together on the last carts, but the doctors had noted the features of the bodies – distinguishing marks, if any, the colour of their hair and their eyes and so on.

As a demonstration of his goodwill, Philip had even allowed the Athenians to bring back some of the weapons in order to facilitate identification of the nameless warriors.

'I envy you, my son,' he said to Alexander as he prepared to set off. 'You are about to see the most beautiful city in the world.'

His companions came to say goodbye.

'Look after Bucephalas for me,' the Prince said to Hephaestion. 'I don't want to tire him out or make him run any unnecessary risks on such a long journey.'

'I'll treat him as if he were a beautiful woman,' replied his friend. 'You needn't worry. I'm only sorry that . . .'

'What?'

'That you haven't asked me to look after Pancaspe as well.'

'Stop it, you fool!' Alexander said as he started laughing. Then he mounted a well-built morel which a squire had just brought for him and gave the signal for the departure.

The long convoy started out with much creaking from the wheels of the chariots. The Athenian prisoners came behind on foot, each one carrying a bundle with a few personal effects and the food he had been able to gather.

Demades was given a horse in recognition of the role he had played in securing the signing of the peace treaty.

The dead Thebans, however, still lay where they had fallen and for days had been prey to the crows and the vultures while at night the wild dogs and nocturnal birds of prey had been at work. All of this was witnessed by the many mothers who had come from the city and had congregated on the edges of the battlefield, their wailing harrowing and terrible. Others, within the walls of Chaeronaea, carried out strange magical rites through which they sought to invoke the worst possible death for Philip.

But their curses and invocations had had no effect whatsoever – the King had steadfastly denied his enemies any hope of having their dead to bury for the simple reason that he considered them all to be traitors.

In the end, convinced by the insistence of his own friends who were afraid of the ultimate consequences of such a heartless policy, the King acquiesced.

The Thebans left their city bedecked in mourning, preceded by the weeping of the hired mourners, and they dug a large pit in which they placed the remains of their young men who had fallen in battle. Over the tomb they piled earth to form a tumulus, alongside which they later erected a gigantic stone statue of a lion to commemorate the courage of their soldiers.

In the end a peace treaty was signed with the Thebans as well, but they had to accept a Macedonian garrison on their acropolis and the dissolving of the Boeotian League as they entered into Philip's pan-Hellenic alliance.

*

Alexander was welcomed to Athens as an important guest and received full honours. As a sign of gratitude for the merciful mission he had carried out and for the way in which the Macedonians had treated their prisoners, the council of Athens decreed that a public statue of him should be installed and the Prince had to pose for the great Athenian sculptor Protogenes, although he had once declared that only Lysippus would ever create his likeness.

Demosthenes, still much loved by his fellow citizens despite the defeat, had been sent to Calauria, an island off the city of Troezen, so as to avoid any meeting that would have been embarrassing for both parties.

Alexander understood and wisely avoided asking for news of Macedon's rival. His official duties over, he wanted to visit the Acropolis, the monuments of which Aristotle had praised so highly, showing him sketches.

He climbed up there one morning after a storm the previous night and was dazzled by the splendour of the colours and the incredible beauty of the statues and the painting. in the middle of the wide open space rose the Parthenon, crowned by its immense tympanum with the group of sculptures by Phidias representing the birth of Athena from Zeus's forehead. The statues were enormous and their postures followed the inclination of the slopes of the roofs: the ones standing up in the centre were the main characters and gradually moving out towards the exterior they appeared kneeling or lying down.

They were all painted in bright colours and decorated with metallic elements in bronze and gold.

Alongside the sanctuary, to the left of the entrance steps, stood a bronze statue by Phidias representing the armed goddess Athena with a golden-tipped spear in her hand – the first thing the Athenian sailors saw when they returned to the port after a voyage.

But what Alexander most wanted to see was the gigantic statue of Athena inside the temple, also created by Phidias.

Alexander entered quietly, respectful of the sacred place, the goddess's dwelling, and there he found himself facing the colossus of gold and ivory, the wonders of which had been described to him ever since he was a child.

The air inside the cella was saturated with the incense that the priests burned continuously in honour of the goddess and the room was immersed in half-shadow. Thus the gold and the ivory of which the statue was made stood out even more – their magical reflections glimmering from the end of the double row of columns that supported the roof.

The goddess's weapons and her *peplum* – stretching down to her feet – as well as her helmet, spear and shield, were all of pure gold while her face, arms and feet were of ivory, in imitation of the colour of skin. Her eyes were of mother of pearl and turquoise, which reproduced the blue-green gaze of the goddess.

Her helmet bore three horse-mane plumes each dyed red – the central one supported by a Sphinx, the two lateral ones by Pegasuses. In her right hand the goddess held an image of winged Victory, as big, he had been told, as a person, which meant that Athena's statue must have been at least thirty-five feet in total height.

Alexander stood there in raptures as he contemplated that splendour and he thought of the glory and the power of the city that had created it. He considered the greatness of the men who had built theatres and sanctuaries, forged bronze and sculpted marble, painted frescoes of wondrous beauty. He thought of the daring of the mariners who for many years had enjoyed uncontested domination of the seas, of the philosophers who had expounded their truths along those luminous porticoes, of the poets and playwrights who had produced their tragedies for thousands of involved spectators.

He felt himself swelling with admiration and feeling and then blushed with shame at the memory of the limping figure of Philip, his father, and his unspeakable victory dance among the dead of Chaeronaea.

26

ALEXANDER VISITED the theatre of Dionysus at the foot of the Acropolis together with the buildings and monuments of the great square in which all of the city's history was represented. But above all else it was the Decorated Colonnades – the huge series of frescoes inspired by the Persian Wars and painted by Polygnotus – which captured his imagination.

The Battle of Marathon was depicted with its famous heroic exploits, including a scene showing Phidippedes, the athlete who ran to Athens to announce the victory only to drop dead from exhaustion.

A little further on were the battles of the Second Persian War – the Athenians abandoning their city, fleeing to the island of Salamis from which they watched in tears as the Acropolis burned and the temples collapsed. And then the huge naval battle of Salamis in which the Athenian fleet had given the Persian navy a good hiding – there was the Great King himself fleeing in terror, followed by black clouds and gale-force winds.

Alexander would have liked to stay in that wonderful place, this treasure chest in which human genius had deposited its most precious cultural valuables, but duty and messages from his father called him back to Pella.

His mother Olympias had also written several times,

congratulating him on the battle at Chaeronaea and telling him how much she missed him. Although she never fully explained her insistence in writing, Alexander understood intuitively that there must be something behind these letters, some new event, some painful torment. He knew his mother well and could read between her lines.

So he left one day at the beginning of summer accompanied by his escort, heading in a northerly direction. They entered Boeotia at Tanagra, passed close by Thebes one sultry afternoon, crossing the plain under the burning rays of the sun, and then rode along the shore of Lake Kopais, shrouded in a thick fog.

Now and then ghost-like herons, their wings flapping slowly, would cut through the mists that covered the swampy shores. The calls of invisible birds penetrated the damp heat like muffled shouts. Black drapes had been hung at the entrances to the villages and at the doors of the houses because war and death had struck many families, carrying off their loved ones.

He reached Chaeronaea at sunset the following day and the city seemed haunted, deserted under the dark sky of the new moon. Alexander found it impossible to conjure up any satisfactory image of Macedon's recent victory there. The cries of the jackals and the hooting of the owls simply brought anguish in the long, nightmare-filled night he spent in the tent pitched in the shade of an enormous, solitary oak.

At Pella his father did not come to meet him because he was in Lyncestis to meet with the heads of the Illyrian tribes, and the young Prince slipped into the palace almost unnoticed, after sunset. Only Peritas came to greet him –

mad with joy, he ran around, rolling on the ground, whining and wagging his tail and jumping up on his master and licking his face and hands.

A pat or two was all that was needed to make him happy and Alexander immediately went to his own apartments where Pancaspe was waiting for him.

The girl ran to Alexander and held him tightly, then she took off his dust-covered clothes and bathed him, her soft hands lingering in massaging his tired limbs. When Alexander left the bath she began to undress, but just then Leptine entered the room; her face was red and she lowered her eyes.

'Olympias would like you to go to her as soon as possible,' she said. 'She hopes you might have supper with her.'

'I will,' replied Alexander. And while Leptine left the room he whispered to Pancaspe, 'Wait for me.'

As soon as she saw him, the Queen pulled him to her in a frantic embrace.

'What's wrong, Mother?' the young man asked as he moved away to take a look at her.

Olympias' eyes were as unblinking and dark as the lakes in her mountain homeland. At that moment her gaze was an unbearably clear mirror of the violently contrasting passions that were boiling deep down in her soul.

She lowered her head and bit her lip.

'What's wrong, Mother?' Alexander asked once more.

Olympias turned towards the window to hide her sorrow and her shame.

'Your father has a lover.'

'My father has seven wives. He is a passionate man and one woman alone has never been enough for him. What's more . . . he is our King.'

'But it's different this time. He has fallen in love with a girl the same age as your sister.'

'She's not the first one. He'll get over it.'

'I'm telling you it's different this time. He's in love, he's lost his mind. It's just like . . .' and she sighed deeply, '. . . it's just like when we first met.'

'What difference does that make?'

'A lot,' replied Olympias. 'The girl is pregnant by him and he wants to marry her.'

'Who is she?' asked Alexander, his expression darkening.

'Eurydice, daughter of General Attalus. Do you see now why I'm so worried? Eurydice is Macedonian, from a noble family . . . she's not a foreigner like me.'

'That doesn't mean a thing. You come from a family of kings, a descendant of Pyrrhus, son of Achilles and of Andromache, Hector's bride.'

'Wishful thinking, my son. Let's suppose the girl gives birth to a boy . . .'

Alexander was speechless, assailed by a sudden feeling of dread.

'Explain what you mean exactly. Tell me what you think – no one can hear us.'

'Let's suppose Philip repudiates me and declares Eurydice Queen, something which is within his power: Eurydice's son becomes the legitimate heir and you are the bastard, the son of the repudiated foreigner.'

'But why should he? My father has always loved me,

he has always wanted the best for me. He has had me groomed for the throne.'

'You don't understand. A beautiful, determined young girl can completely upset the mind of a mature man, and a newborn baby will attract all of his attention because it will make him feel young again. A new son will reverse the inexorable passage of time.'

Alexander was dumbstruck, and it was clear his mother's words had upset him deeply.

He sat on a chair and rested his forehead on his left hand, as though trying to collect his thoughts. 'What do you think I should do?'

'I really don't know,' the Queen admitted. 'I am indignant, humiliated, furious over this affront he has inflicted upon me. If only I were a man . . .'

'I am a man,' Alexander said.

'But you are his son.'

'What do you mean by that?'

'Nothing. The humiliation I must endure is driving me out of my mind.'

'Well . . . in your opinion what should I do?'

'Nothing. There is nothing to be done now. But I wanted to tell you, to put you on your guard, because from now onwards anything might happen.'

'Is she really such a beauty?'

Olympias lowered her head and it was clear how painful it was for her to reply to this question. 'More than you can possibly imagine. And her father Attalus made sure Philip found her in his bed. It's clear he has a definite plan and has many members of the Macedonian nobility on his side. They hate me, I know.'

Alexander stood to take his leave.

'Don't you want to stay for supper? I've had them cook things for you, all your favourite things.'

'I'm not hungry, Mother. And I am tired. Excuse me. We'll see each other soon. Try not to worry about this too much. I really don't think there's much that can be done for the moment.'

This conversation with his mother left him shattered. The idea that his father could suddenly eliminate him from his thoughts and from his plans had never occurred to him, and he would never have expected it at a moment when he was receiving just praise for his crucial role in the great victory at Chaeronaea and in leading the delicate diplomatic mission to Athens.

To chase these unsettling thoughts away he went down to the stables to see Bucephalas and the horse immediately recognized his voice, stamping and neighing. The stall was in perfect order and smelled of fresh hay. The animal's coat was shining, its mane and its tail brushed as carefully as a girl's hair. Alexander moved closer and embraced the animal, stroking his neck and muzzle.

'So you're back finally!' came a voice behind him. 'I knew you'd be here. Well? How does Bucephalas look? See how I've taken care of him? Just as if he were a beautiful woman. I promised I'd do it.'

'Hephaestion, it's you!'

The young man moved towards his Prince and gave him a clap on the back. 'You rogue, I've missed you.'

Alexander returned the gesture. 'I've missed you too, Horsethief!'

They threw themselves into each other's arms and

embraced long and hard, harder than friendship, than time, than death.

That night Pancaspe waited for him in vain.

*

Philip came back a few days later and straight away called Alexander to his rooms where he embraced him warmly as soon as he entered.

'By the gods you look fine! How did things go for you in Athens?' But he immediately sensed his son's unease in returning the affection.

'What's wrong, my boy? Those Athenians haven't made you lily-livered with all their culture, have they? Or have you fallen in love? Oh, by Hercules, you don't mean to say you've fallen in love? Ha! I arrange the most expert of "companions" and he falls in love with . . . with who? A beautiful Athenian? Don't say a word . . . I know, there's nothing to match Athenian charm. Ah, yes, this is a good one, I'll have to tell Parmenion all about this.'

'I haven't fallen in love, Father. But I hear you have.'

Philip suddenly froze for a moment and then began pacing the room with long strides. 'Your mother! Your mother!' he exclaimed. 'She's resentful, consumed by jealousy and by bad faith. And now she's trying to turn you against me. That's what's happening, isn't it?'

'You have another woman,' Alexander stated coldly.

'And so? She's not the first and she won't be the last. She's a rose . . . as beautiful as the sun . . . like Aphrodite. Even more beautiful! I found her naked in my arms – two tits like ripe pears, her body soft, hairless and perfumed, and she opened her legs for me. What was I supposed to do? Your mother hates me, she detests me, she'd spit on me every time she sees me if she thought she could get away with it! And then this girl is as sweet as honey.'

He let himself collapse into a chair and with a rapid flick of his wrist pulled his cloak over his knees, a sure sign he was furious.

'I can't hold you to account for who you take to bed, Sire.'

'Stop calling me "Sire" . . . we're alone here!'

'But this time my mother feels humiliated, rejected, and she is worried.'

'I get it!' shouted Philip. 'I understand! She really is trying to turn you against me. And with no good reason. Come, come with me! Come and see the surprise I'd prepared for you before you ruined my day with this nonsense. Come on!'

He dragged Alexander down a stairway and then to the end of a corridor, near the various workshops of the palace. He threw open a door and almost pushed his son inside.

'Look!'

Alexander found himself in the middle of a room illuminated by a large window to one side. Sitting on a table was a round clay sculpture, a circular relief depicting him in profile and with a crown of laurel around his head, like the god Apollo.

'Do you like it?' asked a voice from a dark corner.

'Lysippus!' exclaimed Alexander, turning suddenly to embrace the artist.

'Do you like it?' repeated Philip behind him.

'But what is it?'

238

'It's the model for a stater, for a gold coin of the realm of Macedon which will be minted from tomorrow onwards as a memorial to your victory at Chaeronaea and your role as heir to the throne. Ten thousand of them will be struck and it will circulate throughout the world,' replied the King.

Alexander lowered his head in bewilderment.

27

PHILIP'S GESTURE and the presence of Lysippus at court for a while helped clear the clouds that had cast their shadow on relations between father and son, but Alexander soon realized for himself just how strong was the bond between his father and young Eurydice.

Nevertheless, pressing political commitments distracted both the King and the Prince from private court affairs.

The response from Arses, King of Persia, had been even more contemptuous than Philip's letter. Eumenes read it to the King as soon as it arrived with the messenger:

Arses, King of the Persians, King of Kings, Light of the Aryans and Lord of the Four Corners of the Earth, to Philip of Macedon.

The actions of my father, Artaxerxes, third of this name, were good and true and rather it is you who should pay us tribute – as did your predecessors – for you are our vassals.

The King immediately called Alexander and let him read the message as he said, 'Exactly as I imagined. My plan is taking shape in all its detail. The Persian refuses to pay compensation for the damage caused by his father and this is more than sufficient excuse for declaring war on him.

My dream becomes reality. I will unite all the Greeks of the homeland and the eastern colonies, I will save Hellenic culture and spread it throughout the world. Demosthenes has not understood my plan and he fought me as a tyrant, but just look around you! The Greeks are free and I have installed a Macedonian garrison only on the acropolis of the Theban traitors. I have protected the Arcadians and the Messenians and more than once I have been the champion of the sanctuary at Delphi.'

'Do you really want to move into Asia?' Alexander asked, having been struck by this affirmation alone in the midst of his father's bragging.

Philip looked into his eyes.

'Yes. And I will announce this enterprise to our allies at Corinth. I will ask all of them to provide men and warships for the undertaking that no Greek has ever managed to complete.'

'And do you think they will follow you?'

'I have no doubt,' replied Philip. 'I will explain to them that the aim of the expedition is to free the Greek cities of Asia from barbarian domination. They won't be able to decline.'

'But is this really the aim of the expedition?'

'We have the strongest army in the world, Asia is enormous, and there is no limit to the glory that a man may conquer, my son,' said the King.

A few days later another guest arrived at Pella – the painter Apelles, who was considered by many people at that time to be the best in the world. Philip had summoned him to have his portrait painted alongside the Queen, naturally with the required corrections and embellishment.

It was an official painting to be hung in the sanctuary in Delphi, but Olympias refused to pose next to her husband and for his preparatory sketches Apelles had to spy on her at a distance.

Philip was in any case very pleased with the final result and he asked the painter to depict Alexander as well, but the Prince refused.

'I'd rather you painted a friend of mine,' he said. 'Nude.'

'Nude?' Apelles asked.

'Yes. I miss her beauty when I am far away. You'll have to paint a picture that isn't too big – so that I can carry it with me – but it must be a good likeness.'

And so it was that Pancaspe, said to be the most beautiful woman in the Greek world, posed nude in all her splendour for the greatest of all painters.

Alexander was impatient to see the result of this extra-ordinary confluence of talent and every day he stopped by to see the progress being made on the work, but he was soon aware of the fact that there was no progress at all, or almost none. Apelles was simply drawing and redrawing his sketches.

'But this painting is like Penelope's shroud, it's never-ending,' the young man commented. 'What's the problem?'

'The fact is, Sire . . . the fact is that I simply cannot bear the thought of ever having to part from such splendid beauty.'

Alexander took a good look at Pancaspe and the artist and he realized that in those long sittings they had been busying themselves with something more than just pic-torial artistry. 'I see,' he said. At that moment he thought of Leptine, whose eyes were always red from crying, and he considered that there would be no shortage of equally beautiful women in the future as and when and how he wanted them. He was also painfully aware of the fact that Pancaspe was becoming more and more petulant and demanding every day. He moved closer to the painter and whispered in his ear: 'I have a proposal to make. You leave me the painting and I'll leave you the girl. That is, of course, if she agrees.'

'Oh, Sire . . .' the great artist started stammering with emotion. 'How can I possibly thank you? I . . . I . . .'

The young Prince clapped Apelles on the back. 'The important thing is that you are both happy and that the painting is a good one.' Then he opened the door and left.

*

Philip and Alexander went down to Corinth towards the end of the summer and they were both hosted at the city's expense. The choice of venue was not a chance one: it was at Corinth some one hundred and fifty years previously that the Greeks had sworn to resist the Persian invaders and it was from there that a new pledge was to be made now, uniting all the Greeks on the continent and the islands into one big mission to invade Asia. This was an undertaking that would make the glories of the Trojan War, as sung by Homer, pale into insignificance.

In a passionate speech to the delegates, Philip recounted the various phases of the history of the conflict between Europe and Asia, even those episodes to be found only in mythology. He recalled the dead of Marathon and Thermopylae, the burning of the acropolis and the temples of

Athens. And although these were all remote events from several generations back, they were still very much alive in popular culture, partly because Persia had never stopped interfering in the Greek states' internal affairs.

But more important than these faded memories of the Persian invasions was Philip's determination to convince them of the necessity of his plan, to make them realize that there was no alternative to his will and that his political method included war as an instrument. The sad fate of Thebes and its allies was still there for everyone to see.

At the end of the assembly the King of Macedon was officially granted his role as pan-Hellenic leader of a great expedition to invade Persia, but many delegates thought it was simply a sort of propaganda stunt. They were wrong.

Alexander was able to see something of Corinth, a city he had never visited before, during the days spent there. He went up with Callisthenes to the acropolis, almost impregnable, and admired the ancient temples of Apollo and Poseidon, the sea god and protector of the city.

The thing that most impressed him was the 'naval tow', the slipway along which ships were hauled so that they could pass from the Saronic to the Corinthian gulfs across the isthmus separating them, thus avoiding the circumnavigation of the Peloponnese with its many rocky headlands and deadly shallows.

The tow was a wooden slide to which ox grease was applied continually as it climbed to the high point of the isthmus and then descended on the other side to the Gulf of Corinth. The ship was dragged by oxen to the top and waited there until another ship arrived below and was then attached to it. The ship at the top was pushed down on the other side so that as it descended it helped pull the second ship up, which in its turn functioned as a brake to the descent of the first. The second ship, having reached the top, then had a third ship attached to it, while the first was able to set sail, and so on.

'Has no one ever thought of digging a canal to connect the two gulfs?' Alexander asked his Corinthian hosts.

'If the gods had wanted there to be sea where there is land, they would have made the Peloponnese an island, don't you think?' the guide replied. 'One is reminded of what happened to the Great King of the Persians at the time of his invasion of Greece. He built a bridge over the sea so that his troops could cross the Straits and he cut the peninsula of Mount Athos with a canal so that his navy could sail through, but then he suffered heavy defeats, punishment for his hubris.'

'It is true,' admitted Alexander. 'My father once took me to see that enormous canal and he told me all about the Great King's achievements. That was exactly why I thought of a canal.'

His hosts also told him that nearby there lived Diogenes, the celebrated cynical philosopher who inspired all sorts of incredible stories.

'Oh yes, I know,' replied Alexander. 'Aristotle explained the theories of the cynics to me. Diogenes maintains that only by depriving oneself of everything that is superfluous can one hope to free oneself of all desire and therefore of all unhappiness.'

'A bizarre theory,' Callisthenes said. 'Depriving oneself of everything not to achieve happiness, but simple imperturbability would seem to me to be a rather dull exercise, not to mention a waste. It's like burning wood just to sell its ash, don't you think?'

'Perhaps,' said Alexander. 'And yet I would like to meet him. Is it true that he lives inside an oil churn?'

'Yes, indeed. During the last war, at the height of your father's siege, all the citizens were rushing about strengthening the walls and busying themselves in all sorts of preparations. Suddenly Diogenes started pushing his churn up a hill and then he let it roll back down again before pushing it once more. "But why are you doing this?" they asked him. And he replied, "For no reason at all. But everyone else seems so busy I didn't want to be seen as a shirker." That just about sums the man up. Imagine – his only household utensil was a little bowl for taking drinking water from the fountain, but one day he saw a boy drinking with his hands cupped together and he threw away his bowl. Are you sure you'd like to meet him?'

'Yes please,' replied Alexander.

'If you really want to,' Callisthenes sighed impatiently. 'I assure you it won't be such an edifying spectacle. You know why Diogenes and his followers are called "cynics", don't you? It's because according to their theories nothing that is natural can be judged obscene and so they do everything in public, just like dogs.'

'Exactly,' their guide confirmed. 'Come, he doesn't live – if we can call it living – very far from here. He's on the edge of the road, where it's easy to receive alms from passers-by.'

They walked for a while along the road that led from

the naval tow to the Sanctuary of Poseidon. Alexander was the first to spot Diogenes from far off.

He was an old man of about seventy, completely naked, and he was sitting with his back against a big terracotta urn in which Alexander could just make out a bed of straw and a tattered blanket. Peritas' kennel, he thought, is certainly more comfortable. Sitting nearby was a little puppy, a small mongrel that probably ate the same food as the philosopher and shared his sleeping quarters.

Diogenes was sitting with his arms resting on his knees, his head leaning back on his wretched home, while the last rays of summer warmed his skinny limbs. He was almost completely bald, but the hair at the back of his neck had grown to reach virtually halfway down his back. His face was thin, furrowed by thick and deep wrinkles, framed by a thin, straggling beard, while his cheekbones stood out and above them his eyes were sunken under his large forehead, which in some way seemed luminous.

His eyes were closed and he sat there completely motionless.

Alexander stopped right there and contemplated the man in silence. The philosopher showed no sign of having noticed the arrival of his visitors and did not open his eyes at all.

The young Prince wondered what thoughts could possibly be passing through that forehead, that ponderous head sitting on that very slender neck, on that thin, fragile body. What had led him, after a life dedicated to research into the human spirit, to lie naked and destitute at the edge of the road, object of derision and pity for passers-by?

He felt moved by this pride in poverty, by this total simplicity, by this body which in the presence of death sought to rid itself of everything, to be as unencumbered as man is at the moment of birth.

He wished Aristotle were with him; he wished he could have witnessed those two minds duelling under the sun like champions with spear and sword. He wished he could say how much he admired him. Instead he came out with a rather unfortunate offer:

'Hail, Diogenes! He who stands before you is Alexander of Macedon. Ask of me what you will and I will be glad to give it to you.'

The old man opened his toothless mouth: 'Anything?' he asked in a high-pitched voice, without even opening his eyes.

'Anything at all,' Alexander repeated.

'Well . . . move over a bit because you're blocking the sun just there.'

Alexander moved immediately and sat down to one side, at Diogenes' feet, like a postulant asking for indulgence from a higher order. He turned to Callisthenes:

'Please leave us alone. I do not know if he will say anything to me, but if he does they will be words that cannot be written, my friend.'

Callisthenes saw that Alexander's eyes were moist.

'Perhaps you're right, perhaps all of this is a waste – burning wood to sell its ash – but I would give anything to know what goes on behind those closed eyelids. And believe me, if I weren't what I am, if I weren't Alexander, I would like to be Diogenes.'

28

No one ever discovered what was said in their conversation, but Alexander certainly never forgot the meeting, and perhaps Diogenes never did either.

Two days later, Philip and his entourage set off again on the northern road towards Macedon and the Prince went with them.

When they reached Pella the King concentrated on preparations for the great expedition to the Orient. Almost every day there was a war council with the participation of the generals Attalus, Cleitus the Black, Antipater and Parmenion, and they worked at organizing the levy of soldiers, their equipment, their supplies. The good relations with Athens now guaranteed them safety at sea and – between the Macedonian navy and the allies' ships – a feasible means of transport to carry the massed army to Asia.

Alexander's time was almost completely taken up by this feverish activity and he didn't seem to be at all preoccupied by Eurydice's pregnancy, nor by his mother's torments, even though Olympias was always sending him messages when he was away from Pella, or sending urgent requests for private talks when he was there.

Olympias was also engaged in lively correspondence with her brother, Alexander of Epirus, with the aim of securing his support. She felt more lonely than ever now – in decline, relegated backstage in her apartments.

She thought of nothing else and her plight was her only topic of conversation with those people who remained loyal to her. Her future stretched out before her as a bleak one of reclusion and total isolation. Indeed, Olympias was acutely aware that from the moment when the new Queen was officially granted her royal prerogatives, she herself would no longer be allowed even to appear in public. She would thus have to relinquish the only satisfaction left to her – the official occasions on which she met foreign guests and delegations, when she would entertain the wives and friends of the visitors in her apartments.

Above all else she was worried that she would lose what was left of her personal power as mother of the heir to the throne.

Alexander was less concerned, surrounded as he was by his friends who continually displayed their devotion and their loyalty.

He also enjoyed the deep and sincere esteem of Generals Parmenion and Antipater, the right- and left-hand men of his father the King. Both generals had seen Alexander in action as a man of government and in combat on the battlefield. They knew that the kingdom would be safe if one day it was left in his hands. But in truth the dynastic situation was not by any means certain: Alexander's cousins, Amyntas and his brother Archelaus, still had some support in certain quarters of the nobility, while his half-brother, Arrhidaeaus, a halfwit, seemed at the moment to pose no threat.

*

The date of Philip's wedding was officially announced at the beginning of winter and although the news had been expected for some time, it came as a thunderbolt.

Everyone was struck by the extraordinary air of gravitas and grand pomp that the King sought to grant the ceremony.

Eumenes was now running the royal office single handed, and he kept Alexander informed of every detail: the rank of invited guests, the expenditure for clothes, the ornaments, the food, the wines, the decorations, the jewels for the bride and her bridesmaids.

Alexander tried to keep most of this from his mother so as to spare her feelings as much as possible, but Olympias was equipped with eyes and ears everywhere and she knew exactly what was going on before he did.

The great day had almost arrived when the Queen and Alexander received official invitations to take part in the ceremony. They were both well aware that an invitation from Philip was effectively an order, and mother and son started preparing themselves, reluctantly, for the ceremony and the sumptuous wedding feast that was to take place immediately afterwards.

Eumenes had performed miracles of diplomatic dexterity in arranging the guests' dining beds and tables so as to avoid contacts that would inevitably have led to arguments or even fights. The tribal chiefs and the Macedonian princes were all lined up more or less on one side or the other and when the wine started flowing, it would be quite possible for the blood to start flowing too as a result of a badly interpreted phrase or gesture.

The bride was enchantingly beautiful, dressed like a true

queen, but the signs of her pregnancy were clearly evident. She wore a golden diadem and her hair was tied up above her neck in a chignon held in place by pins of gold with coral heads; her gown was woven with silver and decorated with extraordinarily beautiful embroidery in imitation of the style of the ceramist painters, reproducing a scene of maids dancing in front of a statue of Aphrodite. Over her face was the nuptial veil which partially covered her forehead.

Alexander, by virtue of his role as heir to the throne, was required to take up position near the King and his new bride and later too, during the banquet, he was expected to stretch out near his father.

Olympias on the other hand, with her own maids, was opposite Philip at the far end of the large dining hall. Alongside her was Princess Cleopatra, who had apparently chosen to remain with her mother because she didn't get on with Eurydice, even though they were of the same age.

The dining beds were arranged along the four sides of a rectangle and only at the end of the long right-hand side was there an opening which allowed the cooks to enter with the dishes and the waiters to keep the wine flowing and the floor clear of leftovers.

A group of flute players had started the music and some dancers were swaying among the tables and in the central area in the middle of the large rectangle of the dining hall. Things were beginning to warm up and Alexander, who hadn't touched a drop of wine, was keeping an eye on his mother without being obvious about it. She was the personification of beauty and pride, her face pale, her gaze icy; she seemed to transcend this bacchanalia, the shouting of the drunken revellers, the piercing music of the flutes. She was like a statue of some implacable goddess of revenge.

She neither ate nor drank throughout, while Philip let himself go in all sorts of debauchery not only with his young bride, whose resistance consisted only of coy giggling, but with the dancers as well as they passed by. All the other guests, especially the Macedonians, did the same.

Then came the moment when everyone had to toast the newly wed couple and, in accordance with ceremonial procedure, it was the bride's father's duty to lift the cup and drink to their health. Attalus was no less under the influence than the others: he stood up, staggered and raised the brimming cup, managing to splash wine not only on his own bed, but also on those of his neighbours. Then, in a rather quavering voice, he said, 'I give you the royal couple! To the groom's potency and to the beauty of the bride. May the gods grant them a legitimate heir to the throne of Macedon!'

This was the most unfortunate thing he could have possibly uttered at that moment. Indeed, it simply reinforced the rumours that were doing the rounds among the Macedonian nobility regarding the Queen's purported infidelity. And of course it was a grievous offence to Alexander, the heir designate.

Olympias turned deathly pale. Everyone who had heard Attalus's toast went silent and turned towards Alexander who had jumped to his feet, his face crimson, in a terrible fit of rage.

'You idiot!' he shouted. 'You son of a bitch! So what am

I then? A bastard? Eat your words or I will slit your throat from ear to ear!' And he drew his sword from its scabbard to give substance to his threat.

At this Philip, furious with Alexander for having insulted his father-in-law and for having ruined his wedding feast, wine-sodden and out of his mind, unsheathed his own sword and set off on the short trip to deal with his son. The hall suddenly filled with shouts, the dancers fled and the cooks ducked for cover in view of the storm that was breaking out.

But as he sought to jump from one dining bed to another to reach Alexander, who stood his ground waiting for the attack, Philip slipped and fell noisily to the floor, pulling drapes, crockery and leftovers with him and ending up in a pool of red wine. He tried to stand up, only to slip once more and fall face down.

Alexander moved closer with his sword still held firmly in his hand. A tomb-like silence descended on the hall. The dancers crowded together trembling in one corner. Attalus was waxen pale and a thread of spit dribbled from the corner of his half-open mouth. The young bride sobbed, 'Stop them, in the name of the gods, someone do something!'

'Here he is!' exclaimed Alexander, laughing. 'Just take a look at the man who wants to move from Europe into Asia and yet isn't even capable of stepping from one bed to another without taking a tumble.'

Philip crawled through the wine and the leftovers of the meal growling, 'I'll kill you! I'll kill you!'

But Alexander didn't bat an eyelid. 'It will already be quite an achievement if you can manage to get up onto your feet,' he said. Then, turning to the servants, 'Pick him up and wash him down.'

Then he went to Olympias. 'We must leave now, Mother, you were right. This is no place for us.'

29

ALEXANDER LEFT the palace quickly, arm in arm with his mother, the pair of them followed by Philip's furious shouting. As soon as they reached the courtyard Alexander asked Olympias, 'Do you feel up to riding or shall I have a carriage prepared?'

'No. I will ride on horseback.'

'Get changed and make sure you're ready at the entrance to your apartments. I'll be with you soon. Don't forget your cloak and your warm clothes. We're heading for the mountains.'

'At last!' exclaimed the Queen.

Alexander ran to the stables to collect Bucephalas together with a Sarmatian bay complete with tack, caparison and satchels for a journey. He took them both to the northern corner of the palace.

'Alexander! Wait!' shouted a voice behind him.

'Hephaestion! Go back, my father will pick on you next if you don't.'

'That doesn't matter . . . I'll be damned if I leave you on your own. Where are you going?'

'To Epirus, to my uncle's.'

'Which road are you taking?'

'Beroea.'

'You go on ahead. I'll catch up with you later.'

'Good. Say goodbye to the others for me and tell Eumenes to look after Peritas.'

'Of course . . . don't worry, I'll take care of it,' and Hephaestion ran off.

'At least one bone every day!' Alexander shouted after him. 'For his teeth!'

His friend made a gesture indicating that he'd understood and disappeared again inside the stables.

Olympias was ready. She had gathered her hair in a bun, put on a leather jerkin and a pair of Illyrian trousers and over her shoulders were two satchels with blankets and supplies and a purse. One of her maids followed her crying, 'But my Queen . . . my Queen . . .'

'Go back inside into your room,' Olympias ordered her.

Alexander handed her the bridle and asked, 'Mother, where is Cleopatra? I can't leave without saying goodbye to her.'

'She sent a maid to say she's waiting for you in the atrium of the women's quarters, but you do realize that every instant we waste could prove fatal, don't you?'

'I won't be long, Mother.'

He covered his head with the hood of his cloak and ran to his sister. She was pale and trembling, still dressed in her wedding feast finery.

As soon as Cleopatra saw him she threw her arms around his neck and started crying:

'Don't go! Please don't go. I'll ask him to forgive you, I'll get down on my knees before him . . . he won't be able to refuse me.'

'Where is he now?'

'They've taken him to his apartments.'

'Dead drunk?'

Cleopatra nodded.

'We must leave now, before he regains consciousness. There is no place for me here now, neither can our mother remain in this palace. I will write, if I can. I love you, little sister.'

Cleopatra burst into even more desperate tears and Alexander almost had to prise himself from her embrace.

'When will I see you again?' the girl shouted after him.

'When the gods will,' replied Alexander. 'But you will always be in my heart!'

He quickly returned to his mother who was still ready and waiting.

'Let's go!' he exclaimed. Then he looked at her quickly and smiled. 'Mother, you're beautiful. You look like an Amazon.'

Olympias shook her head. 'A mother is always beautiful in her child's eye. But thank you anyway, my boy.' She spurred her horse on as Alexander, with an agile leap, mounted Bucephalas and galloped off to join her.

They kept clear of the busiest roads, at one point taking a country lane Alexander had used several times before when he was at Mieza, and they travelled a good distance without encountering any problems before darkness fell.

They stopped a couple of times to let their mounts get their breath back and to water them before reaching the large forest which covered Eordaea and the Haliakmon valley. They took shelter in a cave with a gurgling spring at its entrance and Alexander left the horses to graze freely outside. Then he set to work lighting a fire with two sticks and a bow.

'Aristotle taught me,' he explained. 'The friction creates heat.'

'Was Mieza a good experience for you?'

'They were wonderful years, but a life like that is no life for me.' He arranged some dry leaves around the sticks and started blowing on them when he saw the first smoke rising.

A weak flame started and it grew stronger as Alexander added more and more leaves and sticks.

When the flames had taken good hold, he put larger pieces of wood on the fire and spread his cloak on the ground before it.

'Make yourself comfortable, Mother. I'll get your supper ready this evening.'

Olympias sat and stared, almost spellbound by the dance of the flames in the solitude of the forest, while her son opened the satchels, took out some bread and toasted it on the fire. Then he cut a piece of cheese with his knife and handed it to her.

They began eating in silence.

'This is the best supper I've had in many years,' Olympias said, 'and in a setting more beautiful than any palace. I feel as though I am a child again, up here in my mountains.'

Alexander dipped a wooden cup into the springwater and offered it to her. 'And yet even this wouldn't satisfy you. You would soon miss the politics, your connections, your intrigues. Don't you think?'

'Perhaps. But for the moment just let me dream. The last time you and I slept in the same room you had only just learned to walk. And your father loved me.'

They sat there talking quietly and listening to the rustling of the evening wind through the branches of the oaks and the crackling of the flames in their lone camp. In the end they fell asleep, exhausted by their long, eventful day.

A deep melancholy had descended on both of them: they were exiles and fugitives, homeless and friendless. And they both bitterly resented their separation from a man who was hard, violent, despotic, but capable like no other of making people love him.

During the night Alexander opened his eyes, woken by an almost imperceptible noise, and he was immediately aware that his mother was no longer beside him. He looked round and in the moonlight saw a shadow along the path that wound its way among the age-old oaks. It was Olympias. She was standing in front of an enormous tree and seemed to be speaking to someone. He moved quietly, crawling over the moss until he was close to her and heard her murmuring something in an unknown language, then she would become silent as if receiving a response and then start up again, whispering yet more mysteries.

Alexander stayed there hidden from view, observing her from behind an oak tree, and he saw her set off along a path streaked with the long shadows of branches extended in the diaphanous light of the moon. He followed her, keeping out of sight and making sure he made no noise. She stopped in front of the ruins of an old shrine where the wooden sculpture of the worshipped god was barely recognizable, ruined by the ravages of time and the elements. It was the age-old image of Dionysus, the god of orgiastic fury and rapture, illuminated by the uncertain light of a few lamps, a sign that the site was still frequented.

Olympias moved light-footed towards the statue, almost as though she were about to break into a dance. She placed her hand on the pedestal and as if by magic there appeared a reed flute which she immediately began to play, sending out onto the wind an intense, sinuous note, a magical and arcane melody which soon rose above all the nocturnal voices of the wood, flying far away through the branches which were only just moving in the gentle breeze.

Some time passed and a music came from the forest, seemingly in reply to the Queen's flute. It was an undefinable air that at first was almost indistinguishable from the rustling of the leaves, then from the far off song of the nightingale, before becoming ever clearer and more distinct: first a cascade of notes, dark and muffled like the gurgling of the spring in the cave, then higher and clearer.

This music also came from a flute, or rather many primitive cane flutes, and the sound they played was long and suspended, so much so that it seemed to be engendered by the wind itself.

Olympias placed her instrument on the pedestal, took off her cloak and started dancing to the rhythm of the melody until men and women appeared from the wood, their faces covered with animal masks that made them look like satyrs and maenads. Gradually they started undressing, clinging to one another first dancing and then on the ground, around the statue in the spasms and contortions of wild intercourse.

In the midst of this chaos of sounds and forms, Olympias had suddenly become motionless, just like the wooden statue of Dionysus, like some nocturnal goddess. Masked men, naked in the moonlight and virtually crawling on all fours like animals, came close to her.

Alexander, excited and at the same time upset by this scene, was about to put his hand to the hilt of his sword when he saw something that froze him there in astonishment, against the trunk of the tree concealing him from the people around the statue. An enormous snake had come out from below ground and had slithered to the statue of the god before starting to wind itself slowly about his mother's legs.

Olympias still did not move, her limbs rigid and her eyes staring fixedly into space. It was as though she neither heard nor saw anything of what was going on. Another snake came out from below ground, and then another and another after that and they all wrapped themselves around the Queen's legs.

The biggest of them all, the one which had appeared first, lifted itself up above the others and wrapped its coils around Olympias' body until its head was above hers.

The frenetic music had stopped suddenly, the masked figures had retreated to the edges of the clearing – taken aback, almost frightened by this supernatural event. Then the snake opened its jaws wide, flicked its slender forked tongue and proceeded to make the same noise Olympias had made with her flute: a most fluid, intense note, dark and trembling like the voice of the wind among the oaks.

The lamps went out one after another and in the moonlight Alexander saw only reptile scales flash in the half-shadow and then disappear into nothing. He let out a deep sigh and wiped the cold dripping sweat from his forehead. When he looked again in the direction of the small tumbledown shrine, the clearing was completely empty and silent, as if nothing had happened.

Suddenly he felt someone touch his shoulder and he turned sharply with his sword in his hand.

'It is I, my son,' said Olympias, looking at him with a surprised expression. 'I woke up and I saw that you had gone. What are you doing here?'

Alexander put out his hand towards her, almost as though he didn't believe what he was seeing.

'But what are you doing here?' the Queen asked him once more.

Alexander shook his head as though trying to rouse himself from a dream or a nightmare and he met his mother's gaze, her eyes darker and deeper than the night.

'Nothing,' he replied. 'Let's go back.'

The next day they got up just as the sun was beginning to sparkle in the water of the spring and they set off again in silence towards the west. It was as though neither of them dared speak.

Suddenly Alexander turned towards her: 'Mother . . . people tell strange tales about you,' he said.

'What tales?' Olympias asked without turning.

'They say . . . they say that you take part in secret Dionysian worship and nocturnal orgies and that you have magic powers.'

'And do you believe these things?'

'I don't know.'

Olympias did not reply and they carried on riding, their horses stepping in time, in silence.

'I saw you last night,' Alexander started again.

'What did you see?'

'I saw you summon an orgy with the sound of your flute and I saw you charm snakes from below ground.'

Olympias turned and sent him a lightning cold look, like the light in the eyes of the snake that had appeared in the clearing.

'You gave manifest expression to my dreams there in the woods and you followed my spirit, which is a hollow simulacrum, like the shadows of the dead. This because you are part of me and you have received the gift of a divine force.'

'It wasn't a dream,' protested Alexander. 'I am certain of the things I saw.'

'There are places and times in which dream and reality become confused, there are people who can cross the confines of reality and move into those areas inhabited by mystery. One day you will abandon me and I will have to leave my body and fly through the night to reach you, to see you, to hear your voice and your breath, to be near you when you need me, whenever that moment might be.'

Neither of them said another word until the sun was high in the sky and they had reached the road for Beroea. There they met Hephaestion and Alexander dismounted and ran towards his friend.

'How did you manage to find us?' he asked.

'Your Bucephalas leaves tracks as obvious as a wild bull. It wasn't difficult.'

'Any news?'

'I haven't got much to tell you. I left shortly after you

did. I think the King was so drunk he really couldn't stand up. They must have washed him and put him to bed.'

'Do you think he'll send soldiers after us?'

'Why?'

'Because he wanted to kill me.'

'He was drunk. I bet as soon as he wakes up he'll say, "Where's Alexander?"'

'I'm not so sure. There were some ugly things said. It's going to be difficult for both of us to forget it all. And, even supposing my father is willing to forget it all, there's always going to be someone there to remind him.'

'That's certainly possible.'

'Did you tell Eumenes to look after the dog?'

'That was the first thing I did.'

'Poor Peritas. He'll miss me, he'll think I've abandoned him.'

'He won't be the only one to miss you, Alexander. I for one couldn't bear the idea of being away from you. That's why I decided to come with you.'

They spurred on their horses to catch up with Olympias who had ridden on alone.

'Hail, my Queen,' said Hephaestion.

'Hail, young man,' replied Olympias. And they continued the journey together.

*

'Where's Alexander?'

Philip had just come out of the bath chamber and the women were massaging his shoulders and his back with a linen towel.

The field adjutant came closer: 'He's not here, Sire.'

'I can see he's not here. Go and call him.'

'What I mean, Sire, is that he has gone.'

'Gone? Gone where?'

'No one knows, Sire.'

'Agghh!' cried Philip, dashing the towel to the floor and striding naked across the room. 'I want him here immediately! I want his apologies for the things he said! He made a fool of me in front of my guests and my wife. Find him and bring him here immediately! I'll pummel his face until it's a bloody mess! I'll kick the living daylights out of him! I'll . . .' His field adjutant stood there motionless and in silence. 'Are you listening to me, by Zeus?'

'I am listening, Sire, but Alexander left as soon as he came out of the dining hall and you were too . . . too much in difficulty to do anything about it . . .'

'You're trying to tell me I was too drunk to give orders, are you?' Philip shouted into his face as he turned round to confront him.

'The fact is, Sire, that you gave no orders and . . .'

'Call the Queen! Immediately!'

'Which one, Sire?' the adjutant asked, increasingly at a loss as to what to do and say.

'Which one? You stupid . . . what am I supposed to do with that little girl? Get me the Queen, immediately!'

'Queen Olympias left with Alexander, Sire.'

The King's roar was heard as far as the guard house at the other end of the courtyard. Shortly afterwards the field adjutant was seen rushing down the stairs giving orders left, right and centre. Everyone jumped on horseback and sped off at full tilt in all directions.

That day the foreign guests left with their official delegations and Philip had to receive them one by one and thank them for the fine presents they had brought. This duty took up the whole morning and afternoon.

By the time evening came around he was sick, fed up and tired – not only because of the week of celebrations and the endless feasting – but also because for the first time in his life he felt as lonely as an abandoned dog.

He sent Eurydice to bed, went up onto the roof and for a long time walked back and forth across the great terrace in the moonlight. He presently became aware of an insistent barking coming from the west wing of the palace; it grew into a heart-wrenching howl that seemed to last for ever before dying into a plaintive whining.

Peritas too had realized that Alexander had gone and he was baying all his despair at the moon.

30

IT TOOK A WEEK for the three fugitives to reach the borders of Epirus and they sent word of their arrival to King Alexander.

The young King already knew about events in Macedon because his informers were using a more rapid system of communications and they had no worries about being seen along the way between Pella and Epirus.

He went to meet them in person, and hugged his elder sister and his nephew lovingly before embracing Hephaestion whom he had come to know during the time he spent at court in Pella.

They slept that night in a hunting lodge and set off again the following morning with a full escort in the direction of the royal residence at Buthrotum, a couple of days' journey away. This city was on the sea and was the focal point of all the myths regarding the small kingdom of Epirus. Legend had it that Pyrrhus, son of Achilles, had landed there, bringing with him as slaves Andromache, Hector's widow, and Helenus, the Trojan seer. Pyrrhus had made Andromache his concubine, but later passed her to Helenus. Both of these unions had resulted in offspring who subsequently founded the royal dynasty that still dominated these lands.

On his mother's side, therefore, Alexander of Macedon

was a descendant of one of the greatest of Greek heroes and came from the stock of Priam, ruler of Asia. Such legends were sung by the poets who for several evenings entertained the King and his new guests. Indeed, for a few days Alexander and Olympias enjoyed some diversion and respite from their ordeal, but the King of Epirus knew that such peace could not last; he was well aware that they would soon be receiving visitors.

The first of them was announced one morning at dawn, while they were all still asleep. It was a horseman of Philip's personal guard, covered in mud from head to toe because it had been raining in the mountains.

'The King is furious,' he said, without even accepting the warm bath he had been offered. 'He expected Alexander to come before him the day after the wedding to apologize for his behaviour and for the harsh words he used in deriding him in front of his guests and his bride.'

'My nephew informs me that the King threatened him with his sword drawn and that Attalus called him a bastard. Philip must understand that his son has his own blood in his veins, and consequently has the same pride, the same dignity and a very similar character.'

'The King accepts no excuses and wants Alexander to come before him at Pella to beg his pardon.'

'If I know him well he will not do it.'

'In that case he will have to accept the consequences.'

Alexander was a light sleeper and had heard the noise of the hooves on the stone paving. He had got up, thrown a cloak around his shoulders and was listening now, out of sight, to what his father's messenger was saying.

'And what exactly will the consequences be?' asked the young King.

'His friends will all be sent into exile as traitors or conspirators, with the exception of Eumenes, Philip's secretary, and Philotas, son of General Parmenion.'

'I shall inform my nephew and I will let you know his answer.'

'I shall await your return and then I will set off again immediately.'

'But don't you want to eat and wash? In this house we have always prided ourselves on making our guests most welcome.'

'I cannot spare the time. The bad weather has already held me up,' the Macedonian envoy explained.

The King left the audience chamber and found himself face to face with his nephew and namesake in the corridor.

'Did you hear it all?'

Alexander nodded.

'What will you do?'

'I will not go crawling to him. Attalus offended me in public and my father should have intervened to preserve my dignity. Instead he came after me with his sword drawn.'

'But the price your friends will pay is very high.'

'I know and this pains me greatly. But I have no choice.'

'Is this your last word?'

'Yes.'

The King embraced him. 'It's exactly what I would have done in your position. I will tell the envoy.'

'No . . . wait. I will do it myself.'

He pulled his cloak around himself tightly and, barefoot,

entered the audience chamber. The messenger was slightly shocked at first, then he promptly bowed in deference.

'May the gods keep you, Alexander.'

'And you too, my good friend. Here is my reply for the King, my father. Tell him that Alexander cannot beg his pardon without first receiving an apology from Attalus and an assurance that Queen Olympias will no longer be subjected to such humiliation and that she will receive full respect, befitting her rank of Queen of Macedon.'

'Is that it?'

'That's it.'

The envoy bowed and made his way to the door.

'Tell him . . . tell him that . . .'

'What, Sire?'

'That Alexander says he must take good care of himself.'

'I shall.'

Shortly afterwards there came the neighing of a horse and the noise of galloping which faded into the distance.

'He didn't want to rest or even eat,' came the King's voice from behind Alexander. 'Philip must be very anxious to have your reply. Come, I have had breakfast brought for us.'

They went into a room in the royal apartments where two tables had been prepared alongside two chairs with arms on them. There was fresh bread and slices of mack-erel and swordfish cooked on skewers.

'I have put you in a difficult situation,' Alexander said. 'It was my father who put you on the throne.'

'That's true. But in the meantime I have grown up. I am not a boy any more. I'm the one who looks after his interests in this area and I can assure you it's no easy matter. The Illyrians are often difficult, the coastline is infested with pirates and we're receiving reports of other peoples descending from the north along the Ister. Your father needs me as well. And then I must safeguard the dignity of my sister Olympias.'

Alexander ate some fish and drank a drop of wine, a light sparkling wine from the Ionian islands. He went over to the window that overlooked the sea, continuing to chew on a piece of bread.

'Where is Ithaca?' he asked.

The King pointed towards the south. 'Ulysses' island is down there, about one day's sail in a southerly direction. The island opposite us is Corcyra, the island of the Phaeacians where Ulysses was a guest in Alcinous' palace.'

'Have you ever seen it?'

'Ithaca? No. But there's nothing there to see. Just goats and pigs.'

'Perhaps, but I would like to go there nonetheless. I'd land there towards evening, when the sea changes colour and the ways of land and sea are darkened, and feel what Ulysses felt in seeing it again after such a long time. I could . . . I'm certain I could relive the very same feelings.'

'If you want I can have you taken there. It's not far, as I said.'

Alexander seemed not to hear this and he turned his gaze towards the west, where the peaks of Corcyra were beginning to turn pink in the light of the rising sun as it came over the mountains of Epirus to the east.

'Italy lies over those mountains and beyond that sea, doesn't it?'

The King's face seemed to light up all of a sudden. 'Yes, Alexander, there's Italy and there is Great Hellas. Cities founded by the Greeks, incredibly rich and powerful: Tarant, Locri, Croton, Thurii, Rhegium and many, many others. There are endless forests and herds of livestock of thousands and thousands of head. Fields of grain for as far as the eye can see. And mountains covered with snow all year round which suddenly erupt fire and flames and make the earth shake.

'And beyond Italy lies Sicily, the most fertile and beautiful land known. There stand Syracuse and Agrigentum, Gela and Selinous. And even further on is Sardinia and then Spain, the richest country in the world with its inexhaustible silver and iron and tin mines.'

'I had a dream last night,' said Alexander.

'What did you dream?' asked the King.

'We were together, you and I, on horseback, at the top of Mount Imarus, the highest in your realm. I was astride Bucephalas and you were on Keraunos, your battle charger, and we were both in the midst of a field of shining light because just then there was one sun setting over the sea to the west while another one rose way over to the east. Two suns . . . can you imagine that? A truly moving spectacle.

'Then we said goodbye to each another because you decided to go to where the sun was setting while I opted for the place where the sun was rising. Isn't that something? Alexander of the rising sun and Alexander of the setting sun! And before parting, before each of us spurred on his horse towards his own fiery globe, we made a solemn promise: that we would never meet again before completing our journeys and the place we chose for our meeting was . . .'

'Was where?' insisted the King. 'Where is the place we agreed on for our reunion?'

'Ah! I don't remember that.'

31

ALEXANDER WAS NOT LONG in understanding that his stay in Buthrotum would soon create unbearable complications, both for himself and for his uncle, Alexander of Epirus. Philip continued to send urgent requests to Epirus requiring Alexander to return to Pella, make amends for his misdeeds and beg forgiveness in front of the assembled court.

The young Prince made up his mind to leave.

'But where will you go?' asked the King.

'North. Where he can't find me.'

'You can't. That area is peopled by wild and semi-nomadic tribes, permanently at war with one another. And on top of that the bad weather's just about to start. It snows and snows up there in those mountains, you know. Do you have any experience of white weather? It's a formidable enemy.'

'I am not afraid.'

'We all know that.'

'And so I will go. Don't worry about me.'

'I will not let you leave unless you give me details of the route you're planning to take. If I should need you, I want to know where I can find you.'

'I have studied your maps. I'm going to Lychnidos, on

the eastern side of the lake, and from there I'll head towards the interior along the Drilon valley.'

'When do you plan to set off?'

'Tomorrow. Hephaestion is coming with me.'

'No. You must remain here for another two days at least. I have to prepare everything you'll need for your journey. And I will give you a horse for carrying your supplies; when you have finished the food you'll be able to sell the horse and continue along your way.'

'Thank you,' said Alexander.

'I will give you letters for the Illyrian chiefs of Chelidonia and Dardania. They might be useful to you. I have friends in those regions.'

'I hope one day to be able to repay you for all you have done for me.'

'There's no need to say that. And keep your spirits up.'

That same day the King hurriedly wrote a letter and gave it to the fastest of his messengers with instructions to deliver it to Callisthenes, in Pella.

*

Alexander went to say goodbye to his mother on the morning of his departure. She held him tightly, crying warm tears and cursing Philip from the depths of her soul.

'Don't say these things, Mother,' Alexander begged her, his voice muffled with sadness.

'Why?' shouted Olympias in a voice that came directly from her grief and her pain. 'He has humiliated me, wounded me, he has forced me into exile. And now he obliges you to run away, to set off into the unknown in the midst of winter. I wish him the worst of deaths, if only he could be made to suffer as I have!'

Alexander looked at her and felt a cold shiver run through his blood. If he was afraid of anything, he was afraid of such hatred, a hatred so strong she reminded him of a heroine from the tragedies he had seen many times in the theatre: Clytemnestra wielding the axe with which she kills her husband Agamemnon, or Medea who kills her own children to spite Jason, her husband, to hurt him in the very depths of his love.

At that moment there came to his mind another of the terrible stories about the Queen that had done the rounds at Pella: it was said that during an initiatory ceremony of the cult of Orpheus she had eaten human flesh. He looked into her enormous eyes, full of darkness now, full of such desperate violence that he would have believed her capable of anything.

'Don't curse him, Mother,' he repeated. 'Perhaps it is a good thing that I should suffer solitude and exile, cold and hunger. This is a lesson that I have never had before, one that my father never taught me. Perhaps he wants me to learn this as well. Perhaps it is the ultimate lesson, a lesson that only he can give me.'

With some difficulty he pulled himself from her embrace, leaped onto Bucephalas and dug his heels vigorously into the horse's flanks.

The charger rose up onto his hind legs with a neigh, thrashed his front hooves in the air and then set off at a gallop blowing steamy vapour from his nostrils. Hephaestion lifted an arm in salute and then he too spurred his mount on, keeping hold of the bridle of the third horse as he rode off in pursuit.

Olympias stood there watching as they disappeared, her eyes brimming with tears. Soon all that was left before her was the empty northern road.

*

The letter from the King of Epirus reached Callisthenes in Pella a few days later and Aristotle's nephew opened it impatiently and began reading.

Alexander, King of the Molossians, hails Callisthenes!

I trust this finds you well. My nephew Alexander is enjoying a quiet life here in Epirus, far from the turmoil of military life and the daily pressures of government. He spends his days reading, especially Euripides, and of course Homer, in the boxed edition he received as a present from his teacher and your uncle, Aristotle. Sometimes he amuses himself by playing the lyre a little.

On other occasions he takes part in hunting expeditions . . .

As he read the missive Callisthenes found himself increasingly surprised by its ordinariness and complete irrelevance. There was nothing important and nothing personal in the King's communication. The letter seemed to be a completely futile exercise. But why?

Deeply disappointed, he put the papyrus down on his desk and started pacing the room, trying to understand what the King of Epirus had had in mind when suddenly, as his eyes fell on the sheet, he saw that there were cuts all along its edges, and on looking more closely he saw that these had been made deliberately, with scissors.

He brought the heel of his left hand up to smack his forehead. 'Why on earth didn't I think of it before! It's the intersecting polygon code.'

This was a code that Aristotle had once taught him and he, in his turn, had taught it to Alexander of Epirus, thinking that it might just be useful one day if the young sovereign ever found himself leading a military campaign.

He got a ruler and a set square and started joining all the cuts in order and then all the intersecting points. He then traced perpendicular lines on each side of the internal polygon, thus obtaining further intersections.

Each intersection highlighted a word in the text and Callisthenes rewrote them all following a sequence of numbers that Aristotle had taught him. A simple yet ingenious way of sending secret messages.

When he had finished he burned the letter and ran to Eumenes. He found the secretary up to his eyes in paperwork, reckoning taxes and expenditure forecasts for equipping four more phalanx battalions.

'I need to ask you something,' he said, and he whispered in Eumenes' ear.

'They left ten days ago,' replied Eumenes, lifting his head from the papers.

'Yes, but where did they go?'

'I don't know.'

'You know perfectly well where they are.'

'Who's asking?'

'I am.'

'In that case I don't know.'

Callisthenes moved closer once more and again whispered something in Eumenes' ear, then he added, 'Can you get a message to them?'

'How much time do I have?'

'Two days at the most.'

'Impossible.'

'I'll do it myself then.'

Eumenes shook his head. 'Come on, give it to me then. You reckon you could manage a job like this?'

*

Alexander and Hephaestion wound their way up the Argirinian Mountains, the peaks already dusted with snow, and then descended towards the valley of the River Aoos which shone like a golden ribbon way down below in the depths of the green slopes. The mountainsides, bedecked with forests, were beginning to change colour with the approach of autumn and across the sky flew flocks of cranes, crying as they left their nests on their long migratory journey towards the lands of the pygmies.

They travelled along the Aoos valley for two days, following the river as it flowed northward until reaching the intersection with the Apsos. They started up the river, thus leaving behind them the dominion of Alexander of Epirus and entering Illyria.

The population of this country lived spread out in small villages fortified with dry stone walls and they subsisted on livestock breeding and, occasionally, brigandry. But Alexander and Hephaestion had arrived well prepared – wearing trousers in the barbarian style and rough woollen cloaks. They were hardly a sight for sore eyes, but it was good wet-weather clothing and ensured they fitted in with the people from the area without being noticed.

When they started moving towards the interior mountain chains, snow began to fall and the temperature dropped considerably. The horses blew clouds of vapour from their nostrils and they struggled and slipped on their way up the steep paths, so much so that Alexander and Hephaestion had to dismount and continue on foot, coaxing their animals along the way.

Now and then, on reaching the high point of a mountain pass, they would turn to look backwards and the white sameness and vastness of the snow with only their own tracks spoiling it would send a shiver through their bodies, and not just because of the cold.

At night they had to find shelter where they could light a fire to dry their sodden clothes, spread out their cloaks and rest a while. Often, before falling asleep, they would sit and contemplate in the light of the flames the large white snowflakes as they fell dancing to earth, or they would listen rapt to the call of the wolves echoing through the lonely valleys.

They were just boys, still fresh from their adolescence, and such moments filled them with a deep and harrowing melancholy. Sometimes they would pull the same cloak around their shoulders and hold each other tightly in the dark. In the midst of the boundless fields of snow they remembered their childhood and the nights in which they would climb into each other's beds, frightened by a nightmare or by the lament of a condemned prisoner crying out his torment.

And it was the frozen darkness and the apparent

hopelessness of the future that led them to seek warmth in each other, to lose themselves in their nudity which was both fragile and powerful at one and the same time. Their own proud and desolate solitude left them amazed.

The cold, livid light of dawn called them back to reality and the pangs of hunger drove them to set about finding food.

There were traces of some animals in the snow, so they went to look at the traps they had set and found they had managed to catch a few things: a rabbit or a mountain grouse which they would eat still warm after having first drunk its blood. On other occasions they had to set off with nothing but hunger in their bellies, frozen stiff by the biting cold of those inhospitable lands. And their horses suffered this ordeal as well, eating only the old grass they managed to find by scraping the snow with their hooves.

Finally, after days and days of difficult progress, exhausted by the cold and the hunger, they saw the frozen surface of Lake Lychnidos shining before them like a mirror in the pale light of the winter sky. They proceeded at a walk along the northern shore, hoping to reach the village of the same name before darkness fell. Perhaps they would be able to spend a night indoors, in the warmth, next to a blazing fire.

'See that smoke on the horizon?' Alexander asked his friend. 'I was right . . . there must be a village down there. There'll be hay for the horses and food and a straw mattress for us.'

'Too good to be true, I must be dreaming,' replied Hephaestion. 'Do you really believe we'll have all these things?'

'Oh yes. And there might even be women. I once heard my father say that the barbarians from the interior some-times offer them to strangers as a mark of hospitality.'

It had started snowing again and it was drifting, so that the horses struggled now through the whiteness. The cold air penetrated through their clothes to the very bone. Suddenly Hephaestion pulled the reins of his horse. 'Oh, by the gods . . . look!'

Alexander threw his hood back and looked into the thick blizzard: there was a group of men blocking the way forward, motionless on their horses, their shoulders and their hoods covered in snow, all of them armed with javelins.

'Do you think they're waiting for us?' asked the Prince, putting his hand to his sword.

'I think so. And in any case we will soon know,' replied Hephaestion, drawing his own sword and spurring his horse into a walk again.

'I'm afraid we're going to have to clear a way through,' Alexander said.

'I'm afraid so too,' replied Hephaestion quietly.

'I was so looking forward to a plate of warm soup, a bed and a fire. And maybe even a fine wench. And you?'

'Me too.'

'On my signal?'

'All right.'

But just as they were about to launch into their charge, a shout rang out in the great silence of the valley.

'Alexander's troop salutes its leader!'

'Ptolemy!'

'Sire!'

'Perdiccas!'

'Sire!'

'Leonnatus!'

'Sire!'

'Craterus!'

'Sire!'

'Lysimachus!'

'Sire!'

'Seleucus!'

'Sire!'

The last echo faded away over the icebound lake and Alexander looked at the six men on horseback, motionless in the snow, and his eyes filled with tears. Then he turned towards Hephaestion and shook his head in amazement. 'By Zeus!' he said. 'It's my lads!'

32

THREE MONTHS AFTER the wedding, Eurydice gave birth to a baby girl who took the name Europa. Shortly afterwards Eurydice fell pregnant again. Philip, however, wasn't able to enjoy his newly rediscovered fatherhood for very long on account of developing political and personal affairs. His health was a problem too: his left eye, which had been wounded in battle but never adequately treated, was blind by now.

That winter he received a visit from his informer Eumolpus of Soloi. He had faced the sea voyage in bad weather because the news he carried was simply too important to wait. He was used to the stable, mild climate of his city, and was frozen through now. The King had him sit near the fire and ordered a cup of strong sweet wine to revive him and loosen his tongue a little.

'Well then . . . what news do you bring me, my old friend?'

'The goddess of Fortune is on your side, Sire. Just let me tell you what has happened at the Persian court. As predicted, Arses, the new king, was quick to realize exactly who the real master of the palace was and, finding this reality hard to accept, arranged to have Bagoas poisoned.'

'The eunuch?'

'Precisely. But Bagoas had been expecting a move of

this kind. He foiled the plot and took countermeasures, successfully poisoning the King. After that he had all Arses' children killed.'

'By the gods, that ball-less wonder is deadlier than a scorpion when he sets his mind to it.'

'Indeed. But at that point the dynastic line had come to an end. Between those killed by Artaxerxes III and those killed by Bagoas there was no one left.'

'So?' Philip asked.

'So Bagoas picked up on an old lateral lineage and put one of them on the throne with the name of Darius III.'

'And who is this Darius III?'

'His grandfather was Ostanes, the brother of Artaxerxes II. He is forty-five years old, and he appreciates both women and boys.'

'I'm not sure how relevant that news is,' commented Philip. 'Haven't you got anything more interesting to tell me?'

'At the time of being nominated King he was Satrap of Armenia.'

'A difficult province. He must be a tough specimen.'

'Let's say a robust one. It appears he killed a rebel of the Kadusian tribe in hand-to-hand combat.'

Philip ran his hand over his beard. 'I think the ball-less wonder might well have bitten off more than he can chew this time.'

'Exactly,' nodded Eumolpus who was just beginning to warm up. 'It seems Darius has every intention of taking full control of the Straits and of reaffirming his right to rule over all the Greek cities of Asia. There is even a rumour that he wants a formal act of submission from the

Macedonian crown, but I wouldn't worry about that much. Darius is certainly not an opponent of your stature: as soon as he hears you roar he'll run cowering to his bed.'

'We shall see,' said Philip.

'Do you need anything else, Sire?'

'Excellent work you've done, but the difficult part starts now. Stop by at Eumenes' desk and make sure you're paid. Take extra money, if required, to pay some informers. Nothing of what goes on at Darius' court must escape your notice.'

Eumolpus thanked the King and left, anxious to return to the warmth of his fine city by the sea.

Some days later, the King summoned his war council in the hall of the royal armoury – Parmenion, Antipater, Cleitus the Black and his father-in-law, Attalus.

'Not one word of what I am about to tell you must go beyond these walls,' was Philip's opening. 'Arses, King of the Persians, has been assassinated and a prince of a side branch of the family has been put on the throne; his name is Darius III and, as far as we know, he is not lacking in dignity but, for a considerable period of time, he will be very busy consolidating his own power.

'This is therefore the right moment for us to act. Attalus and Parmenion will leave as soon as possible with an army of fifteen thousand men. They will move into Asia, occupy the eastern shore of our sea and announce my proclamation of freedom for the Greek cities currently under Persian rule. In the meantime I will complete the mobilization of the army before joining you and beginning the invasion.'

The rest of the meeting was dedicated to considering details of the logistical, political and military problems related to the initial campaign. But what struck those present more than anything was the King's muted tone, the absence of the enthusiasm and the drive they had become accustomed to.

The King was so out of sorts that Parmenion, before leaving, approached him. 'Is there something wrong, Sire? Perhaps your health is troubling you?'

Philip put a hand on his general's shoulder as he accompanied him to the door. 'No, my old friend, no, everything's fine.'

*

Philip was lying. Alexander's absence, something he hadn't even considered initially, was a growing torment with every day that passed. As long as the boy had been in Epirus with his mother and his uncle, Philip had only worried about forcing him to return and submit publicly to his will. But Alexander's refusal to do so and now his flight northwards had brought anger, apprehension and worry.

If anyone tried to intercede for Alexander, Philip became furious when he thought about the outrage he had suffered. But then if no one spoke about the affair he fretted over the lack of news. He had activated his spies everywhere, he had sent messengers to the kings and tribal chiefs of the north, his clients, asking them to keep him continually informed of the movements of Alexander and Hephaestion. Thus he discovered that the group had grown with the arrival of another six young warriors who had arrived from Thessaly, from Acarnania and Athamania – it wasn't difficult to guess who they were.

Alexander's troop was almost completely reunited and Philip was always warning Parmenion to take care that Philotas, his son, didn't slip off to join that band of wretches wandering purposeless through the snows of Illyria. And he was also suspicious of Eumenes, almost as though he expected him to abandon his office and his papers from one moment to the next in favour of adventure.

Sometimes, completely alone, he travelled to the old palace at Aegae. He would sit for hours watching the white flakes of snow as they fell on the silent countryside, on the woods of blue firs, on the small valley from which his dynasty originated, and he thought of Alexander and his friends travelling through the frozen villages of the north.

It was as though he could actually see them struggling through blizzards, their horses sinking up to their bellies in the snow, the wind cracking through their torn clothes, encrusted with ice. He turned his eyes to the great stone fireplace, to the big oak logs that surrendered their heat to the ancient walls of the throne room as they burned, and he imagined his boys piling up sodden logs in make-do shelters, struggling for ages, exhausted, just to light a meagre fire. Or at night, sleepless, standing guard with their spears ready when the howling of the wolves came too close for comfort.

Then, with the approach of spring, the news really did start to become more worrying, but not in the way that everyone might have expected. Not only had Alexander and his troop managed to survive the hardships of the winter, but they had now offered themselves as allies of some of the tribal chiefs who lived on the Macedonian border and had taken sides in the internecine struggles of these peoples, helping them secure pacts of friendship or even surrender on the battlefield. These developments, sooner or later, could even have posed a threat to Philip's sovereignty.

There was something irresistible in the boy that charmed all those who came into contact with him – men, women, and even animals. Bucephalas was a case in point: how to explain his having been able to mount that black demon and tame him at the first attempt as if he were a lamb?

And how could one explain the fact that Peritas, a beast capable of shattering a thick pork bone with one snap of his jaws, lay there pining, eating virtually nothing, guarding the road along which his master had disappeared?

Then there was Leptine, the girl he had saved from the hell of Mount Pangaeos: every day she prepared Alexander's bed and bath, as if he was due to return at any moment. And she never had anything to say to anyone.

Philip also began to worry about the stability of his relations with the realm of Epirus, seriously compromised by the presence of Olympias alongside the young King, her brother. The all-consuming hatred she held within could easily push her to carry out any madness simply to harm him, to upset his political and his familial plans. King Alexander was certainly a friend, but there was no doubt he also felt close to his nephew, a homeless exile drifting through barbarian territory. Alexander of Epirus had to be made to feel some further bond with Pella, while Queen Olympias, with her malevolent influence, had to be isolated. For Philip there was only one possible solution and there was no time to lose.

One day he sent for his daughter Cleopatra, the last member of his first family who remained at court in Pella.

The Princess was in the full ripeness of her eighteen years. Her eyes were large and green, her hair long with copper highlights and her body was worthy of an Olympic goddess. There was no Macedonian nobleman who didn't dream of taking her as his bride.

'It is time you married, my child,' Philip said to her.

Cleopatra lowered her head. 'I imagine you have already chosen my husband.'

'Indeed,' Philip confirmed. 'King Alexander of Epirus, your mother's brother.'

The girl stood motionless in silence, but it was clear that she was not too disappointed in her father's decision. Her uncle was a handsome and valiant young man, much esteemed by his subjects and similar to Alexander in terms of character.

'Have you nothing to say?' the King asked her. 'Perhaps you were expecting someone else?'

'No, Father. I know that this choice is your prerogative and therefore I would never have thought of considering anyone in particular because I would never want to go against your wishes. There is just one thing I would like to ask you.'

'Tell me, my child.'

'Will my brother Alexander be invited to the wedding?'

Philip abruptly turned his back to her, as if he had suddenly been on the receiving end of a whiplash: 'As far as I am concerned, your brother no longer exists,' he said in a cold voice.

Cleopatra burst into tears. 'But why, Father? Why?'

'You know why. You were there. You saw how he humiliated me in front of the representatives of all the Greek cities, in front of my generals and all the notables of Macedon.'

'But, Father, he . . .'

'Don't you dare defend him!' shouted the King. 'I summoned Aristotle here to educate him, I commissioned Lysippus to sculpt his image, I minted coins bearing his portrait. Do you understand what all that means? No, my child, the insult and the injury have been too great, too much . . .'

'Father . . .' the girl insisted again.

'I told you not to speak up for him!'

'But I have every intention of doing so. Yes . . . I was there that day and I saw my mother as pale as a corpse as she watched you, drunk, cup the breasts of your little bride in your hands and proudly caress her belly. And Alexander saw Mother too and he truly loves her. Is there some reason why he shouldn't? Should he wipe her from his life in the same way you have?'

Philip went wild with anger. 'It's her. It's Olympias who has turned you against me! Isn't that it?' he shouted, red with anger. 'You're all against me now!'

Cleopatra threw herself at his feet and hugged his knees. 'It's not true, it's not true, Father, all we want is for you to come back to your senses. Alexander has certainly made mistakes . . .' and with these words Philip seemed to quieten down for a moment. 'But don't you understand?

Can't you just make one attempt to understand your son? What would you have done in his place? If someone in public had treated you as if you were illegitimate . . . a bastard? Wouldn't you have defended your own and your mother's honour? Isn't that what you had always taught your son to do? And now that he resembles you, now that he behaves in the way you had always expected him to, you reject him. You wanted Achilles!' continued Cleopatra, turning her face, moist with tears, towards her father. 'You wanted Achilles and you've got him. Alexander's wrath is Achilles' wrath, Father!'

'Fine! If Alexander's is Achilles' wrath, then mine is the wrath of Zeus himself!'

'But he loves you, he loves you and he is suffering because of all this, I know . . .' and she sobbed as she fell to the floor.

Philip looked at her in silence for a moment, tightening his lips. Then he turned to leave.

'Get ready,' he said when he reached the door. 'The wedding will take place in six months' time,' and he left.

Eumenes saw Philip return to his study with his troubles written all over his face, but he acted as though nothing were wrong and continued down the corridor, his arms full of rolls of papyrus.

Then, as soon as he heard the door shut, he turned back and put his ear to it. The King was crying.

33

EUMENES WALKED AWAY in silence to his own room in the royal archives. He sat and thought for a long time with his elbows on his desk and his head in his hands. Then he made his decision.

He picked up a small packet from the archive, settled his cloak on his shoulders, passed his hand through his hair, went out again into the corridor and walked straight to the King's study.

He took a deep breath and knocked.

'Who is it?'

'Eumenes.'

'Come in.'

Eumenes entered and closed the door behind him. Philip's head was bent over a document there in front of him.

'Sire, we have received a proposal of marriage.'

The King suddenly lifted his head. His face was haggard and his single remaining eye was red with fatigue, with anger, with crying.

'Who's it from?' he asked.

'The Persian Satrap who is also King of Caria, Pixodarus, he offers his daughter's hand to a prince of the royal house.'

'Tell him to forget it. I don't deal with the Persians.'

'Sire, I really think you should. Pixodarus isn't exactly Persian. He governs a coastal province of Asia Minor for the Great King and controls the fortress of Halicarnassus. If you are preparing to cross the Straits, this marriage may well constitute an important strategic move. Especially now that the Persian throne is still in uncertain hands.'

'Perhaps you're right. My army will set out in a few days.'

'All the more reason.'

'Who would you choose?'

'Well . . . I was thinking of . . .'

'Arrhidaeaus. That's who we'll give them. My son Arrhidaeaus is a halfwit, he isn't capable of creating trouble. And if he can't manage the bed chamber stuff, I'll take care of the bride personally. What's she like?'

Eumenes took a small portrait on a tablet from the bag, certainly the work of a Greek painter, and showed it to him.

'She looks very pretty, but you can never trust these things; then when you see them in real life you get the fright of your life . . .'

'What shall I do?'

'Write and tell them that I am moved and honoured by the proposal and that for the girl I have chosen the valiant Prince Arrhidaeaus – young, courageous in battle, of high sensibility and all the rest of that waffle you're so good at writing. Then bring me the letter to sign.'

'It is a wise decision, Sire. I will take care of it immediately,' said Eumenes as he made for the door. But then he stopped, as though he had suddenly remembered something very important. 'May I ask you a question, Sire?'

Philip looked at him with suspicion written all over his face. 'About what?'

'Who will command the army you are sending to Asia?'

'Attalus and Parmenion.'

'Excellent. Parmenion is a great soldier and Attalus . . .'

Philip stared at him pointedly.

'I wanted to say that sending Attalus away might favour . . .'

'One word more and I'll have your tongue cut out.'

Eumenes continued undeterred: 'It's time you called your son back here, Sire. There are many good reasons.'

'Silence!' shouted Philip.

'Firstly, and above all else, it makes sense politically: how can you possibly convince the Greeks that they should live peacefully in a common alliance when you can't even keep the peace in your own family?'

'Silence!' the King roared, banging his fist loudly on the table.

Eumenes felt his heart shrink and was certain his time had come, but he thought that in such a desperate situation it made sense to continue and die like a man and so, 'Secondly, from a purely personal point of view, we all miss the boy terribly, your own self more than anyone, Sire.'

'One more word and I'll have the guards lock you up.'

'And Alexander himself is suffering terribly because of all this.'

'Guards!' shouted Philip. 'Guards!'

'I assure you, it's true. And Princess Cleopatra is permanently in tears as well.'

The guards entered with their weapons rattling.

'I have a letter here from Alexander in which . . .'
The guards were just about to grab hold of him.

Alexander to Eumenes, Hail!

Philip made a gesture to stop his men.

I was glad to hear the things you wrote about my
father – that he is well and that he is about to begin
the great expedition against the barbarians in Asia.

The King made another gesture and the guards left the
room.

But having said this, the news also brings me great
sadness.

Eumenes stopped and looked at the King: he was in
some sort of shock, overcome by strong emotion, and his
tired cyclops eye shone out from under his frowning
forehead like a dying ember.
'Continue,' he said.

My dream has always been to follow my father in
this grand enterprise and to ride by his side to show
him how much I have tried, throughout my life, to
live up to his valour and his greatness as King of
Macedon.
    Unfortunately, circumstances led me to make an
irreparable gesture and anger pushed me beyond the
limits that a son should always respect.
    But certainly there is a god who wills such things,
because when men lose control of their actions, then
they do the things they are destined to do.
    My friends are all well, but, like me, they are

downcast because of the distance between us and our homeland and our dear ones; and you, good Eumenes, are most certainly among them. Help the King as much as you can. Unfortunately I cannot help him at all. Keep your spirits up.

Eumenes put the letter down and looked at Philip who had covered his face with his hands.

'I took the liberty . . .' he began again after a while.

The King lifted his head suddenly. 'What liberty exactly have you taken?'

'Of preparing a letter . . .'

'By Zeus! I will kill this Greek, I will kill him with my own hands!'

Eumenes at that moment felt like the captain of a ship who, after having struggled for a long time with the waves in the midst of a storm – the sails torn, the hull battered – was now nearing harbour, but still a last almighty effort was required from his exhausted crew. He drew a deep breath, took another sheet from the pack and started reading under Philip's incredulous gaze.

Philip, King of Macedon, to Alexander, Hail!

What happened on the day of my wedding has been for me a fount of infinite bitterness and I had decided, despite the affection which ties me to you, to exclude you from my presence for ever. But time is a great healer and it soothes the sharpest pains.

I have reflected for a long time on what happened and, convinced as I am that those who are older and have more experience should provide examples for young people who are often blinded by their passions,

I have decided to put an end to the exile to which I had condemned you.

The same exile is hereby also revoked for those of your friends who, greatly offending me, decided to follow you.

It is a father's clemency which here reigns over the rigour of the judge and the Sovereign. In exchange I ask you only to express your regret for the outrage I had to endure and to assure me that your filial love will prevent any such situation arising in the future.

Take good care of yourself.

Eumenes stood motionless in the middle of the room, his mouth open, not knowing at that stage what to expect. Philip said nothing, but it was obvious he was seeking to conceal the emotional turmoil in which he found himself. Indeed, he held his head in such a way that Eumenes could see only his blind, tearless eye.

'What do you think, Sire?' Eumenes finally found the courage to ask.

'I couldn't have written it better myself.'

'In that case, if you would be so kind as to sign it . . .'

Philip put out his hand, picked up a reed pen and dipped it in the ink, but then stopped as his anxious secretary watched on.

'Is there anything wrong, Sire?'

'No, no,' said the King as he signed the letter. Immediately, however, he turned the sheet over and started scribbling away with the pen in a corner at the bottom. Eumenes took the missive once more, dusted it down with ash, blew the excess off and, bowing, made for the door, rapidly and light-footed, before the King changed his mind.

'One moment,' Philip called him back.

He had changed his mind.

Eumenes stopped. 'Yes, Sire?'

'Where will you send that letter?'

'Well . . . I took the liberty of maintaining contacts, of discreetly collecting some information . . .'

Philip shook his head. 'A spy . . . that's who I pay for looking after my administration. I will strangle this Greek, sooner or later. By Zeus, I swear I will choke the life out of him with these hands!'

Eumenes hurriedly managed another bow and left the room. As he rushed towards his study his eyes fell on the words the King had added below his signature.

Try it just once more and I really will kill you.
    I miss you.
        Father

34

ATTALUS AND PARMENION moved into Asia without meeting any resistance and the Greek cities of the eastern shore welcomed them as liberators, dedicating statues to the King of Maccdon and preparing great celebrations.

The news coming in from his informers now pleased Philip – the timing of his expedition into Asia could not have been better. The Persian empire was still in difficulty due to its recent dynastic crisis, while Philip had at his disposal a powerful national army, unique in terms of valour, loyalty, cohesion and determination, and a group of generals of the highest tactical and strategic calibre, trained in his school of warfare. He was also equipped with an heir to the throne who had been educated according to the ideals of Homer and in full respect of the rationality of philosophical thought – a proud and invincible Prince.

And now the moment had come to set off on the last and greatest adventure of his life. The decision had been taken and everything was ready. He would welcome Alexander back to the fold, strengthen ties with the realm of Epirus through the unforgettably extravagant wedding of his daughter Cleopatra with his brother-in-law and then he would join his navy beyond the Straits for the great leap.

And yet, now that everything seemed to have been resolved, everything seemed to be proceeding well, now that Alexander had sent word saying that he would soon be at Pella and would be present for the grand event of his sister's wedding, Philip felt a strange sense of anxiety which kept him awake at night.

One day, early in spring, he sent for Eumenes, telling him to go to the stables and to be ready for a horse ride: there were things to discuss. This was an unusual request, but his secretary of course accepted the idea and kitted himself out with Thracian trousers, a Scythian jerkin, boots and a hat with a wide brim; he had the squires prepare an old mule, quiet and easy to ride, and was ready and waiting when Philip arrived.

'Where do you think you're off to? To conquer Scythia?' said the King, looking at him askance.

'My valet gave me some advice, Sire.'

'Yes. I can see that. Come on, let's get going,' and the King spurred his charger into a gallop, disappearing down a path that led out of the city.

The peasants were already in the fields, weeding the wheat and the millet and tending to the vines.

'Look around you!' exclaimed Philip as he brought his horse to walking pace. 'Just look around you! In one single generation I have transformed a semi-barbaric, mountain people, shepherds basically, into a nation of farmers who live in towns and villages with efficient, orderly administrations. I have given them the pride of belonging to their country. I have forged them as the blacksmith forges metal, I have made invincible warriors out of them. And Alexander repudiated me because I got a bit drunk, he accused me of being incapable of stepping from one bed to another . . .'

'Stop fretting about it, Sire. You have both suffered. It's true that Alexander said some things he shouldn't have, but he has been severely punished for that. You are a great King, the greatest, and he knows this and is proud of the fact, I assure you.'

Philip fell silent and proceeded at a walk. When he came to a stream whose waters ran clear and cold from the snow melting on the mountain tops, he dismounted and sat on a rock, waiting for Eumenes to arrive.

'I'm going away for a while,' he announced to his secretary.

'Away? Where?'

'Alexander won't be back for twenty days or so and I want to go to Delphi.'

'No . . . keep clear of that place, Sire. They'll drag you into another sacred war.'

'There will be no more war in Greece for as long as I am alive, neither sacred nor profane. I'm not planning on going to the council of the sanctuary. I am going to the sanctuary.'

'To the sanctuary?' Eumenes repeated in amazement. 'But, Sire, the sanctuary is yours. The oracle says what you want it to say.'

'Do you think so?'

The day was beginning to warm up. Eumenes took off his jerkin, dipped a handkerchief in the water and wiped his forehead.

'I don't understand you. Of all people you ask me this question, after you have seen the council manoeuvre the oracle according to its wishes so that the god says things useful for a particular policy or for certain military alliances.'

'That's true. And yet the god, sometimes, manages to tell the truth, despite the falsity and the shamelessness of the men who should serve him. Of this I am certain.' He rested his arms across his knees, lowered his head and listened to the gurgling of the stream.

Eumenes was speechless. What did the King mean? A man who had lived life to every excess, who had witnessed every imaginable type of corruption and duplicity, who had seen human malice at work in all sorts of atrocities – what could this man, covered in scars both visible and invisible, possibly hope to find in the Vale of Delphi?

'Do you know the inscription on the façade of the sanctuary?' the King asked.

'I do, Sire. It says, "Know thyself".'

'And do you know who wrote those words?'

'The god?'

Philip nodded.

'I understand,' said Eumenes, without having understood.

'I'll set off tomorrow. I have left instructions and the royal seal with Antipater. Sort out Alexander's apartments, have his dog and Bucephalas' stable cleaned, polish his armour and make sure that Leptine prepares, as usual, my son's bed and his bath. Everything must be just as it was when he left. But no feasts, no banquets. There is nothing to celebrate. We are both full of grief.'

Eumenes nodded. 'Don't worry, Sire. Everything will

be taken care of as you have asked for and in the best possible way.'

'I know,' murmured Philip. He clapped a hand on his secretary's shoulder before leaping onto his horse and disappearing off at a gallop.

*

He left the following day at dawn with a small escort, and took the road to the south, crossing the Plain of Macedon before entering Thessaly. He reached Delphi from Phocis after seven days' journey and found the city full, as it always was, of pilgrims.

They came from all parts of the world, even Sicily and the Adriatic gulf where the city of Spina stood on an island in the middle of the sea. Along the sacred road leading to the sanctuary there were many small temples dedicated to Apollo from the various Greek cities, adorned with sculptures, and often in front of them or to the side there were spectacular statuary groups in bronze or in painted marble.

There were many stalls full of merchandise – animals to be offered sacrificially, statues of all sizes for consecration in the sanctuary, and reproductions in bronze or terracotta of the statue of the god inside the temple, or of other masterpieces nearby.

Alongside the sanctuary was the gigantic tripod of the god with an enormous bronze bowl standing on three twisted serpents, also of bronze, melted from the arms the Athenians took from the Persians at the battle of Plataea.

Philip queued up with the postulants, covering his head with the hood of his cloak, but it was impossible to hide anything from the priests of Apollo. Soon the news passed from mouth to mouth, from the servants to the ministrants of the cult hidden away in the darkness of the interior, secret part of the temple.

'The King of Macedon, head of the sanctuary council, is here,' announced a young, breathless follower of the cult.

'Are you sure of this?' asked the priest who that day had the job of ministering the functions of the cult and the oracle.

'It is not easy to mistake Philip of Macedon for another man.'

'What does he want?'

'He is queuing up with the postulants and wants to question the god.'

The priest sighed. 'This is incredible. Why were we not warned? We cannot be taken off guard by the request of such a powerful man . . . Quick!' he ordered. 'Put out the insignias of the sanctuary council and bring him to me immediately. The victor of the sacred war, supreme head of the council, has absolute precedence here.'

The youngster disappeared through a small side door. The priest put on his vestments, wrapped the sacred bands round his head, leaving them to fall down to his shoulders, and then entered the temple.

The god Apollo was there before him, sitting on his throne, his face and his hands of ivory, a crown of silver laurel leaves on his head, his eyes of mother of pearl. The enormous simulacrum wore an astonished expression, absent in the fixity of its gaze, and its lips opened slightly in an enigmatic, at times scornful smile. A brazier at its feet burned incense and the smoke rose in a bluish cloud up to an opening among the joists of the ceiling through which a small piece of sky could be seen.

A band of light came in through the entrance, slicing the darkness of the interior, striking the gilded profiles of the Doric columns and illuminating a myriad of particles suspended in the dense, heavy air.

Suddenly a massive figure stood in the doorway, his shadow falling long, almost to the priest's feet. He advanced towards the statue of the god and the limping steps of his studded footwear resounded through the deep silence of the sanctuary.

The priest went towards him and recognized the King of Macedon. 'What are your wishes, Sire?' he asked deferentially.

Philip lifted his eyes to the impassive gaze of the statue that loomed there before him. 'I wish to question the god.'

'And what is your question?'

Philip gave the priest a look from his only eye, a look that must have penetrated his soul, if he had a soul.

'I will ask my question of the Pythia directly. Take me to her.'

The priest lowered his head in confusion, surprised at this request which was impossible to deny.

'Are you sure you wish to expose yourself directly to the voice of Apollo? Many are those who have not been able to bear the experience. It can be sharper than a war horn, stronger than thunder . . .'

'I will bear it,' replied Philip peremptorily. 'Take me to the Pythia.'

'As you wish,' replied the priest. He moved towards a

bronze triangle hanging from a column and struck it with his staff. The metallic sound bounced off the walls in a complex game of echoes until it reached the most intimate and most secret sanctum of the entire temple: the *adyton*.

'Follow me,' he said when the sound had died away, and he started walking.

They passed behind the pedestal of the statue and stopped in front of a bronze sheet which covered the rear wall of the cell. The priest struck it with his staff, creating a dark reverberation which seemed to be swallowed up by an invisible subterranean space. Then the sheet of bronze turned silently, revealing a narrow stairway that plunged steeply underground.

'No one, during the course of this generation, has ever entered here,' continued the priest without turning round. Philip went down the steep, uneven steps until he found himself at the centre of a hypogeum, an underground chamber poorly lit by a few lamps.

At that moment, from the total darkness of the far wall, there entered a dishevelled figure covered by a long red gown reaching to her feet. Her face was ashen pale and her heavily made-up eyes moved rapidly, full of suspicion, like a hunted animal. Two ministrants held her, almost carrying her towards a sort of bowl on a tripod. They placed her inside it.

Then they struggled to open a stone hatch in the floor, uncovering the mouth of an abyss from which pestilentially smelly vapours began to exude.

'This is the *chasma ghes*,' said the priest, his voice

trembling, this time without any pretence, in sheer terror. 'This is the fount of night, the last mouth of primeval chaos. No one knows where it ends and no one who has ever gone down there has ever come back.' He picked up a pebble from the rough floor of the cave and threw it into the opening. There was no sound at all.

'The god is about to penetrate the body of the Pythia. He is about to fill her with his presence. Watch.'

The seer inhaled the vapours that came out of the chasm and her breath came in fits and spasms that tormented her body and at moments she writhed inside the bowl, letting her arms and legs hang loose, showing the whites of her eyes. Then, suddenly, she began trembling in pain and gave out a sort of rattle that became sharper and sharper until it was like the hiss of a snake. One of the ministrants put a hand on her chest and nodded to the priest.

'You may question the god now, King Philip. The god is present now,' said the priest in a quiet voice.

Philip moved forward until he was almost touching the Pythia's hand.

'Oh god, we are preparing a solemn rite in my house and I am about to avenge the outrage that the barbarians once inflicted upon the temples of the gods in our lands. But my heart is leaden and my sleep is troubled by nightmares. What is the answer to my worry?'

The Pythia let out a long moan, then, slowly, she lifted herself up, leaning on both hands, until her head was at the edge of the bowl and she started speaking, with a strange, trembling and metallic voice:

'Wreathed is the bull.

All is done.

Ready is the one who will smite him.'*

Then she fell backwards, motionless and inert like a lifeless body.

Philip looked at her for a moment in silence, then he turned to the stairway and disappeared in the pale light that came down from above.

* Diodorus Siculus, XVI.91.2.

35

THE MESSENGER ARRIVED in the middle of the night at a gallop, leaped to the ground in front of the guard house and gave his sweaty mount, its flanks lathered, to one of the squires.

Eumenes, who always slept lightly, immediately got up, threw a cloak around his shoulders, took a lamp and went down the stairs to go and meet him.

'Come,' he ordered as soon as he saw him enter under the portico, and he led him towards the armoury. 'Where is the King now?' he asked as the man followed him, still breathless.

'He is a day's march away, no more. You know why I lost time on my journey.'

'All right, all right,' Eumenes cut him short as he unlocked a small iron-clad door. 'Come in here, we won't be disturbed.'

It was a large, bare room, a storehouse for weapons that were due for repair. Along one side were two or three stools arranged around a stump that was used as an anvil. Eumenes handed one to his companion and sat down in his turn.

'What have you found out?'

'It wasn't easy and it cost me a lot. I had to bribe two of the ministrants who have access to the *adyton*.'

'Well?'

'King Philip's arrival took them by surprise, he almost succeeded in hiding himself, queuing up with the other postulants until someone recognized him and then he was taken directly to the sanctuary. When the priests realized that he wanted to question the oracle, they tried to have the question first so as to prepare a suitable answer.'

'That's normal practice.'

'Indeed. But the King refused: he asked to consult the Pythia directly and wanted them to lead him to the *adyton*.'

Eumenes covered his face with his hands. 'Oh! Great Zeus!'

'The priest who was officiating that day didn't even have the time to inform the council. He had no choice but to agree to his request. Therefore Philip was accompanied to the *adyton* and he put his question to the Pythia once she had entered her ecstatic state.'

'Are you sure?'

'Absolutely sure.'

'And what was her response?'

'Wreathed is the bull. All is done. Ready is the one who will smite him.'

'Nothing else?' asked Eumenes, his face darkening.

The man shook his head.

Eumenes took a purse full of money from his cloak and handed it to his informer. 'It's what I'd promised, but I am sure you must have kept the change after paying off the ministrant.'

'But I . . .'

'Forget it, I know how these things work. Just remember that if you breathe as much as one word about this, even if you find yourself only tempted to speak about it with someone, have no fear that I will find you wherever you are and I will make you regret ever having been born.'

The man picked up the money, swearing and promising that he would never speak about it to anyone, and he left.

Eumenes was alone in the big, empty, cold room, in the lamplight, and he thought for a long time on an interpretation of the oracle's response that might be a good omen for his King. Then he too left the room and returned to his bed chamber, but he didn't manage to get back to sleep.

*

Philip reached the palace the following day, late in the afternoon. Eumenes used the excuse of some documents to be signed to make sure he was there to meet him.

'May I ask you about the outcome of your mission, Sire?' he asked as he was passing the sheets to him one by one.

Philip lifted his head and turned towards him. 'I'd bet ten silver talents against a pile of dogshit that you know already.'

'Me, Sire? Oh, no, I'm not as clever as all that. No, these are delicate matters, there's nothing to joke about here.'

Philip stretched out his left hand for another document and pressed the seal onto it.

'Wreathed is the bull. All is done. Ready is the one who will smite him.'

'Was that the response, Sire? But that's extraordinary, it's magnificent! Just now when you're planning to move into Asia! The new emperor of the Persians has just been crowned and what is the symbol of Persepolis, the capital? The bull, the winged bull. There is no doubt, he's the bull. So his end is nigh because the one who will smite it, the one who will sacrifice the bull, is ready. And you are the one who will smite it. The oracle has seen your imminent victory over the Persian empire.

'In fact, Sire, shall I tell you what I think? It's too good to be true. I'm afraid the priests, tricksters as they are, must have concocted a tailor-made reply for you. But it is still a good omen, don't you think?'

'They didn't concoct anything. I arrived there suddenly, I took a ministrant of the cult by the collar, I made him open the *adyton* and I saw the Pythia, out of her mind, her eyes white, her mouth foaming as she inhaled the vapours from the *chasma*.'

Eumenes nodded repeatedly. 'Certainly . . . a lightning manoeuvre, worthy of your own self. Anyway, better still if the reply was a genuine one.'

'Exactly.'

'Alexander will arrive in a couple of days' time.'

'Good.'

'Will you go to meet him at the old border?'

'No. I will wait for him here.'

'May I go with Callisthenes?'

'Yes, of course.'

'Perhaps I could also take Philotas with a dozen guardsmen. Just a small escort of honour . . .'

Philip agreed.

'Good, Sire. Well, if there's nothing else, I'll be off,' said Eumenes as he gathered his documents and started to leave.

'Do you know what my soldiers used to call me when I was young, when I used to go through two women in one night?'

Eumenes turned to look at the King's wounded gaze.

'They used to call me "the Bull".'

Eumenes was lost for words. He reached the door and went out, bowing hurriedly.

*

The small welcoming party reached the Beroea road where they crossed the old frontier of the realm of Amyntas I. Near the Haliakmon ford Eumenes signalled to the others to stop because Alexander and his troop had no choice but to cross the river there.

They all dismounted and left their horses free to graze on the grass. Some members of the escort pulled out their water flasks to quench their thirst, others, given the time of day, took bread, cheese, olives and dried figs from their satchels and sat on the ground to eat. One of the men was sent up a nearby hill to look out for Alexander.

They spent several hours there and the sun began to descend towards the horizon, over towards the Pindus mountains, and still there was no sign of anything happening.

'It's a terrible road, believe me,' Callisthenes was saying. 'It's teeming with brigands. I wouldn't be surprised if . . .'

'Oh, the brigands!' exclaimed Philotas. 'But that lot eat brigands for breakfast. They've survived a winter up in the mountains of Illyria, do you know what that means?'

But Eumenes was looking up at the hill and at the lookout who had started waving a red cloth.

'They're on their way,' he announced, almost in a whisper.

Shortly after, the lookout fired an arrow that landed in the ground not far from them.

'That means they're all present,' said the secretary. 'Not one of them is missing.' And he said this as though he didn't really believe what he was saying. The lookout in the meantime had come back down.

'Men! On your mounts!' Philotas ordered, and all twelve of the horsemen leaped onto their chargers and arranged themselves along the road, spears in hand.

Eumenes and Callisthenes, without their horses, set off walking along the road just as Alexander and his troop appeared from a declivity of the hill.

All eight advanced side by side and the rays of the sun as it set behind them wrapped them in a halo of purple light, a gilded cloud. The distance and the drumming of their gallop in the light-filled dust created a strange optical effect, as though they were riding suspended in the air, as if they came from another time, from a magic, far-off place, from the ends of the earth.

They reached the riverbank at full tilt and threw themselves at top speed into the ford, as though unable to bear being separated from their homeland for one instant more. The horses' hooves, in the wild churning of the water, lifted up an iridescent spray coloured by the dying rays of the great setting globe.

Eumenes wiped the arm of his tunic across his eyes and blew his nose noisily. His voice trembled. 'Oh gods above . . . it is them . . . it is them.'

Then a figure with long golden hair, shining in its

glowing copper armour, leaped from the water in a boiling of spray and spume, leaving the group behind and plunging into a breakneck gallop astride a stallion whose hooves made the earth tremble.

Philotas shouted, 'Guard . . . attention!' And the twelve warriors lined up one next to the other, their heads held high, their backs straight, the points of their spears directed skyward.

Eumenes could not contain his emotion.

'Alexander . . .' he stammered through his tears. 'Alexander is back.'

36

Eumenes and Callisthenes accompanied Alexander all the way to the threshold of the King's study. Eumenes knocked, and when he heard Philip's voice inviting his son to enter, he put a hand on his friend's shoulder and said, somewhat embarrassedly, 'If your father should make mention of the letter you wrote to me, don't show any surprise. I took the liberty of making the first move in your name, otherwise you would still be up a mountain in a snowdrift.'

Alexander looked at him in amazement, finally realizing what had happened, but at that point all he could do was enter Philip's study and enter he did.

He found his father there before him and he saw that he had aged a great deal. Although his exile had lasted a little less than a year, it seemed to him that the furrows across Philip's forehead were deeper and his hair was turning white prematurely.

He spoke first: 'I am glad to find you in good health, Father.'

'And you,' replied Philip. 'You look more substantial and I am happy you have returned. Are your friends well?'

'Yes, they are all well.'

'Sit down.'

Alexander obeyed. The King picked up a jug and two cups: 'Some wine?'

'Yes, thank you.'

Philip moved nearer and Alexander found himself face to face with his father; now he saw his dead eye and now there was no doubt about the fatigue sculpted over his forehead.

'To your health, Father, and to the enterprise you are embarking on in Asia. I have heard about the great prophecy of the god at Delphi.'

Philip nodded and took some wine.

'How is your mother?'

'She was well, last time I saw her.'

'Will she come to Cleopatra's wedding?'

'I hope so.'

'Me too.'

They stood in silence staring at one another and both of them felt a strong desire to abandon themselves to their feelings, but they were also two men hardened by much pain and resentment, by a moment of rage that had passed now but which was still terribly alive. Father and son were aware that at that precise moment they could easily have fallen to blows to the point of spilling each other's blood.

'Go and say hello to Cleopatra,' Philip said suddenly, breaking the silence. 'She has missed you very much.'

Alexander nodded and left the room.

Eumenes and Callisthenes were positioned at the end of the corridor, waiting for an explosion of either violence or joy: the unreal silence left them puzzled.

'What do you think?' asked Callisthenes.

'The King said to me, "No feasts, no banquets. There is

nothing to celebrate. We are both crippled by grief." That's what he said to me.'

Alexander walked through the palace as though he were in a dream. As he went by everybody smiled and nodded, but no one dared approach him or speak to him.

Suddenly a loud barking came from the great courtyard and Peritas came rushing into the internal portico like a fury unleashed. He leaped up on Alexander, almost dashing him to the ground, and continued barking and making a general fuss.

The young Prince was moved by the animal's demonstration of its affection for him – so open and enthusiastic – in front of everyone. He petted him for a long time, scratching his ears and trying to calm him. Argus, Ulysses' dog, came to mind, the only one who recognized the hero on his return after many years away, and Alexander felt his eyes moisten.

His sister threw her arms around him crying in full flood as soon as she saw him in the doorway of her room.

'My child . . .' Alexander murmured as he held her to him.

'I've cried so much . . . I've cried so much . . .' the girl sobbed.

'That's enough. I'm back now and I'm even hungry. I was rather hoping you might invite me to stay for supper.'

'Of course!' exclaimed Cleopatra, drying her tears and sniffing. 'Come in.'

She had him sit down and gave orders for the tables to be laid immediately and for a basin to be brought so that her brother might wash his hands, his arms and his feet.

'Will Mother come to my wedding?' she asked when they were reclining to eat.

'I hope so. Her daughter and her brother are getting married to each other – she should be there. And then perhaps Father would be pleased if she came.'

Cleopatra seemed encouraged by this and they talked about all they had been through in the year during which they had been separated from each other. The Princess shivered every time her brother told her about a particularly exciting adventure or about dangerous chases through the rocky gorges of the Illyrian mountains.

Now and then Alexander would interrupt his stories to ask her about herself and how she was planning to dress for the wedding and what her life would be like in the palace at Buthrotum. Or he would sit quietly and look at her, with his light smile and that curious way he had of leaning his head towards his right shoulder.

'Poor Perdiccas,' he said at a certain point, as though suddenly plunged into serious thought. 'He's hopelessly in love with you and when he heard about your wedding he fell into despair.'

'I am sorry. He's a fine young man.'

'More than fine. One day he will be one of the best Macedonian generals, if I know anything about my men. But there's nothing to be done about it all – everyone has his or her own destiny written.'

'Quite,' said Cleopatra as she nodded.

A sudden silence came over the two young people who had been laughing together after their long separation. Each one sat listening to the voice of his or her own feelings.

'I am sure you will be happy with your husband,' Alexander began again. 'He's intelligent and young and brave and can dream. For him you will be like a dew-kissed flower, like the smile of spring, like a pearl mounted in gold.'

Cleopatra looked at him, her eyes moist with tears. 'Is that how you see me, brother of mine?'

'That's it. And I'm sure that's how he must see you too, I'm certain.' He brushed her cheek with a kiss and left.

It was late now as he returned to his room for the first time in a year: he smelled the fragrance of the flowers that adorned it and the perfume of his bath.

The lamps spread a warm, collected light. His strigil, his comb and his razor were all lined up in order alongside the bathtub and Leptine was sitting on a stool dressed only in a short *chiton*.

She ran to him as soon as he entered and threw herself at his feet, hugging his knees, covering them with kisses and tears.

'Don't you want to help me have my bath?' Alexander asked her.

'Yes . . . yes of course, Sire. Straight away.'

She undressed him and waited while he got into the big tub, then she began rubbing him gently with the sponge. She washed his straight, soft hair, dried it and over his head poured a precious oil that had been brought all the way from distant Arabia.

When he came out of the water she covered him with a towel and had him lie down on his bed. Then she too undressed and massaged him for a long time to loosen his limbs, but she didn't use perfume because there was nothing more beautiful and pleasant than the natural scent of his skin. When she saw that he had let himself go and his eyes were beginning to close, she lay down alongside him, naked and warm, and began kissing him all over.

37

EURYDICE GAVE BIRTH to a boy towards the end of spring, not long before the date fixed for the wedding of Cleopatra and Alexander of Epirus. The new arrival made the already difficult relations between the Prince and his father even more strained.

The misunderstandings and the disagreements increased, aggravated by Philip's decision to keep his son's closest friends at a safe distance from the court, in particular Hephaestion, Perdiccas, Ptolemy and Seleucus.

Philotas, who at that moment was in Asia, had been rather cold with Alexander following his return. He even started spending time with his cousin Amyntas, who had been heir to the throne before Alexander's birth.

All of these facts, together with his lost sense of familiarity with court life and an acute feeling of isolation, created in Alexander a dangerous sense of insecurity which in its turn pushed him towards clumsy initiatives and unjustifiable behaviour.

When he learned that Philip had put forward his mentally deficient half-brother Arrhidaeus as husband of the daughter of the Satrap of Caria, he simply didn't know what to think. In the end, after much thought and having decided that the King's manoeuvre was in some way linked to the expedition to Asia, he sent a messenger to Pixodarus offering to marry the girl himself. The King heard of Alexander's initiative from his informers, however, and flew into a tremendous rage. The proposed matrimonial alliance – a project which was already tottering – had to be abandoned.

Eumenes gave Alexander the bad news.

'But why on earth did you do such a thing?' he asked him. 'Why didn't you speak to me . . . why didn't you tell me about your ideas? I would have told you that . . .'

'What, exactly, would you have told me?' Alexander snapped, worried and resentful. 'All you ever do is follow my father's orders! You never speak to me, you keep me in the dark about everything!'

'You're out of your mind,' Eumenes replied. 'But how can you ever imagine that Philip would waste his heir to the throne by marrying him off to the daughter of a servant of his sworn enemy, the King of the Persians?'

'I no longer know if I am Philip's heir. He has never told me, he tells me nothing. All his time is taken up with his new wife and his newborn son. And you . . . you have all abandoned me too. You're all afraid of spending time with me because you think that when it comes to it I will no longer be the King's heir! Look around you: how many children does my father have? Someone might decide to support Amyntas – after all, he was heir before my birth, and recently Philotas has been spending much more time with him than with me. And didn't Attalus suggest that his daughter would give birth to the legitimate heir to the throne? Well, now they have a boy.'

Eumenes said nothing. He watched Alexander pacing the room with his long strides, and waited for him to calm down. When he saw the Prince stop in front of the window and stand there looking out, he spoke: 'You have to face your father, even if he would like to strangle you right now.'

'Don't you see? You're on his side!'

'Stop it! Stop treating me like this! I have always been loyal to your family. I have always sought to keep the peace among you because I believe your father is a great man, the greatest Europe has known in the last hundred years, and also because I love you, you stubborn specimen! Come on then, tell me just one thing I've ever done to harm you, just one letdown I have inflicted upon you in all the years we have known each other! Speak now . . . come on, I'm waiting.'

Alexander could not reply. He wrung his hands and did not turn to face Eumenes so as not to show the tears welling up in his eyes. And with the tears he felt the anger rising, and he was aware that his father's anger still frightened him, just as it had done when he was a boy.

'You must face him. Now. Now that he is furious for this thing you have done. Show him that you are not afraid, that you are a man, that you are worthy of sitting on his throne one day. Admit to your error and apologize. This is what true courage is.'

'All right,' Alexander accepted. 'But remember that Philip has already tried to attack me with his sword drawn once before.'

'He was drunk.'

'And what sort of state is he in now?'

'You are unfair. He has achieved the impossible for you.

Do you have any idea how much he has invested in you? Do you know? I know because I keep the books and I look after his archives.'

'I don't want to know.'

'At least a hundred talents, an incredible sum: one quarter of the treasure of the city of Athens when it was at the height of its splendour.'

'I don't want to know!'

'He lost an eye in battle and will limp for the rest of his days. He has built the greatest empire the world has ever seen west of the Straits – he did that for you and now he's offering you Asia. But you have chosen to obstruct his plans, you resent the few pleasures that a man of his age can still hope to enjoy in life. Go to him, Alexander, and speak to him, before he comes to you.'

'Very well! I will go to him!' and he left, slamming the door behind him.

Eumenes came running after him along the corridor: 'Wait! Wait I say!'

'What is it now?'

'Let me speak to him first.'

Alexander let him past and watched him shaking his head as he rushed off towards the eastern wing of the palace.

Eumenes knocked and entered without waiting for a response.

'What's wrong?' Philip asked, his face thunderous.

'Alexander wants to speak to you.'

'What?'

'Sire, your son is sorry for his actions, but try to understand him – he feels alone and isolated. He no longer feels close to you, he feels he no longer has your affection. Can you not forgive him? After all, he is little more than a boy. He believed you had abandoned him and fear got the upper hand.'

Eumenes had been expecting an explosion of uncontrollable wrath, but he was amazed to see the King perfectly calm. He was almost shocked by this.

'Are you well, Sire?'

'I am fine . . . I am fine. Show him in.'

Eumenes went out and there was Alexander waiting, his face pale.

'Your father is under great strain,' he said. 'He is perhaps even more alone than you are. Remember this.'

The Prince crossed the threshold.

'Why did you do it?' Philip asked.

'I . . .'

'Why?' he shouted.

'Because I felt I had been excluded from your decisions, from your plans, because I was alone, without anyone to help me, to guide me, give me advice. I felt I had to affirm my own dignity, my own self.'

'By offering to marry the daughter of a servant of the King of Persia?'

Eumenes' very words, Alexander thought to himself.

'But why not speak to me?' Philip continued in a calmer tone of voice. 'Why not speak with your father?'

'But you had already chosen Arrhidaeus over me – my halfwit half-brother.'

'Exactly!' shouted Philip, banging his fist on the table. 'Don't you think that means something? Is this how Aristotle taught you to reason?'

Alexander stood there in silence and the King stood up and started limping up and down the room.

'Is the damage I have done so severe?' asked the Prince after a while.

'No,' replied Philip. 'Even though a matrimonial alliance with a Persian satrap would be extremely useful to me just now when I am planning to move into Asia. But there is a solution to every problem.'

'I am sorry. It will not happen again. I will wait for you to let me know what my place will be at Cleopatra's wedding.'

'Your place? A place befitting the heir to the throne, my son. Go to Eumenes, he has everything in hand and has organized the ceremony down to the tiniest detail.'

Alexander's face turned deep red at those words and he found himself wanting to embrace his father as he did when Philip used to come and visit him at Mieza. But he wasn't able to overcome his diffidence and the embarrassment he now felt in his father's presence since the fateful day on which their relations had taken their turn for the worse. Nevertheless, he looked at his father with a pained expression, almost pleading, and Philip understood. He said, 'Now clear off and let me get on.'

*

'Come,' Eumenes invited him. 'You must see what your friend is capable of. This wedding will be my masterpiece. The King has dispensed with masters of ceremony and chamberlains and has entrusted me with all the organization. And now,' he said as he opened a door and gestured for Alexander to enter, 'just look at this!'

The Prince found himself inside one of the two rooms of the royal armouries which had been almost completely emptied to make room for a large table on trestles on top of which there was a scale model of the royal palace in Aegae, with the sanctuaries and the theatre.

The roofs had been taken off the rooms, exposing the interiors with coloured terracotta figures representing the various personages who were to take part in the grand ceremonies.

Eumenes walked forward and picked up a pointer from the table. 'Here,' he explained, indicating a large open room on a colonnaded portico, 'the wedding will take place here and then the great procession, an extraordinary event, something that has never been seen before.

'After the ceremony, while the bride is led by her maids to the nuptial chamber for the ritual bath and the dressing of her hair, the procession will take place. The statues of the twelve gods of Olympus will come first, these statues you see here, carried by the ministrants on their shoulders, and among them will be the statue of your father, symbolic of his devotion to the gods and his function as tutelary leader of all Greeks.

'Then, in the centre, will be the King himself, wearing a white cloak, with a crown of golden oak leaves on his head. A little ahead, on his right, will be your place as heir to the throne, and to the left Alexander of Epirus. You will all proceed towards the theatre. Here it is.

'The guests and the foreign delegations will take their places at dawn and will be entertained up until the arrival of the procession by shows and recitals by famous actors who have been summoned specially from Athens, from

Sycion, and from Corinth, including Thessalus, who I'm told is the actor you admire most.'

*

Alexander rearranged the white cloak on his shoulders and exchanged a quick glance with his uncle. They were both walking slightly ahead of Philip, who was accompanied by his bodyguards. The King of Macedon was dressed in a red tunic, its hem embroidered in gold ovals and palmettes, and over this a rich white cloak, his ivory staff in his right hand, the crown of golden oak leaves on his head. He looked exactly like the small statue Eumenes had shown Alexander in the scale model inside the weapons room.

The royal shoemakers had prepared a pair of tragic actor buskins for him – shoes with very thick soles that were hidden by the hem of his gown and went some way towards correcting his limp and increasing his height.

Eumenes had taken up position on a high wooden structure erected on the highest part of the bowl of the theatre and he signalled to the master of ceremonies using coloured flags to coordinate the impressive procession.

He looked to his right over the large semi-circle, teeming with more people than he ever thought possible, and then, down at the bottom of the access road, he could make out the front of the procession with the statues of the gods. These were wonderfully made by the greatest craftsmen and wore real clothes and real crowns of gold, flanked by their sacred animals, the eagle of Zeus, the owl of Athena, the peacock of Hera, all reproduced with impressive realism – almost as though they might take to the air at any moment.

Behind came the priests decked in their sacred bands, censers in hands, and then a chorus of beautiful young boys as naked as little cupids, singing nuptial songs to the accompaniment of their flutes and drums.

Next came the King preceded by his son and his brother-son-in-law. Bringing up the rear were the seven royal bodyguards in parade dress.

Eumenes gave the signal, the master of ceremonies nodded to the heralds to sound their instruments, and the procession got under way.

It was a splendid sight, which the sun and the extraordinarily clear day made even more spectacular. The beginning of the procession was entering the theatre now and one by one the statues of the gods passed through the semi-circle of the orchestra before being positioned in rows in front of the stage.

As each part of the procession passed under the entrance archway alongside the stage, Eumenes would lose sight of it until it reappeared in the sun inside the theatre.

The priests passed in a cloud of incense and then the young boys dancing and singing their hymns to love for the bride: Eumenes saw them disappear under the arch and re-emerge on the other side among exclamations of wonder from the audience.

Now Alexander of Macedon and Alexander of Epirus passed by and the King came nearer. As planned, Philip gave orders to his bodyguards not to follow him under the arch because he did not want to present himself to the Greeks flanked by his guard like a tyrant.

Eumenes saw the two young men reappear inside the theatre to rapturous applause, just at the moment when the King disappeared into the shadow of the archway on the other side. Out of the corner of his eye he saw the bodyguards pull back and he took a quick look at them, but immediately found himself looking more carefully: there was one missing!

At that very instant Philip emerged into the sun inside the theatre and Eumenes, having realized what was about to happen, started shouting at the top of his voice, but the roar of the public acclamation was too strong. It all happened in a flash: the missing bodyguard suddenly appeared out of the darkness, a short dagger in his hand, jumped on the King and plunged the weapon into his side, right up to the hilt, and then began to run away.

Alexander realized that something terrible was happening by the shocked expression on the faces of the audience. He turned round just an instant after his father had been stabbed and saw his face, suddenly pale like the gods' ivory masks. He saw Philip teeter and hold his side as the blood flowed freely and stained the white cloak.

Behind Philip a man ran off in the direction of the meadows along the road. Alexander hurried towards his father who was falling to his knees now, and Alexander of Epirus ran past them shouting, 'Stop that man!'

Alexander reached Philip before he collapsed into the dust and he held him while the blood flowed strong and red, wetting his clothes, his arms and his hands.

'Father!' he shouted as the sobs came, and he held him tight. 'Father, no!' and Philip felt his son's burning tears on his bloodless cheeks.

The sky above him burst into a myriad bright points of light and then, suddenly, it all went dark. At that moment he saw himself once more at the very centre of a room immersed in darkness while he held a newborn baby to his chest. He felt the smooth skin of the little one against his bristly cheek, felt the baby's lips on his scar-furrowed shoulder and in the air there was an intense perfume of Pierian roses. Then he sank into darkness and silence.

38

THE ASSASSIN, breathless, ran towards a thicket where other men were waiting for him with a horse, obviously accomplices, who galloped off in their turn as soon as they saw that he was being followed.

The man, alone now, turned round and realized they were closing in on him. Alexander of Epirus had thrown off his cloak and was running with his sword drawn and held high in the air, shouting, 'Take him alive! Take him alive!'

He started running again, as fast as he could this time, and then, just a few strides away from his horse, he attempted a flying mount but tripped on the root of a vine and went crashing to the ground. He got up immediately, but the guards were already on him and they ran him through many times, killing him instantly.

As soon as the King of Epirus saw what they had done he shouted at the top of his voice, 'You idiots! I told you to take him alive!'

'But, Sire, he was armed and he tried to attack us.'

'Follow the others!' ordered the King. 'Follow the others at least and get hold of them!'

By this time Alexander had arrived as well, his clothes still stained with Philip's blood. He looked at the assassin and then at the King of Epirus and said, 'I knew him. His name was Pausanias and he was one of my father's bodyguards. Undress him, hang him from a pole at the entrance to the theatre and leave him there to rot until there's nothing left but bones.'

In the meantime a crowd had formed around the body – onlookers, men of the royal guard, army officers and foreign guests.

Alexander immediately returned to the theatre, which was rapidly emptying now, and there he found Cleopatra, still wearing her wedding dress, sobbing in despair over their father's body. Eumenes, standing not far off, his own eyes full of tears and one hand over his mouth, shook his head continually as though simply unable to take in what had happened. There was still no sign of Queen Olympias who had been expected since that morning.

Alexander had the fall-in signal sounded for all the combat units in the surrounding area, then he gave orders to remove his father's body and to prepare for the funeral rites. He had Cleopatra accompanied to her apartments and requested that armour be found for himself and for his brother-in-law.

'Eumenes!' he shouted, rousing his friend from his state of shock. 'Find the royal seal and bring it to me. And send messengers immediately for Hephaestion, Ptolemy, Perdiccas, Seleucus and the others – I want them all here by tomorrow evening.'

The armourers arrived shortly afterwards and the two young men put on their breastplates and greaves, strapped their swords and scabbards on and set off through the crowd, followed by a group of select troops, to occupy the palace. All the members of the royal family were put under strict guard in their quarters, with the exception of Amyntas who appeared dressed in his armour and ready to follow Alexander's orders: 'You can count on me and my loyalty. I want no more blood to be spilled.'

'Thank you,' replied Alexander. 'I will not forget this gesture.'

The gates of the city were occupied by groups of shieldsmen and cavalry units. Philotas voluntarily reported to the palace and immediately asked for his orders.

Halfway through the afternoon, Alexander, flanked by the King of Epirus and his cousin Amyntas, appeared before the assembled army. He was armed and dressed in a royal cloak and crown. The message was loud and clear.

The officers had the trumpets sound and the men shouted their salute:

'Hail, Alexander, King of Macedon!'

Then, at another signal, they started banging their spears against their shields, so that the porticoes of the palace resounded with a deafening clangour.

Having received the salute from the assembled divisions, Alexander gave orders for Bucephalas to be prepared and made ready for departure. Then he summoned Eumenes and Callisthenes, who had also been present at the ceremony.

'Eumenes, you will take care of my father. Make sure he is washed and embalmed so that his body is well preserved until the funeral, which you yourself will organize. And you will receive my mother, should she arrive. Call an architect and have work begin as soon as possible on the royal tomb.

'Callisthenes, you will stay here and find out everything you can about the assassin. Look for his friends, his accomplices, try to find out where he went and what he did in the hours before the killing. Interrogate the guards who killed the assassin against my brother-in-law's orders. If necessary, use torture.'

Eumenes came forward and handed a small casket to Alexander: 'The royal seal, Sire.'

Alexander took it, opened it and slipped the ring onto his finger. 'Do you love me, Eumenes? Are you loyal to me?'

'Of course, Sire.'

'In that case you must continue to call me Alexander.'

He went out into the parade ground, leaped astride Bucephalas and, leaving a garrison at Aegae under Philotas' orders, left with his brother-in-law for Pella to take possession of the throne and to demonstrate to the court nobles that he was the new King.

At that stage of the fateful day the theatre was completely empty. Only the statues of the gods remained, abandoned on their pedestals, and, in the diminishing light of the sunset, the statue of Philip whose expression had the same fixed stare as a forgotten divinity.

Suddenly, as darkness began to fall, a shadow seemed to appear from nowhere – a man, his head covered by the hood of his cloak, entered the deserted arena and spent a long time examining the bloodstain that was still there on the ground. Then he turned back and passed through the archway adjacent to the stage. His eyes were drawn to a metal object, bloody and half-hidden in the sand. He bent over to study it with his small, grey, darting eyes, then he picked it up and hid it away among the folds of his cloak.

He proceeded out into the open and stopped in front of the pole to which the assassin's body had been nailed. Everything was wrapped in darkness now and out of it came a voice behind him:

'Uncle Aristotle, I never imagined I'd find you here.'

'Callisthenes. A day that was supposed to have been so full of joy has ended up in such sadness.'

'Alexander had hoped to see you once again, but so much has happened so quickly . . .'

'I know. I am sorry too. Where is he now?'

'He is on horseback, leading his troops towards Pella. He wants to make sure there is no possibility of a coup on the part of some groups in the nobility. But what are you doing here? This is not an edifying sight.'

'Regicide is always a critical point in human events. And, as far as I have heard, there was a premonition from the oracle at Delphi: "Wreathed is the bull. All is done. Ready is the one who will smite him."' And then, turning to Pausanias' mutilated body, 'Here he is, the one who smote the bull. Who would have thought that this was the meaning of the prophecy!'

'Alexander has asked me to investigate the crime,' said Callisthenes, 'to try to discover who was behind the assassination of his father.' Far off in the distance, from the sanctums of the palace, came the lugubrious wailing of the mourners crying for the death of the King. 'Would you like to help me?' Callisthenes asked. 'Everything seems so absurd.'

'That is the key to the crime,' affirmed Aristotle. 'Its very absurdity. Why on earth choose such a public form – an assassination in a theatre, like a scene in a tragedy interpreted in real life, with real blood and . . .' he pulled something from the folds of his cloak, '. . . a real knife. A Celtic dagger, to be precise.'

'An unusual weapon . . . but I see that you have already begun your investigation.'

'Curiosity is the key to knowledge. What do you know about him?' he asked, indicating the body again.

'Very little. His name was Pausanias and he was from Lyncestis, originally. He had been recruited to the King's bodyguard because of his physical prowess.'

'Unfortunately he won't be able to tell us anything, and this is surely part of the plan. Have you interrogated the soldiers who killed him?'

'One or two, but I didn't get much from them. They all maintain they didn't hear King Alexander's order not to kill him. The shock of Philip's death had made them furious, they were in a blind rage and as soon as he showed the slightest sign of trying to defend himself, they massacred him.'

'It's a credible story, but it's probably not true. Where is the King of Epirus?'

'He left with Alexander, they're on their way to Pella together.'

'So he has relinquished his first night with his bride.'

'For two reasons, both of them understandable: to support his brother-in-law at this critical juncture in the succession, and as a mark of respect for Cleopatra's bereavement.'

Aristotle brought a finger up to his mouth as a signal to his nephew to keep quiet. The sound of a horse galloping reached them ever more distinctly as it came nearer.

'Let's move,' said the philosopher. 'Let's get away from here. Whoever believes himself to be unobserved behaves more naturally.'

The sound of the gallop changed into the gentle rhythmic steps of a horse at a walk and then it stopped altogether. A figure draped in black leaped to the ground, walked forward until it stood in front of the corpse nailed to the pole, and then pulled back the hood of its cloak to reveal a fine head of wavy hair.

'Gods above! It's Olympias!' whispered Callisthenes in his uncle's ear.

The Queen moved closer still, pulled something from the folds of her cloak and then stood up on tiptoes in front of the body. When she turned round to join her escort again, there was a garland of flowers around Pausanias' neck.

'Oh, by Zeus!' Callisthenes said. 'But then this means . . .'

'You think you know what it all means?' Aristotle shook his head. 'It's not so clear at all. If she had commissioned the assassination do you think she would have made such a gesture in front of her escort, well knowing that someone was probably keeping Pausanias' corpse under surveillance?'

'But if she's aware of all this, then she might behave in such an absurd way precisely to lead whoever is investigating to dismiss her on these very grounds.'

'This is true, but it is always wiser to attempt to discover the motives that may have pushed a suspect to commit a crime rather than quiz oneself on what that person thinks other people are thinking,' observed Aristotle. 'Find me a lamp or a torch and let's go to the place where Pausanias was killed.'

'But wouldn't it be best to wait for the light of day?'

'Too many things might happen before dawn. I'll wait for you down there.'

The philosopher set off towards the wood of oak and elm that was near the place where the assassin had been massacred.

39

HEPHAESTION, PTOLEMY, Seleucus and Perdiccas, all four dressed in their armour, arrived tired and dripping with sweat as darkness fell. They gave their horses to the attendants and quickly went up the stairs of the palace to the council chamber where Alexander was waiting for them.

Leonnatus and Lysimachus were to arrive the following day because they were travelling all the way from Larissa, in Thessaly.

A guard let them all into the chamber where the lamps had already been lit and Alexander was already waiting together with Philotas, General Antipater, Alexander of Epirus, Amyntas and some commanders of the phalanx battalions and the Companions cavalry. All of them, including the King, were wearing their armour and they kept their helmets and their swords at hand on the table in front of them – a sure sign that the situation was still critical.

Alexander, visibly moved, came towards them. 'My friends . . . finally we are back together again.'

Hephaestion spoke for all of them: 'We are deeply sorry for the death of King Philip and our grief is most strong. We no longer resent the exile he inflicted upon us. We remember him as a great King, the most valiant of soldiers and the wisest of rulers. He was like a father to us – strict and unyielding, but also generous and capable of most noble gestures. We grieve for him most sincerely. It has been a terrible event, but now you must take his inheritance in hand, and we recognize you as his successor and as our King.'

This short speech over, Hephaestion walked to Alexander and kissed him on both cheeks, as did all the others. Then he saluted King Alexander of Epirus and those officers present and they all took seats around the table.

Alexander picked up where he had left off: 'It will not take long for news of Philip's death to spread everywhere because the assassination took place in the presence of thousands of people. The reactions that it will inevitably provoke are difficult to predict, but we must be ready to move equally rapidly to prevent anything and everything that might weaken the realm or threaten my father's achievements in any way. This is my plan.

'We must gather intelligence on the state of the northern borders, on the reaction of our new Athenian and Theban allies and . . .' at this point he turned to Philotas with a knowing look, 'on the intentions of the generals who command our expedition to Asia – Attalus and Parmenion. Since they have at their disposal an army of fifteen thousand men, it makes sense to clarify their intentions immediately.'

'What are you thinking of doing?' asked Philotas with a certain degree of apprehension in his voice.

'I don't want to put any of you in difficult positions: I will give my message to a Greek officer by the name of Hecataeus, who is in our service in the Straits area with a small division. I have decided to relieve Attalus of his command and I am sure you will all understand the reasoning behind that.'

No one objected. Indeed, the scene that had been played out a year previously at Philip's wedding was still vivid in their memories.

'I believe,' said Alexander, 'that the consequences of the King's death will soon make themselves felt. Some people will see this as an opportunity to move backwards in time, to restore old ways, and we will have to persuade them that they are wrong. Only once we have dealt with this danger will we be able to start again with my father's plans.'

Alexander fell silent and at that moment everyone realized that time had in fact stopped, that in this very room a future beyond anyone's imagination was being prepared. The young man Philip had had educated and groomed through years of hard work and sacrifice now sat on the Argead throne and, for the first time in his life, the devastating power that he had only ever seen wielded by the heroes in epic poems now rested firmly in his hands.

*

Alexander went with his namesake brother-in-law to Aegae, leaving command of the various units of the phalanx and the *Hetairoi* cavalry to his friends, while Hephaestion was entrusted with the royal palace. Philip still had to be buried and there were other serious matters to be dealt with in the old capital.

Halfway there they met a messenger who had been sent by Eumenes with an urgent despatch.

'It is just as well I found you, Sire!' exclaimed the messenger, handing him a sealed roll of papyrus. 'Eumenes wants you to read it immediately.'

Alexander unrolled it and read the succinct message:

Eumenes to Alexander, King of Macedon, Hail!

Eurydice's baby boy has been found dead in his cradle and I fear for the life of Eurydice herself.

Queen Olympias arrived here the night you left for Pella.

You must come immediately.

Take good care.

'My mother arrived there immediately after we left? Did you know about that?' Alexander asked his brother-in-law.

The King of Epirus shook his head. 'She said nothing to me when I left Buthrotum, but I never thought she really intended to go to the wedding. For her it was another affront. She thought this was Philip's way of alienating her completely, since I would be formally obliged to provide him with security for his western borders following the wedding. I never thought she really meant to join me at Aegae.'

'In any case, she's there now. And it appears she has taken some very drastic initiatives. Let's move, before she does something completely irreparable,' said Alexander, and he spurred Bucephalas into a gallop.

They reached Aegae the following evening, as the sun was setting, and from a distance they could hear heart-rending cries coming from the palace. Eumenes came to meet them at the entrance.

'She's been crying like that for two days. She says it was your mother who killed her boy. And she refuses to relinquish the body. But time passes and . . . you can imagine . . .'

'Where is she?'

'In the southern wing,' replied Eumenes. 'Come with me.'

Alexander nodded to his bodyguard to follow and strode through the palace, every sector of whicwas heavily guarded by armed soldiers. Many of them were from Epirus – members of his brother-in-law's escort.

'Who posted them all here?'

'Your mother, the Queen,' replied Eumenes as he walked, breathless, behind Alexander.

As they approached, the wailing became louder. Now and then it would explode into raucous shouting, then fade into a long, drawn-out sobbing.

They came to the door and Alexander opened it without hesitating, but what he found in the room froze him instantly. Eurydice was lying in a corner, her hair dishevelled, her eyes swollen and red, a mad look in her eyes. She was holding the lifeless body of her baby to her breast. The boy's head and arms dangled backwards and the blue colour of his limbs was a sure sign that decomposition had already started.

Her clothes were torn to shreds, her hair was plastered with dried blood, her face, her arms and legs were covered in bruises and cuts. The whole room exuded a revolting stench of sweat, urine and putrefaction.

Alexander closed his eyes for an instant and saw Eurydice at the height of her splendour as she sat alongside the

King his father – a young girl who was loved, spoiled, envied by everyone. He felt the horror rise in his mind and wrath fill his chest and the veins in his neck.

He turned to Eumenes and asked, his voice cracking with anger, 'Who did this?'

Eumenes lowered his head in silence.

Alexander shouted, 'Who did this?'

'I do not know.'

'Call someone to take care of her immediately. Bring Philip, my physician, and tell him to attend to her, to give her something to make her rest . . . to make her sleep.'

He started to move away, but Eumenes held him back. 'She won't leave the child. What can we do?'

Alexander stopped and turned towards the girl, who crouched down even lower in the corner, like a frightened animal.

He moved towards her slowly and knelt down in front of her, his eyes fixed on hers. Gently he moved his head to one side as if to lessen slightly the strength of his gaze, as if to envelop her in an aura of compassion. Then he put out his hand and gently caressed her cheek.

Eurydice closed her eyes, leaned backwards until her head rested on the wall and let out a long, painful sigh.

Alexander held out his arms and said quietly, 'Give him to me, Eurydice, give me the little one. He's tired, don't you think? We have to put him to bed.'

Two big tears slipped slowly down the young girl's cheeks until they reached her lips. She whispered, 'Sleep . . .' and loosened her grip on the child's body.

Alexander took him carefully, as if he really were asleep, and went out into the corridor.

Eumenes, in the meantime, had sent for a woman who arrived just then. 'Give him to me, Sire,' she said. Alexander put the baby in her arms and ordered, 'Lay him alongside my father.'

★

'Why?' he shouted as he burst into the room. 'Why?'

Queen Olympias stood there before him, her eyes burning with rage: 'You dare enter my rooms armed?'

'I am the King of Macedon!' shouted Alexander. 'And I go wherever and however I like! Why did you kill the child and why did you do those barbaric things to his mother? Who gave you the right?'

'You are the King of Macedon precisely because that child is dead,' replied Olympias impassively. 'Isn't that what you wanted? Have you forgotten how you fretted when you were afraid you had fallen out of Philip's favour? Have you forgotten what you said to Attalus on the day of your father's wedding?'

'I haven't forgotten, but I don't kill children and I don't attack defenceless women.'

'There is no other way for a king. A king is always alone. There is no law which lays down who should succeed to the throne. Any group of noblemen could have decided to take the child under their wing and to govern in his name until he came of age. If that had happened, what would you have done?'

'I would have fought to conquer the throne!'

'And how much blood would have been spilled? Answer me that! How many widows would be mourning their husbands, how many mothers their prematurely dead sons, how many fields would have been burned to cinders, how many villages and cities sacked and razed to the ground? And in any case the entire empire which Philip built at the cost of just as much blood and just as much destruction would have come apart at the seams.'

Alexander regained his composure, thunder rolling into his face as if the massacres and the mourning evoked by his mother suddenly weighed on him, all at once, depressing his spirit.

'It is destiny,' he replied. 'It is destined that man should bear wounds and illnesses and pain and death before plunging into the void. But to act with honour and to be merciful whenever it is possible to do so . . . these things are in man's power and they are real choices. This is the only dignity that is granted to man during his time on earth; the only light before the darkness of an endless night . . .'

40

THE FOLLOWING DAY Eumenes announced to Alexander that Philip's tomb was ready and that the funeral could now take place. In truth only the first part of the great sepulchre had been completed so quickly. A second chamber was envisaged to contain all the precious objects that would accompany the King on his journey to the beyond.

Philip was dressed in his finest clothes and a crown of gold oak leaves was placed on his head. His soldiers arranged the body on the funeral pyre. Two battalions of the phalanx and a squadron of Companions paid tribute.

They used wine to extinguish the flames and then wrapped the ashes and the bones in a purple and gold cloth in the shape of a Macedonian military cloak, a *chlamys*. The bundle was then placed in a solid gold chest with feet in the shape of lion's paws and the sixteen-point Argead star on the lid.

Inside the tomb they arranged his breastplate, made of iron, leather and gold, his bronze greaves, his gold quiver, his parade shield lined with gold laminate and decorated with a Dionysian scene of satyrs and maenads, carved in ivory. His weapons – his sword and his spearhead – were thrown into the altar fire and then ritually bent so that they could never be used again.

Alexander deposited his personal tributes: a magnificent jug of solid silver, its handle adorned with a bearded satyr's head, and a two-handled silver cup of such beauty and lightness that it seemed weightless.

The entrance to the sepulchre was closed with a huge double door made of marble, flanked by two Doric pilasters, reproductions of the entrance to the royal palace at Aegae, while an artist from Byzantium was working on a frieze depicting fine hunting scenes on the architrave.

Queen Olympias did not attend the funeral rites because she did not want to make any votive offering on her husband's pyre or in his tomb and because she did not want to meet Eurydice.

Alexander cried when the soldiers closed the great marble doors; he had loved his father and he felt that his own youth was being buried in that tomb.

Eurydice simply gave up, she never ate again and died of hunger together with young Europa, her daughter. Philip the physician tried everything he possibly could, but it was all in vain.

Alexander had a fine tomb built for her as well and gave instructions that the throne his father used when sitting as a judge under the oak tree at Aegae should be placed inside. It was splendid, with golden griffins and sphinxes and a four-horse chariot painted on the backrest. His duty done, his soul full of sadness, Alexander returned to Pella.

*

General Antipater was an officer of Philip's old guard, loyal to the throne and completely reliable. Alexander had given him the job of keeping track of Hecataeus' mission in Asia to Parmenion and Attalus, and he was most anxious about the outcome.

He knew that the barbarians of the north – the Triballians and the Illyrians who had recently been quashed by his father – could rise up at any moment, and that the Greeks had accepted the Corinth peace pact only because of the massacre at Chaeronaea. He was also aware that all of his enemies, Demosthenes in particular, were still alive and kicking, and then there was the fact that Attalus and Parmenion had control of the Straits and were leading an expeditionary force of fifteen thousand men.

As if these threats were not enough, news had reached him about Persian agents having made contact with anti-Macedonian groups in Athens and offering enormous sums of money for anyone who was able and willing to instigate uprisings.

Instability was rife and if all these potential problems were to materialize into real problems at one and the same time, the new King would find himself in serious difficulty.

The first response to his questions came at the beginning of autumn. Antipater immediately asked for an audience with the King and Alexander received him in the study which had been his father's. Although a military man through and through, Antipater did not enjoy making a show of his status and he normally dressed just like any ordinary citizen. This fact was a manifestation of his equilibrium and self-confidence.

'Sire,' he announced on entering the room, 'here is the news from Asia: Attalus refused to cede command and to return to Pella, he put up armed resistance and was killed. Parmenion assures you of his loyalty.'

'Antipater, I would like to know what you really think of Parmenion. You know that his son Philotas is here at court. In some way Parmenion might consider him my hostage. In your opinion is this what lies behind his declaration of loyalty?'

'No,' replied the old general with no hesitation whatsoever. 'I know Parmenion very well. He is fond of you, he has always loved you, ever since you were a child and you used to come and sit on your father's knees during the war councils in the royal armoury.'

Alexander suddenly remembered the rhyme he used to sing every time he saw Parmenion's white hair:

> The silly old soldier's off to the war
> And falls to the floor, falls to the floor!

He felt a deep sadness come over him as he considered how power can dramatically change relations between people.

Antipater continued, 'But if you have doubts about the matter there is one way to satisfy them.'

'Send Philotas to him.'

'Exactly, since his other two children, Nicanor and Hector, are already there with him.'

'That's what I'll do. I'll send him Philotas with a letter calling him back to Pella. I need him, I think there's a storm about to break out.'

'That sounds like a very wise decision, Sire. Parmenion appreciates one thing above all others – trust.'

'What news from the north?'

'Bad news. There is an uprising among the Triballians and they have burned some of our frontier outposts.'

'What do you think I should do?'

'I have had warnings sent. If they should ignore them, hit them as hard as you can.'

'Of course. And from the south?'

'Nothing good there either. The anti-Macedonian wing is growing in strength everywhere, even in Thessaly. You are very young and there are some who think . . .'

'Spit it out, Antipater.'

'They think you're just a boy with no experience and that you'll never manage to maintain Philip's hegemony.'

'They'll have to eat their words.'

'There is one other thing.'

'What is it?'

'Your cousin Archelaus . . .'

'Continue,' Alexander encouraged him, his expression becoming darker.

'He has been involved in a hunting accident.'

'Is he dead?'

Antipater nodded.

'When my father succeeded to the throne, he spared both Archelaus and Amyntas, even although they were both then in the line of succession.'

'It was a hunting accident, Sire,' repeated Antipater impassively.

'Where is Amyntas?'

'Down below, in the guard house.'

'He must not come to any harm; he was at my side immediately after the assassination of my father.'

Antipater nodded to show that he had understood and set off towards the door.

Alexander got up and stood there before Aristotle's

grand map – he had had it set up in his study. West and east were safe, looked after by Alexander of Epirus and Parmenion respectively, assuming he really could trust the old General. But the north and south still represented two serious threats. He had to strike as quickly as possible and in such a decisive way as to leave no doubts about the fact that the new King of Macedon was every bit as strong as Philip.

He went out onto the north-facing balcony and looked out towards the mountains where he had spent his exile. The forests were just beginning to change colour with the arrival of autumn and soon the first snow would be falling: all would be quiet up there until spring. For the moment the job in hand was to scare the Thessalians and the Thebans. He thought out a plan of action while he waited for Philotas and Parmenion to return from Asia.

He summoned his war council a few days after their return.

'I will enter Thessaly with an army ready for war. I will make sure I am reconfirmed as *Tagos*, the title my father enjoyed, and I will push on as far as the walls of Thebes,' he announced. 'I want the Thessalians to understand that they have a new leader, and as for the Thebans, I want to frighten them to death – they have to be aware of the fact that I can strike at will, whenever, however, wherever.'

'But there is a problem,' Hephaestion intervened. 'The Thessalians have closed off the Vale of Tempe with fortifications to the left and right of the river. We are blocked.'

Alexander moved towards Aristotle's map and indicated the mass of Mount Ossa and the precipice over the sea.

'I know,' he replied. 'But we will pass through here.'

'How?' asked Ptolemy. 'None of us has wings, or at least we didn't last time I looked.'

'We have mallets and chisels,' replied Alexander. 'We will cut a stairway in the rock itself. Have five hundred miners from Mount Pangaeos brought here – the best of them. Feed them well, give them clothes and shoes and promise them their freedom if they finish the job in ten days: they will work shifts, non-stop, from the sea upwards. The Thessalians won't be able to see them.'

'Are you serious?' asked Seleucus.

'I never joke during war councils. And now, let's get moving.'

All those present looked at one another in amazement; it was obvious that no obstacle, no human or godly barrier would ever stop Alexander.

41

'ALEXANDER'S LADDER' was ready in seven days and, under cover of darkness, the assault troops of the shieldsmen slipped onto the Plain of Thessaly without once raising their weapons.

A few hours later a messenger on horseback delivered the news to the Thessalian commander, but without any explanation because the simple truth was that at that point in time no one had any explanation to offer.

'Are you telling me that we have a Macedonian army led by the King himself on our backs?'

'Yes, Sir.'

'And how do you think they managed that?'

'No one knows, Sir, but the soldiers are certainly out there, and there are a lot of them.'

'How many?'

'Between three and five thousand, well equipped and armed. There are even some horses – not many, but there are some.'

'It's impossible. There's no way through from the coastal side, and no way through the mountains either.' The commander, whose name was Charidemus, was still speaking when one of his soldiers reported that two battalions of the phalanx and one squadron of the *Hetairoi* cavalry were coming up the river towards the fortification.

This meant that before nightfall they would be crushed between two armies. Shortly afterwards, another soldier came to inform him that a Macedonian officer by the name of Craterus had asked to parley.

'Tell him I'll be with him immediately,' ordered Charidemus, and he left through a back door to go and meet the Macedonian.

'My name is Craterus,' the officer introduced himself, 'and I am here to ask you to let us pass through your territory now. We have no desire to harm you, we simply want to rejoin our King and his men who are in your territory and are on their way to Larissa, where he will summon a council of the Thessalian League.'

'I don't have much choice,' said Charidemus.

'No, it's true, you don't,' replied Craterus.

'Very well, let's negotiate. But there is something I'd like to know.'

'If I can, I will provide an answer,' Craterus declared in a very formal tone.

'How did your infantry manage to get here?'

'We cut a stairway into the seaward face of Mount Ossa.'

'A stairway?'

'Yes. A throughway, a passage we required in order to maintain contact with our Thessalian allies.'

Charidemus was completely taken aback, but, as he himself had admitted, he had no option other than to let them through.

Two days later Alexander reached Larissa, summoned the council of the Thessalian League, and had himself confirmed as *Tagos* for life.

He then waited for the arrival of other divisions of his army so that they could proceed across Boeotia and parade under the walls of Thebes in a great show of strength.

'I want no bloodshed,' he stated. 'But we must scare the living daylights out of them. You take care of it, Ptolemy.'

And so Ptolemy had the army line up in the same formation as at the Battle of Chaeronaea. He asked Alexander to put on the same armour his father had worn and made ready the gigantic war drum on wheels, drawn by four horses.

The grim drumbeat could be heard clearly from the walls of the city, within which, just a few days previously, the Thebans had made an attempt to storm the Macedonian garrison on the Cadmean citadel. Memories of their casualties and fear of the threatening army helped calm down the hotter heads, but it wasn't enough to quench fully the hatred and the desire for revenge.

'Will this be enough?' Alexander asked Hephaestion as they marched below Thebes.

'For the moment. But don't delude yourself. What will you do about the other cities where our garrisons have been ejected?'

'Nothing. I want to be the Greeks' leader, not their tyrant. They must understand that I am not an enemy, that the enemy lies across the sea, the enemy is Persia who persists in denying the Greek cities of Asia their freedom.'

'Is it true you've ordered an investigation into the death of your father?'

'Yes, I've asked Callisthenes to deal with it.'

'And do you think he'll get to the bottom of it?'

'I think he'll do his best.'

'And if he were to discover that the Greeks were responsible? The Athenians, for example?'

'I'll decide what has to be done when the time comes.'

'Callisthenes has been seen with Aristotle, did you know about that?'

'Of course.'

'And how do you explain the fact that Aristotle hasn't come to speak to you in person?'

'Speaking with me of late hasn't been easy for anyone. Or perhaps he simply wants to maintain complete independence in evaluating the situation.'

The last division of the Companions disappeared with the thumping of the drum as it faded away and the Thebans held their important decision-making council. A letter from Demosthenes had arrived from Calauria, exhorting them not to give up hope and to prepare for the moment when they would rise up once more.

'The throne of Macedon,' he wrote, 'is occupied by a little boy and the situation now is clearly in our favour.'

The orator's words pleased almost everyone, but there were some members of the Theban council who were inclined to be more prudent. An old man who had lost two sons at Chaeronaea asked to speak and said, 'This "little boy", as Demosthenes calls him, has reconquered Thessaly in three days without any combat whatsoever and has sent us a clear message with this parade under our walls. I think we should listen to him.'

But the angry voices that then made themselves heard

from various quarters drowned out this invitation to reason, and the Thebans prepared to strike as soon as the opportunity arose.

Alexander reached Corinth completely unobstructed, summoned the council of the pan-Hellenic League and asked to be reconfirmed as general of the confederate armies.

From the chair that had once been his father's, he issued a proclamation: 'Each member state will be free to govern itself as it wishes and there will be no interference in its internal laws and its constitution. The only aim of the League is to free Asian Greeks from the Persian yoke and to maintain lasting peace among the Greeks of the peninsula.'

All the delegates signed the motion, with the exception of the Spartans, who hadn't supported Philip's previous motion either.

'We have always been used to leading the Greeks, not to being led,' their envoy declared to Alexander.

'I am sorry,' replied the King, 'because the Spartans are magnificent soldiers. Today, however, the Macedonians are the strongest of all the Greek peoples and it is only right that they should be leaders and enjoy hegemony.' But there was some regret in these words because he was well aware of Spartan valour at Thermopylae and Plataea. He was also fully aware that no power can ever resist the ravages of time – the only thing that grows over time is the glory of those who have lived honourably.

On the return journey Alexander visited Delphi and was greatly charmed and impressed by the wonders of the sacred city. He stopped in front of the façade of the sanctuary of Apollo and studied the gilded words engraved there:

KNOW THYSELF

'What do you think it means?' asked Craterus who had never given much thought to philosophical questions before.

'It's obvious,' replied Alexander. 'To know ourselves is the most difficult of enterprises because it involves not reason alone, but our fears and our passions too. If we are capable of truly knowing ourselves then we will be able to understand others and the reality that surrounds us.'

They watched the long procession of the faithful who had come from all over bearing offerings and questions for the god. There was no part of the Greek world that did not have some representative there.

'Do you believe the oracle tells the truth?' Ptolemy asked.

'My ears are still ringing with the answer it gave my father.'

'It was an ambiguous answer,' Hephaestion said.

'But true in the end,' replied Alexander. 'If Aristotle were here he would say that prophecies can actually make the future come true, rather than predict it . . .'

'That's quite probable,' Hephaestion nodded. 'I once heard one of his lessons at Mieza: Aristotle trusts no one, not even the gods. For him everything is based on his own mind.'

*

Aristotle leaned back in his chair, interlocking his fingers with his hands resting on his belly. 'And the oracle at

Delphi? Have you thought about the Pythia's answer? That's rather suspicious too. Remember, an oracle lives on its own credibility, but to construct this credibility it requires an unlimited wealth of knowledge. No one alive has as much knowledge as the priests of the sanctuary of Apollo – this is why they can predict the future. Or why they can determine it. It's the same thing in the end.'

Callisthenes was holding a tablet on which he had listed the names of all those who up until that moment could be suspected of having ordered the King's assassination.

Aristotle spoke again: 'What do you know of the assassin? Who did he spend time with in the period immediately before he killed the King?'

'There's a nasty twist to the story there, Uncle,' Callisthenes said. 'Attalus, Eurydice's father, is involved in it. In fact let's say he's in it right up to his neck.'

'And Attalus has been killed.'

'Exactly.'

'And Eurydice is dead too.'

'Indeed, Alexander had a fine tomb built for her.'

'What's more,' said Aristotle, 'he argued violently with his mother, Olympias, because she attacked Eurydice and because she was probably responsible for the death of the child.'

'This clears Alexander.'

'But at the same time these deaths have favoured him in the succession.'

'Do you suspect him?' Callisthenes asked.

'On the basis of what I know of him, no. But sometimes knowing about or suspecting a criminal event without doing anything to prevent it can be a form of guilt.

'The real problem is that so many people had motives for assassinating Philip. We must continue to gather information. In this way we might reach the truth through the simple weight of evidence that accumulates against one or other of the suspects. Continue your enquiries on Attalus' involvement and then let me know. But let Alexander know as well – he's the one who commissioned the job.'

'Shall I tell him everything?'

'Everything. And make sure you don't miss any of his reactions.'

'Can I tell him that you're helping me?'

'Of course,' replied the philosopher. 'In the first place because he'll be pleased to hear it. And in the second place because he already knows.'

42

GENERAL PARMENION came back to Pella together with his son Philotas towards the end of autumn, after having made sure that the Asia expeditionary force would be able to winter without any serious problems.

Antipater received him because at that moment it was he who held the royal seal and was acting as official regent.

'I was most sorry not to be able to attend the King's funeral,' said Parmenion. 'And I must also say that Attalus' death brought me considerable grief, but I cannot say I didn't expect it.'

'In any case, Alexander demonstrated his complete trust by sending Philotas to you. He wanted you to be free to take whatever decision you felt you had to.'

'That is exactly why I have returned. But I confess I am surprised to see you with the royal seal on your finger – the Queen Mother has never loved you and I hear she still exerts considerable influence over Alexander.'

'That is true, but the King knows his own mind, he is his own man. Right now what he wants is that his mother should keep out of politics. Completely.'

'And what about the politics?'

'What do you think? In three months he has managed to re-establish the Thessalian League, frighten the Thebans, reinforce the pan-Hellenic League and recoup General

Parmenion, the key to the East. Not bad at all, for a boy, as Demosthenes would have it.'

'You're right, but the north is still a problem. The Triballians are now allied with the Getae, who live along the lower reaches of the Ister, and together they have been carrying out raids on our territory almost continually. Many of the cities founded by King Philip have been lost.'

'I believe this is exactly why Alexander has called you back to Pella. He intends to march north in midwinter to catch the enemy off guard, and you will be asked to lead the front-line infantry. He will put his friends at your disposal as battalion commanders – he wants them to learn from a good teacher.'

'And where is he now?'

'The latest news is that he is crossing through Thessaly. But before that he went to Delphi.'

Parmenion's face darkened. 'Has he consulted the oracle?'

'In a way, yes.'

'What do you mean by that?'

'The priests probably wanted to avoid another incident like Philip's visit, so they told Alexander that the Pythia was not well and that she couldn't answer his questions. But Alexander simply dragged her bodily to the tripod with the intention of obliging her to give him a prophecy.' Parmenion's face and eyes were a picture of incredulity as he listened. 'By that stage the Pythia was out of her mind with rage and started shouting wildly, "But there is absolutely nothing that can hold you back, my boy!" Alexander stopped then, struck by these words, and simply said, "That'll do fine as a response." And then he left.'

Parmenion shook his head. 'That's a good one . . . a line worthy of a great actor.'

'And that's exactly what Alexander is. Or rather, he's a great actor among other things. You'll see.'

'Do you think he believes in the oracles?'

Antipater rubbed his hand through his bristly beard. 'Yes and no. The rationality of Philip and Aristotle live in Alexander, together with the mysterious, instinctive and barbaric nature of his mother. But he saw his father fall like a sacrificial bull before the altar, and at that moment the words of the prophecy must have exploded like a thunderclap in his mind. He won't forget them for as long as he lives.'

Evening was falling and the two old soldiers found themselves in the grip of a sudden, deep melancholy. They felt that their time had reached its twilight with the death of King Philip, as if their days had been consumed in the vortex of flames around the pyre of the assassinated King.

'Perhaps if we had been at his side . . .' Parmenion suddenly murmured.

'Don't say another word, my friend. No one can alter fate's design. Our only thoughts must be that our King had prepared Alexander to be his successor. All that remains of our days belongs to him.'

*

The King returned to Pella leading his troops and he paraded through the city in the midst of two lines of joyous onlookers. It was the first time in living memory that an army had returned victorious from a campaign without having been involved in combat, without having suffered any losses. This handsome young man – his face, his clothes, his armour all resplendent – was for everyone the virtual incarnation of a young god, an epic hero. And in his companions as they rode alongside him the people saw the same light reflected; their eyes seemed to burn with the same intense and febrile gaze.

Antipater went to meet him and return the seal and tell him that Parmenion had returned.

'Take me to him right away,' ordered Alexander.

The General mounted his horse and led the way to an isolated villa just outside the city.

Parmenion came down the stairs with his heart in his mouth as soon as the King's arrival was announced and it was explained that he hadn't even been to the palace yet after his journey. When Parmenion came out of the door he found Alexander there before him.

'Soldier! My old Soldier!' Alexander greeted and embraced him. 'Thank you for coming home.'

'Sire,' replied Parmenion with a lump in his throat, 'your father's death was a terrible blow. I would have given my life to save him, had it been possible. I would have shielded him with my body . . . I would have . . .' but he couldn't continue because his voice had started cracking.

'I know,' nodded Alexander. Then he put his hands on Parmenion's shoulders and looked straight into his eyes. 'I would have done the same thing, had it been possible.'

Parmenion looked down.

'It was like a lightning bolt, General, organized by a genius, a ruthless genius. There was a lot of fuss and noise just at that moment and I was ahead of him together with

King Alexander of Epirus. Eumenes shouted something to us, but I didn't understand, I couldn't hear, and when I realized something was happening and I turned round, he was already falling to his knees, falling into his own blood.'

'I know, Sire. But let's not speak of such sad things. Tomorrow I will go to Aegae, I will make a sacrificial offering on his tomb and I hope he will hear me. Why have you come to see me now?'

'I wanted to greet you and to invite you to supper. Everyone will be there and I intend to illustrate my plans for the winter. This will be our last enterprise in Europe, after which we will march towards the East, towards the rising sun.'

He leaped onto his horse and went off at a gallop. Parmenion went back into the villa and called for his manservant: 'Prepare my bath and my best clothes,' he ordered. 'This evening I am to dine with the King.'

43

In the days following these events, Alexander joined in military training and took part in several hunts, but he also had occasion to realize just how much his authority was now recognized even in remote countries. He received delegations not only from the Greeks in Asia, but from Sicily and Italy as well.

A group of cities on the Tyrrhenian Sea, for example, brought him a golden bowl as a gift and petitioned for his help.

Alexander was much flattered and asked them where they came from.

'From Neapolis, Medma and Poseidonia,' they explained in an accent that he hadn't heard before, but which reminded him somewhat of the way people spoke on the island of Euboea.

'And what can I do for you?'

'King Alexander,' replied the eldest representative, 'there is a powerful city to the north of us and it goes by the name of Rome.'

'I have heard of it,' replied Alexander. 'They tell me it was founded by Aeneas, the Trojan hero.'

'Indeed, but in the Romans' territory, on the coast, there is a city peopled by pirates who are causing terrible disruption to our sea traffic. We want to put an end to this situation and we would like you to intervene. Your fame has spread everywhere and we believe that your opinion would carry substantial influence in the matter.'

'I will do it gladly. And I hope they will take heed. Make sure you let me know the result of this initiative.'

Then he nodded to his scribe and started dictating.

Alexander, King of Macedon, pan-Hellenic leader, to the people and the city of Rome, Hail!

Our brothers of the cities of the Tyrrhenian Gulf tell me they are suffering grievous harm at the hands of some of your subjects who engage in piracy.

I would therefore ask you to resolve this as soon as possible or, if you are not able to resolve it yourselves, to let others deal with it.

He pressed his seal on the letter and gave it to his guests who thanked him profusely and left satisfied with their mission.

'I wonder what effect this letter will have?' Alexander asked of Eumenes who was sitting near him. 'And what will these Romans think of such a distant King who interferes in their internal affairs?'

'Not so very distant,' said Eumenes. 'You'll see that they will reply.'

Other emissaries and other news, much worse, came from the northern border: the alliance between the Triballians and the Getae had been consolidated and was now jeopardizing all of Philip's conquests in Thrace. The Getae were especially formidable because they believed themselves to be immortal and fought wildly and furiously and with utter disdain for personal danger. Many of the colonies founded by Alexander's father had been attacked and plundered, the populations massacred or enslaved. At that particular moment, however, the situation seemed calm and the northern warriors had all gone back into their villages to get ready for the harsh winter cold.

Despite the unfavourable season, Alexander decided to bring forward their departure and to put his plan into action. He sent word to the Byzantine fleet to proceed up the Ister for five days' sail, until they reached the confluence with the River Peukes. In the meantime he mobilized all of his army's units in Pella, put Parmenion in charge of the infantry, and personally took command of the cavalry before setting off.

They crossed Mount Rhodope, went down into the Vale of Europos and then started out on a forced march towards the Haemon passes which were still covered with a thick blanket of snow. As they advanced they saw ruined cities, devastated fields, bodies hanging on poles, others tied up and burned; the wrath of the Macedonian King grew like the implacable fury of a river in flood.

In a completely unexpected manoeuvre, Alexander descended with his cavalry onto the Getaen plain, burning villages and camps, destroying harvests, massacring livestock.

The people, terror stricken, retreated in panic towards the Ister and sought refuge on an island in the middle of the river, where they thought Alexander could never reach them. But the Byzantine fleet arrived, and ferried the assault troops, the shieldsmen and the Vanguard cavalry.

The battle on the island was a fierce one. The Getae

and the Triballians fought desperately and with superhuman energy because they were defending not only their last scrap of land, but also their wives and children. Alexander in person, however, led the attack on their positions, in the teeth of the icy wind and the rough waves of the Ister which was swollen by torrential rain. The smoke from the fires mingled with the sheets of rain and sleet, while the shouts of the soldiers, the cries of the wounded, and the neighing of horses melded with the crash of thunderclaps and the whistle of the northern wind.

Those under attack had formed a tight circle by uniting their shields and planting the shafts of their spears in the ground to create a barrier of spikes against the cavalry charges. Behind this were the archers who let off clouds of deadly arrows on command. But Alexander himself was possessed of an awesome strength.

Parmenion, who had seen him fight at Chaeronaea three years previously, was shocked as he watched him fight hand-to-hand, oblivious to everything, as if gripped by an uncontrollable fury. The King was animated by an inexhaustible energy – shouting, mowing down the enemy with sword and axe, pushing Bucephalas, with his bronze armour, against the opponents' lines to open a breach through which he could lead the heavy cavalry and the assault infantry.

Surrounded, scattered, hounded one by one like fleeing beasts, the Triballians surrendered, while the Getae continued to the bitter end, to the last spark of their vital energy.

When it was all over the squall that had been moving

down from the north reached the island and, on coming into contact with the humidity of the Ister, it quietened somewhat. Then, as if by magic, it started snowing. Initially it was a form of sleet, tiny crystals of ice falling with rain, and then they became ever bigger and thicker and developed into large flakes. The bloody mess on the ground was soon covered by a white blanket, the fires were quenched and everywhere a grim silence fell, broken only here and there by some muffled shout or by the snorting of the horses as they moved through the blizzard.

Alexander returned to the riverbank, and the soldiers he had left on guard at the jetty saw him appear suddenly out of the curtain of snow and fog. He had lost his shield, but he still held his sword and his double-bladed axe and he was covered with blood from head to toe. The bronze plates on Bucephalas' chest and forehead were splashed with red too and thick steam came from the stallion's body and his nostrils. He looked like some beast from a warped imagination, a creature from a nightmare.

Parmenion was with Alexander in an instant, consternation written all over his face. 'Sire, you shouldn't have . . .'

The King took off his helmet, freeing his hair into the icy wind, and the old General didn't recognize his voice when he said, 'It's over, Parmenion, let's go back.'

*

Part of the army was sent back home along the same road they had taken on the way north. Alexander, however, led the rest of the soldiers and the cavalry westwards along the Ister until he came upon the Celts, a people whose origins lay far away on the banks of the northern ocean, and he established an alliance with them.

He sat under a tent of tanned animal skins with their chief – a huge, blond-haired man sporting a helmet with a bird on top whose wings went up and down with a slight creaking every time he moved his head.

'I swear,' said the barbarian, 'that I will be faithful to this pact for as long as the earth does not sink into the sea and the sea does not rise to cover the earth and the sky does not fall on our heads.'

Alexander was surprised by this formula which he had never heard before and asked, 'Which of these things do you fear most?'

The Celtic chief looked up and the bird's wings moved up and down as he thought for a moment before saying, very seriously, 'That the sky might fall on our heads.'

Alexander never discovered the whys and wherefores of that one.

He then crossed the lands of the Dardanians and the Agrianians, wild peoples of Illyrian stock who had reneged on their alliance with Philip and had joined forces with the Getae and the Triballians. He quashed them and forced them to provide troops because the Agrianians were famous for their ability to climb, fully armed, up the steepest mountain faces. The young King thought that making use of these skills might be more convenient than cutting stairways out of rock for his infantry as he had done on Mount Ossa.

The army took a long time marching and riding its way through the many valleys and woods of those inhospitable lands, so much so that rumours began to circulate about the King having fallen into an ambush and having been killed.

This news travelled like lightning and reached Athens first, by sea, and then Thebes.

Demosthenes returned to Athens immediately from Calauria where he had taken refuge and he gave an impassioned public speech. Messages of support were sent to Thebes together with supplies of heavy armour for their infantry, something the city was completely lacking in. Indeed, the Thebans rose up in arms and besieged the garrison occupying the Cadmean citadel, digging trenches and building barriers all around it so that the Macedonians who were blocked in there had no hope at all of receiving supplies from outside.

But Alexander came to hear about the uprising and was furious when he heard about Demosthenes' speeches against Macedon and her new King.

It took him thirteen days to travel from the banks of the Ister and he appeared beneath the walls of Thebes just when the defenders of the Cadmean citadel – much weakened by the siege – were about to capitulate. They couldn't believe their eyes when they saw the King astride Bucephalas, ordering the Thebans to hand over the ring-leaders of the uprising.

'Hand them over!' he shouted. 'And I will spare your city!'

The Thebans went into council to decide. The representatives of the democratic grouping, exiled by Philip, had returned and were determined now to wreak their revenge on Macedon.

'He's only a boy. What are you afraid of?' asked one of them, who went by the name of Diodorus. 'The Athenians are with us, the Aetolian League and even Sparta itself might well join forces with us before long. Now is the moment to rid ourselves once and for all of the Macedonian tyranny! Even the Great King of Persia has promised his support – arms and money to bolster our uprising are on their way to Athens as I speak.'

'In that case why don't we wait for reinforcements?' asked another citizen. 'In the meantime the garrison in the Cadmean citadel may well surrender and then we will be able to use those men in negotiations – letting them go free in exchange for a definitive withdrawal of the Macedonian troops from our territory. Or we might wait until an ally's army is positioned behind Alexander and attempt an attack.'

'No!' Diodorus persisted. 'Every day that passes goes against us. All those who believe they have suffered injustice or oppression at the hands of our city will unite with the Macedonian. As I speak, troops are coming from Phocis, from Plataea, from Thespiae, from Oropus, and they all hate us to the point of seeking our total ruin. Have no fear, Thebans! We will avenge the dead of Chaeronaea, once and for all!'

The citizens, fired by these passionate words, stood up in unison and started chanting, 'War!' Without even waiting for the federal magistrates to bring the assembly to its official conclusion, they all ran off to their homes to make ready their weapons.

Alexander summoned a war council in his tent.

'All I want is to force them to negotiate,' he began, 'even though they refuse to do so.'

'But they've issued a challenge!' Hephaestion objected. 'Let's attack now and show them who's the strongest!'

'They already know who is the strongest,' Parmenion said. 'We are here with thirty thousand men and three thousand horses, all of them veterans who have never lost any battle. They will negotiate.'

'General Parmenion is right,' said Alexander. 'I don't want blood. I am about to invade Asia, and all I want to leave behind me is peace among all Greeks and to know that perhaps I have their support in my venture. I will give them time to mull it over.'

'Then why on earth have we just put ourselves through thirteen days of forced marching? To sit here under the tents and wait for them to decide what they want to do?' Hephaestion asked.

'My aim was to demonstrate that I can strike whenever I want and at short notice; to show them that I will never be far enough away for them to organize their defences. But if they ask for peace, I will gladly give it to them.'

But the days passed and nothing happened. Alexander decided to intimidate the Thebans more decisively, to put more pressure on them to negotiate. He had his army line up in battle formation, marched them up to the walls and then sent forward a herald who proclaimed:

'Thebans! King Alexander offers you the peace that all other Greeks have accepted, together with your independence and whatever political system you may prefer. But, should you reject this offer, he will still offer refuge to those of you who wish to leave Thebes now to live in peace without hatred and without bloodshed!'

The Thebans' response was not long in coming. One of their heralds shouted from the top of a tower:

'Macedonians! Whomsoever wishes to join us and the Great King of the Persians in freeing the Greeks of all tyranny is welcome here in Thebes and we will open our gates to let them in.'

These words hurt Alexander deeply. They made him feel like the barbarian oppressor he never had been and had never had any ambition to be. In an instant the Theban proclamation reduced all the dreams and efforts of his father Philip to nothing. Rejected and humiliated, Alexander's fury knew no bounds and his eyes darkened like a sky in which a storm is brewing.

'That's it!' he exclaimed. 'They leave me no choice. I will make such an example of this city that no one will ever dare break the peace I have created for all Greeks.'

In Thebes, however, not quite all of the voices that called for the city to negotiate had been silenced, and several ominous portents had spread anxiety throughout the population. Three months before Alexander's arrival beneath the walls with his army, an enormous spider's web had been seen in the temple of Demeter – it was in the shape of a cloak and it shone all around with iridescent colours, just like a rainbow.

On being questioned about it, the oracle at Delphi gave this response:

The gods to mortals all have sent this sign;
To the Boeotians first, and to their neighbours.

The ancestral oracle of Thebes was also consulted and responded:

> The woven web is bane to one, to one a boon.*

No one had succeeded in interpeting those words, but on the morning Alexander arrived with his army, the statues in the market square at Thebes had started sweating, and soon they were covered with big drops of liquid that ran slowly to the ground.

The city representatives also received reports that a sort of moaning sound had been heard coming from Lake Kopais, and in the water near Dirke some ripples had appeared, such as when a stone is thrown into the water, but these had the colour of blood and they then extended over the whole surface of the lake. And last but not least, some travellers from Delphi recounted that the Theban temple at the sanctuary, built in thanks for the spoils taken from the Phocaeans during the sacred war, had bloodstains on its roof.

The seers who busied themselves with these omens said that the spider's web inside the temple meant that the gods were planning to abandon the city, while the fact that it shone in many colours was a presage of a variety of disasters. The sweating statues prefigured a looming disaster and the bloodstains indicated an approaching massacre.

It was felt therefore that since these were all bad omens then nothing should be done to tempt fate on the battlefield, but rather a negotiated settlement should be sought.

---

* Diodorus Siculus, XVII.10.3.

And yet, despite all of this, deep down the Thebans were not particularly worried. Indeed, they were very much aware of their reputation as being among the best fighters in Greece and the memories of their great historical victories were very much alive. They were completely in the grip of a sort of collective madness and they acted more out of blind courage than out of sagacity and reflection, and thus it was that they dived headlong into wrack and ruin, bringing about the destruction of their city and its lands.

In just three days Alexander made ready all his plans for the siege and the machines for breaching the walls. The Thebans then came out lined up for battle. On the left wing was their cavalry protected by a palisade, in the middle and to the right was the front-line heavy infantry. Inside the city the women and children took refuge in the temples, where they prayed to the gods for salvation.

Alexander split his forces into three divisions – the first had the job of attacking the palisade, the second was to take on the Theban infantry while he held the third back in reserve, under Parmenion's command.

When the trumpets sounded the battle erupted with a violence that was even worse than the fateful day at Chaeronaea. Indeed, the Thebans were well aware of their having gone beyond the mark and they knew that if the Macedonians achieved victory they would be shown no quarter. It was clear that in defeat their homes would be sacked and burned, their wives raped, their children sold. They fought with reckless disregard for their own safety, courageously looking death square in the face.

The reel of the battle, the shouts of the commanders,

the high-pitched sound of the trumpets and the whistles rose up to the sky, while from the depths of the valley came the grim, rhythmical thumping of the enormous Chaeronaea drum.

Initially the Thebans had to retreat a little because they simply couldn't withstand the impact of the infantry phalanx, but when they came to fight hand-to-hand on rougher ground they demonstrated their superior ability, so that for hours and hours the battle seemed to be in the balance, almost as though the gods had put the two sides on the scales in perfect equilibrium.

At that stage Alexander sent his reserves into the battle – the phalanx that had been fighting up until that moment split in two and let the fresh troops advance. But the exhausted Thebans, rather than being daunted by the prospect of having to fight on against the new reinforcements, found their second wind.

Their officers shouted at the tops of their voices, 'Look at this, men! It takes two Macedonians to defeat one Theban! Let's send these new ones back where they came from, just as we did with the first lot.'

Thus they unleashed all their energies in an attack that would decide not only their own individual fates, but the fate of their entire city.

Just then, however, Perdiccas, out on the left flank, saw that a side door in the walls had been opened up to let out reinforcements for the Theban lines. He sent a division to take it and immediately sent as many Macedonians as possible inside the walls.

The Thebans ran back to close the breach, but there were too many of them all at once and they ended up piled one on top of the other, horses and men, wounding one another and unable to stop the enemy troops from spreading throughout the city.

In the meantime, the Macedonians trapped inside the Cadmea citadel managed to break out in a sortie and catch their opponents from behind as they fought hand-to-hand in the narrow winding streets in front of their own homes.

Not one of the Thebans surrendered, not one of them fell to his knees to beg for his life, but this desperate courage in no way inspired any act of clemency from the Macedonians. Indeed, nothing would have availed to stop the cruel vendetta. Blind with rage and drunk with blood and violence, they entered the temples, tore the women and the children from the altars and committed every possible type of atrocity on them.

The streets of the city echoed with the cries of boys and girls pleading for help from their parents, men and women who, even if they heard, simply could not help them.

The Macedonians were not alone now in that they had been joined by all the Greeks, Boeotians and Phocaeans who had suffered Theban oppression in the past. These people, even though they spoke the same language and the same dialect as the Thebans, proved to be the cruellest of all, continuing to inflict violence even when there were piles of bodies on every corner and in every square.

Only the arrival of nightfall, together with exhaustion and drunkenness, brought the massacre to an end.

On the following day Alexander united the council of the League to decide what was to be done with Thebes.

The delegates from Plataea were the first to speak: 'The Thebans have always been traitors to the Greeks' common cause. They were alone among our peoples, during the Persian invasion, in forging an alliance with the Great King against our brothers who were fighting for freedom. They showed no pity then, when our city was destroyed by the barbarians and razed to the ground, when our women were violated and our children were taken as slaves to countries so far away that no one will ever be able to find them.'

'And the Athenians,' said the Thespian delegate, 'they helped the Thebans only to abandon them in their moment of need, when the just punishment approached . . . perhaps the Athenians have lost all memory of the occasion when the Persians burned their city, razing the temples of the gods to the ground?'

'To make a punitive example of one single city,' the Phocaean and the Thessalian representatives suggested, 'will help prevent future wars, and will deter others from violating the peace out of hatred and blind partisanship.'

The decision was taken by a large majority, and although Alexander himself was against it, he could not oppose it because he had proclaimed that he would respect the council's motion.

Eight thousand Thebans were sold as slaves. Their age-old city, celebrated by Homer and Pindar, was razed to the ground. Thebes was wiped from the face of the earth as if it had never existed.

44

ALEXANDER LET HIMSELF FALL to the ground from his horse and then he dragged himself off to his tent. His head was full of bloodcurdling cries, of laments and pleas, his hands were covered in blood.

He declined food and water, unstrapped his weapons and threw himself onto his bed where his body was wracked by terrible spasms. It was as if he had lost control of his muscles and his senses – nightmares and hallucinations passed before his eyes and moved through his soul like a storm destroying everything in its path, a hurricane blew through his mind, uprooting any thought that appeared there just as soon as it had begun to take shape.

These were the hours immediately after the storming of Thebes and the pain and despair of an entire Greek city torn up by the roots weighed on his soul like a millstone. The sense of oppression was so strong it exploded in an almost feral cry of delirium and suffering. For those who heard it, however, it was no different from the many other cries that cut through that accursed night, its darkness haunted by drunken shadows, by blood-sodden spirits.

Ptolemy's voice suddenly broke into his consciousness.

'It was nothing like a battle in an open field, was it? It wasn't like the battle on the Ister. And yet the fall of Troy as sung by your Homer was no different from this, and neither was the destruction of many other glorious cities of which not even any trace of memory remains.'

Alexander said nothing. He had sat up on the bed as Ptolemy talked and the expression on his face was that of a man possessed, almost mad. All he managed was to murmur, 'I . . . I didn't want to.'

'I know,' said Ptolemy as he lowered his head. 'You didn't enter the city,' he began again after a short silence, 'but I can assure you that the worst ones, the cruellest, the ones who mutilated these wretches were their very own neighbours – the Phocaeans, the Plataeans, the Thespians, all of them kin to the Thebans, if not identical, in terms of language, stock, tradition and belief.

'Seventy years ago Athens was defeated and was forced to surrender unconditionally to its opponents – Spartans and Thebans. And do you know what the Thebans wanted to do? You do know, don't you? They wanted to burn Athens and to demolish the city walls, to slay the population or sell them off into slavery. If the Spartan Lysander had not been so firm in his opposition to their plans, then today the glory of the world, the most beautiful city ever built, would be nothing but a heap of ash and even its name would have been lost.

'The cruel fate invoked by the Thebans' ancestors against a helpless, harmless enemy has today come home to roost with their descendants. It is their inexorable nemesis. And yet today the circumstances are different – you had even offered them peace in exchange for minimal limitation of their freedom.

'And now, out there, their neighbours, the members of the Boeotian Confederation, are already arguing over how to split up the territory of their mother city and they are calling for your arbitration in this process.'

Alexander moved towards a basin full of water and plunged his head into it. Then he dried his face and said, 'Is this why you have come? I don't want to see them.'

'No. I came to tell you that the house of the poet Pindar, as you ordered, has been spared and I managed to save a certain number of works from the flames.'

Alexander nodded.

'I also wanted to tell you that . . . Perdiccas is close to death. He was seriously injured in yesterday's attack, but he didn't want you to be informed.'

'Why?'

'Because he didn't want to distract you from the responsibilities of your command at such a crucial moment. But now . . .'

'So that's why he hasn't been here to report to me! Oh, by the gods!' exclaimed Alexander. 'Take me to him immediately.'

Ptolemy went out and the King followed him to a tent at the far western end of the camp where lamps were burning.

Perdiccas lay on his bed, out of his mind, soaked in sweat and burning up with fever. Philip the physician was sitting by him and was squeezing a clear liquid from a sponge into his mouth.

'How is he?' Alexander asked.

Philip shook his head. 'His temperature is very high and he has lost a lot of blood. It's an ugly wound – a spear under his collar bone. It didn't catch his lung, but it cut through several muscles and the bleeding is terrible. I've cauterized it, stitched and dressed it, and now I'm trying to give him some liquid mixed with a medicine that should calm the pain and keep the fever down. But I don't know how much of it he actually absorbs and how much is lost . . .'

Alexander came nearer and put a hand on Perdiccas' forehead.

'My friend, don't go, don't leave me.'

Together with Philip he sat up all night to watch over Perdiccas, even though he was exhausted and hadn't slept for two whole days. At dawn, Perdiccas opened his eyes and looked around. Alexander elbowed Philip who had dropped off to sleep.

The doctor woke up, took a look at the wound and placed his hand on his patient's forehead – he was still very hot, but his temperature had come down considerably.

'Perhaps he'll make it,' said Philip before going back to sleep.

Shortly afterwards Ptolemy came in.

'How is he?' he asked quietly.

'Philip thinks he might make it.'

'That's good. But you should rest now – you look terrible.'

'Everything here has been terrible, these have been the worst days of my life.'

Ptolemy came nearer, as if wanting to say something, but he couldn't quite bring himself to.

'What's wrong?' asked Alexander.

'I . . . I don't know . . . if Perdiccas had died then I wouldn't have said anything, but since he might survive, I think you should know . . .'

'What? By the gods . . . don't drag it out so much.'

'Before he lost consciousness, Perdiccas gave me a letter.'

'For me?'

'No. For your sister, the Queen of Epirus. They were lovers, and in the letter he asks her never to forget him. I . . . we all joked about this infatuation of his, but no one ever thought that they really . . .' Ptolemy handed over the letter.

'No,' said Alexander. 'I don't want to see it. It's all water under the bridge. My sister was a young girl full of life, and I don't see anything wrong in her having desired a man she liked. She's no longer an adolescent and she is embarking on a marriage with a husband she loves. As for Perdiccas, I certainly can't take him to task for having wanted to dedicate his last thoughts to the woman he loves.'

'And what am I to do with this?'

'Burn it. But if he asks you, tell him it was delivered straight to Cleopatra in person.'

Ptolemy went over to a lamp and held the papyrus sheet over the flame. Perdiccas' declaration of love was consumed in the flames and disappeared with the smoke into the air.

*

The ruthless punishment of Thebes provoked horrified reaction throughout Greece: never had such an illustrious city been wiped from the face of the earth. Thebes' roots ran so deep that they mingled with the very myths of Greek origin. The despair of the few survivors became the despair of all Greeks, who identified their homeland with the city. in which they were born. The sanctuaries, the springs, the squares where, every memory of their origins was guarded lovingly.

The city was everything for the Greeks – images stood at every street corner, ancient simulacra worn by time which in one way or another were linked to myths, to events that were all part of their common heritage. Every fount had its own sound, every tree its voice, every stone its history. Everywhere there were traces of the gods, of the heroes, of the ancestors, everywhere there were people venerating their relics and their effigies.

To lose one's city was like losing one's soul, like dying before one's time, like becoming blind after having long enjoyed the light of the sun and the colours of the earth. It was worse than being a slave, because often slaves have no memory of their past.

The Theban refugees who managed to reach Athens were the first to bring the news and it plunged the city into deep anguish. The people's representatives sent heralds everywhere to summon the assembly because they wanted everyone to hear the accounts of what had happened from eye witnesses and not through second-hand tales.

When the truth was clear to everyone in all its frightful drama, an old military admiral by the name of Phokion – the man who had led the Athenian expedition in the Straits against Philip's fleet – stood up to speak.

'It seems clear to me that what has happened at Thebes could happen here in Athens too. We have reneged on our pact with Philip exactly as the Thebans had. And, what's more, we armed the Thebans. Why should Alexander show any leniency towards us?

'It is also true that those responsible here for these decisions – those who persuaded the people to vote for these measures, who incited the Thebans to challenge the King of Macedon and then abandoned them to face him alone and who now expose their own city to a terrible risk – it is true that these people should bear in mind that the sacrifice of a few is always preferable to the extermination of many, or of an entire city. They ought to be brave enough to hand themselves over and to confront the fate that they have so recklessly tempted.

'Citizens, when I spoke against these decisions I was accused of being a Macedonian sympathizer. When Alexander was still in Thrace, Demosthenes said that a little boy had climbed up onto the throne of Macedon – then he became a youngster when he reached Thessaly and then a young man when he appeared beneath the walls of Thebes. Now that he has demonstrated all his devastating power, how would you describe him? How do you intend to address him? Will you finally recognize that this is a man in full possession of his own immeasurable power and abilities?

'I have only one last thing to say. I believe firmly that it is necessary to have the courage both of one's actions and of one's convictions.'

Demosthenes stood up to defend his own actions and those of his supporters by appealing, as he always did, to the sense of freedom and democracy which had been born in Athens, and he concluded by letting the assembly decide his own fate:

'I am not afraid of death. I have already looked death

square in the face on the field at Chaeronaea, where I barely survived by hiding in the midst of piles of bodies and then fleeing through the mountains. I have always served this city and I will continue to serve it now in these difficult moments. If the assembly asks me to hand myself over, I will do so.'

Demosthenes had been adroit as always – he had offered himself up for sacrifice, but in truth he had spoken so skilfully that for all those listening such a choice would have been almost a form of sacrilege.

The assembly discussed the situation for some time and the various heads of the opposing political factions were given the time necessary to persuade their own supporters.

Two well-known philosophers were also present – Speusippus, who had become director of the Academy on Plato's death, and Demophanes.

'Do you know what I think?' said Speusippus to his friend with a sardonic smile. 'I think that when Plato and the Athenians denied Aristotle the directorship of the Academy, he, out of a sense of revenge, went ahead and created Alexander.'

The assembly voted against the proposal to hand over Demosthenes and his supporters to the Macedonians. They also decided, however, to send a delegation made up of those men who would have the greatest chance of being listened to, and Demades was chosen to lead it.

Alexander met him on the road to Corinth, where he intended to summon once again the representatives of the pan-Hellenic League to have himself reconfirmed, after the events at Thebes, as supreme commander in the war against the Persians.

He was sitting in his tent and Eumenes was at his side.

'How is your wound, Demades?' was the first thing he asked, leaving all the onlookers stunned.

The orator lifted up his cloak and showed the scar. 'It has healed perfectly, Alexander. A true surgeon couldn't have done any better.'

'It's all credit to my teacher, Aristotle, a man who was once your fellow citizen. In fact, don't you think it's about time you dedicated a statue to him in your market place? Athens doesn't have one, does it? A public statue of Aristotle?'

The delegates looked at one another, even more stupefied now.

'No. We haven't taken care of that yet,' admitted Demades.

'Think about it. And one more thing – I want Demosthenes, Lycurgus and all those who led the revolt handed over to me.'

Demades lowered his head. 'Sire, we expected this request and we understand your state of mind. You well know that I personally have lobbied for peace, even though I have always done my duty and have fought just like any other citizen whenever the city has asked us to. Nevertheless, I am convinced that Demosthenes and the others acted in good faith, like true patriots.'

'Patriots?' shouted Alexander.

'Yes, King Alexander, patriots,' repeated Demades with conviction.

'In that case why do they not hand themselves over? Why don't they accept responsibility for their actions?'

'Because the city voted against it and the city is ready

to face any danger and any challenge. Listen, Alexander, Athens is ready to accept reasonable requests, but don't push us to desperate measures because even if you should win, your victory will be much more bitter than any defeat.

'Thebes is gone and Sparta will never ally with you. If you destroy Athens or you make the city your enemy for all time, what will be left of Greece then? Clemency, very often, goes much further than force or arrogance ever will.'

Alexander did not reply but stood up and paced back and forth in his tent. Then he sat down once again and asked, 'What do you want?'

'No Athenian citizen will be handed over and there will be no retaliation against the city. We also ask to be allowed to grant asylum and aid to the Theban refugees. In exchange we will renew our membership of the pan-Hellenic League and the common pact of peace. If you move into Asia you will need our fleet to cover your back – yours is too small and too inexperienced to manage unaided.'

Eumenes moved closer to Alexander and whispered in his ear, 'They all seem like reasonable proposals to me.'

'In that case draw up a document and sign it,' ordered Alexander as he stood up. He slipped the seal ring off his finger and put it in Eumenes' hand before leaving.

45

Aristotle closed his satchel, took his cloak from the wall where it was hanging and unhooked the door key from a nail. He took one last look around the room and said to himself, 'I don't think I've forgotten anything.'

'So you really are leaving then?' asked Callisthenes.

'Yes. I have decided to return to Athens since the situation there seems to have quietened down.'

'Do you know where you'll be staying?'

'Demades has taken care of all that and he's found me quite a big building near Lycabettus with a covered portico, similar to Mieza, where I can set up a school. There is enough space to house a library and the natural science collections and there will be a section dedicated to musical research. I have already had all the materials carried to the port and all that's left to do is for me to set sail.'

'And so you're leaving me to deal with the investigation on my own.'

'Quite the opposite. In Athens I'll be able to garner much more information than in Macedonia. I've already learned all there is to be learned here.'

'Which is?'

'Sit down,' said Aristotle as he took some sheets full of notes from a drawer. 'The only sure thing, up to now, is that Philip's death caused such upset that it raised a cloud of whisperings, rumours, calumnies, insinuations, just like an enormous stone falling to the muddy bed of a clear pond. One has to wait for the mud to settle before being able to see clearly through the water again.

'Pausanias' actions originated – and this was foreseeable – in some murky affair of male love, the most dangerous of all loves. To make a long story short, Pausanias – a fine young man, skilful with his weapons – manages to join up with Philip's bodyguards. The King notices him and takes him as his lover. In the meantime Attalus puts his daughter, poor Eurydice, into the King's bed and Philip finds her irresistible.

'Pausanias is driven wild by jealousy and, during a meeting with Attalus, actually has a screaming fit, but the General shrugs off this insubordination and indeed seems to take it all in his stride. As a sign of good faith he invites Pausanias to dine with him after a hunting expedition in the mountains.

'The place is very isolated. The wine flows freely and everyone is merry and excited. At a certain point Attalus disappears and leaves Pausanias in the hands of his huntsmen, who strip him naked and rape him repeatedly throughout the night in all the ways they can possibly imagine. Then they abandon him, more dead than alive.

'This outrage drives Pausanias out of his mind and he asks Philip to avenge it, but the King certainly cannot consider any action against his future father-in-law, a man he anyway greatly respects. Pausanias would like to kill Attalus himself, but this is no longer possible because Philip has put him in command, together with Parmenion, of the Asian expeditionary force. Pausanias therefore turns his rage against the only target left to him – Philip. And he kills him.'

Aristotle let his left hand fall on the sheaf of papyrus with a thump, to drive home his conclusion.

Callisthenes stared into the philosopher's little grey eyes, which shone with an undefinable expression some way between the knowing and the ironic.

'I can't make up my mind if you believe all of this or if you're just pretending to believe it.'

'One must never underestimate the impetus of the passions, which are always a strong motivating factor in human behaviour, especially the behaviour of an individual who is lacking in mental equilibrium as an assassin inevitably is. Furthermore, the complexity of the tale is such that it might even be true.'

'It might be . . .'

'Indeed. But there are many things that don't make sense. Firstly, there has been much talk about Philip's affairs with men, but no one has ever recounted anything definite beyond occasional episodes . . . not even this time. And in any case can you imagine that a man in Philip's position would be so stupid as to take on a hysterical madman as his bodyguard?

'Secondly, if things really did happen this way, why did Pausanias wait so long before carrying out his act of revenge and why did he do it in such a reckless manner? Thirdly, who is the key witness to all of this? Attalus, of course, but Attalus is conveniently dead. Murdered.'

'So?'

'So the most likely thing is that the person who commissioned the assassination actually invented a complex, but basically plausible story which puts the blame on a person who, being dead, can neither prove nor deny his innocence.'

'As clear as mud, basically.'

'Perhaps. But there is something that's beginning to take shape.'

'What?'

'The personality of the man or woman behind it all, and the type of circle out of which these events arose. I have a copy of my notes here in my bag, so you must keep hold of these, Callisthenes, and make good use of them. I will continue the investigation from another vantage point.'

'The fact is,' his nephew replied, 'that I may find myself with no time left to continue my enquiries. Alexander is now completely taken with the Asian expedition and he has asked me to follow him. I am to write the history of this enterprise.'

Aristotle nodded and half-closed his eyes. 'This means that Alexander has taken the past and its burden of significance and has put it behind him. He is rushing towards the future now, which is to say, in essence, that he is rushing towards the unknown.'

He picked up his bag, threw his cloak over his shoulders and went out onto the road. The sun was just rising over the horizon and far off in the distance it was beginning to give shape to the bare peaks of Mount Kissos, beyond which lay the vast Plain of Macedon with its capital and the secluded retreat at Mieza.

'It's strange,' he remarked as he walked to the small carriage that was waiting to take him to the port, 'there simply hasn't been the time for Alexander and me to meet again.'

'But you are always in his thoughts and perhaps one day, before he leaves, he will come to visit you.'

'I doubt it,' said the philosopher as if thinking to himself. 'He is drawn by his longing for adventure like a moth to the flame of a lamp. When he truly feels he wants to see me, it will be too late for him to turn back. In any case, I will send you my address in Athens, so that you may write to me whenever you like. I am sure Alexander will do everything in his power to maintain a line of communication with the city. Farewell, Callisthenes, take good care of yourself.'

Callisthenes hugged his uncle. As Aristotle moved away, just before he climbed onto the carriage, Callisthenes thought he saw, for the first time ever, a spark of sentiment in those little grey eyes.

46

THE ANCIENT SANCTUARY was just visible in the evening darkness, there at the edge of the wood. It was illuminated from below by lamps and torches, and the painted wood of its columns displayed all the ravages of time and the elements to which it had been exposed for centuries.

The coloured terracotta decorations of the architrave and the tympanum depicted the deeds of the god Dionysus, and the flickering reflections of the torch- and lamplight seemed to lend them movement, almost as though calling them to life.

The door was open and inside – within the cella and through the half-light – the figure of the statue of the god could be made out, solemn in its age-old immobility. Two seats had been prepared at its feet and another eight were arranged, four on each side, along the lateral colonnades that supported the ceiling joists.

Ptolemy arrived first, then Craterus and Leonnatus together. Lysimachus, Seleucus and Perdiccas, still not completely recovered, came not long afterwards and shortly behind them Eumenes and Philotas, who had also been invited to the meeting. Alexander, astride Bucephalas, arrived last of all together with Hephaestion.

Only then did they all enter and take up position along the colonnades of the deserted and silent temple.

Alexander sat down, had Hephaestion join him to his right and then signalled to the others to do the same, all of them excited and impatient to know what the purpose of this night-time meeting might be.

'The moment has come,' the King began, 'to set out on the enterprise my father long dreamed of, but which was denied him by a sudden, violent death – the invasion of Asia!'

A gust of wind blew through the main door and the flames of the lamps burning beneath the statue of the god flickered wildly, animating Dionysus's enigmatic smile.

'Our meeting place here tonight is not by any means coincidental. Dionysus – the god who travelled with his cortege of satyrs and sileni, bearing crowns of vine-leaves – will show us the way to distant India where no Greek army has ever been.

'The conflict between Asia and Greece is an age-old one that has neither winners nor losers. The Trojan War lasted ten years and ended with the sack and the destruction of just one city, and the most recent invasions – attempts made first by the Athenians and then by the Spartans to free the Greeks of Asia from Persian domination – failed, just as the Persian attempts at invading Greece failed in their turn. But all of these events involved no shortage of massacres, fires and raids which did not even spare the temples of the gods.

'Times have changed now. *We* are the most powerful army that has ever existed and *we* are the strongest, best-trained soldiers, but above all else,' he said as he looked into their faces one by one, '*we*, those of us sitting here tonight, are united by the common bond of deep and sincere friendship. We grew up together in the palace at Pella, we played together as children, we went to the same school, together we learned how to face our first trials and our first dangers.'

'We all had a taste of the same cane!' added Ptolemy, provoking laughter all round.

'Quite right!' said Alexander.

'Is that why you haven't invited Parmenion?' asked Seleucus. 'If I remember well, you and I both copped it once from the old General on specific orders from your father.'

'By Zeus! I see you have a good memory,' Alexander laughed.

'And who could ever forget that cane?' asked Lysimachus. 'I think I've still got the marks on my back.'

'No, that is not the reason why I haven't invited Parmenion,' Alexander began again after having regained his companions' attention. 'I have no secrets to keep from him, however, and that is why his son, Philotas, is here with us tonight.

'Parmenion will be the linchpin of our enterprise, our counsellor, the repository of all the skills and experience my father accumulated. But Parmenion is a friend of my father's and Antipater's, while you are *my* friends, and here and now I ask you, before Dionysus and all the gods, to follow me and to fight with me wherever we must go. Even if that means to the ends of the earth!'

'Even to the ends of the earth!' they all shouted, getting to their feet and gathering round the King.

A powerful excitement had spread through them, an irrepressible agitation, a burning desire for adventure that had become all the more urgent for their having seen and had physical contact with Alexander, for he more than anyone seemed to nurture Philip's dream.

'Each one of you,' the King continued when they had calmed down a little, 'will take command of a division of the army, but each one of you will also bear the title of King's "bodyguard". Never before have such young men borne such enormous responsibility. But I know that you are up to this because I know you, because I grew up with you and because I have seen you in combat.'

'When do we set off?' Lysimachus asked.

'Soon. This spring. So get ready . . . in body and in spirit. And if any of you should have second thoughts, or should change your minds completely, do not be afraid to tell me. I will need trusted friends back home as well.'

'How many men will you lead into Asia?' asked Ptolemy.

'Thirty thousand foot soldiers, and five thousand horses and everything we can take with us without leaving Macedonian territory too exposed. And I am still not sure how far we can actually trust our Greek allies. In any case, I have asked them to provide a contingent, but I don't think they'll manage any more than five thousand men.'

'We don't need them!' exclaimed Hephaestion.

'But we do,' replied Alexander. 'They are excellent soldiers and we all know that. What's more, this war is our response to the Persian invasions of Greek territory, to the continued threat posed by Asia over Hellas.'

Eumenes stood up. 'May I speak too?'

'Let Mister Secretary General speak!' Craterus laughed.

'Yes. Let him speak,' said Alexander. 'I want to know what he thinks.'

'It won't take long for me to tell you what I think, Alexander. The fact is that if I work solidly from here to the beginning of the expedition I will manage to scrape together enough resources to sustain the army for one month, no more than that.'

'Eumenes is always thinking about money!' shouted Perdiccas.

'It's just as well someone does,' replied Alexander. 'That's what I pay him for. Indeed, the point he makes is no laughing matter, but it is something I have already given some thought to. The Greek cities of Asia will help us, given that we are embarking on this to help them as well. After that we'll see.'

'We'll see?' asked Eumenes as if he couldn't believe his ears.

'Didn't you hear what he said?' Hephaestion chipped in. 'Alexander said, "we'll see". Isn't that clear enough?'

'Not in the slightest,' mumbled Eumenes. 'If I have to organize provisions for forty thousand men, including our Greek allies, and five thousand horses then I'd like to know where the money's going to come from, by Hercules!'

Alexander clapped him on the back. 'We'll find it somehow, Eumenes, don't you worry. I assure you we'll find it. You just busy yourself getting everything ready for the off. It won't be long now.

'Friends, a thousand years have passed since my ancestor Achilles first set foot in Asia to fight the city of Troy together with other Greeks, and now not only will we accomplish a feat of the same magnitude, but we are sure to surpass it. There may well be no Homer to pen our story, but our valour will be none the less for all that.

'I am certain that you can equal the deeds of the heroes of the *Iliad*. We have dreamed of them many times together, have we not? Have you forgotten how in our dormitory we would get up after Leonidas had done his rounds and we would all tell stories about the adventures of Achilles, Diomedes and Ulysses? We would stay up late into the night, until we fell asleep exhausted.'

Silence fell in the temple, because they were all filled now with memories of their youth, gone now but still near them. And together with the memories was a slight trepidation for an impending, unknown future, and the awareness that Death and War always ride together.

They looked at Alexander, at the changing colour of his eyes in the weak glimmer of the lamps, and they read there a mysterious perturbation, a burning desire for endless adventure, and it came to them there and then that they really would soon be setting off on an adventure, but they knew not when and indeed whether they would ever return.

The King moved closer to Philotas. 'I will speak to your father. I would rather you didn't tell him about this evening.'

Philotas nodded. 'You're right, you must speak to him. And I am glad you asked me to take part.'

The atmosphere had suddenly become leaden and Ptolemy broke it with a simple, 'I'm hungry now. What would you all say to the idea of eating a skewered partridge down at Eupithos' tavern?'

'Yes! Good idea!' they all agreed.

'Eumenes is paying!' shouted Hephaestion.

'Yes! Yes! Eumenes is paying!' they all repeated, including the King.

Shortly afterwards the temple was again deserted and all that could be heard was the galloping of their horses fading into the night.

*

At that same moment, far away in the palace at Buthrotum on a cliff above the sea, Cleopatra was about to open the doors of her bed chamber and her arms to her husband. The period of mourning required for a young wife had come to its end.

The King of the Molossians had been welcomed by a group of maids dressed in white and bearing torches, symbols of burning love, and they led him along the stairs up to a half-open door. One of them took his white cloak from his shoulders and gently pushed the door. Then they all disappeared down the corridor together, as light as nocturnal butterflies.

Alexander saw a golden, trembling light come to rest on a head of hair as soft as sea foam – Cleopatra. He remembered the shy little girl he had caught glimpses of so many times as she secretly observed him in the palace at Pella, only to run away on her slender little legs if he turned to look at her. Two maids were attending to her – one was combing her hair, while the other was undoing the belt of her nuptial gown and was opening the gold and amber buckles that held it on her ivory-smooth shoulders. And then the young Queen turned towards the door, wearing only the lamplight.

Her husband entered and moved closer to study the beauty of her statuesque body, to drink deep of the brightness that emanated from her divine countenance. She held his ardent eyes without lowering her long, moist lashes – just at that moment her gaze burned with the wild force of Olympias and the visionary ardour of Alexander and the King was completely lost in her eyes before he took her in his arms.

He gently caressed her face and her full breasts with his hand. 'My bride, my goddess ... how many sleepless nights have I spent in this house dreaming of your honey mouth and your body. So many nights ...'

His hand moved down to her smooth belly, over her downy sex, while with his other arm he held her tightly to his body and then guided her forcefully to the bed.

He opened her lips with a fiery kiss and she responded with equal passion, with an ever more intense and ardent strength, and when he took her, he realized that she was not a virgin, that another had had her before him, but he didn't pull back. He continued to give her all the pleasure it was in his power to give and luxuriated in their union, in her perfumed skin, sinking his face into the soft cloud of her hair, seeking her neck with his lips, kissing her shoulders and her fine breasts.

He felt as though he were lying with a goddess, and no mortal can ever ask anything of a goddess, he can only ever be grateful for what he receives from her.

He lay exhausted at her side when he had finished, while the flames of the lamps died one after another, leaving the opalescent half-light of the moon to penetrate the room.

Cleopatra fell asleep on her husband's ample chest, exhausted by the length of their pleasures and by the sleepiness that suddenly weighed on her maidenly eyes.

For days and nights the Molossian King only had thoughts for her, he dedicated all his time to her and paid her every possible attention, every consideration, even though deep in his heart he felt the stabs of pain that were his jealousy. But then something unexpected arose to revive his interest in the outside world once more.

He was with Cleopatra up on the walkways of the palace enjoying the evening breeze, when suddenly he saw a small fleet sailing from the open sea towards his port. There was one large vessel with a magnificent figurehead in the shape of a dolphin escorted by four warships carrying archers and foot soldiers all armoured with bronze.

Shortly afterwards a guard came to him. 'Sire, the foreign guests come from Italy, from an important city by the name of Tarant, and they have asked for an audience with you tomorrow.'

The King looked at the red sun which was slowly disappearing below the horizon and replied, 'Tell them I will gladly meet with them.'

He then poured a cup of light, sparkling wine for Cleopatra, the same wine her brother enjoyed, and he asked her, 'Do you know this city?'

'Only by name,' replied the girl as she put the cup to her lips.

'It is a very rich and powerful city, but it has always been weak in war. Would you like to hear its story?'

The sun by now had descended beneath the sea and all that was left on the waves was a purple reflection.

'Certainly, if you're the one who tells it to me.'

'Good. What you must know to start with is that a long time ago the Spartans besieged the city of Ithome in Messenia. The siege lasted years and they simply couldn't break the deadlock. The Spartan leaders were worried because back in their own city very few babies were being born as a result of the prolonged absence of the thousands and thousands of soldiers being used at Ithome. It was felt that the day would come when there simply wouldn't be enough young men for their army and the city would find itself unprotected.

'So they came up with a solution – they went to Ithome, chose a group of soldiers, the youngest and strongest, and gave them orders to return home to carry out a much more pleasurable mission than a long drawn out siege. More pleasurable, but no less demanding.'

Cleopatra smiled knowingly. 'I think I can guess what it was.'

'Exactly,' continued the King. 'Their mission was to make all the city's virgins pregnant. They accomplished it with the same sense of duty and with the same ardour they displayed in combat. They were so successful that the following year a veritable litter of babies was born in Sparta.

'But the war finished shortly afterwards and on returning to their homes all the other soldiers sought to make up for lost time, resulting in yet more babies. As all these children grew up, however, the legitimate ones claimed that all those born of the virgins should not be considered true citizens of Sparta, but ought instead to be treated as bastards.

'Indignant, the children of the virgins started planning an uprising, led by a strong and daring young man by the name of Taras. Unfortunately for them, their plans were discovered and they were ordered to leave their homeland. Taras questioned the oracle at Delphi who directed him towards a place in Italy where they would be able to found a city and live off the fat of the land. The exiles did indeed found the city and it still stands there today – Tarant, which takes its name from Taras.'

'It's a lovely story,' said Cleopatra with just a shade of sadness in her eyes, 'but I wonder what they want.'

'I'll let you know as soon as I have met with them,' said the King as he stood up and took his leave with a kiss. 'And now I must go and give instructions so that our guests are put up in a fashion worthy of their status.'

The small Tarantine fleet left two days later, and only when the sails had disappeared over the horizon did Alexander of Epirus return to his bride's bed chamber.

Cleopatra had prepared supper in her room – specially perfumed with lilies – and she had stretched out on the dining bed wearing a gown of transparent linen.

'What did they want?' she asked as soon as her husband was stretched out next to her.

'They came to ask for my help and . . . to offer me Italy.'

Cleopatra said nothing, but her expression darkened.

'Will you be going away?' she asked after a long silence.

'Yes,' replied the King. And inside he felt that this expedition and the war and perhaps even the risk of death in battle would afflict him less than the thought, which was growing day by day, that Cleopatra had once belonged to another man and that perhaps she still remembered him, or perhaps she loved him.

'Is it true that my brother is also about to set off on an expedition?'

'Yes. Towards the East. The invasion of Asia.'

'And you are to go towards the West and I will be left alone.'

The King took her hand and caressed it for a while in silence. Then he said, 'Listen. One day, when Alexander was a guest here in the palace, he had a dream which I want to tell you about now . . .'

*

Parmenion looked Alexander in the eyes with disbelief written all over his face. 'You can't be serious.'

Alexander put a hand on his shoulder. 'I have never been so serious in all my life. This was the dream of Philip, my father, and it has always been my dream. We will set off with the first winds of spring.'

'But, Sire,' Antipater said, 'you cannot begin an expedition in this manner.'

'Why not?'

'Because in war anything can happen and you have neither a bride nor an heir. You must first take a wife and leave an heir to the throne of Macedon.'

Alexander smiled and shook his head. 'I hadn't given it

the slightest consideration. Taking a wife is a very long process. We would have to evaluate all the possible candidates for the role of Queen, spend time deciding on the chosen one and then deal with the difficult reactions of all those families who would be excluded from the much sought-after family tie with the throne.

'There would be the wedding to be prepared – the guest list, the ceremony and all the rest, and then I'd have to make the girl pregnant, which wouldn't necessarily happen straight away. And then, even if it were to happen, it wouldn't by any means be certain that it would be a boy and so perhaps I'd have to wait another year. And when my son was finally born I would have to do what Ulysses did with Telemachus – leave him as an infant and see him once again after who knows how long. No, I must set off immediately. My mind is made up.

'I have called you here not to discuss my wedding, but my expedition to Asia. You two are the pillars of my kingdom, just as you were for my father, and I intend to confer on you duties which carry the very highest responsibility, and I hope you will accept them.'

'You know, Sire, that we are loyal to you,' said Parmenion, who never managed to call the young King by his first name, 'and we have every intention of serving you for as long as our strength allows us to do so.'

'I know,' said Alexander, 'and I know that this fact makes me a fortunate man. You, Parmenion, will come with me and you will have general command of the entire army, a command second only to that of the King. Antipater will remain in Macedon with all the prerogatives and powers of regent. Only in this way can I leave Pella with peace of mind, safe in the certainty that I am leaving my throne in the hands of the best man possible.'

'You honour me too much, Sire,' replied Antipater, 'especially because the Queen, your mother, will remain at Pella and . . .'

'I know perfectly well what you are alluding to, Antipater. But please do not forget the words I am about to pronounce – my mother must not be involved in any way with the government of the kingdom. She is to have no official contact with the foreign delegations and her role will be exclusively representative.

'Only on your request will she have any part to play in diplomatic relations, and even then under your strictest supervision. I want no interference from the Queen in any affairs of a political nature. You will deal with all such things personally.

'I want her to be respected and honoured and her every wish should be satisfied whenever possible, but everything must go through your hands – you, and not the Queen, will hold the royal seal.'

Antipater nodded. 'As you will, Sire. I only hope that this does not create conflicts – your mother is a very strong character and . . .'

'I will make a public announcement of the fact that you are the one who holds power in my absence and therefore you will be accountable to me and me alone for your decisions. In any case, we will be in constant contact. I will keep you informed of all of my actions and you will do the same, informing me of what happens in the cities of our Greek allies, and what happens among our friends and

our enemies alike. And for this reason we will be careful
to maintain safe lines of communication open at all times.

'There will be time to set out all the details of your
duties, Antipater, but the fact remains that you are a man
I trust and therefore you will have complete freedom in
making your decisions. The purpose of this meeting was
simply to discover whether the two of you agree to my
proposal, and I am very glad you do.'

Alexander got up from his seat and the two old generals
did the same as a sign of respect. But before the King left
the room, Antipater spoke: 'Just one thing, Sire. How long
do you think the expedition will last and how far do you
intend going?'

'I have no answer to that question, Antipater, because I
myself do not know the answer.'

And with a nod he left. The two generals stood alone
in the deserted royal armoury and Antipater said, 'You
know, don't you, that you will have enough provisions
and money for just one month?'

Parmenion nodded. 'I know. But what could I say? His
father, in his day, was even worse.'

*

Alexander returned to his apartments so late that night
that all the servants were asleep, apart from the guards
watching over his door and Leptine, who was waiting with
a lighted lamp to give him his bath, the water already
warm and perfumed.

She undressed him and waited for him to climb into the
big stone tub, then she poured water on his shoulders
from a silver jug. This was something the physician Philip

had taught her – the action of the water was an even more delicate massage than her own hands, it soothed him and relaxed the muscles in his shoulders and neck, the points where all the tiredness and tension concentrated.

Alexander let himself go gradually until he was completely stretched out, and Leptine continued pouring water on his belly and his thighs until he made a sign for her to stop.

She placed the jug on the edge of the bath and, even though the King had not yet said a word to her, she dared to speak first:

'They say you are about to set off on an expedition, Sire.'

Alexander did not reply and Leptine took a deep breath before continuing, 'They say you're going to Asia and I . . .'

'You?'

'I would like to go with you. I beg you – only I know how to look after you, only I know how to welcome you back home in the evening and get you ready for the night.'

'You will come,' replied Alexander as he got out of the bath.

Leptine's eyes filled with tears, but she said nothing and started drying him delicately with a sheet of linen.

Alexander lay down naked on his bed stretching out his limbs and she stood there for a moment looking at him as if enchanted and then, as she usually did, she undressed and lay down beside him, fondling him gently with her hands and her lips.

'No,' said Alexander. 'Not like that. Tonight I will take you.' He opened her legs carefully and slid on top of her. Leptine clung to him, gripping his hips in such a way that it was clear she didn't want to miss an instant of this intimacy which was so dear to her; with her hands she guided the long, continuous thrust of his back, the power of his hips, the very same force which had tamed Bucephalas. And when he relaxed and lay still her face was covered by his hair and she enjoyed its scent as she took deep breaths through it.

'Will I really be able to come with you?' she asked when Alexander stretched out on his back by her side.

'Yes, until at some stage on our march we come across a people whose language you understand – the mysterious language you sometimes speak in your sleep.'

'What do you mean, Sire?'

'Turn over,' Alexander ordered. Leptine turned her back and he took a lamp and held it above her.

'Did you know that you have a tattoo on your shoulder? I've never seen anything like it before. Yes, you will come with me and perhaps one day we will find someone who will make you remember who you are and where you come from, but there is one thing you must be aware of now: when we are in Asia things won't be as they are now. It will be another world – other people, other women – and I too will be different. We have come to the end of one period in my life and another one is beginning. Do you understand what I mean?'

'I understand, Sire, but for me it will be enough simply to be near you and to know that you are well. I ask no more from life, because I have already had much more from it than I could ever have hoped for.'

47

ALEXANDER MET the King of Epirus one month before setting out for Asia, at a secret rendezvous in Eordaea. The appointment had been arranged by means of a rapid exchange of messengers and they had not seen each other for more than a year, since Philip's assassination. Much had happened in that time, not only in Macedon and in Greece, but in Epirus too.

King Alexander had succeeded in uniting all of the tribes of his small mountainous homeland in a confederation that had recognized him as supreme leader and had given him command of and responsibility for training its army. The soldiers of Epirus were all trained after the Macedonian fashion – divided into phalanxes of heavy infantry and squadrons of cavalry – while the monarchy had adopted Greek models in terms of ceremony, in minting gold and silver coin, and in dress and behaviour. The King of Epirus and the King of Macedon were now very much mirror images of each other.

As the moment set for the meeting approached, shortly before dawn, the two young men recognized each other from far away and spurred their steeds towards the large plane tree that stood solitary near a spring in the middle of a vast clearing. The mountain shone with a dark yet strangely luminous green colour because of the recent rains and the approaching change of season, while across the sky, which was still dark, a mild wind pushed large white clouds that had come from the direction of the sea.

They dismounted, leaving the horses free to graze, and embraced with youthful enthusiasm.

'How are you?' asked Alexander.

'Fine,' replied his brother-in-law. 'I understand you are about to set off.'

'I hear you are too.'

'Did Cleopatra tell you?'

'Rumours.'

'I wanted to let you know in person.'

'I understand . . . thank you.'

'The city of Tarant, one of the richest in Italy, has asked for my help against the western barbarians who have been making incursions into their territory – the Brutians and the Lucanians.'

'I too am responding to a call for help from the Greek cities of Asia in their resistance against the Persians. Isn't it remarkable? We two have the same name, the same blood, we are both kings and leaders of armies and we are setting off on similar adventures. Do you remember my dream of the two suns?'

'It's the first thing that came to my mind when the envoys from Tarant explained their problem. Perhaps in all this there is some message from the gods.'

'I am certain of it,' replied Alexander.

'And so you are not against my going westward?'

'The only one who might oppose it is Cleopatra. My poor sister – she has seen her father assassinated on her wedding day and now her husband sets off on an adventure and leaves her abandoned and alone.'

'I will try to earn her forgiveness. Are you really not against it?'

'Against it? I am all for it. Listen: if you had not asked me for this meeting, I would have asked you. Do you remember Aristotle's big map?'

'There's a reproduction of it in my palace at Buthrotum.'

'Greece is the centre of the world in that map, and Delphi is the fulcrum of Greece. Pella and Buthrotum are equidistant from Delphi, and Delphi is equally distant from the extreme West – from the Pillars of Hercules – and from the far East – where the waters of the motionless, waveless Ocean lie.

'You and I must make a solemn oath here, calling on the sky and the earth as witnesses: we must promise to go forth – myself towards the East and you towards the West – and we must never stop until we reach the shores of the all-encircling Ocean. And we must swear that should one of us fall by the way, the other will take his place and will continue with our undertaking. We are both setting off without heirs, my friend, and therefore we will each be the other's heir. Are you willing to do this?'

'With all my heart, *Aléxandre*,' said the King of the Molossians.

'With all my heart, *Aléxandre*,' said the King of Macedon.

They unsheathed their swords, made incisions on their wrists, and mixed their blood in a small silver cup.

Alexander the Molossian poured some of it onto the

soil and then gave the cup to Alexander of Macedon, who threw the rest up into the air, towards the sky. Then the King of Macedon said, 'The sky and the earth have witnessed our oath. There can be no stronger, no more urgently binding tie. All that remains now is for us to take our leave and to wish each other good luck. We know not when we will see each other again. But when we do, it will truly be a great day, the greatest day the world has ever known.'

The springtime sun was coming into view just at that moment from behind the mountains of Eordaea and it flooded the vast landscape of peaks, valleys and torrents with a sharp, clear light. It made every single drop of dew sparkle, as if the night had rained pearls on the meadows and on the branches of the trees, as if the spiders had woven webs of silver in the dark.

The western wind responded to the appearance of the radiant face of the god of light by making waves in the great sea of grass that extended there before them, caressing the tufts of golden reeds and the purple crocuses, the red petals of the mountain lilies. Flocks of birds took to the air and flew towards the centre of the sky, standing out against the cirrus clouds which soared high and white like dove wings, and herds of deer came out of the forest and ran towards the sparkling torrents and the pastures.

At that moment there appeared, at the top of a hill, the agile figure of an Amazon, clad only in a short *chiton* over her naked, slender legs, a young girl with long golden hair astride a white horse with a flowing tail and mane.

'Cleopatra wanted to see you,' said the King of Epirus. 'I couldn't say no.'

'There was no need to say no. I too wanted to see her more than anything. Wait for me here.'

He jumped onto his steed and galloped to the young girl who sat waiting for him, trembling with emotion, resplendent like a statue of Artemis.

They dismounted, ran to each other and embraced, kissing on the cheek, kissing each other's eyelids, their hair; they hugged each other with a mutual sweetness and concern that was deeply moving.

'My beloved, my sweet, my gentle sister . . .' Alexander said as he looked at her with infinite tenderness.

'My Alexander, my King, my Lord, my beloved brother, light of my eyes . . .' and she couldn't bring herself to finish the sentence. 'Will I ever see you again?' she asked, her eyes moist with tears.

'No one can know the answer to that question, my sister, for our destiny lies in the hands of the gods. But I swear that you will always be in my heart – in the deep silence of the night as in the clamour of battle, in the burning of the desert as in the mountain cold. I will call your name every evening before going to sleep, and I hope the wind will carry my voice to you. Fare thee well, Cleopatra.'

'Farewell, Brother. I will go up every evening to the highest tower in the palace and I will listen out until the wind brings me your voice, and the scent of your hair. Fare thee well, *Aléxandre* . . .'

Cleopatra sped off in tears on her steed, unable to bear the sight of her brother's departure. Alexander returned slowly to his brother-in-law who was waiting for him below, leaning on the trunk of the giant plane tree. He dismounted and gave both hands to his namesake; his voice when he spoke was full of emotion:

'And so we must leave each other here. Farewell, King of the West, King of the Red Sun and of Mount Atlantis, King of the Pillars of Hercules. When we see each other again it will be to celebrate a new era for all humanity. But if fate or the envy of the gods should deny us that meeting, may our embrace now be stronger than time, stronger than death, and may our dream burn for ever like the flames of the sun.'

'Farewell, King of the East, King of the White Sun and of Mount Paropamisus, Lord of the Far Ocean. May our dream burn for ever, whatever be the destiny that awaits us.'

They embraced, overcome by emotion, while the breeze entwined their lions' hair, while their tears mingled just as their blood had mingled. It was a solemn, poignant rite in the presence of the sky and the earth, in the midst of the wind's strength.

Then they jumped astride their steeds and spurred them on – the King of the Molossians off towards the Evening and Sunset, the King of Macedon towards the Morning and the Dawn. At that moment not even the gods knew what fate awaited them because only Fate, the inscrutable, can ever know all the highways and the byways of such great men.

48

THE ARMY BEGAN to assemble with the arrival of the first spring winds, starting with battalions of the heavy infantry of the *pezhetairoi*, fully equipped, with their enormous *sarissae* on their shoulders. In the front lines were the young men, lined up with the shining copper Argead star on their shields, then came the more experienced soldiers sporting the bronze star and then, last but not least, the veterans, the shields on their arms bearing the silver star.

They all wore helmets in the shape of a Phrygian cap with a short visor, together with red tunics and cloaks. And when they took part in military exercises, carrying out turns or simulating attacks in the field, the *sarissae* would clash one against the other, creating a tremendous noise, as if the wind were blowing through the branches of a forest of bronze. And when the officers ordered them to lower their pikes, the immense phalanx looked horrifying, like a porcupine bristling with spines of steel.

The *hetairoi* cavalry were drawn from among the nobility, district by district, equipped with heavy armour covering them down to their abdomens and with Boeotian helmets with wide brims. They rode magnificent Thessalian horses, raised on the rich pastures of the plain and along the banks of the great rivers.

The fleet gathered in the northern ports and was joined

by Athenian and Corinthian divisions because there was some fear of an attack by the Persian imperial navy, led by a Greek admiral called Memnon, a formidable man in terms of cunning and experience, but above all else a man of his word who would respect his commitments, no matter what the outcome.

Eumenes had met him in Asia and warned Alexander one day when the King came to inspect the fleet aboard the flagship: 'Be careful, Alexander, Memnon is a principled mercenary who only ever sells his sword once and to one person only. His price is high, but then it's as if he has sworn loyalty to a new homeland – nothing and no one will ever make him change allegiance and flag.

'His fleet has both Greek and Phoenician crews and he can count on the clandestine support of the considerable number of adversaries you still have in Greece. Imagine what might happen if he were to unleash a surprise attack while we are ferrying our army from one side of the Straits to the other.

'My informers have created a system of reflected light signals between the Asian and European coasts so as to raise an immediate alarm should Memnon's fleet approach. We know that the Persian satraps from the western provinces have confirmed his supreme command of all their forces in Asia. His mission is to engage and neutralize your invasion force, but for the moment we have no news of his battle plans – we only have very limited information.'

'And how long will it take to gather more?' asked Alexander.

'Perhaps a month.'

'That's too long. We are setting out in four days' time.'

Eumenes looked at him in amazement. 'Four days? But that's madness, we don't have enough supplies yet. I told you – what we have now is only enough for a month, more or less. We must at least wait until the new deliveries arrive from Mount Pangaeos.'

'No, Eumenes. I will wait no longer. With each day that passes the enemy has more opportunity to organize his defences, to muster troops, to employ mercenaries . . . Greek ones even. We must strike as soon as possible. What do you think Memnon will do?'

'Memnon has already fought successfully against your father's generals. Ask Parmenion just how easy it is to predict his moves.'

'But what do you think he will do?'

'He will lead you far away landwards,' said a voice behind Eumenes, 'towards the interior, razing the earth in his wake, and then his fleet will sever your seaward communications and supplies.'

'Do you know Admiral Nearchus?' asked Eumenes.

Alexander shook the man's hand. 'Hail, Admiral!'

'Excuse me, Sire,' said Nearchus, a robust Cretan with broad shoulders and black hair and eyes. 'I was busy with preparations and wasn't able to reach you until now.'

'Is what you have just told us your sincere view of this situation?'

'Frankly . . . yes. Memnon knows that to challenge you on the open field would be dangerous because he doesn't have sufficient numbers of troops to deal with your infantry, but he almost certainly knows that you are lacking in reserves.'

'And how would he know that?'

'Because the Persians' intelligence-gathering system is second to none – they have spies everywhere and they are extremely well paid. What's more, they can count on many friends and sympathizers in Athens, in Sparta, Corinth and even here, in Macedon. All he need do is gain a little time and then instigate skirmishing operations by land and by sea behind you – we will find ourselves in trouble, and perhaps even in a trap.'

'Do you really think so?'

'I simply want you to be on your guard, Sire. What you are about to undertake is no ordinary enterprise.'

The ship was moving offshore with its prow breaking the waves of the open sea, the spray flying. The chief oarsman was beating the rhythm and the rowers bent and straightened their shining backs under the brightness of the sun, alternately immersing and raising the long oars.

Alexander appeared lost in listening to the rhythm of the drum and the calls of the rowers as they sought to maintain their timing.

'It seems this Memnon inspires fear in everyone,' he suddenly said.

'Not fear, Sire,' Nearchus asserted. 'We are simply considering a possible scenario. Indeed, in my opinion it is a most likely one.'

'You are right, Admiral. We are weakest and most exposed at sea, but on land we are invincible – no one can beat us.'

'For now,' said Eumenes.

'For now,' admitted Alexander.

'And so?' asked Eumenes again.

'Even the most powerful of fleets has need of ports, is that not the case, Admiral?'

'There is no doubt of that at all, Sire, but . . .'

'To cut him off you would have to occupy all the ports of call along the coast from the Straits to the delta of the Nile,' said Eumenes.

'Exactly,' replied Alexander, without batting an eyelid.

*

On the eve of their departure the King returned from Aegae in the dead of night. He had been there to offer a sacrifice on Philip's tomb and he went straight to his mother's apartments. The Queen was still awake, embroidering a cloak by lamplight. When Alexander knocked at her door she went to him and embraced him.

'I never imagined this moment would come,' she said, trying to conceal her emotion.

'You have seen me set off on other expeditions, Mother.'

'But it's different this time. I feel it. I have had strange dreams, difficult to interpret.'

'I can imagine. Aristotle says that dreams are the offspring of our minds and so we must search for the answer within our own selves.'

'I have sought it there, but for some time now I have found that looking within myself gives me a sense of vertigo, almost fear.'

'And I'm sure you know why.'

'What do you mean by that?'

'Nothing. You are my mother, and yet you are the most mysterious being I have ever known.'

'I am simply an unhappy woman. And now you are setting off on a long war, abandoning me here. But it was written that these things would happen, and that you should accomplish extraordinary, superhuman feats.'

'What does that mean?'

Olympias turned towards the window as if searching for images and memories among the stars or on the face of the moon. 'Once, before you were born, I dreamed that a god had touched me as I slept alongside your father in our bed chamber and one day, at Dodona, while I was expecting you, the wind that blew through the branches of the sacred oaks whispered me your name

Aléxandros.

'There are some men born of mortal women whose destinies are different from those of ordinary mortals, and you are one of these, my son, I am sure of it. I have always felt it is a privilege to be your mother, but saying farewell to you is no less bitter for that.'

'Neither is it for me, Mother. I lost my father recently, remember? And someone has told me that you were seen placing a garland around the neck of the assassin.'

'That man avenged the cruel humiliations that Philip had inflicted upon me, and by his actions he also made you King.'

'That man was carrying out someone else's orders. Why don't you put a garland of flowers around that person's neck too?'

'Because I don't know who that person is.'

'But sooner or later I will find out, and I will nail him to a pole.'

'And if your real father was a god?'

Alexander closed his eyes and saw Philip once more, falling into a lake of blood, he saw him collapse slowly as in a dream and he could clearly distinguish every crease that the pain wrote so cruelly on his father's face before it killed him. He felt burning tears come welling up in his eyes.

'If my father is a god then one day I will meet him. But certainly he will never be able to do for me what Philip did. I have offered sacrifices to his wrathful shadow, Mother.'

Olympias looked out to the sky and said, 'The Oracle at Dodona gave an omen for your birth. Another oracle, in the midst of a burning desert, will presage another birth for you, for a new life that will never perish.' Then she turned and suddenly threw herself into his arms. 'Think of me, my son. For I will think of you every single day and every single night. My spirit will shield you in battle, heal your wounds, lead you through the dark, defeat all malign influences, salve your fevers. I love you, Alexander, more than anything in this world.'

'I love you too, Mother, and I will think of you every day. And now let us take our leave, because we set out before dawn.'

Olympias kissed him on the cheeks, on his eyelids and on his forehead and she continued to embrace him as though she simply could not bear to let go.

Alexander extricated himself gently from the embrace with one last kiss and said, 'Farewell, Mother. Take good care.'

Olympias nodded while copious tears ran down her

cheeks. And only when the King's steps had faded into the distance of the palace corridors did she manage to murmur:

'Farewell, *Aléxandre*.'

She stayed up all night just to see him one last time from her balcony. He put on his armour by torchlight, fitted his crested helmet, strapped his sword to his side, slipped his arm through the straps of his shield which bore the golden star of Argead. All of this while Bucephalas neighed and stamped impatiently and Peritas barked desperately as he tried to break free of his chain.

And Olympias stood there immobile watching her son as he sped off astride his stallion. She waited until the last echo of his gallop disappeared far off, swallowed up by the darkness.

49

ADMIRAL NEARCHUS gave orders for the royal standard to be raised and the trumpets to sound, and the great quinquereme slipped smoothly through the waves. At the base of the main mast, in the centre of the deck, the gigantic drum of Chaeronaea had been fitted and four men beat the rhythm of the rowing with enormous mallets wrapped in leather. The thumping noise was carried on the wind and reached all the fleet as it followed behind.

Alexander stood at the bow wearing armour covered with silver laminate and on his head was a shining helmet of the same metal, but in the shape of a lion's head with its jaws wide open. His greaves bore an embossed pattern and he carried a sword with an ivory hilt which had belonged to his father. In his right hand he gripped a spear with an ash-wood shaft and a head of gold; it flashed light at his every movement, like Zeus's thunderbolt.

The King seemed intent on his dream and he stood there letting the brackish wind and the clear light of the sun caress his face, while all his men, from each of the one hundred and fifty ships of the fleet, kept their gaze firmly on the resplendent figure on the prow of the flagship. He looked like a statue of a god.

But suddenly he heard something and he cupped his hand to his ear. He turned round, worried, as if looking for something. Nearchus came closer. 'What is it, Sire?'

'Listen . . . can't you hear it as well?'

Nearchus shook his head. 'I can't hear anything, Sire.'

'Yes . . . listen. It's like . . . but it can't possibly be.'

He came down off the prow and walked along the gunnels until he heard, clearer now, but increasingly weak, the barking of a dog. He looked back into the foamy waves and saw Peritas swimming desperately, on the verge of going under. He shouted, 'It's my dog! It's Peritas, save him! Save him, by Hercules!'

Three sailors dived in immediately, tied ropes around the animal and hauled him aboard the ship.

He lay almost lifeless on the deck and Alexander, deeply moved, knelt next to him, petting and caressing his faithful dog. There was still a piece of chain around his neck and his paws were bleeding from the long journey.

'Peritas, Peritas,' he called, 'don't die.'

'Don't you worry, Sire,' reassured an army vet who had hurried to offer assistance. 'He'll make it. He's just half-dead from exhaustion.'

When the sun's rays had dried and warmed him, Peritas began to show some signs of life and it wasn't long before he was making himself heard once more. As the dog barked, Nearchus put his hand on the King's shoulder, 'Sire . . . Asia.'

Alexander started and ran to the prow. Ahead loomed the Asian coast, marked by small bays and dotted with villages nestling up in wooded hills and arranged around sunny beaches.

'We are preparing to land,' Nearchus added, while the sailors lowered the sail and made the anchor ready.

The ship continued forwards, cutting through the foamy

waves with its big bronze rostrum, and Alexander looked intently at the land which was now ever closer, as if the dream he had cherished for so long was about to become reality.

The captain shouted, 'Ship oars!'

And the rowers raised the dripping oars from the water, letting the craft slide under its own momentum towards the coast. When they were close to, Alexander grasped his spear, took a run up along the deck and let it fly with all his might.

The pointed shaft glided through the air in a wide arc, glinting in the sun like a meteor, then the golden head turned and plummeted straight earthward, gaining speed all the way until suddenly it landed and stuck deep, vibrating, in Asia.

ALEXANDER: THE SANDS OF AMMON

Continuing the epic saga of Alexander the Great, *The Sands of Ammon* brilliantly describes Alexander's quest to conquer Asia, the limitless domain ruled by the great King of the Persians.

Journeying over land and sea to the mysterious land of Egypt, Alexander discovers the Oracle of Ammon, which will reveal an amazing truth. One that will change his already amazing life.

Turn the page to read the first chapter . . .

1

FROM THE TOP OF THE HILL Alexander turned towards the beach and beheld a scene that was almost an identical repetition of one that had been played out a thousand years earlier. Hundreds of ships were lined up along the coast, carrying thousands and thousands of soldiers, but the city behind him – Ilium, heir to ancient Troy – rather than preparing for years of siege and resistance, was now getting ready to open its gates and welcome him, descendant of Achilles and of Priam.

He saw his companions coming up towards him on horseback and spurred Bucephalus on towards the top. He wanted to be the first to enter the ancient shrine of Athena in Troy and he wanted to do it alone. He dismounted, handed the reins to a servant and crossed the threshold of the temple.

Inside, objects glimmered in the darkness, difficult to make out, draped deep in the half-shadow. Their shape was indefinite and his eyes took some time to become accustomed to the gloom because up to just a moment before they had been coping with the dazzlingly bright sky of the Troad region with the sun at its highest.

The ancient building was full of relics, of weapons displayed in memory of the war described by Homer in his epic of the ten-year siege of the city built by the gods themselves. On each of the time-worn souvenirs was a dedication, an inscription: Paris's lyre was here, as were Achilles's weapons and his great shield.

He looked around, his eyes resting on these mementoes which unseen hands had kept shining for the reverence and the curiosity of the faithful over the centuries. They hung from the columns, from the ceiling beams, from the walls of the cella – but how much of all this was real? How much was simply the product of the priests' cunning, of their will to exploit it all for their own ends?

At that moment he felt as though the only genuine thing in the confused jumble – more like the clutter of objects displayed in a market than fitting décor for a sanctuary – was his own passion for the ancient blind poet, his boundless admiration for the heroes who had been reduced to ashes by time and by the countless events that had taken place between the two shores of the Straits.

He had arrived out of the blue, just as his father Philip had done one day at the temple of Apollo, at Delphi, when no one was expecting him. He heard some light footsteps and hid behind a column near the statue of Athena, a striking image of the goddess carved in stone, painted in various colours and bearing real metal weapons: this primitive simulacrum was sculpted from a single block of dark stone, and her mother-of-pearl eyes stood out starkly from a face darkened by the years and by the smoke of the votive lamps.

A girl wearing a white peplum, her hair gathered into a headdress of the same colour, moved towards the statue. She carried a bucket in one hand and a sponge in the other.

She climbed up on to the pedestal and began wiping the surface of the sculpture, spreading as she did so an intense, penetrating perfume of aloe and wild nard throughout the temple. Alexander moved up to her silently.

'Who are you?' he asked.

The girl jumped and the bucket fell from her hand, bouncing once and then rolling over the floor before coming to a halt against a column.

'Do not be afraid,' the King reassured her. 'I am only a pilgrim who seeks to pay homage to the goddess. Who are you? What is your name?'

'My name is Daunia and I am one of the sacred slaves,' replied the young girl, intimidated by Alexander's appearance, which was certainly not what one would have expected of an ordinary pilgrim. His breastplate and greaves glinted under his cloak and when he moved there came the noise of his chainmail belt clanking against his armour.

'A sacred slave? I would never have guessed. You have fine features – aristocratic – and there is such pride in your eyes.'

'Perhaps you are more used to seeing the sacred slaves of Aphrodite: they really are slaves, before being sacred, slaves of men's lust.'

'And you aren't?' asked Alexander as he picked up her bucket from the floor.

'I am a virgin, like the goddess. Have you never heard of the city of women? That is where I am from.'

She had an unusual accent that the King had never heard before.

'I had no idea there was such a place as the city of women. Where is it?'

'In Italy, it bears the name of Locri and its aristocracy is exclusively female. It was founded by a hundred families, all originating from Locris in Greece. They were all widowed and legend has it they formed unions with their slaves.'

'And why are you here, so far from home?'

'To atone for a sin.'

'A sin? But what sin can such a young girl have committed?'

'Not my sin. A thousand years ago, on the night of the fall of Troy, Ajax Oileus, our national hero, raped Princess Cassandra, daughter of Priam, right here on the pedestal bearing the sacred Palladium, the miraculous image of Athena that had fallen from the heavens. Since then the Locrians have paid for Ajax's sacrilege with the gift of two maids from their finest aristocracy, both of whom serve for a full year in the goddess's shrine.'

Alexander shook his head as if unable to believe what he was hearing. He looked around while outside the cobbles surrounding the temple resounded with the noise of horses' hooves – his companions had arrived.

Just at that moment, however, a priest entered and immediately realized who the man standing before him was. He bowed respectfully.

'Welcome, most powerful lord. I am sorry you did not let us know of your arrival – we would have given you a very different welcome.' And he nodded to the girl to leave, but Alexander gestured for her to stay.

'I preferred to arrive this way,' he said, 'and this maid

has told me such an extraordinary story, something I could never have imagined. I have heard that in this temple there are relics of the Trojan War. Is this true?'

'It certainly is. And this image you see before you is a Palladium: a likeness of an ancient statue of Athena that fell from the heavens and granted the gift of invincibility to whichever city held it in its possession.'

At that moment Hephaestion, Ptolemy, Perdiccas and Seleucus entered the temple.

'And where is the original statue?' asked Hephaestion as he came nearer.

'Some say that the hero Diomedes carried it off to Argos; others say that Ulysses went to Italy and gave it to the King, Latinus; and then others again maintain that Aeneas placed it in a temple not far from Rome, where it is still housed. However, there are many cities which claim the original simulacrum as their own.'

'I can well believe it,' said Seleucus. 'Such conviction must be a considerable source of courage.'

'Indeed,' nodded Ptolemy. 'Aristotle would say that it is conviction, or the prophecy, which actually generates the event.'

'But what is it that distinguishes the real Palladium from the other statues?' asked Alexander.

'The real simulacrum,' declared the priest in his most solemn voice, 'can close its eyes and shake its spear.'

'That's nothing special,' Ptolemy said. 'Any of our military engineers could build a toy of that kind.'

The priest threw him a disdainful look and even the King shook his head. 'Is there anything you believe in, Ptolemy?'

'Yes, of course,' replied Ptolemy, placing his hand on the hilt of the sword. 'This.' And then he placed his other hand on Alexander's shoulder and said, 'Together with friendship.'

'And yet,' the priest said, 'the objects you see here have been revered between these walls since time immemorial, and the tumuli along the river have always contained the bones of Achilles, Patroclus and Ajax.'

There came the sound of footsteps – Callisthenes had joined them to visit the famous sanctuary.

'And what do you make of it all, Callisthenes?' asked Ptolemy as he walked towards him and put his arm around him. 'Do you believe that this really is Achilles's armour? And this, hanging here from that column, is this really Paris's lyre?' He brushed the strings and the instrument produced a dull, out-of-tune chord.

Alexander no longer seemed to be listening. He was staring at the young Locrian woman as she now filled the lamps with perfumed oil, studying the perfection of her figure through the transparency of her peplum as a ray of light came through it. He was captivated by the mystery that glowed in her shy, meek eyes.

'You well know that none of this really matters,' replied Callisthenes. 'At Sparta, in the Dioscurian temple, they have an egg on display from which Castor and Pollux, the two twins, brothers of Helen, were supposedly born, but I think it's the egg of an ostrich, a Libyan bird as tall as a horse. Our sanctuaries are full of relics like this. The thing that matters is what the people want to believe and the people need to believe and need to be able to dream.' As he spoke he turned towards Alexander.

The King moved towards the great panoply of bronze, adorned with tin and silver, and he gently stroked the shield carved in relief, with the scenes described by Homer and the helmet embellished with a triple crest.

'And how did this armour come to be here?' he asked the priest.

'Ulysses brought it here, filled with remorse for having usurped Ajax's right to it, and he placed it before the tomb as a votive gift, imploring Ajax to help him return to Ithaca. It was then gathered up and housed in this sanctuary.'

Alexander moved closer to the priest. 'Do you know who I am?'

'Yes. You are Alexander, King of Macedon.'

'That's right. And I am directly descended, on my mother's side, from Pyrrhus, son of Achilles, founder of the dynasty of Epirus, and thus I am heir to Achilles. Therefore this armour is mine, and I want it.'

The priest's face drained of all colour. 'But Sire . . .'

'What!' exclaimed Ptolemy with a grin on his face. 'We're supposed to believe that this is Paris's lyre, that these are Achilles' weapons, made by the god Hephaestus in person, and you don't believe that our King is a direct descendant of Achilles, son of Peleus?'

'Oh no . . .' stammered the priest. 'It's simply that these are sacred objects which cannot be . . .'

'Nonsense,' said Perdiccas. 'You can have other identical weapons made. No one will ever know the difference. Our King needs them, you see, and since they belonged to his ancestor . . .' and he opened his arms as if to say, 'an inheritance is an inheritance.'

'Have it brought to our camp. It will be displayed before our army like a standard before every battle,' came Alexander's orders. 'And now we must return – our visit is over.'

They left in dribs and drabs, hanging on to look around at the incredible jumble of objects hanging from the columns and the walls.

The priest noticed Alexander staring at the girl as she left the temple through a side door.

'She goes swimming every evening in the sea near the mouth of the Scamander,' he whispered in his ear.

The King said nothing as he left. Not long afterwards the priest saw him mount his horse and set off towards the camp on the seashore, which was teeming with activity like some giant anthill.

*

Alexander saw her arrive, walking briskly and confidently in the darkness, coming along the left-hand bank of the river. She stopped just where the waters of the Scamander mixed with the sea waves. It was a peaceful, calm night and the moon was just beginning to rise from the sea, drawing a long silver wake from the horizon to the shore. The girl took off her clothes, undid her hair in the moonlight and entered the water. Her body, caressed by the waves, glowed like polished marble.

'You are beautiful. You look like a goddess, Daunia,' Alexander said quietly as he came out of the shadow.

The girl went in deeper, up to her chin, and moved away. 'Do not harm me. I have been consecrated.'

'To do penance for an ancient act of rape?'

'To do penance for all rapes. Women are always obliged to endure.'

The King took off his clothes and entered the water, as she crossed her arms over her chest to hide her breasts.

'They say that the Aphrodite of Cnidus, sculpted by the divine Praxiteles, covers her breasts just as you are doing now. Even Aphrodite is demure ... do not be afraid. Come.'

The girl moved towards him slowly, walking over the sandy bed and, as she came nearer, her divine body emerged dripping from the water and the surface of the sea receded until it embraced her hips and her belly.

'Lead me through the water to the tumulus of Achilles. I don't want anyone to see us.'

'Follow me then,' said Daunia. 'And let's hope you are a good swimmer.' She turned on to her side and slipped through the waves like a Nereid, a nymph of the salty abyss.

The coast formed a wide bay at that point, the shoreline already illuminated by the campfires, and it ended in a promontory with an earthen tumulus at its tip.

'Don't you worry about me,' replied Alexander as he swam alongside her.

The girl struck out offshore, cutting straight across the bay, aiming directly for the headland. She swam elegantly, graceful and flowing in her movements, almost noiseless, slipping through the water like some marine creature.

'You are very good,' said Alexander, himself breathless.

'I was born on the sea. Do you still want to go as far as the Sigeus headland?'

Alexander did not reply and continued swimming until

he saw the foam of the breaking water in the moonlight on the beach, the waves stretching up rhythmically to the base of the great tumulus.

They came out of the water holding each other by the hand, and the King led them closer to the dark mass of Achilles's tomb. Alexander felt, or he believed he felt, the spirit of the hero penetrate him and he thought he saw Briseïs with her rosy cheeks when he turned towards his companion, who was now standing before him in the silver moonlight, searching for Alexander's gaze in the darkness that enveloped him.

'Only the gods are allowed moments like this,' Alexander whispered to her and turned towards the warm breeze that came from the sea. 'Here Achilles sat and cried for the death of Patroclus. Here his mother, the ocean nymph, deposited his arms, weapons forged by a god.'

'So you do believe in it after all?' the girl asked him.

'Yes.'

'So why in the temple . . .'

'It's different here. It's night and those distant voices, long silenced, can still be heard. And you are resplendent here before me – unveiled.'

'Are you really a king?'

'Look at me. Who do you see here before you?'

'You are the young man who sometimes appears in my dreams while I sleep with my friends in the goddess's sanctuary. The young man I would have wanted to love.'

He moved closer and held her head on his chest.

'I will leave tomorrow, and in a few days' time I will have to face a difficult battle – perhaps I will be victorious, perhaps I will die.'

'In that case, take me if you want me, take me here on this warm sand and let me hold you in my arms, even if we will regret it later.' She kissed him long and passionately, stroking his hair. 'Moments like this are reserved for the gods alone. But we are gods, for as long as this night lasts.'

savagely as he'd done to Martin Sweet? And on the other hand, kill so stealthily we weren't even sure that those patients at Municipal *had* been murdered?

I wondered if I'd ever know? But I did have one good lead. Maybe it would work out.

'Where are you, Lindsay?' Claire asked me.

'Right here, Butterfly.'

She pressed my hand. 'No, really,' she said.

'I was thinking about Garza and his dark, crazy eyes,' I said. 'He's forty-five years old. He'll die in prison. He'll never hurt anyone ever again.'

Yuki put her arms around me and hugged me really hard.

'I can't thank you enough,' she said. 'Thank you for taking my mom's death to heart, Lindsay. Thank you for chasing Garza down.'

Yuki took a breath, then slowly let it out. 'When my dad came home from the war, he was changed in many ways. He told my mom about the Four Horsemen of the Apocalypse – Death, Famine, Pestilence and War – you know. But he said the Fifth Horseman was Man, and that Man was the most dangerous of all. You got Garza, Lindsay. You got the Fifth Horseman.'

EPILOGUE

Unfinished Business

Chapter One Hundred and Thirty-Nine

I t was the start of the midnight-to-8:00 a.m. shift at Peachtree General, the largest hospital in the metropolitan Atlanta area.

The nurse stepped into a single room in the crowded cardiac wing and approached a patient who was lying restless and awake in the dark. She turned on the lamp at her bedside.

'How're you doing tonight, sweetheart?'

'Just like I told you yesterday. I'm depressed as hell,' said Mrs Melinda Cane. She was a middle-aged white woman with gold hair extensions, looking at Botox or a facelift pretty soon. 'With Frankie dead and gone, and my kids living God knows where, I might as well be dead myself.'

She twisted her heavy gold wedding band as if that might bring her husband back.

'Look around,' she continued. 'See any flowers in the room? Any happy helium balloons? No one cares about me.'

'Now, I don't want you to be so worried,' said the nurse. 'I've brought you something to help you sleep through the night.'

'Luz, keep me company while I drift off,' said Mrs Cane.

'Tell you what,' Luz said. 'Take your meds. I'll see to my other patients and come back.'

Melinda Cane smiled, took the cup of pills, the glass of water, and, being a good girl for Luz, swallowed all her medicine.

The Night Walker tucked the blankets up to the woman's chin, thinking how much she liked her new identity. Wondering at how easy it had been to get all that new ID for only $175. Not that anyone ever did much of a background check on a nurse.

She walked down the hall with her rolling cart, stopping in every room, checking beds, dispensing medication, saying good night. Then she returned to Melinda Cane's room.

She closed the door behind her and walked out of the shadows to the bed just as the patient began to gasp for breath.

Melinda Cane reached out to her, patting the air frantically with her hands.

'Something's wrong, Luz,' she wheezed. 'Help me. I can't breathe. Please help me!'

The Night Walker took the woman's hand and squeezed it gently. 'It's all right, lovey. Luz is right here with you.'

Melinda Cane strained desperately for air, the cords of her neck standing out, her hands clutching at the blue flannel blankets as the opiate paralyzed her central nervous system.

She looked up at the nurse with disbelief, tried to pull her hand away, to reach for the call button beside the bed.

The Night Walker moved the call button to the nightstand, but she stayed with Mrs Cane the whole time, winding the lady's blond ringlets around her fingers.

She steeled herself for the spasms when they came, and in just a few moments, Melinda Cane was still.

Luz Santiago had also been Marie St Germaine, and before that, Yamilde Ruiz, and way before that, she'd been born and raised LaRaine Johnson of Pensacola, Florida.

It was truly a gift to have this power over life and death, and also to be invisible to everyone.

In a few minutes, the Night Walker straightened the woman's body in her bed, arranged the bedding.

Then she reached into her pocket and took out a small black doll. She'd hidden the buttons there, inside the rough woolen strands.

She took the buttons out from between the threads of the

doll, put one on each of the dead woman's eyes. The caduceus, serpents around the winged staff, symbol of the medical profession.

'Good night, princess,' she said. 'Good night.'

The Night Walker stepped out into the hallway – and saw the police waiting there for her. A half dozen officers, at least.

She even recognized one of them, the lieutenant from California.

The tap on her shoulder from behind surprised her even more than the police waiting in the hallway. She turned to see Melinda Cane. Melinda was very much alive, and she was holding a gun.

'Put your hands in the air, Luz. Or whatever your name is. You're under arrest for attempted murder. I'm Detective Cane.' Then the Atlanta Homicide detective smiled. 'You probably remember Lieutenant Lindsay Boxer from San Francisco. She's the one who nailed you to the wall.'

4th of July

James Patterson with Maxine Paetro

Detective Lindsay Boxer and the Women's Murder Club make a courageous return for their most thrilling case ever – one that could easily be their last.

In a late-night showdown, Lindsay has to make an instantaneous decision: in self-defence she fires her weapon – and sets off a chain of events that leaves a police force disgraced, a city divided and a family destroyed. Now everything she's worked for her entire life hinges on the decision of twelve jurors.

To escape the media circus, Lindsay retreats to the picturesque town of Half Moon Bay. Soon after, a string of grisly murders punches through the community. There are no witnesses; there is no pattern. But a key detail reminds Lindsay of an unsolved murder she worked on years ago. As summer comes into full swing, Lindsay and her friends in the Women's Murder Club battle for her life on two fronts: in court, and against a ruthless killer.

Working with MAXINE PAETRO, JAMES PATTERSON fine-tunes the tension like never before in this breathtaking addition to the bestselling detective series.

Praise for JAMES PATTERSON'S No. 1 bestselling novels:

'The sort of street-sharp dialogue you can slice your page-turning finger to the bone on . . . This is murder mystery at its best' *Mirror*

'Brilliantly terrifying . . . so terrifying I had to stay up all night to finish it' *Daily Mail*

'Unputdownable. It will sell millions' *The Times*

0 7553 0583 3

headline

3rd Degree

James Patterson with Andrew Gross

The No. 1 bestselling mystery series of the past decade comes roaring back with 3RD DEGREE, a shockingly suspenseful thriller featuring the Women's Murder Club.

Detective Lindsay Boxer is jogging along a beautiful San Francisco street as a ferocious blast rips through the neighbourhood. A townhouse owned by an internet millionaire explodes into flames, three people die and a sinister note signed 'August Spies' is found at the scene. Soon a wave of violence sweeps through the city – and it seems that whoever is behind it is intent on killing someone *every three days*.

Even more terrifying, the four friends who call themselves the Women's Murder Club discover that the killer has targeted one of them. And Lindsay learns that one member of the club is hiding a secret so dangerous and unbelievable that it could destroy them all.

Working with Andrew Gross, James Patterson delivers the breakneck pace and never-saw-it-coming plot twists that have made him the top-selling and most addictive suspense writer at work today. 3RD DEGREE is another searing and unforgettable thriller from this internationally acclaimed author.

'A novel which makes for sleepless nights' *Daily Express*

'A master of the suspense genre' *Sunday Telegraph*

'Unputdownable' *The Times*

0 7553 0025 4

headline

2nd Chance

James Patterson with Andrew Gross

Lindsay Boxer, San Francisco's only woman homicide detective, is back in *2nd Chance* – the mind-blowing new thriller in the international No. 1 bestselling Women's Murder Club series.

I moved in closer and knelt over the body. Tasha's blouse was soaked with blood, mixed with falling rain. Just a few feet away, a rainbow-hued knapsack still lay on the grass. Bullet holes were everywhere, splintered glass and wood. Dozens of kids had been streaming out to the street . . . All those shots, and only one victim.

The tragic end of the honeymoon murder case left Lindsay Boxer unsure if she could ever return to work. But when a little girl is shot outside a San Francisco church, she knows it's time to reconvene the Women's Murder Club. Working with reporter Cindy Thomas, assistant DA Jill Bernhardt, and medical examiner Claire Washburn, Lindsay starts to track a mystifying killer who quickly turns his pursuers into his victims.

Acclaim for James Patterson's novels

'Unputdownable' *The Times*

'Makes Kay Scarpetta's lot look positively fairytale' *Mirror*

'A master of the suspense genre' *Sunday Telegraph*

0 7472 6693 X

headline